Black Iron

Black Iron

a novel by
Franklin Veaux and Eve Rickert

Thorntree Press

Black Iron

Copyright ©2018 by Franklin Veaux and Eve Rickert

Thorntree Press, LLC
P.O. Box 301231
Portland, OR 97294
press@thorntreepress.com

Thorntree Press's activities take place on traditional and ancestral lands of the Coast Salish people, including the Chinook, Musqueam, Squamish and Tsleil-Waututh nations.

Cover illustration ©2018 by Julie Dillon
Cover design by Franklin Veaux | Interior design by Jeff Werner
Copy-editing by Roma Ilnyckyj | Proofreading by Hazel Boydell

Library of Congress Cataloging-in-Publication Data

Names: Veaux, Franklin, author. | Rickert, Eve, author.
Title: Black iron / Franklin Veaux and Eve Rickert.
Description: Portland, OR : Thorntree Press, LLC, 2018. |
Series: Impious Empires ; book 1 |
Identifiers: LCCN 2018004206 (print) | LCCN 2018009297 (ebook) |
  ISBN 9781944934668 (epub) | ISBN 9781944934675 (mobipocket) | ISBN
  9781944934682 (pdf) | ISBN 9781944934644 (hardcover) | ISBN
  9781944934651 (softcover)
Subjects: | GSAFD: Alternative histories (Fiction) | Black humor (Literature)
  | Humorous fiction.
Classification: LCC PS3622.E39 (ebook) | LCC PS3622.E39 B58 2018 (print) |
  DDC 813/.6--dc23
LC record available at https://lccn.loc.gov/2018004206

10 9 8 7 6 5 4 3 2 1

Printed in the United States of America on acid-free paper that is certified by the Sustainable Forestry Initiative.

Certified Chain of Custody
Promoting Sustainable Forestry
SUSTAINABLE
FORESTRY www.sfiprogram.org
INITIATIVE SFI-01268
SFI label applies to the text stock

To Kay, Harry, and Whiskers

and to Stella, empress of our hearts

1

It was the rain that woke him.

At least he hoped it was rain. When you find yourself lying on the street with something wet falling on your face, you can't always be sure. There were other possibilities, but he preferred not to think about them.

His head hurt. So did his shoulder. His back, that hurt too. He could probably postpone worrying about the throbbing in his knee, at least for now, though it might present a bit of a problem when it came time to stand. With a bit of luck, he wouldn't need to run, though that, too, was something you couldn't always take for granted. Something in his pocket was poking most unpleasantly into his thigh, but he didn't quite feel up to moving his leg just yet.

First things first. Where was he?

Reluctantly, with great effort, he opened his eyes.

The wetness falling on him was rain, an endless dreary drizzle of it pattering on the rough cobblestone around him. It pooled in the cracks between the stones. It formed larger rivulets that set out in search of the mighty Thames, that enormous body of what was in theory water, or had once been water, or had water as one of its less odiferous components. Tiny fingers of cold water detoured on their trip to the storm grates and thence to the sluggish mud-colored river of maybe-water just long enough to flow into his pant leg and send icy wet misery down his back.

They trickled from his collar to rejoin the rest of the water making its indirect way toward the river.

Everything around him was gray. Okay, that seemed right. Buildings towering above him, drab brick faces daubed with soot. Above them, a tangle of electrical wires, strung in hodgepodge fashion from building to building. Far above the buildings, an enormous zeppelin floated in the flat gray sky, angling down for landing. Its signaling lamp strobed a frantic staccato of brilliant light toward the ground.

New Old London, then. The wires were a dead giveaway. That was surprising. He was used to waking up across the river, in Old New London.

It hadn't always been called New Old London. Once, it had simply been London. The city, driven by an ever-increasing population, had grown rapidly, sprawling helter-skelter until it fetched up against the banks of the Thames. It paused for a bit at the river's edge, like a great swarm of termites gathering its strength. Then, all at once, it sprouted bridges across the river like tendrils of brick and metal. The moment those tendrils touched down on the opposite bank, the city resumed its growth with vigor.

For a while, the bit of London on the far side was called New London, which made the older bits Old London. Then, about the time the now-reigning monarch Her Most Excellent Majesty Queen Margaret the Merciful, who had been granted that particular honorific by some unknown poet in an exuberance of artistic license, was just graduating from wetting herself to speaking in complete sentences, her father, the now-late Royal Majesty King John the Proud, had decided Old London was a bit fusty and by royal decree had ordered much of it razed and rebuilt.

A handful of people objected to his bold—some said "audacious"—approach to civil engineering, questioning both the cost and the small but nevertheless still important matter of what to do with all the people displaced by it, but a few beheadings soon sorted that out. A man can accomplish quite a lot when he commands both the royal treasury and the headsman's axe. And it certainly helps when that royal treasury is groaning under the vast weight of gold sent home in a never-ending stream from the colonies of the New World.

So Old London became New Old London, which meant New London was now Old New London, and there you had it.

He moved his arm, the one pressed quite uncomfortably against the curbstone. His father had always said that any day you woke up looking down at the gutter instead of up at the gutter was a good day. By that measure, this was not shaping up to be a good day.

His father. That's right, he'd had one of those, once.

A clue, then. He probably wasn't an orphan. Orphans didn't have memories of their fathers, did they? Maybe he would ask the next one he caught trying to pick his pocket. Having a father implied being birthed by human beings, which meant he wasn't an animate, one of the not-quite-living constructs stitched together out of bits of the dead and then zapped back into existence with electricity and foul-smelling chemicals. And the fact that he was thinking about it clinched the deal. Everyone said animates didn't have thoughts at all. They were frightfully expensive, and as beasts of burden they were only moderately useful, but they'd been all the rage since that doctor from Geneva had started making them a couple of years back. All the trendiest aristocrats employed one or two for menial tasks like carrying firewood, and a few inventive folks suggested they might have utility in some of the messier parts of home security. He found them creepy, with their weird and often mismatched eyes and their occasional bursts of unprovoked violence.

Not that humans were necessarily any better in the unprovoked violence department, but at least their eyes usually matched.

I think; therefore, I am not an animate.

That seemed a safe bet.

He still wasn't quite sure who he was or what he was doing lying face-up in a gutter in New Old London, but he didn't feel an undue sense of urgency about it. At the moment, he seemed not to be bleeding from anywhere, and nobody was chasing him. Might as well take advantage of this unexpected luxury, he thought.

He looked down the length of his body. Both legs present and accounted for, and in more or less the correct shape. Nothing obviously broken. But what were those ridiculous things on his feet? The shoes were gaudy, made of different kinds of leather assembled in a patchwork collage that was probably the current height of fashion among those who cared about that sort of thing, which he felt he most probably did not. They had bright red clasps and pointed metal tips. They were, he thought, certainly not the sorts of things he would wear under ordinary, or indeed even extraordinary, circumstances. They seemed quite impractical for either running or creeping, two things he had a vague sense that he did rather a lot of. Yet there they were, buckled to his feet in all their gaudy monstrosity.

Another mystery. That made two so far, and he'd barely been conscious for a minute. He hated days like this, or at least he thought he probably did.

The thing in his pocket poked into him with greater urgency. Time to do something about that.

He closed his eyes, took a deep breath, then, with titanic effort, flopped over onto his side. That should sort out the problem with whatever was in his pocket.

He paused, breathing heavily. This new position squashed his hand rather unfortunately beneath him. It wouldn't be long before he had to move again. Life was so unfair.

Baby steps.

A loud, clattering sound came down the alley. He blinked. A huge machine stomped past, all copper and black iron. Smoke poured from its chimney. A clanker. Two-legged, this one, vaguely human-shaped, or it would be if humans stood eleven feet high and had smokestacks protruding from the tops of their heads. A newer model, then. Its driver, high up in his cage, didn't even spare him a glance. The thing wheezed and stomped down the alley, dragging a cart piled high with freshly fired bricks behind it.

Alley. Another clue.

New Old London was arranged in a grid, the late and much-lamented King John being of a mind more than a little obsessed with perfect geometry. It was said he could not eat unless every table setting was properly arrayed, all the plates precisely centered in front of each chair, the service perfectly parallel, the chairs exactly the same distance from their neighbors. There were rumors of an unfortunate noble who had moved his plate from its appointed place before His Royal Highness had been seated and consequently lost his title, or perhaps his head, depending on which version of the story you believed.

More precisely, New Old London was arranged in two grids. You would, if you were to look down on it from one of the many zeppelins drifting through the ashen sky above, see an alternating pattern of streets and alleys. The streets were broad and level, with wide sidewalks fronting tidy storefronts well-lit by gas lamps or, in the more fashionable districts, electric arc lamps. The alleys were narrower and more potholed, without sidewalks or lighting. The rows of buildings faced the streets, with the alleys running behind them.

Street, alley, street, alley: two different grids, slightly offset from each other. The people who mattered—aristocrats, merchants, skilled tradesmen: people with money, all—used the streets. Those without money used the alleys. Two different classes of people flowing along two different grids, living in two different cities, in a manner of speaking. It all made sense to somebody. Somebody in the former class, most likely. It seemed that wherever you went, the rich were willing to travel extraordinary distances to look at poor people but went to equally extravagant lengths to avoid looking at poor people close at hand.

He felt at home in alleys.

His hand throbbed. Time to do something about that. He rose to his knees and then, with another Herculean effort, to his feet.

He closed his eyes, panting. This must be what the heroes of Greek stories felt like, after they'd just skinned a hydra or defeated a twelve-headed lion or whatever it was they did.

There was a fabulously complex tangle of black silk and exquisitely spidery, jointed bamboo struts lying wet and broken on the rough cobblestone where he'd just been lying. Strange, that.

He leaned against a wooden refuse-dump, trying to catch his breath.

Its side was caved in, its contents spilling across the ground around the black silk whatever-it-was. By some stroke of fortune, the refuse that oozed wetly to the cobblestones was mostly vegetative. There were far less savory refuse-dumps, like those behind the laboratories where the animate-makers plied their arts, creating those animated creatures of flesh from whatever raw materials the street offered up.

He looked up. Something had happened to the roof of the building above him. It looked as though a large, heavy object had struck it with considerable force, shattering the red clay tiles in a vaguely circular area several feet wide. A broad swath of dislocated tiles made a path from the point of impact to the edge of the roof, just above the refuse-dump, where the gutter had given way and was swinging forlornly from metal rivets. His eyes followed the path of destruction down, from the edge of the roof into the refuse-dump, and then to the street, right about…

Aha! He smiled grimly. That explained the various aches and pains, then. From the looks of things, he'd hit the roof plenty hard before he'd skidded over the edge into the refuse-dump, taking a bit of the gutter with him, and from there, come to rest in the alley.

At least it explained the "how," if not the "why."

No, he thought, scratch that, it didn't even explain the "how." Where precisely had he fallen onto the roof *from?*

More immediately, why was he wearing this ridiculous getup? A sodden black jacket with tails—tails, for the love of all that was holy!—hung wetly from his narrow frame. A couple of feet down the alley was what had once been, and was still trying against all odds to be, a top-hat. He had a vague sense that it belonged to him, though he could not imagine why he would own such a thing. He was still a bit hazy on who he was, exactly, but he was quite certain he was not the sort of chap who habitually engaged in the wearing of top-hats.

Nor in the habit of falling from the sky into a refuse-dump, he had to admit to himself, so perhaps he shouldn't be too hasty with the assumptions.

A party. He had been to a party. In a top-hat and the absurdly impractical shoes—shoes he was certain he would never wear absent the most dire need.

He frowned, adding it all up. A party, a top-hat, shoes, a long fall onto a roof, a sudden slide into a rubbish-bin, and the wreckage of some silk and bamboo contraption that he knew, with abrupt clarity, had once been a gigantic kite.

A zeppelin. The party had been on a zeppelin. And he had left the party with some alacrity. Planned, evidently, to do so. From the look of things, he'd made arrangements in advance to depart over the side of the airship, rather than waiting for it to land as might be more traditional when one debarked from a flying vessel.

Damn, he thought, it sure would be nice if he could remember who he was.

The thing in his pocket intruded into his consciousness again. The pants he was wearing were just as ridiculous as the shoes. Like much of what the upper class wore, they had been designed to show off the fact that their owner had no need to do anything as profane as work, and therefore need not carry around anything larger than a pocket watch. The pockets, as a result, were vestigial, barely more than slits with a small pouch sewn inside. Whatever was in his pocket, it was larger than anything the tailor had meant for it to accommodate.

And it had sharp edges, or so it seemed. He would, he ruefully supposed, probably have quite a large bruise to show for it.

He stuck a hand in his pocket and drew it out.

Memory poured into him like wine into a glass.

He, Thaddeus Mudstone Ahmed Alexander Pinkerton, ne'er-do-well and ruffian of the most despicable sort, had just robbed, though only by the skin of his teeth and at, evidence suggested, great personal peril, Her Most Excellent Majesty Queen Margaret the Merciful.

And lived, apparently also by the skin of his teeth, to tell about it.

He picked up the battered top-hat, set it atop his head at a rakish angle, and walked, or more correctly limped, down the alley, whistling.

Perhaps this was going to be a good day after all.

2

In the air high above New Old London, the Lady Alÿs de Valois was not having a good day. Cold, wet wind gusted in through the yawning doorway, tearing at the folds of her deep blue gown. The huge loading door, normally barred shut against the possibility of an unfortunate guest tumbling to an unfortunate end, banged against the wooden body of the airship. The whistling wind almost drowned out the low mutter of the great engines that turned the enormous airscrews. Her mouth was still hanging open.

"Right. My lady, I think you should come with me."

The owner of that slightly nervous voice was dressed in the ceremonial bronze breastplate and white cape of the Royal Guard. His name was Roderick Hamsbender, and he, too, was not having a good day.

Roderick was, generally speaking, of slightly nervous disposition all around. Indeed, that was one of the reasons he'd joined the Royal Guard in the first place. When you were in the Guard, almost nothing exciting ever happened.

Roderick's father, a trader in imported cloth, had never been completely happy with his lot in life. He wanted the best for his only son, and had insisted that Roderick become a real man—the process of which involved, apparently, taking up the sort of profession in which one carried a weapon and helped rid the world of threats to King and Country (or more accurately, Queen and Country, times being what they were) in a suitably manly and heroic fashion. That left only a handful of possible careers. Members of the municipal police force dealt with dangerous criminals who had nothing to lose. Soldiers had lives that were mostly boring, interspersed with brief moments of excitement that were very exciting indeed...sometimes terminally so. The Royal Guard, on the other hand, spent almost all of their time watching noble types doing nobly-type things, like taking dancing lessons, raising taxes on the poor, and eating complicated little bits of food from the ends of small wooden skewers. As jobs went, it was prestigious, it was honorable, and best of all, it was *dull.*

Exactly what he wanted.

He had succeeded in the Guard by being clever enough not to show anyone how clever he was, and by honing a highly advanced deference to his betters. He was also tall, and had the strength that came from lifting heavy baskets. That helped, but it was mostly those other things that had facilitated his progression through the ranks.

The job did come with certain duties beyond standing still and deferring to his betters, and one of those duties was reporting infractions of the law. Roderick was not aware of any area of the law that specifically covered ladies of high birth assisting unknown gentlemen in leaving the Queen's airship by means of the loading door while the ship was in flight, but there were rules that covered "suspicious activity," and jumping out of the back of an airship, he reasoned, might be at least a bit suspicious. He figured he really ought to do something. Problem was, from the looks of it, doing something meant detaining a young lady who was not only of noble birth, but the daughter of King Philip xviii of France, and on top of that was due to marry the Queen's half brother. No part of that looked good for Roderick's career prospects.

On the whole, he would have preferred to live his life hawking the finest imported silks. Imported silks, he thought with perhaps understandable naivety, seldom tried to kill you.

The wind drove a hard slap of rain into his face, threatening to knock his helmet off. He righted it absently, frowning.

The Lady Alÿs drew herself to her full height. Most people became more imposing when they did that, but in her case, it still left her a bit short of five feet tall. Her curly black hair, which usually tended toward frizzy even when sternly disciplined by comb and tie, managed to pull itself together long enough to stream imperiously in the damp breeze. "Do you have any idea who I am?" she demanded.

"Oh yes, I do, my lady," Roderick said, bowing very slightly. "I do indeed." His voice sounded a bit rueful. "Meaning no offence, my lady, but I would be remiss in my duties if I didn't report this…" He glanced out the gaping cargo door into the gray rain outside. "This…um, this whatever-it-is to Her Majesty. I think it might be best for both our sakes if you come along with me. We'll let her sort this out." His cape billowed behind him dramatically.

From Alÿs's perspective, the day was going inexplicably sideways. And it had started out so well. The Queen's flying parties were famous, and this party promised to be posh even by the normal standards of the Court. Queen Margaret was entertaining a special guest, namely the ambassador from the Ottomans, and had gone to considerable lengths to impress. There was to be a grand buffet, part meal and part (the better part, truth be told) an opulent display of wealth, with long tables of polished oak groaning under the weight of food so fancy that it was, in some cases, not even entirely clear which bit went into your mouth.

The Queen herself was dressed to impress as well, in a long but form-hugging brocaded dress with a lot of complicated and fussy bits on the front that somehow managed to conceal all the things a dress was supposed to conceal while still exposing enough to have set tongues wagging even five years ago.

But fashion is a mercurial thing, and one of the nice things about being a monarch was that you got to set the fashion. Many of the same women of the Court who would a few years back have found Margaret's dress entirely *outré* were, this evening, just as outrageously dressed themselves, as it ever has been with those who cleave close to the bosom of power.

After the meal, there would be an all-evening dance attended by the various barons, dukes, earls, and viscounts who made up that part of the royal Court that mattered. There would be subtle flirting and endless gossip to catch up on. Alÿs's betrothed, His Excellency Sir Leo the Duke of Byron-on-shire, would be there, but no matter: His Excellency the Duke had scarcely passed his eleventh birthday and would be tucked somewhere out of sight the moment the first dance finished.

The decision that Alÿs would marry the Duke had been met with some small degree of shock and more than a few whispers behind exquisitely gloved hands. Alÿs was three years older than His Excellency, and some felt that an older woman with a younger man was distressingly modern, even scandalous. But the union of the French and English royal houses carried with it no small advantages, and Alÿs, being the youngest of four siblings, was the most available to be sent off to a distant land for political purpose, so there it was. What could you do?

Such evenings were not without their charms. Alÿs had been looking forward to gossiping with the Lady Eleanor de Revier, the Queen's favored lady-in-waiting. Alÿs had heard a rumor that Viscount Thomas Holland of Huntingdon was feuding with Baron William Marlboro, he of the bulbous red nose, over something involving the upcoming marriage of the good baron's daughter. As a result, Holland was making noises about withdrawing his support for Marlboro's son Bernard to attend the Academy of Military Arts, which would in all probability mean that the appointment would go to Richard, the son of the Duke of Barnstaple, instead. The Duke's family was in good graces with the Baron of Harringworth, whose brother had just been killed in that dreadful war in Afghanistan that never seemed to end, so he would be bound to have a spirited opinion on the subject. Lady Eleanor would surely know every detail.

The zeppelin tilted up away from its mooring, making for the early evening sky. The city slipped away beneath them. Eleanor sidled up to Alÿs at the buffet to whisper hints of something even bigger than the developing feud between the Huntingdons and Marlboros.

Something, she said, she had just learned about Charles Rathman, Earl of Shrewsbury, uncle to Her Most Royal Majesty and overseer of the evening's festivities. "Find me later," she giggled, and scurried away. Alÿs nodded, momentarily distracted by a minor kerfuffle at the far end of the buffet line, where an odd little man had set off a wave of tittering by picking up the wrong fork.

This was exactly the sort of gaffe that would, in more ordinary times, have attracted the sustained attention of Alÿs and the entire rest of the Court for days. For those born to the aristocratic class, silverware was a serious matter, rivaling in complexity the *Philosophiæ Naturalis Principia Mathematica* that Alÿs had struggled through with her frustrated tutors. It existed almost entirely as one of the many little rituals the upper crust of society created to separate themselves from the more beastly sorts of people, and only incidentally to assist in the pragmatic matter of conveying comestibles from plate to mouth.

But these were not usual times. The matter of the fork could not hope to compete with the matter of the Turks.

Margaret had personally invited Tahkir, the Ottoman ambassador, aboard her airship, setting many brows furrowing and many tongues wagging. He sat at the end of the table like some great exotic masthead carved in the prow of a ship, wearing an extraordinary outfit of yellow and blue, woven through with gold thread and decorated exquisitely with gemstones.

The ambassador smiled easily and often as he moved through the people, chatting with nobles and servants alike. He was surrounded by half a dozen members of his own personal guard, all dark eyes and sleek black hair, who smiled far less often than the ambassador did. They too were dressed in robes of yellow and blue that set them apart from the Queen's aristocratic guests in their opulent dresses and fashionable suits.

Alÿs looked forward to dancing with the ambassador later that evening. She had met him twice before at Margaret's parties. She found him an excellent dancer and a charming conversationalist, always eager to listen to whatever she had to say, however trivial or gossipy. He seemed to take genuine delight in hearing her stories about her family back in France, about the goings-on in Margaret's Court, and about anything else she wanted to talk about.

There was talk, though it was more whispered than spoken aloud, that Margaret planned to make an Ottoman a member of her Guard, an unprecedented departure from tradition that caused the narrowing of many eyes. Compared to that, the strange little man with his clumsy inability to navigate the tricky shoals of proper dinner etiquette was more footnote than main story.

The feast ended. The band assembled on the edge of the dance floor. Her Royal Highness and her guests moved to the airship's Great Hall, where the members of the Court arrayed themselves under the curious eyes of the Ottomans.

Alÿs and her betrothed shared the first dance, as was the custom. The young Duke was a quick-witted lad with dark eyes and dark hair, only slightly taller than Alÿs herself. The Duke was a fine dancer, despite his age. Alÿs glowed with pleasure as they whirled together on the dance floor, soaking up the attention from the assemblage of aristocrats.

Alÿs noticed the man after her dance. The shoes were the first things that caught her eye. They were fetchingly designed, made of several different kinds of leather cunningly arrayed in a carefully crafted artifice of randomness. They were tipped with metal points, slightly upturned, in a style currently the rage back home in Paris.

The shoes were attached to the feet of the strange man who had very nearly used a dessert fork in place of a fruit fork, to his unending shame at this and every future Court function at which he might appear until the end of time.

She looked him up and down. He seemed to have been purpose-built as the exemplar of the word "nondescript." Dark hair, dark eyes, not unlike the Ottomans standing to one side of the dance floor. Slight of build, with one of those faces that you forget the moment you look away.

She didn't recall ever having seen him before this evening. That piqued her interest. She was intimately acquainted with all the members of the Queen's Court and could tell you, were you of a mind to listen, their titles, crests, histories, and endless minutiae of who favored whom and who was most likely at a moment's notice to challenge whom to a duel, the outcome of which would be talked about for weeks. She was acquainted with the ever-changing swirl of consorts, attendants, squires, lackeys, and various hangers-on that buzzed around the noble families like a cloud of hopeful, gaily dressed flies. She knew the comings and goings of the ambassadors, lesser diplomats, and other functionaries who made their living operating the vast machinery of the state, and could even recognize in passing the couriers and servants whose jobs were likely to bring them in contact with civilization's more refined elements.

And this man was a complete, utter mystery.

If there was one thing that intrigued the Lady Alÿs, it was a mystery. Preferably the sort of mystery that could be turned into a juicy bit of gossip of the sort that was the standard medium of exchange among her peers.

"Who are you?" she asked, curiosity making her bold.

He bowed, looking flustered. "I'm sorry," he said, "I have—"

"It's 'I'm sorry, my lady,'" Alÿs said. "And I insist." She had a way of insisting that hinted darkly of unfortunate events to those who failed to obey her. It was a strategy that cut straight through her combined disadvantages of stature and youth. "I am Lady Alÿs de Valois, and I would very much like to make your acquaintance."

She offered her gloved hand. He took it gingerly, as though he expected it to crawl off her arm and do something hideous.

The man reached out and shook her hand in the manner of a carpenter or a fruit purveyor or some other member of the coarser classes. Alÿs was most thoroughly and astonishedly shocked.

"I saw you at dinner earlier," she said when she had reclaimed her appendage. "You seemed to be having difficulty managing your tableware. Who are you?"

"I am, that is…" He hesitated. "I am the second cousin once removed of the Earl of Glaucaster, visiting London from Canterbury." He had the look of one reading from a script at an audition.

"Oh? Charles has a cousin? I had no idea!" Alÿs said mischievously. "So you know his sister, Gertrude, then?"

"Of course!" the strange little man said. "Gertrude. Yes, of course, I know Gertrude well. Lovely woman."

"His sister's name is Francine," Alÿs said. "She's quite a nasty woman. Who are you really?"

"I told you! I'm—"

"I know what you told me," Alÿs said. "I asked who you were."

The little man bowed awkwardly several times. "I would love to stay and chat, but I must be off. Thank you, Your Eminen—Your Gr—that, is, um, m'lady," he said.

"Oh, no you don't," Alÿs said. "Who are you really?" She looked him up and down. "Where do you really come from?"

"I really have to go, um, m'lady," the strange man said. His brown eyes carried the desperate look of a rabbit in a snare.

"Before we get to know each other? I think not. I want you to stay so I can learn all about you." Alÿs moved to take his hand.

But then the Earl of Tuscón slipped smoothly between them, bowing deeply enough to be obsequious. "The pleasure of a dance, my lady?" he said. Before Alÿs could protest, the strange man in the fetching shoes melted away like a ghost.

As they whirled around the dance floor, Alÿs kept scanning the crowd for the odd little man. The earl was a consummate dancer, and if he noticed Alÿs's distraction, he was far too much of a gentleman to remark upon it. Not that he was really much of a gentleman; Alÿs had heard from Eleanor that she had it on good authority from none other than the Lady Jane Holland, the second daughter of the Viscount Thomas Holland, that the earl was running about in scandalous fashion with a lady of the evening from Highpole Street, and with his wife expecting their second child in just a few months—the inhumanity of it!

The dance ended. Alÿs disentangled herself from the Earl of Tuscón's damp grasp and headed off in the general direction the strange man had gone. He was nowhere to be seen. Odd, that. The Queen's zeppelin was the largest airship ever constructed, but it was not so large it offered many places to hide.

She made excuses, waving her hand vaguely in the direction of the zeppelin's privies with an expression that suggested she would be unavailable for a time, and set out on a serious search. Now that she had both hands wrapped firmly around a genuine mystery, she was reluctant to let go.

She found him, finally, in the last place it would occur to her to look, a part of the vessel ordinarily only visited by members of the servant class. He was unfolding a large, complicated-looking structure made of bamboo and black silk, a great delta-winged kite so large its wingtips almost brushed the storeroom's walls. The large doors, used for provisioning the zeppelin with food for the banquets and normally secured for flight, hung wide. Cold wind howled outside.

"Who are you?" she demanded, gripping the doorway.

He looked wildly around the room. "Me? Um…I'm, that is…"

"What are you doing with that contraption?"

"What? This? Oh. I was just going to…" He sighed. "It's a long story." He fumbled in his pockets. "How do people wear these pants?"

"You don't belong here," Alÿs said conversationally. She felt like this was one of those situations where she ought to be afraid, but she had never quite got the hang of fear.

"You have no idea how right you are," the man said ruefully. He fiddled with something on the contraption he was holding. "Here, can you hold this for a second?"

He passed her a smooth bamboo strut. She took it, bemused. "Okay, so, this cloth bit wraps around here, like this, see," he said. "And then this part comes down here like this, see? And then I just fasten this harness around my chest and I just hold on to this bit, and…thank you. I can take that back now." He took the strut from Alÿs and fitted it into the frame of the kite.

"Hey there! Stop right there! What do you think you're up to, then?"

Alÿs turned. The guard loomed in the doorway, watching the two of them with suspicion.

"I think that's my cue," the stranger said. "Sorry, lovely talking to you, can't stay. Goodbye!" He turned and leapt through the door into the yawning chasm below. Alÿs heard the flutter of silk, then nothing but the wind.

Alÿs and Roderick watched in open-mouthed astonishment.

Roderick recovered his wits first. "Right. My lady, I think you best come with me," he said.

✦

Her Royal Highness was mightily displeased, and more than a little disbelieving. "He did what, Alice?" she said, deliberately mispronouncing the name just to show her displeasure. Alÿs felt her face grow hot. There was a cluster of people, mostly lords and ladies from the dance but also a handful of the Royal Guard, gathered around them. Someone sniggered. Alÿs felt an urge to stomp her foot.

"Jumped, Your Grace." She stared resolutely at a point just behind Margaret's left ear.

"What did this…man look like?"

"Well, he was—he had—" Alÿs stammered. She closed her eyes, but could produce nothing more than a vague recollection of the kind of bland, unextraordinary face that seldom leaves anything but vague recollections. "He had exquisite shoes. Your Grace."

"Just so there is no mistake, you are saying that a strange man with—" she frowned "—with exquisite shoes snuck aboard our zeppelin, to attend our party, a party whose invitation list was carefully overseen by none other than the Cardinal himself, a man known to your father, as we recall—and then jumped out a window?"

"It was the loading door, Your Grace."

Roderick nodded enthusiastically. "'S true!" he said. "I saw it with me own eyes. She helped that man put together some sort of apparatus. Like a big kite or something. I saw her! Then he went right out the doo—out the window, Your Grace. Boom! Just like that. The two of them were in cahut—cehoot—working together, Your Grace."

The Queen's face grew cold. "Is that so?"

This time Alÿs did stomp her foot. "Absolutely not! I have no idea who he was. I was trying to find out what he was up to before this big oaf scared him off. I am not in cahoots with anyone. Your Grace."

The Queen turned away from Alÿs. "Search the airship," she commanded. "Every square inch. As for you," she returned her gaze to Alÿs, "we shall decide what to do with you when we land. You!" She pointed to Roderick. "See to it that Alice does not go leaping out of any windows."

The problem with a life of shady dealings, in Thaddeus Mudstone's considered opinion, was that it invariably involved association with shady characters. Not that being shady was a bad thing, necessarily. Thaddeus wasn't exactly a beacon of light himself, and besides, you could hardly have light without some shade, right? But shady characters could be uncomfortable sorts, and the man in front of Thaddeus was one of the shadiest Thaddeus had ever met. Light seemed to slink away from him. His demeanor suggested a personality that had gone past shady into downright opaque.

This man, his most recent employer, had been quite clear that Thaddeus was to report to him the moment the job was done. No going home first, no talking to anyone, or half his pay would be forfeit. Do the job, come right here, get his money, and be on his way.

He'd been tempted to go home anyway, just to replace the ridiculous things on his feet with something a bit more sensible, but his better judgment (or, more accurately, his greed, which in his line of work was an adequate substitute) overruled him. For what he was being paid, he figured he could wear absurd shoes for another hour.

And now here he was.

The dock district of Old New London had a logic all its own. It was the logic of commerce, in whose service every square inch of space had been sanctified. Entire neighborhoods sprawled in a rambly sort of unpremeditated fashion, buildings growing and merging almost like living things, all driven by the need for more: more places to store the crates and casks and barrels coming off the endless barges that made their long, slow ways up and down the Thames; more ways to obfuscate the flow of money that changed hands at every step of complex multitiered transactions, the better to hide it from the Crown's revenue collectors.

The space wasn't really a room in the conventional sense of the word. Sure, it had a roof, and walls, and a door, but it was a small place formed when someone had roofed over an odd little corner of space where two buildings, driven to expand by the relentless demands of the great machinery of commerce, had met at an odd angle. It was a private space, easy to overlook, and did not seem to clearly belong to anyone in particular—a deliberate and quite delicate state of affairs. On the docks, a great deal of business happened in spaces that did not clearly belong to anyone.

A small lantern glowed on the floor. Its light seemed reluctant to touch the man, sliding away as though wanting no truck with him. The man's face was entirely concealed by a heavy black cowl. Not that there was anything unusual about that; in Thaddeus's line of business, this was one of those things one got used to. Thaddeus was often not entirely clear on who his clients were.

"Please, sit down." The words slithered from the man's lips and oozed into Thaddeus's ear.

A bony white hand extended from a heavy sleeve to point to the empty chair that made up the only furnishing in the room.

Over the years, Thaddeus had developed a set of instincts as precise and cunningly fashioned as a jeweler's pocket watch. They told mood instead of time, reading intent and motive in every subtle motion around him. Right now, they were jangling a warning. "If it's all the same to you, I'll stand," he said.

"Suit yourself." The man's hand vanished into its sleeves. "Is it done?"
"Yes."
"You placed the ring in the Queen's chambers?"

"Yes."

"You took nothing and disturbed nothing, exactly as you were instructed?"

Thaddeus felt the bulge of the ornamented case in his pocket. The way he saw it, the people who retained his services tended not to be the most honest sorts and were almost always up to no good. These kinds of people didn't have any grounds to expect honesty. In fact, deceiving such persons was, in Thaddeus's moral code, a virtue. If you tell a lie to a duplicitous man, well, that was hardly a sin, right? In fact, you could argue it was quite the opposite. Dishonesty to such persons was almost a civic duty! And they knew he was a dishonest man himself, so if they didn't take that into account, well, that was on them, wasn't it? Honor among thieves made one a poor thief indeed, in his experience.

"Yes," he lied.

"Nobody saw you? You spoke to nobody?"

"Not a soul," Thaddeus said solemnly. "I was in and out like a mouse." His face was the very picture of honest innocence.

"Good. It is so nice to know there are reliable people in this world. And now on to the matter of your payment."

Thaddeus leaned forward. This was always his favorite bit, though it was also the most fraught. If someone was going to double-cross you, it was usually here. Well, here or at the bit where you're slipping into the alleyway expecting your accomplice to distract the guards at the other end, but often here. Shady men could rarely be counted on in such moments, and that, Thaddeus thought, was a damn shame. Where would you be if you couldn't trust the people you worked with?

The man's hand dipped into the pocket of his robe and came out with a bulging coin purse. "I believe we had agreed on two hundred," he said. The words crawled off his tongue like vipers leaving their nest.

"Yes."

"Here you are, then." He extended the heavy bag toward Thaddeus. Thaddeus reached to take it.

The man was fast, far faster than anyone had any right to be. A flash of bright steel whirred toward Thaddeus's throat. Thaddeus jumped back, turning away as he did. The dagger brushed past him, slicing through his jacket without effort. Its edge was so sharp it barely slowed down.

Stupid. Stupid, stupid, stupid. He'd been stupid, Thaddeus thought. He should have seen it coming. Oldest trick in the book. Show a man the prize in your left hand, and he won't pay attention to what's in your right. Thaddeus had done the same thing himself countless times. Stupid.

The dagger reversed, arcing back toward Thaddeus. Thaddeus was off balance, encumbered by the ridiculous clothes he was wearing. He ducked and kicked out with one leg. His foot connected solidly with the chair, sending it crashing into the man's knees. He fell sideways. The coin bag hit the floor. Two hundred shillings' worth of gleaming gold spilled across rough wood planks. For the tiniest fraction of a second, Thaddeus hesitated.

In that instant, the man was already up again and coming at him fast.

Priorities, Thaddeus thought. Gold was nice. Life was better. Time to do what he did best.

He turned and bolted, feeling a swish of air as the dagger passed through the space he had just vacated. A moment later he was through the door and in the warren of tiny, confusing alleys that together made up the dock district of Old New London.

The sun was nearly gone. Sensible people were heading home, and people of Thaddeus's sort were not yet out. Thaddeus chose a direction at random and plunged off as fast as he could, weaving through the crowd of laborers and merchants of the petty sort. Behind him, the door to the tiny shack, really little more than a pile of planks coaxed by a trick of the carpenter's artifice into believing it was a storeroom, banged open.

Run now. Think later.

The dock district was a tangle of lanes and alleys, some of them little more than crevices between rows of warehouses. It hadn't been built so much as thrown up. The engine of commerce was constantly arranging and rearranging the architecture, and many of the pathways seemed more like accidents of urban geography than anything intended to conduct traffic.

Thaddeus saw an opening between two buildings on his left, completely deserted. He darted through it and flattened himself against the wall. His pursuer flashed by the opening, a blurred shape in the failing light. Thaddeus exhaled slowly. That should buy him a few moments.

He crept carefully down the alley, cursing his shoes. The hard soles, so practical for walking down broad, well-paved streets, slapped on the rough cobblestone. Even a blind rat could follow him, Thaddeus thought.

The passageway opened up into a wider space, with alleys heading off in all directions. A young girl, perhaps in her tenth year, looked up at Thaddeus with an expression of suspicion. She was dressed entirely in rags.

"D'you have a shilling, mister?"

Thaddeus paused for a moment, panting. "No. I don't have a shilling. I should have a lot of shillings, but I don't. Listen, there's a bad man chasing me. Which way should I go?"

She looked Thaddeus up and down appraisingly. "That's a rum qab y'got."

"What?"

"I ken your qab." She held out her hand. "Give it t'me."

Thaddeus looked around wildly. He could hear feet pounding down the alley toward him. He took off his top-hat and handed it to the girl. "Which way do I go?"

She examined the hat with a critical air. Thaddeus felt his hands curl into fists.

"There," she said, pointing. "That way."

"Thank you, little girl. Don't tell the bad man where I am, okay?"

She nodded.

Thaddeus ran down the alley she had pointed to as though all the legions of Hell were behind him. Not that there was much difference between that and one person hell-bent on murder behind him. Past a certain point, it stopped mattering how many people were trying to kill you.

The alley extended barely twenty yards before it ended in a rough brick wall. Thaddeus stopped. The girl had sent him down a dead end. Refuse-dumps lined both sides.

Behind him, he heard a voice, glutinous and sibilant. "Little girl, have you seen a man run this way?"

"Maybe," she said. "D'you have a shilling?"

"Oh, yes. I have a shilling for you," came that slithery voice.

There was a pause. Then, "He's that way. Down Ambush Alley."

Thaddeus felt his heart freeze in his chest. *Oh, you impudent little urchin*, he thought to himself. He flattened himself against the wall, as far in the corner as he could get. The refuse-dumps were almost empty and offered little cover. He crouched in the deepest part of the shadow, holding his breath.

A shadow loomed in the far end of the alley, a man-shaped hole in the fading light. He was nearly silent. It was easy, when you have the proper footwear. The knife gleamed in his hand.

Thaddeus held himself still. The shape glided closer. He willed himself to melt into the shadow.

Another step closer. Another. The man was cautious, wary of cornered prey. Closer.

Thaddeus exploded out at him. The man reacted almost instantly, the dagger thrusting up and out.

Fortunately, there is a world of difference between "almost instantly" and "instantly."

They crashed into each other. The dagger flashed and gleamed. Thaddeus brought his foot up. The hard metal tip collided hard with a particularly sensitive portion of the man's body.

The man fell, eerily silent. The dagger skittered across the cobblestones. Thaddeus leapt past him, heading back the way he had come.

The child was still standing where she had been. Thaddeus's top-hat sat on her head, nearly covering her eyes. She looked solemnly at him. "D'you have a shilling now?" she asked.

"You nit little hackie," Thaddeus said. He snatched the top-hat from her head as he sailed past.

She spun to face him, hands on her hips. "Hey! Tha' *mine!*" But he was already on his way out.

She started after him. "Oi! Mister! Tha' my hat!" she yelled. "You give tha' back or I'll call the posies on you! Mist—*oof!*"

Thaddeus spared a backward glance. The man in the cowl had collided full-speed with her, sending them both sprawling. How was that possible? A kick like that should have kept him down for at least five minutes, curled up around the family jewels. How was he still moving?

Run now. Think later.

A right, a left, another left, a quick right, a direction that wasn't really right or left so much as sideways, and he emerged in a broad alley behind the grain silos, filled with the slow-motion traffic of tired people heading away from backbreaking jobs. The last light faded. No sign of pursuit.

He held his breath for a count of ten. His pursuer failed to appear.

Ten more beats. His pursuer continued to not appear.

The tension inside him uncoiled slowly. "Thaddeus, my boy," he said to himself, "that was a close one and no mistake." He placed the top-hat, beaten almost beyond recognition, back on his head. He turned toward home, where a stiff drink and his own shoes awaited.

✦

Thaddeus took a circuitous route, wary of followers with sharp steel. By the time he reached his destination, night had finished its long fall and was lying sprawled out over the disorganized heap of Old New London. Rows of gas lamps created uneven pools of light along the roads. Deep shadows lurked between.

He was less than a block from home when a shadow detached itself from the wall and moved toward him menacingly. "Oi there, who's this, then?" came a voice, heavy with implicit violence. "Got any money on you?"

"Put a cork in it," Thaddeus said. "It's been a long day."

"Ha! Muddy! Didn't recognize you." The shadow stepped under a gaslight, where it resolved itself into the shape of a young man, tall and broad and thick with muscle. "Why're you dressed like that? You look a complete prat."

"I don't want to talk about it," Thaddeus said. "Long day, remember?"

"No day long enough to make me go out lookin' like that. 'Eard you coming a mile off. Thought you were some nobleman lost his way."

"Around here? No nobleman's ever been that lost," Thaddeus said. "Hey, listen, Jake, you seen anyone looking for me who doesn't belong?"

Jake scratched his enormous head with an enormous hand. Everything about Jake was enormous: his hands, his feet, his height, his strength, his club, his library of creative violence. His expression tightened with the exertion of thought. "Nope," he said after a while.

Thaddeus felt himself relax a bit more. "Good."

"Why're you dressed up like a ninny, anyway?" Jake said.

"I was on the Queen's airship," Thaddeus said. "Went to a dance with the nobles."

"Oh." Jake pondered the idea. "Hur hur hur. You dancin' with the high and mightily. Just say you don't want to tell me. No need makin' up stories."

"I'm going to bed," Thaddeus said. "Don't hit too many people over the head."

"Why not?" Jake looked puzzled.

"You might strain your arm."

Jake brightened. "Naw. I got a new club. Ergonometric."

"Good man," Thaddeus said.

"No I ain't."

Home, for Thaddeus, was a small room on the ground floor of a tiny ramshackle wood building with a pitched roof wedged between the imposing brick faces of two larger structures that had once been warehouses. They'd been put to new use as times and the city had changed. Nowadays, the one on the left was used as a tannery, and the one on the right was home to a textile mill. Granted, it took a bit of time to get used to the smell. Once you'd done that, it wasn't a bad place, at least if you didn't mind neighbors like Jake.

That was the rub. People did not live next to a tannery because they enjoyed the aroma. Thaddeus's neighbors, like Thaddeus, lived where they lived only because they lacked the means to live anywhere else. But for the most part, the folks in the neighborhood recognized a certain kinship in one another and, more importantly, understood that nobody else had anything worth taking, so they mostly left each other alone.

Like Randall McAddams, Thaddeus's upstairs neighbor. He hardly bothered anyone except on the nights when he drank too much and reenacted the Siege of Kabul in his bedroom, with much crashing about and occasional small explosions, but that rarely happened more than three or four times a week. Post-stress disorder of the trauma, he called it.

The bedroom where Thaddeus lived, which was also his living room, his dining room, his study, and his kitchen, was a bit wider than his bed. He had easy access to the privy behind the tannery, not that he needed it, because he had a chamber pot of his very own he kept beside the bed so he wouldn't have to brave the night air. It wasn't like he was *poor*, after all.

There was a small coal stove to keep out the chill and a tiny table next to the bed that was barely large enough for a chipped china plate. Above it, scraps of wood had been nailed to the wall to form something that approximated a set of shelves, and on those shelves Thaddeus kept his good shirt (which, to a casual observer, was nearly indistinguishable from his less-good shirt), a collection of small bits of metal that looked like a pile of scrap to a layperson but in the hands of a man like Thaddeus became magic keys to almost any lock, and a small brown bottle topped with a bit of cork.

Thaddeus pulled the door closed and fastened it with a bit of string. He heaved a great sigh and sat down on the edge of his bed, which creaked beneath him. Finally, he could relax for a moment, take off those ridiculous shoes, and—

The door crashed open.

Everything slowed.

Thaddeus was aware of a large shape coming at him with the unspoken promise of mayhem. Of more immediate interest was the club held tightly in the shape's hand. It was banded with iron and had an exuberance of spikes all over it, like someone had found a morning star and said, "but it doesn't look *menacing* enough!"

He was also aware, in a peripheral sort of way, of two more shapes just outside the door, both crowding to get in. His room was barely big enough for just him alone, Thaddeus thought. Four would be absolutely intolerable. Particularly if three of them wanted to kill him.

And he was aware that his foot was already extended, and could with only the most modest effort be moved to the side. Just a little bit, like that, and...

The intruder with the spiked club collided with his foot and went sprawling. His head hit the coal stove with a loud *splorch!* Thaddeus grimaced and looked away.

That left two more people, both of whom were now halfway into the room. One of them held a club, a bit less extravagantly menacing than his still-twitching companion's but solid and serviceable nonetheless. The other carried a dagger.

Four murderous assailants in one day. A new personal record, Thaddeus thought mirthlessly. Plainly he was moving up in the world.

He launched himself up from the bed, straight through the window next to the door. This was a lot less dramatic than it sounded, as the window was little more than a hole in the wall covered with a scavenged bit of oilskin that tore easily. Thaddeus felt a pang of sorrow for the tuppence it would cost him to replace it, then he was swinging over the wooden railing onto the stairs leading up to the room above. Best not to try to run straight down the street, he thought. Not in these shoes. Two men in practical footwear against one in aristocrat's shoes? Those odds didn't look good.

The two remaining assailants pounded up the stairs after him. Thaddeus took the stairs two at a time, careful to skip over the stair just below the top landing.

The closer of the two pursuers hit the step. It collapsed. He let out a brief cry and disappeared, plunging to the cobblestones below. His cry ended with an unpleasant crunching noise. A gleeful, giddy laugh came from inside the top-floor room.

Two down, one to go. Thaddeus breathed a silent thanks to good old Randall and his broken stair. Post-stress disorder of the trauma had made him paranoid—a healthy and eminently sensible attitude, Thaddeus believed.

Thaddeus paused on the landing in front of Randall's door. There was a crude wooden ladder, hardly more than slats of wood nailed to the side of the ramshackle house, leading up to the roof. Thaddeus started to climb. Don't look back. That was important, when men were chasing you with murderous intent. Look forward. Find an escape route. Never look back.

He was just crawling over the edge of the roof when the final pursuer started climbing. That was worrisome. The man should have been at least halfway up the ladder by now. He was smarter than his recently departed accomplices and had become more careful. Very worrisome indeed. Thaddeus preferred recklessness in his adversaries.

He slipped as he started up toward the top of the roof. His knees came down hard on the rough shingles. He cursed. The roof was steeply pitched, its peak almost level with the flat roofs of the buildings on each side. A broad plank of wood, barely visible in the dark, connected the peak of the roof to the roof of the tannery next door.

Thaddeus scrambled up toward the plank, cursing the aristocracy and their vagaries of taste. He reached it just as the dark shape of his pursuer appeared over the edge of the roof.

Thaddeus ran out onto the plank. Something whistled past his ear.

He ducked. A second something whirred over his head. The man chasing him swore and began to scramble up to the peak, racing to reach the plank before Thaddeus could make it across to the other side.

It was a race he could not win. Even shod as he was, Thaddeus was still far faster on the flat plank than his assailant was on the steep roof. Thaddeus hopped onto the tannery roof. The man pursuing him was still only halfway across the plank.

Thaddeus turned. He placed one foot casually on the end of the plank. The other man, realizing his predicament, stopped instantly. He was little more than an inky outline against the dark, overcast sky.

"Well, this is awkward," the man said.

"Three against one," Thaddeus said. "Hardly seems sporting."

"You're right," the man agreed glumly. "We should've brought more."

"Don't suppose you would mind telling me who sent you? Or perhaps why you're trying to kill me?"

"I'm a dead man if I do."

"Consider your options."

The man looked down over the edge of the plank. It wasn't that far down onto the roof of the house. The pitch of the roof was steep, sure, but still, he might be able to keep from rolling down off the edge and onto the ground below…

"Sorry. Professional confidentialism and all."

"How much did they offer you?"

"Two hundred shillings."

"And my mum said I'd never amount to anything," Thaddeus said. "Payment in advance?"

"On completion."

"Creepy guy, bony hands? Voice that sort of crawls into your ear and turns your brain inside out?"

The man remained silent.

"Watch yourself with him," Thaddeus said. "He's fast with a knife. And he doesn't like to pay his bills."

"So noted," the man said. "Thanks for that. Listen," he added after a time, "I don't suppose we could just call it a day? Pretend this whole thing never happened?"

Thaddeus considered this. "I doubt your friends are that good at pretending."

"Ah, good point. But y'know, I never really liked those guys anyway."

"I take it you're out of throwing knives?" Thaddeus asked.

"I packed light. Didn't think I'd need them, what with my compatriots and the clubs and all."

"That was probably a mistake."

"Probably."

There was an uncomfortable silence. Finally, Thaddeus asked, "Do you happen to have any oilcloth on or about your person?"

"Oilcloth? I don't think so. Tell you what, I could just nip over there and check."

"That won't be necessary." Thaddeus gave the plank a shove with his foot. The would-be assassin plummeted out of sight with a shriek. Thaddeus heard a thud as he hit the roof. He didn't bother to see whether the man managed to stop himself before continuing over the edge.

He set off unsteadily across the tannery roof. His knees screamed at him. The last ragtag ends of adrenaline burnt themselves out of his system, leaving his nerves quivering.

Couldn't go back home. Too dangerous. Too many dead people lying about too. He felt quite strongly that he should not have to be the one to clean them up, as he had not, technically speaking, been responsible for putting them there.

On the other side of the building, an iron drainpipe made an easy slide to the street—easy, at any rate, when he was well rested and not still shaking from a string of recent attempts on his life. He hit the ground hard, cursing. Then, he picked himself up again and limped off down the road.

If his route home had been circuitous, the path he took now was positively labyrinthine. He went down Boggs Road until it met up with Glevinshire Lane, then doubled back along the alley behind the baker's to Sentinel Avenue, and from there 'round past Kingsway to Foursquare Street. He was careful to stick to the darkness, out of the light of the gas lamps.

Eventually, he made his way to Hammersmith Street. He kept going, following the road until at last he came to a large brick building with a fat chimney protruding from its roof. Electric arc lamps glowed from a high window. A rust-streaked metal sign hanging out front proclaimed "Bodger & Bodger Iron Fittings."

Thaddeus hammered on the door.

"Go away!"

He hammered again.

There was a thump from inside, followed by the sound of footsteps. The door opened an inch. A suspicious face looked out at him. The face was several inches above his own. It was connected to a tall person of indeterminate gender, wearing clothes so caked in grime it appeared that if they ever saw the inside of a washtub, they might disintegrate entirely. A heavy leather apron was tied over top of them, probably to keep them from crawling off their owner's body to do unfortunate things.

"Claire Bodger! It's a delight to see you on such a fine night."

"Muddy!" Claire threw open the door. "Er..." She lowered the crossbow, looking a bit apologetic. "You shouldn't maybe be coming around at night. I might have put a bolt in you. Where on earth did you get that hat? You look a complete tosser."

"That's a bit of a story," Thaddeus said. "Not as interesting as the bit that comes after. Is Donnie around? I—" He felt the last of the adrenaline flowing out of him. "I think I'm in trouble. It's been a bad day..." The world wavered, then turned sideways and slid past him fast. Claire slung the crossbow over one shoulder, slung Thaddeus over the other, and disappeared inside.

In the shadows across the street, a pair of eyes watched the door close. Eventually, the light upstairs went out.

4

High in the skies above New Old London, Her Royal Majesty Queen Margaret the Merciful was very unhappy. As was customary when people in positions of power were unhappy, the people standing closest to her—in this case, one on each side of her—were also unhappy. Say what you want about the monarchy, in some ways those born to power are very generous. It was a matter of perspective which of the three of them was having the worst of it.

"Release me at once!" she demanded. "You will pay for this treason! Guards! Execute these men!"

The man holding her right arm felt that, as these things went, he was probably having a worse day than she was. His name was Julianus Oysterson, and he was dressed in the white cape and plumed helmet of the Royal Guard. "I'm sorry, Your Grace," he said. "It is the Law." He pronounced the capital *L*.

"You treasonous imbecile!" the Queen snapped. "We *are* the law!"

Julianus sighed. "I swore my oath to the Kingdom, Your Grace. Not to you."

This was a point, Julianus felt, few people properly understood. It was all well and good to have a government, and if you had to have a government, it stood to reason that someone should be at the head of it. But there was a difference between representing the law and *being* the law. Even the greatest of leaders, he thought, should still be subject to the rules of civilization. Many of his fellow Guardsmen thought this notion to be entirely too bohemian, but Julianus was firm in his conviction. In Julianus's view, people who felt the law was something to be applied to others tended to turn it into an instrument of barbarism rather than civilization.

"And I swore my oath to Her Most Excellent Majesty the Queen," said the man holding the tip of his sword against Julianus's ceremonial breastplate. He was dressed exactly like Julianus, save for the red stripe that bisected his white cape from corner to corner. The plume in his helmet was red rather than white.

They were standing in the middle of the airship's enormous grand ballroom. Like everything else on the airship, the grand ballroom was opulent in the way that could be possible only to those with limitless wealth and limited taste. The floor was made of narrow strips of the finest hardwoods, shipped at great expense from the vast forests of the New World colonies. The walls were painted with colorful murals depicting the British exploration of the New World: British surveyors crossing the American continent to the far sea, British merchants establishing trading posts in rugged mountains, British soldiers keeping the Spanish heathens at bay while natives looked on with gratitude. The walls curved gently upward to meet a ceiling tiled with rose-colored French marble.

Julianus had one hand on the hilt of his sword. His other was holding the Queen. His lieutenant, Albert Besthammer, was holding her other arm. Albert was the son of a solidly working-class fishmonger from the dock district who believed the greatest duty of a man was to know his place, even if that place was up to his elbows in fish guts at five o'clock every morning, and who would have been shocked into speechlessness to see his son arresting the monarch. Albert's sword was drawn in a nonchalant kind of way, as though he just happened to have it in his hand at that moment. It was a small sword, mostly ceremonial, not exactly the kind of thing one would want in a full-on brawl, and he had very little confidence that if things went too far around the bend it would do him very much good at all. Still, it was better than nothing, which was his only other choice given that the Queen strictly forbade firearms aboard her airship.

A tight cluster of very cross men had formed around the three of them, crowding in as close as was prudent when gathering around men with swords. The rest of the Queen's personal guard, wearing helmets with red plumes and cloaks with red stripes, made up the inner tier. Around them was a second ring of people, identically dressed but with white plumes and white cloaks. There were more of these than the men with red, but no reasonable man would bet on numbers alone; the Queen's personal guard were chosen for their single-minded zealousness. It also didn't hurt that she chose the tallest and strongest men for her personal guard, a habit she'd picked up from the French.

And then beyond them was nearly everyone else aboard the airship, save only for a small handful of people upon whom the operation of the great zeppelin relied. Dukes and counts, ladies and servants all stood shoulder to shoulder, craning their necks to see who was going to be first to have his head detached from his shoulders. The Ottoman ambassador Tahkir, surrounded by his own bodyguards, watched from the edge of the dance floor, arms crossed, lips pursed with disapproval. Even the serving maids were there. There is little that unites the disparate classes of humanity more quickly than a Spectacle.

Many of the people in the ballroom were having bad days, save for a small handful of people unaware of the chaos that tended, historically speaking, to accompany changes in the status quo of a monarch's court and who therefore saw this as nothing but feedstock for the rumor mill.

Julianus thought about how easy life had once been. In those carefree days, fifteen minutes ago, he had been standing at the back of the ballroom, watching the noblemen dance and gossip, and wondering if a certain serving wench was on duty tonight. Things had been simple then. His duty was to keep an eye on the assembled noblemen (or, as Albert referred to them, "that motley bag of criminal buggers," though only when they were safely out of earshot and usually when he had so much Longfellow ale in him that it came out as "tha' motley bag of buggered

35

blaggers! Bugg'r'm!") in case one of them should suddenly turn out to be a foreign assassin or something—something that had happened only once, to his knowledge, many years ago, and caused some excitement for a time and maybe a war or something.

Now, those days seemed so far away he could scarcely remember them. Fifteen minutes doesn't seem like a long time ago until you're in a situation where you don't expect to be alive fifteen minutes from now.

All because of a ring.

They'd searched the airship, just as the Queen had commanded. Albert, good old reliable, unimaginative Albert, had been the one to search her quarters. Personally.

He'd found the ring. Personally.

And, because he followed rules without imagination or thought to consequences, he'd reported it to Julianus. He could have given it to one of the Queen's personal guard, whose loyalty lay with her and not the Kingdom and who in any event were likely to have better sense, which in situations like this principally meant a sense of self-preservation. Or he could have just stuck it in his pocket or thrown it out a window or something. Anything but reported it to Julianus.

But no. Albert was assertive in his incuriosity. He possessed the kind of mind that, confronted by anything out of the ordinary, simply kicked it up the chain of command to let someone else deal with it. He was not often bothered by thoughts of the consequences of his actions; that sort of thinking, he reasoned, was best left to his betters.

He'd recognized the symbol on the ring, and somewhere in his mind a thought had formed that it might perhaps mean something, but he didn't quite know what. So he'd fallen back on his routine and given it to Julianus, and, well…

Respect for the law was an integral part of Julianus, as much a part of his DNA as his dark, piercing eyes. And judging from the way the evening was unfolding, it might just end up breeding itself out of the species.

"The Law is clear, Your Grace. Those known or suspected of

36

association with the pretender in Rome shall be detained until a court can be convened to determine their guilt or innocence," he said.

"You stupid, pointy-nosed little man, I am not a heretic!" the Queen said.

"That is not for me to decide, Your Grace," Julianus said. He touched his nose self-consciously. "My duty is to detain you until the matter of your guilt or innocence can be determined."

Queen Margaret was positively vibrating with a seething fury barely contained. "You lowbred offspring of a lowbred imbecile," she said, enunciating each word more precisely than Julianus thought was strictly necessary. "I will have your head on a pike before sunup tomorrow." There was a mutter of assent from the guards with the red stripes on their capes. The point of the sword resting on Julianus's breastplate slid up an inch.

Bag the blag of buggered blaggers.

"You may at that, Your Grace," he said. "But that does not change the Law."

Alÿs scurried over to her friend Eleanor, who was standing on her tiptoes. Eleanor was trying to look over the shoulder of the portly Lord Bombardier, a man almost as wide as he was tall and considerable in both dimensions. Roderick scurried after her. He had been assigned to guard Alÿs to prevent her from throwing herself out a window. As the standoff had developed out there in the middle of the dance floor, he had discovered within himself a newfound devotion to obeying orders. Especially as Alÿs seemed disinclined to get any closer to the ring of angry men with swords, or to the Queen. The look on the Queen's face suggested a sleepless night for the headsman.

"Oi now, where do you think you're going?" he said to Alÿs.

"I just thought I'd nip off and throw myself out the window," Alÿs said. "You don't mind, do you? Oh, don't look at me like that. I'm not serious. Don't you have any sense of humor?"

"Not to my knowledge, my lady. It's discouraged in the Royal Guard," Roderick said.

"Oh, I see—hah. You're entirely too clever."

"Mum's the word, my lady. Now, where are you going?"

"To the privy, if you don't mind," Alÿs said. "And the Lady Eleanor needs to go too. No, hush, you do. Will you be accompanying us, Roderick? No? I thought not. Please do feel free to wait outside the door if it will make you feel any better, there's a good man." She took Eleanor's arm firmly in hers and half-led, half-dragged the taller girl toward the privy.

"Are you mad?" Eleanor complained when the door had closed behind them. "We're missing the good part!"

"Shush!" Alÿs said. "I think we can do more than just watch." She looked at herself in the tall, gilt-edged mirror and adjusted the front of her dress.

"What do you mean?"

"I mean, those idiots out there are going to turn this into a bloodbath. They're all nice and civil now, mostly, but you watch. As soon as we land, things will turn nasty," Alÿs said.

"So?"

"I think we should do something."

"Us? Save the day? Ooh, how exciting!" Eleanor's eyes gleamed. "What should we do?" She leaned forward conspiratorially.

"We need to get a message to the ground. We need to tell the Cardinal what's going on. He'll know what to do."

"You mean like a secret plot?"

"I really wouldn't suggest putting it quite like that, exactly...oh, okay," Alÿs said, seeing Eleanor's expression, "we can call it that if you want. Just not in front of anyone else, alright? Now, what do we say?"

"Help, the Guard has gone berserk and arrested the Queen!" Eleanor suggested.

"I was thinking something a little less likely to get all of London in an uproar," Alÿs said. She thought for a moment. Then she slipped her small silk handkerchief from its place in her sleeve.

"What are you doing?" Eleanor asked.

"Plotting." Alÿs dug out a small pouch from its hiding place in her dress and fished out a small pot of lip paint. Working quickly with a fingernail, she scribbled a note on the handkerchief. "Here. Take this forward. There's a little door in the end of the hall that opens onto a ladder that goes down to the signal room. Show this to the boy there. His name is Gerry. Gerry Highlander. Tell him to send this message to the Cardinal. He knows how to work the signaling lamp." She pushed the scrap of cloth into Eleanor's hands.

"You want me to go into the commoner's area?" Eleanor looked shocked.

"Yes. Take this down to the signal room—"

"Where the commoners are?" Eleanor's mind had latched doggedly onto this detail of the plot and seemed disinclined to let go.

"Yes. Just show this to Gerry."

"Is he a commoner?"

"Who, Gerry or the Cardinal?"

"Gerry! I know the Cardinal is no commoner."

"Yes!" Alÿs sighed with exasperation. "He's a commoner. Don't be that way. Sometimes secret plots mean talking to commoners. Go!"

"Why can't you do it?"

"Because I have Roderick the Fierce, Protector of the Realm, following me around to make sure I don't fling myself out a window. I don't want anyone to know the message came from me. That's why it's secret, right?"

Eleanor studied the cloth, brows knotted. "What does it say?"

"It's a secret message. It's not supposed to be easy to figure out."

"Why is it in Latin? Nobody speaks Latin! I mean, besides…oh." Understanding dawned on Eleanor's face. "Right. Clever!"

"Yes. Get rid of this after he sends it."

"How?"

"I don't know! Use your imagination. Throw it in the fire or something." Alÿs turned this way and that, examining herself in the mirror.

When she was convinced she looked suitably presentable, she said, "Okay, let's go."

They left together. Roderick, who had been waiting dutifully outside the door, picked Alÿs up the moment they passed through. He was not going to shirk his duty, oh no, especially not when the Queen herself had given him a command. And if the pursuance of his duty kept him away from the angry men with swords drawn in the center of the ballroom, well, that was just the way these things went sometimes.

He fell into step beside her. She ignored him. Eleanor headed toward the far exit, where a door opened on to a steep set of narrow stairs leading forward and down. She crept down the stairs with aggrandized caution, a bit disappointed that the whole of the Court's attention was so tied up with the spectacle of the Queen's arrest that there was nobody left to not notice her exit.

The standoff hadn't changed much. There was still an air of wary tension, though it was a little more relaxed. The opposing forces seemed to have come to an unspoken agreement that things would remain as they were until the airship landed. Nobody could really go anywhere until then, and open violence would in all likelihood end up with some deaths that could prove inconvenient or even troublesome to the Kingdom. There was no immediate advantage for any side to provoke violence until they were on the ground, though after that, what would happen was anyone's guess.

Presently, Eleanor sidled up to Alÿs and gave her an exaggerated wink. "It's done," she said in a stage whisper.

"What's done?" Roderick demanded.

"Nothing," Alÿs said. "Girl stuff."

"Oh," Roderick said. He didn't know exactly what Girl Stuff was, but he had three sisters, so he knew that it was something he didn't want to press for too many details about. Often, in his vague understanding, Girl Stuff involved the contents of handbags and other unmentionables, whose mysteries he didn't fully understand and didn't really want to. He had tried once, as a young boy, to find out what Girl Stuff was. The girls had shown him. For weeks afterward, everyone called him Roderick Rosylips. It wasn't an experience he was keen to repeat.

Time passed. The floor tilted as the airship descended toward its mooring. The standoff in the ballroom had changed very little, except that the Guardsmen with red plumes were gathered more tightly around the Guardsmen with white, and everyone looked a bit more tense. The ambassador's bodyguards were wary, hands hovering near the hilts of their daggers, but they did not seem keen to interfere.

The Queen herself looked a bit…smaller than Alÿs remembered. Of course, it was always more difficult to look commanding when two people with swords had you by the arms. Power lies in the hands of the person who wields it, after all. Sometimes those hands could change very quickly. Throughout the ballroom, little hurts were being remembered, little professional jealousies were being relived, the philosophies of those whose allegiance lay with a person were coming up against those whose allegiance lay with an idea, and somewhere in all that, the person who was Her Most Excellent Majesty Queen Margaret the Merciful had all but been forgotten. Power was on the move, trying to decide which hand best suited it.

The thrum of the great engines changed pitch. The floor vibrated. The airship tilted down more steeply, then straightened. A couple of the more eager Guardsmen used the brief change in attitude to shift, ever so slightly, to more advantageous positions. Hands tightened on sword hilts. *So this is what it comes down to,* Alÿs thought. *The Queen has the divine right to rule, right up until the right person thinks up a reason she doesn't.*

Seemed about par for the course. Alÿs had read enough history to know that divine rights were nothing if not transitory.

The vibration grew stronger, then stopped. The floor shifted again. There was a thump.

And so it begins, Alÿs thought.

There were several heavy, muffled thuds from outside. The curved wall of the ballroom split open. The broad steps descended.

"Make way for the Queen's Guard!" A tight triangle of men, all in white cloaks with red stripes, came up the steps and stopped abruptly. They took stock of the situation quickly. A mutter went through them. Swords were loosened in their sheaths.

The man at their head had the look of a person who was accustomed to being obeyed and took it as his right to stab anyone who disagreed. His name was Max. Like many of his species, he had come empirically, via the time-honored scientific process of hypothesis and observation, to the conclusion that he should always be obeyed. That is, he had spent a great deal of time punching, kicking, stabbing, and occasionally biting people, and observed that the more he did these things, the more people listened to him. And since making that observation, he'd seen no reason to change his ways.

Some of his men called him Max the Axe. He pretended not to hear them. Secretly, it pleased him. Max the Axe. It summed up his approach to command nicely.

"What's this, then?" he said.

The tight spiral of angry armed men unfolded like one of those complicated choreographed synchronized dances, only with more swords. People managed to point at Julianus without really pointing at him. He took a deep breath and straightened fractionally. "I have placed the Queen under arrest. And now, if you will step aside, I will escort her to her quarters, where she will be confined until an inquiry can be convened."

Max narrowed his eyes. He felt on familiar and comfortable ground here. He knew exactly what to do: shout orders until people did what he wanted, and stab any people who didn't.

Go with what works.

"Men, draw your swords!" he called. The air was filled with the metallic scrape of deadly intent.

"Stand back," Julianus said. "I am operating under authority of the Law. I have detained the Queen pending an investigation of heresy. Stand down your men." He spoke with the conviction of one who believes the law is always just, the truth will always win, and puppies and kittens always go to heaven.

"Is this really what you want?" Max said, in a tone that suggested he fervently hoped the answer was yes.

"The Queen has been detained by due authority of the Law, pending an investigation of association with heretics," Julianus repeated. "The truth of the matter will be determined by a lawfully appointed council." He kept his grip on the Queen's arm. The tip of his sword moved up slightly, still not quite pointed at anyone in particular.

"Good enough," Max said. "Men, adv—"

"Make way for His Eminence!" thundered a voice from outside.

Outside, on the landing pad, another large group of men appeared, striding toward the airship with purposeful intent. These men wore red robes edged with gold, and high, pointed steel helmets that identified them as members of the Pontifical Swiss Guard. Being of a more practical disposition than the Queen's Guard, they were armed with rifles, not swords.

A tall, thin man with white hair brought up the front of the procession. His narrow face seemed habituated by years of hard experience to wearing a perpetual frown. Behind his eyes lurked the kind of intelligence that misses little and approves of less.

Max turned. This was *not* familiar and comfortable ground. The rifles had an uncomfortable advantage of range, and the bayonets at the ends suggested further discomfort to those who survived the opening salvo.

"Your Eminence," he said. A complex assortment of emotions battled like opposing armies for control of his face. "This is a matter for the Queen's Guard. There's no need for a man of the cloth to be here on such an unpleasant night."

The Cardinal strode forward. His name was René de Gabrielli, but few people knew that and still fewer called him that. To the majority of London, he was simply "the Cardinal."

His men spread out smartly into a loose semicircle, providing flanking cover. They moved, Max noted with surprised dismay, like disciplined and competent soldiers, especially for men of a religious persuasion. Max was a simple man, and like many simple men, he lacked a commanding grasp of history. He had never learned just how closely the martial and theological pursuits tended to follow one another.

"I have heard reports of a certain…matter that might engage the interest of the Holy Church," the Cardinal said.

"I have this under control," Max said.

"Yes, I see that. All the same, indulge an old man. What is going on here?"

"These traitors—" Max began.

"I wasn't speaking to you." The Cardinal took another step forward, hands folded inside his heavy red robes. "You there! What is your name?"

"Julianus, Your Eminence," Julianus said.

"Can you tell me what you are doing?"

"I have placed the Queen under arrest on suspicion of heresy," Julianus said.

"I see," the Cardinal said. "What an extraordinary thing to do. Do you have extraordinary evidence to support this extraordinary claim?"

"Heretical associations, Your Eminence," Julianus said. "I have reason to suspect the Queen of association with the Catholic Church of Rome." A gasp went through the crowd. Behind him, people whispered to one another.

The Cardinal raised an eyebrow. "Do please go on."

"We found a ring, Your Eminence," Julianus said. "It bears the seal of the pretender in Rome. It was found in the Queen's personal effects."

The Cardinal's long, sour face soured more. "This might seem a minor detail, probably unimportant as such, but it is the nature of the ecclesiastical mind to be troubled by these trifling things. What, precisely, were you doing in the Queen's quarters?"

"We had been ordered to search them. There was suspicion of an… intruder, Your Eminence."

"An intruder. On an airship? How very interesting." The Cardinal paced back and forth, appearing to take little notice of the tense standoff around him. The guards behind him adjusted their positions smoothly, maintaining their fields of fire. "And where might this intruder be now?"

"We don't know, Your Eminence. Apparently, there is a report that he may have, if I have this right, jumped out a window."

"Surely not," the Cardinal said. "Even if we do not consider the most probable outcome of such an act, the windows of this airship seem quite small. Inadequate, I think, to permit the passage of an intruder. Unless this intruder was a mouse. A suicidal mouse, perhaps. Was this intruder a suicidal mouse?"

Roderick stepped forward. As the only member of the Guard to witness the event in question, he felt duty bound to help set the record straight. "It was the door, Your Eminence. He went out the door. In the back. Where they load all the food and such," he added helpfully.

"Ah, the door. Yes. That makes far more sense."

"Thank you, Your Em—"

"It appears we have a misunderstanding," the Cardinal said. "I'm sorry, that's entirely my fault. That was sarcasm. But perhaps our invited guests can offer some insight about our uninvited guest, hmm?" He nodded toward the ambassador's party. "What do you have to say on this matter?"

One of the ambassador's men started forward, hand on the hilt of his knife. "I resent your implication," he said. Two of the Cardinal's guard pivoted smoothly in place to cover him with their rifles.

The Cardinal raised his hands. "I mean to imply no disrespect. Being that you are not part of the Queen's Court, and therefore not party to the, how shall I say this delicately..." He clasped his hands behind his back. "To the political ambitions some here might harbor, it is my hope you might be able to lend a bit of clarity to this matter."

The ambassador laid his hand on his bodyguard's arm. "I am Tahrik Khaldun, ambassador for Caliph Rashid Mahmud. Alas, I fear I cannot make transparent what these men have made opaque. The events I have seen are as this man Julianus describes. As for the fate of those who leap from airships, I cannot say."

45

The Cardinal nodded. "No, of course not." He turned to Julianus. "To charge a reigning monarch with heresy is quite serious. One might even say career-limiting. Perhaps, had I not arrived so fortuitously, terminally so. You appear to take the law quite seriously."

"I do, Your Eminence," Julianus said. "The Law is the Law. Where would we be without it?"

"Where indeed. The world needs people like you, Julianus. Your kind are very useful. Invaluable, even." He appeared lost in thought for a moment. Finally, he turned toward Max the Axe. "You will stand down. The Queen will be taken into custody until an ecclesiastical tribunal can be convened. The law, as our excitable friend here says, is the law."

"But, Your Eminence—" Max began.

"No, I insist. It is the correct thing to do. There are procedures." He turned to leave, then seemed to notice the pontifical soldiers arrayed around him for the first time. "Also, my men will kill you if you don't."

Max the Axe growled. He felt the evening rapidly slipping away from him, and he didn't much like the feeling. Not only was nobody listening to him, there didn't even seem to be anyone he could punch.

For Her Most Excellent Majesty Queen Margaret the Merciful, the evening was also going sideways. She did not say a word as her red-striped guards sheathed their swords and stood aside. Julianus escorted her off the airship. As they left, the Church guards flowed seamlessly behind them, creating a band of red and gold between the Queen and her personal guard. Max the Axe growled again. He tried to push forward, but the wall of red capes and high helmets did not yield.

Lords and ladies and serving maids streamed out behind her. Some chattered excitedly; others, of a more thoughtful disposition, reflected on what the Queen's changing fortunes might mean for theirs. The small cluster of people around the ambassador watched, whispering amongst themselves.

Alÿs followed after most of the throng had left, but not so late as to be behind the more common sorts of folks. Roderick kept step with her, not really escorting her, but making it clear that he was with her all the same.

The Cardinal stepped in beside Alÿs, so smoothly it almost seemed he had simply materialized out of the mist next to her. He looked at Roderick. "Shouldn't you be helping to escort the Queen to her tower?"

"I've been ordered to…" He glanced at Alÿs. "That is, the Queen told me to make sure Alÿs didn't jump out of a window. And she said she would decide what to do with her when we landed."

"I'm not sure the Queen will be deciding any such thing at the present moment. So I assume your duty has been discharged?"

"I—" Roderick looked back and forth between him and Alÿs.

"Did she jump out a window?"

"No, Your Eminence."

"Or out a door?"

"No, Your Eminence."

"Well then," the Cardinal said with the tone of a man who has just pronounced a matter settled. "Your job here is done."

"But, Your Eminence…" Roderick said helplessly.

"Are you familiar with the history of the Reformed Holy Catholic Church?" the Cardinal asked casually.

"Um…it split off from the Roman Catholic Church a couple hundred years ago," Roderick said cautiously. "Big to-do about the French cardinals not being at a meeting or something."

"Ah," said the Cardinal, "it was more like three hundred years ago, but no matter. Now, do you know what I have learned during the time I have served the Reformed Holy Catholic Church, helping to guide her through her dealings with the heretics and usurpers in Rome?"

"What's that?" Roderick said.

"The world respects a man of God," the Cardinal said, "but it respects a man of God with an army at his back far more." He glanced at the two men with red robes and rifles, who, like him, seemed to have the disconcerting skill of materializing right out of a space where you were sure a moment ago there was naught but darkness.

"Ah. I see. Good lesson," Roderick said. "I guess now that my oble-gash—obilgash—my duty is discharged…" He looked around. "Good evening, Your Eminence. My lady." He tipped his helmet to Alÿs and hurried away.

The Cardinal smiled at Alÿs. At least, that's what she thought the expression was supposed to be. "*Regina in tribulatione arma indiget auxilio*?" he said.

"Your Eminence?" Her expression revealed nothing.

"The Queen is in trouble, I gathered that," he said, switching to their native French. "But I'm not sure it was her weapons that needed help. You do have an idiosyncratic relationship with the Church's Latin."

Alÿs stopped and spun on her heel to face him, addressing him in French. "You let them arrest her! You know she's not a Roman sympathizer."

"Do I?"

"These charges—it's absurd!" she said. "Something's going on. Find the man who jumped out of the airship. He wasn't supposed to be there. I bet it has something to do with him."

"Ah, yes, a mysterious man who jumps out a window. Excuse me, my lady, my mistake. A door. Of an airship. In flight. Yes, I'm sure such a man could answer many questions."

Alÿs stomped her foot. "Queen Margaret is not a heretic! Or a traitor!"

"Then I'm sure she has nothing to worry about." The Cardinal took her arm. "But you, my dear, have other things to focus on."

"Such as?"

"Covering your tracks. Let's start with Latin conjugation."

5

It was the banging that woke him. Loud, repetitive, metallic banging that echoed through the vast brick space, came sideways into his head, and took up bouncing around inside his skull.

Thaddeus opened his eyes. He was sprawled on a simple bed, just a cloth mattress stuffed with straw over a rude cast-iron frame. The place smelled of industry. Industry had a certain essential odor, made up of equal parts machine oil, grease, burning coal, and steam, seasoned generously with the metallic tang of hot iron.

He was lying on his back, staring up at the distant ceiling. The space above him was packed with a mind-bending array of machinery. An enormous engine, not steam powered but electrical, spun a gigantic iron wheel wider than Thaddeus was tall. A belt from that wheel fed power to a huge shaft that ran nearly the entire length of the building. From that axle sprouted a bewildering profusion of pulleys, driveshafts, and gears, which turned still more axles that fed power down to who knew what down below. A complex network of ladders and catwalks was strung throughout the ceiling like strands of a great metal spiderweb.

He swung his feet off the bed and stood. He was on a platform high up on one wall of the shop, looking down over the main floor of Bodger & Bodger below. There were two narrow beds on the loft, the one he had slept in and a second just like it. A rickety flight of stairs made from planks of wood driven into the wall led down to the floor below.

He had vague memories of Claire half-carrying him up the stairs and dumping him without ceremony into her bed. He wondered where she'd slept. Probably hadn't, he thought.

Thaddeus had slept the dreamless sleep of the exhausted and terrified. He'd fallen asleep in his clothes, with those ridiculous shoes still on his feet. Thaddeus had heard that the winds of fashion shifted rapidly for those at the pinnacle of society. For people of his socioeconomic stratum, fashion seemed entirely too persistent.

His eyes followed the path of a belt that led from the great driveshaft overhead down to a smaller shaft, where a smaller belt fed power to another, smaller driveshaft that turned a wheel that drove an even narrower belt that spun a still smaller shaft, until finally a thin chain no bigger than his pinkie descended to the loft, where it disappeared into a round white fountain-shaped bowl on the floor. Water circulated in the bowl, emerging from a jet in the top and flowing into a shallow depression in the front. A large, surly-looking orange cat was curled up on the floor beside the bowl.

"Shoo!" Thaddeus said. He pointed. This might have worked with a dog; after all, dogs will usually look in whatever direction you point. Cats merely look at your finger.

The cat stared at Thaddeus for just long enough to convey that it was not impressed, then yawned and went back to sleep.

The metallic hammering filled the building, bouncing off the walls and reverberating through his aching head. His eyes vibrated in their sockets. Thaddeus put on his top-hat on and looked over the edge of the rough wooden balcony into the yawning space below.

The main workshop of Bodger & Bodger was a throng of activity, a huge, noisy, open space, lit by giant electric arc lamps that hung from the ceiling, filled with all manner of machinery. An assortment of clankers, both two-legged and four-legged, were scattered across the workshop floor in various states of disassembly, access plates removed to reveal boilers and handles and great iron gears. Workbenches, covered with tools with purposes Thaddeus couldn't even begin to guess at, lined both walls.

The Bodger twins were both hard at work. Claire had opened the shutters that led into the courtyard behind the building, where the enormous brick forge squatted, belching fumes. She was banging a long, flat strip of red-hot iron on one of those big metal things with the pointy bit on the end—an anvil, that's what it was.

The apprentices swarming around the various machines were as varied as the machines themselves. They were all boys, but quite a collection of different sorts they were. Thaddeus saw Scots with fair skin and ginger hair, dusky Moors, and a couple of people of ancestry as muddled as his own. There was even a young man with long black hair and a face that suggested he might be a native of one of the New World colonies. The Bodgers cared for little beyond technical skill and enthusiasm. Rumor had it that they would even employ an Italian, if he knew his way around a forge and had an interesting technique or two to teach them.

A boy of perhaps fourteen, wearing grubby overalls and a striped cap, was halfway inside a bizarre iron vehicle that rested on a strange, continuous steel belt wrapped around a row of small gears, quite unlike any clanker Thaddeus had ever seen.

Of course, there was quite a lot Thaddeus had never seen. He wasn't the most inventive soul ever to walk the noisome streets of London. Which is not to say he lacked the creative spirit; he just typically applied it to the area of financial affairs, and more specifically to property allocation, rather than to the making of things. In fact, he was a bit foggy on the whole process by which the making of things happened. It seemed to him that a lot of it involved beating glowing metal with a hammer, though to what purpose he had never quite grasped. He didn't know if this was because the metal needed to be hammered into submission before it agreed to become other things, or if the hammering was some bizarre ritual designed to vent frustration when things went wrong, which they seemed to do quite often for those who, like the Bodgers, practiced the mechanical arts. Claire had tried to explain it all to him, using words like "malleability" and "forging," but the arcane knowledge of ironworking never found a home within Thaddeus's head.

Donnie Bodger walked by beneath the loft, dragging a wheeled cart filled with enormous gears and pulleys and something that looked a little bit like an ox head made of steel.

The Bodger twins were both formed of the same mold, roughly speaking. There was a familial resemblance, but you had to look pretty closely to tease it out. They'd started from the same template: strong, dark of skin, with wavy black hair. They both had eyes the color of the sky at midnight. They both had round faces that smiled easily.

But at some point after the template had been made, the gods had decided to do some customization. Claire Bodger had been stretched tall and thin, where her brother had been squashed a bit, giving him a lower center of gravity. Where she looked like someone built for speed, he more resembled a cross between a barroom brawler and one of those breeds of dog that's wider than it is tall and can pull a steam locomotive out of a ditch.

Not that anyone would say that to his face.

One thing they shared in common was the sort of intellect that can look at a pile of levers and springs and see something that nobody had seen before. Their devices were legendary among the tinkers of London. Some of them even worked.

Donnie looked up at Thaddeus and waved. Thaddeus waved back, his mind elsewhere.

Going home seemed a bad idea. Not just on account of the two, or perhaps three, inconveniently deceased would-be assassins who were probably in that stage of death where they'd gone all stiff and were beginning to smell a bit fusty, but also because they had known where he lived. Which meant that their employer, who had, from the look of it, recently been his employer as well, also knew where he lived.

Rule one of staying alive: don't be where the men who want you dead want you to be.

Clank. Clank. Clank. Clank. Claire's hammer argued with hot metal, coaxing it into submission.

Claire and Donnie would be happy to put him up for a time, but only for a time. They were the sorts who, if he stayed too long, might start talking about "work" and "rent" and other uncharitable things that made one despair at how the milk of human kindness had been squeezed from the hearts of man.

Clank. Clank. Clank. Clank.

The whole thing had been weird from the get-go. Thaddeus liked to think he had a certain reputation among London's underworld. Thaddeus Mudstone, the man who gets things done! Thaddeus Mudstone, the man who sneaks into and out of impossible places! Thaddeus Mudstone, the one to turn to if nobody else can do it! So of course, when someone wanted something placed among the Queen's personal effects, his was the first name that came up, right? Doing it on an airship and sneaking away uncaught, well, that required no ordinary man. Who besides Thaddeus would even consider such a thing? That had to be it.

Clank. Clank. Clank. Clank.

Thaddeus took the object he'd stolen from the Queen's personal effects out of his pocket and looked at it. He'd been right there, on the Queen's airship, in the Queen's chambers. Her quarters on the zeppelin were more spacious than any place Thaddeus had ever lived in. Hell, they were probably bigger than the last three places Thaddeus had lived, put end to end and then doubled. And so much gold! And silk! Monarchs were, as a species, known to have an affinity for gold and silk. It was a well-known affliction of royal blood. Thaddeus shared that affliction, but that was beside the point. Margaret took the general monarchical tropism for precious metals to a whole new level. Thaddeus didn't know how the airship could even get off the ground, what with all the gold that covered every surface in the Queen's quarters.

Clank. Clank. Clank. Clank.

He had been right there, and it had been right there, sitting on a shelf next to the Queen's jewelry box. It was handily pocket-sized, and

Thaddeus was firmly of the opinion that pocket-sized objects of obvious value that weren't already in his pockets rightfully belonged there. So by taking it, he was righting a universal wrong. Dynamic reallocation of resources, that's what it was.

Thump thump thump.

He had snuck aboard—well, really, walked aboard, holding an invitation given to him by his employer, with an official seal and everything, albeit a bit stiffly with the folded-up kite neatly strapped to his back underneath his tailcoat. But that was okay; it lent him a far more solid, imposing appearance than his compact frame might otherwise have commanded. He'd done the job, then made good his escape, with nobody the wiser except for that noblewoman who didn't really count because she was scarcely more than a child and no one listens to children, and that guard who also didn't count because he was a member of the Queen's Guard and everyone knew they weren't, you know, *real* guards. The Queen's Guard was there for show, or why else would they have those ridiculous plumes on the tops of their helmets?

That was the easy part. The part where his employer kept sending people to kill him was the hard part.

Thump thump thumpthumpthump.

Well, there was just nothing for it but to get to the bottom of what was going on, then. Clearly, he would—

Bang bang bang.

Thaddeus became aware of a great deal of shouting down below. It sounded like only one person was shouting, but that person was doing quite a lot of it, and pounding on the door while he was at it. "Open up in the name of the London Metropolitan Police!" he was saying.

Cold fear grabbed Thaddeus by the spine and squeezed.

He peered cautiously over the rail. The whole workshop had stopped working. Everyone was looking at Donnie.

Donnie wandered unhurriedly to the door and opened it. "Ah, Commander," he said, his voice carrying easily over the hum of machinery. "Welcome. Couldn't hear you o'er the hammerin'. What can I do for you fine upstandin' protectors of civility?"

Thaddeus stashed the jeweled, enameled case under the rough mattress he'd slept on. Donnie glanced up toward him, then back down.

Three men pushed their way past him. This was no mean feat, given how the entryway was piled high on both sides with ingots of metal that formed a narrow corridor almost completely filled by Donnie's broad bulk. The fact that all three of them were holding swords probably didn't hurt.

Donnie stood aside and let the men pass, his face a mask of calm, trustworthy, and above all *law-abiding* helpfulness. He'd learned that when you're built like a rottweiler, people tended to treat you like a rottweiler, no matter how nonthreatening and cheerful of disposition you happened to be. Where other people might have learned to behave more aggressively, Donnie had taken the opposite lesson. Sure, he built machines that could fling a manhole cover through a brick wall at two hundred yards, but he would smile at you beatifically even as he pulled the lever. In person, he tried to be as unassuming as his inventions were intimidating.

The three men fanned out. Donnie glanced up at the loft again. One of the men followed the direction of the glance and immediately headed for the stairs.

Bugger.

Thaddeus brushed dirt and straw off his trousers, placed the top-hat atop his head, and plastered his best nonthreatening smile on his face. He feigned surprise at seeing the policeman. "Good afternoon!" he said. "Always pleased to see an officer of the peace. What brings you here?"

The man looked him up and down. "Oi!" he called. "Found him! Looks just like the description! You, sir, come with me. We have some inquiries we would appreciate your assistance with."

"Of course," Thaddeus said in what he hoped was a reasonable tone, rather than a slightly panicky and desperate one. "Always happy to assist."

The cat opened both golden eyes. Calmly, deliberately, it stood. It carefully folded its ears back, one after the other. It arched its back, stuck its tail in the air, and spat at the policeman. Then, having expressed its opinion to its satisfaction, it curled back up again and went to sleep.

Thaddeus followed the constable down the steps. The other two policemen converged on him in a way that made his heart leap into his throat. It was that expression, polished to perfection by police the world over, that said *This is it, the jig is up.* Thaddeus wondered if they all practiced it in the mirror.

"I believe this is the suspect, sir!" said the man leading Thaddeus. The smile froze on Thaddeus's face.

The three were standard-issue London Metropolitan Police, which is to say, they were nothing at all like the Queen's Guard. No ceremonial armor and long white robes for them, oh no. Those things were for people who rarely grappled with anything more dangerous than an overbaked loaf of bread. These representatives of London's finest looked out at the world with the alert, wary eyes of men who had seen real scuffles and come out on top.

The commander surveyed Thaddeus silently, stroking his chin. That chin was covered in a day's worth of stubble, except where it was creased with a small scar almost exactly in the center. His lips were thin and pressed tightly together in a disapproving frown. His eyes were deep brown and seemed permanently cast in a slight squint.

Thaddeus waited for him to speak. Let them get in the first word. That was key. If you started talking first, you were apt to start babbling, and that would do you no good at all.

The moment stretched until it threatened to snap. Thaddeus fought off the urge to run. Donnie leaned against a pile of pig iron ingots, smiling placidly. Claire, hammer still in her hand, watched the three officers with bright, alert eyes.

Finally, the commander cleared his throat. "State your name," he said. He sounded bored.

"Thaddeus Mudstone Ahmed Alexander Pinkerton," Thaddeus

found himself saying. He had intended to stop after the first word, but the rest just tumbled out as if afraid to let the first bit go out alone.

"Thaddeus Mudstone Ahmed Alexander Pinkerton," the commander repeated. He shook his head slightly. "Whitechapel or Highpole?"

"Whitechapel born and bred," Thaddeus said.

"Hm." The commander nodded. "Tell me, Thaddeus Mudstone Ahmed Alexander Pinkerton, where were you last night before sundown?"

"Oh, you know," Thaddeus said, "here and there. Out and about. No place in particular. I had a social engagement."

"What was the nature of this social engagement?"

Thaddeus ratcheted his smile wider. "Drinking. At the pub. With some mates."

"Does this pub have a name?"

"I'm sure it does," Thaddeus said. "I was too drunk to notice. What I can do for you?"

"We have received a complaint," the policeman said. "Care to comment on that?"

Thaddeus forced the smile wider still, until his face threatened to split. "A complaint?" he said. "I can't imagine why. I'm certain I paid my tab, Officer...?"

"Skarbunket," he said. "Commander Skarbunket, London Metropolitan Police. These are my associates, Officer Bristol," gesturing to the man who had confronted Thaddeus in the loft, "and Officer Mayferry. May I examine your hat, please?"

"My...hat?" The question threw Thaddeus off balance.

"Yes. The complainant gave a detailed description of the hat. And your shoes." The police commander looked down. "Those are very... *distinctive* shoes."

Thaddeus took off the top-hat and handed it over to the commander, who turned it over and looked inside.

"May I inquire as to what—" Thaddeus began.

"Is this your hat?" Commander Skarbunket said.

"I can't imagine who else it would belong to," Thaddeus said.

"Hmm, I imagine not. And those are your shoes, are they?"

"Yes."

"Brundel and Sons, Pemmerton Street?"

"Beg pardon?"

"Your shoes," Commander Skarbunket said. "You can tell a lot about a man by the clothes he wears. You can tell even more about a man by how he wears them. Those shoes, they are very fine shoes. Very expensive. Way beyond a working stiff like me. Made by Brundel and Sons over on Pemmerton Street, as anyone who cared enough about shoes to wear such a pair would know. Me, I don't care about shoes. But those are the shoes of someone who cares very much about shoes. Which is why I find it odd, and I mean no disrespect by saying this, sir, but I find it odd they're on the feet of someone like you. Odd and perhaps a little suspicious. Can you tell me where you were yesterday?"

"I told you already. Out and about."

"Ah, yes, you did say that." He nodded again. "Though now that I think about it, that doesn't really tell me very much at all."

"Is there a point to all this?" Thaddeus snapped through his bolted-on smile.

"We have received a report," the commander said. "A peculiar report. One of the most peculiar I have heard in quite some time, and I have to tell you, sir, just so you really appreciate the full impact of what that means, I have to tell you I have heard some very peculiar reports in my time. Like a report that a flying creature as big as a horse dropped an egg on old Mrs. Havelhutt's roof in the middle of the night. That report described a creature covered with scales and, if I recall correctly, with eyes that glowed like red fire. Excuse me, I ramble sometimes. Anyway, last night I received a report so peculiar that I almost paid it no mind. But the report was very specific on some of the details, you see. And the chief inspector has been encouraging us to be more proactive in our duties. And I happened to be in the area..."

"Of course you did," Thaddeus said bitterly. "With two other officers."

"Just so. As I said, this report was specific on some details. Such as your shoes. And this hat." He looked down at it as though he'd forgotten it was in his hands. "Black top-hat, purple sash, exactly as the report said. Are you quite sure you don't want to tell me where you were yesterday? Besides 'here and there,' I mean."

Thaddeus weighed his options. He could bolt out the back and be on the other side of the forge before they had time to react. From there, he could veer left, around the long, low building where the apprentices slept, then past the shed where the Bodgers kept the coal, and then down the street toward the bridge. But there were three of them, and besides, those shoes, those absolutely ridiculous shoes, would slow him down.

He could jump the man, Thaddeus thought. Maybe take his sword. And then the other two would run him through.

He could try to push past them, make a break for it out the front, try to lose himself in the alleys—

"I wouldn't recommend it, sir," said Commander Skarbunket.

Thaddeus carefully rearranged his face. He made a mental note to start breathing again. Damn and blast. The man could see right through him.

Thaddeus felt giddy. He knew that somewhere, an officer of the law was asking him questions he had no good answers for. He knew that this officer had come with backup, which suggested he'd known all along that Thaddeus would not have good answers, because he already knew the answers, or else why ask the questions? He knew his connection to this earth was now very tenuous, and likely to end with a short, sharp jerk. The knowledge made him free.

"Now see here," Thaddeus heard himself say. "I have no idea what you think you're getting on about, but I had an invitation, see, and…"

"Invitation, sir?" The watch commander's face was unreadable.

Thaddeus's train of thought ran into a wall. The cars jumped the tracks and collided with one another, tumbling over each other in a slow-motion catastrophe that strewed wreckage across his mental landscape. He carefully scrubbed all trace of expression off his face. "Is this about the party?"

"I'm sure I don't know anything about that, sir."

"Then what—"

"We have received a report that as of sundown last night, sir, a gentleman matching your description, sir, did in or about the intersection of Harrington Way and an alley often referred to by the locals as Ambush Alley, sir, steal a top-hat of the following description: black, felt, with red silk lining and a purple sash, in good repair but with some damage, sir, from a young lady by the name of...of..."

"Missy Ellington," Officer Mayferry supplied.

"Missy Ellington," the commander continued. "This gentleman appeared well-to-do, and was reportedly wearing very expensive shoes of a particular style made, as your shoes were, sir, by Brundel and Sons of Pemmerton Street. Said hat, sir, was gifted to Missy Ellington by her late departed father, may he rest in peace, upon the occasion of his death some years ago, and owned by her, sir, as her sole possession in all this earth. And I had to wonder, sir, what kind of monster steals a hat from a young orphan girl who has nothing? Ordinarily, we do not involve ourselves with certain types of petty crime. But as I said, sir," and he coughed, "this was a most peculiar report. One does not normally see the nobility stealing from the poor by such..." he coughed again "... direct means. The removal of what little property might be in the possession of the poor is ordinarily done at a greater...remove. Sir."

The last syllable, for such a simple sound, packed an entire lifetime of experience: a hard climb up from a humble beginning, an unending drive for self-improvement, disillusionment and bitterness at the unjust scales of life, and, most of all, a driving contempt for the rapaciousness of the wealthy in their eternal scorched-earth crusade to accumulate more.

Thaddeus had not even known it was possible to squeeze so much into one word.

"You have me all wrong," Thaddeus said.

"I'm sure I do." There was a strained silence. Then Skarbunket said, "You mentioned a party, sir?"

6

A heated argument filled the guardroom just off the main passageway into the Queen's Palace, sharp words echoing off stone walls. This was the normal way of things. Throughout history, palaces have always had guardrooms, and heated conversations have always taken place in them. Sometimes, these conversations are of the "no, please don't, I swear I don't know anything" variety; sometimes they're of the "where did that ace come from?" variety; but heated conversations are and always have been as much a part of a guardroom as bad lighting and scarred wooden furniture. Monarchs come and monarchs go, but those who guard the monarchs are ever the same.

Max the Axe was angry. This was also the normal way of things. Men like Max the Axe are always angry. It's practically a natural law.

At the moment, Max the Axe's anger was pointed in two different directions. Some might feel that rage would be reduced by this division, under the reasonable but uninformed hypothesis that anger aimed at two targets would mean each of them received half his wrath. In truth, the anger of men like Max the Axe, following its own mathematical logic, multiplies rather than divides. Being angry at two people made him twice as mad at each.

Half his anger—or, rather, double his anger—was aimed at Julianus. It wasn't just that Julianus was there, standing in front of him rather than rotting in a dungeon or swaying gently at the end of a rope. It was that

Julianus *existed*. People are never as unique as they think they are. If Julianus existed, other people like Julianus also existed. In Max's world, people like Julianus had no business existing. People like Julianus were loyal to an idea instead of being loyal to their betters, as was just and proper. That made them untrustworthy. Ideas changed. A man loyal to an idea might shift his allegiances. How was it possible to rely on such men?

The other two parts of his multiplicative rage were aimed, somewhat more carefully, in the direction of the Cardinal. It was not usually safe to point one's anger in the direction of the Cardinal except from a great remove, and preferably while wearing armor. Max was trying very hard not to let his feelings show. The unfamiliar effort was beginning to fray his nerves. The Cardinal watched him calmly from across the table, and as near as Max could tell, the man had utterly taken leave of his senses.

The Cardinal sighed and spoke again, this time very slowly, as if addressing an especially stubborn and slightly dim child. "It is the position of the Church that any investigations must adhere to a very high standard of accountability. Therefore, I would like to insist that you include the arresting member of the Royal Guard in all your activities from this point forward."

"But that means you want me to let Julianus follow my men."

"No. Not just follow your men. I want you to take him *with* your men."

Max blinked, not sure if he could believe the reports coming from his own ears. "You want him to go wherever my men go."

"That is correct, yes."

"That means he will know everything we do."

"Yes. That—"

"And talk to everyone we talk to," Max continued. The sheer effrontery of this man was…was…what was that word that meant annoying and French? *Gauling*—that was it.

"Captain, this is for your own protection. There are those who would say that you have a motive not to uncover anything that might implicate the Queen, or to be less than forthright about it if you do. So your fail-ure to learn anything of use might, ahem, become a cause of suspicion among the more imaginative members of the Court. Those who see con-spiracy at every turn regard lack of evidence as evidence of conspiracy. Whereas if your investigations are accompanied by the very individual who made the arrest, well…he does not share your motivations."

"But he arrested the Queen."

"So he did, yes. Which is why—"

"He arrested the Queen," Max said again, this time more slowly, for emphasis. "You can't trust a man who would do such a thing."

"Now that's not entirely—"

"He *arrested* the *Queen*," Max said.

The Cardinal rose and leaned forward. His long, pinched face looked even more sour than normal, which was no small feat. "Yes," he said, "exactly right. And that is why you will include him in your search for this mysterious man who leaps out of windows. Or doors. Or whatever it is he leaps out of."

Julianus stood ramrod-straight, staring at a point on the wall just beyond Max's head. He didn't like either man, and he felt that there were better uses for his time than searching for someone who in all probability did not exist, or if he did, was doubtless being cleaned up off the streets by scavengers looking for squidgy bits to sell to the animate-makers. Roderick was a good enough chap: solidly unimaginative, not terribly bright, but competent. He said he'd seen a man fling himself out the loading door of a zeppelin in flight. Then again, he also said he'd seen a cat with six legs in an alley near the pub on Pinebutton Street. And he swore it wasn't the Longfellow ale he'd put down, because if he were seeing double, it should have been eight legs, right? And the Queen did keep some very good wine in her airship, not that you were supposed to drink it when you were on duty, or even when you weren't, but still…

"Are we agreed?"

"Your Eminence?" Julianus hastily rewound the last few seconds of conversation in his mind. "Yes, Your Eminence," he said. "I will

accompany representatives of the Queen's personal guard on all enquiries regarding a falling and/or flying man who may or may not have
jumped out a door, a window, or other points of egress from the Queen's
airship in or..." he coughed. "...above New Old London."

"Good." The Cardinal had the look of a man who'd just discovered the
carcass of a dog in his stewpot. "I will not impede your enquiries, then."

Max the Axe, Julianus noted, was absolutely trembling with rage. A
vein on his head looked as though it might burst forth of its own accord
and start strangling people. So at least there was one small spot of light
in this whole ridiculous business.

"Where do we start?" Julianus asked, smiling pleasantly at a spot
somewhere just above Max's head. Max growled, his entire body
quivering. "Partner?" Julianus added.

It took two junior members of the Queen's Guard half an hour to
clean up all the splinters from the shattered table, on account of some of
them being stuck, inexplicably, to the ceiling.

7

"Excuse me, sir. I hate to bring this up, but...what exactly are we doing here?"

Commander Skarbunket looked at Bristol with an expression of surprise. "Surely it is plain what we're doing, Mister Bristol? We're upholding law and order by investigating a criminal complaint."

"Ah, yes, of course, sir. Upholding the law, righting wrongs, championing the defenseless, all that. It's just..."

"Yes, Mister Bristol?"

"Forgive me if I'm out of line, sir, but I just can't help feeling that this matter is a bit beneath our pay grade, you know?"

"Ah. Hmm, yes." Skarbunket dusted off the hat he held in his hands and squinted at it as if trying to decipher the secrets of the universe from the crisscrossed pattern of creases in the velvety blackness of rich but rumpled felt. They were standing in a crowded street that wound its circumlocutious way along the docks, following both the river and its own inner logic. "Mister Bristol, how long have you been on the Force?"

"Five long years, sir, though sometimes it feels more like decades."

"I know what you mean. And Mister Mayferry, how long have you been one of us?"

"Nine years, seeing as how I lacked the advantage of Mister Bristol's military commission. You know this very well, sir. What's your point?"

"Ah, yes, my point. All in good time, Mister Mayferry." He threaded his way through the streaming traffic, nimbly evading a cart loaded with casks of wine being shoved through the crowd by a burly man dressed in blue and white, who handled it with the careless indifference of a sea captain plowing his icebreaker through a sheet of ice.

The presence of the three officers was cause for no small amount of open consternation among the press of people surrounding them. The three of them were the targets of suspicious and occasionally openly hostile stares. There was a certain order, a certain informal agreement between those who enforced the law and those who worked the intricate machineries of commerce here in the docks. The very existence of law enforcement was viewed, by those whose jobs revolved around this place, as an unfortunate necessity of life. Sure, they were sometimes good to have around in case someone took it into his head to get *too* greedy, but most of the time, they were more like sand in the machinery of trade.

Over time, a complex system of graft, bribery, and tacit understandings had evolved here, a quiet, informal way to make sure that business was not unduly hampered by the intrusions of law and order. The presence of Commander Skarbunket and his men was a violation of that delicate system. There were certain places the arm of the law was not expected to reach, certain times when the good citizens of the docks could safely assume that they could perform their job duties without worrying that representatives of the London Metropolitan Police would be around, and the three men, merely by their presence, were violating that natural order of things. There were many who considered their presence a personal affront.

If Skarbunket noticed the narrowing of eyes and the clenching of fists, he gave no sign.

The three men, moving against the flow of traffic, turned away from the river and up one of the close, winding alleys.

"Can't say I'm too crazy about venturing into a place called 'Ambush Alley,'" Bristol observed.

"What's the worst thing that could happen?" Mayferry said. "Other than the obvious, I mean."

"It's the obvious I'm worried about," Bristol said dryly.

Skarbunket turned the hat around and around in his large hands. "Does anything about this—not meaning to interrupt you gentlemen—but does anything about this strike you as odd?"

"About the hat?" Bristol said. "No, sir. Seems an ordinary enough hat to me."

"Yes, I suppose it is. It's the people concerned with the hat I am thinking of."

"Well, sir, if I may be so bold—"

"Please be bold, Mister Bristol."

"If yonder Thaddeus Mudstone Ahmed Alexander Pinkerton belongs in that outfit he was wearing, I'll eat that hat."

"Indeed, Mister Bristol, indeed."

"On the other hand," Mayferry said, "if it belonged to young Miss Ellington's pa, I'll join Bristol here in his repast."

"A most apt perception, Mister Mayferry. Which brings me to the next question, to wit: what did you make of our friend Thaddeus Mudstone Ahmed Alexander Pinkerton's tale?"

"He is a quick dissembler, sir, no doubt. I find it not at all likely that the likes of him would be invited to a dinner party of the Royal Horticultural Society."

"Mm," Skarbunket said. "Don't think so small, Mister Mayferry. I find it highly unlikely that the Royal Horticultural Society exists. Or that, if it did, its idea of a formal dinner party would involve a trained monkey."

"Not for nothing, sir, but this whole situation is peculiar, trained monkeys notwithstanding," Bristol said. "Since when do street urchins come to us about anything?"

"Never in my memory, Mister Bristol, never in my memory. Ah, here we are."

They made their way into the space where the alleys opened up. A light mist drifted down onto them from the ashen sky above.

"My qab!" Missy said. A grin of delight split her grubby face. She leapt to her feet, hands out imploringly.

"I beg your pardon?" Skarbunket said.

"She means her hat, sir," Mayferry said.

Missy made an exasperated noise. "It's what I said! My qab! Give it t'me!"

Mayferry took the hat from Skarbunket and peered into it. "Aye, it's a rum qab for a brim couch as yourself." He set the hat on Missy's head. It fell until it nearly covered her eyes. "Where do you get it?"

"I tole you!" Missy said. "It was my pa's."

"That's a rumple kaddie, lass," Mayferry said. "Don't snap me for a bemmer. Where did you really get it?"

Skarbunket and Bristol looked sideways at each other. "Well, well, Mister Mayferry, you never cease to amaze," Skarbunket said. "What the blazes are you two talking about?"

"Thank you, sir. I told her it's a very fine hat for a young child, but I know she's lying about where she got it, sir," Mayferry said.

"Obviously she's lying," Bristol said. "We're wasting our time."

Skarbunket held out his hand. "No day in which we learn something is a wasted day. Today we have learned something interesting about Officer Mayferry, I think. Pray continue, Mister Mayferry."

Missy squinched up her face. "'Pray continue, Mister Mayferry.' 'E talks like a jeeve."

"That's not a very nice thing to say," Mayferry said. "He got you back your hat."

Missy looked from Mayferry to Skarbunket and back again. "Aight, I s'pose 'e's jayed 'nuff."

"It's not nice to rim your friends," Mayferry said.

"Posies ain't my friends," Missy shot back.

"These posies got you your hat back."

Missy looked doubtful. "Well…"

"That's what the posies are for, isn't it? That's why you came to us. To help you get what was rightfully yours. And you have it back!"

Her grin returned. "My qab!"

"We're not going to take it away," Mayferry said. "We just want to know where you got it for real."

"It's *mine!* I tole you already!" She folded her arms defiantly in front of her. "My pa gave it t'me! Now you go away!"

Mayferry spread his hands. "Okay. Tell us about the hackie cove who cleved your qab."

Missy's face darkened. "'E didn't give me a shilling."

"How did you know where he was when you came to us?"

"I followed him, I did! 'E's a fox an' duckie for sure. Went all over like 'e had a shortie waking 'im. I was too duckie for 'im. I waked 'im all the way." Her small face beamed with pride.

"Translation, if you please, Mister Mayferry?" Skarbunket said.

"She's saying she followed him. Apparently he went to some trouble not to be followed."

"Did he go from here to Bodger & Bodger?"

Missy shook her head. "No! 'E went home first. There was bullybeaters lay about an' jig. Three of 'em! 'E went right out through the window. Tore it right off! And then 'e kilt 'em."

Skarbunket and Bristol exchanged looks. "Take us there," Skarbunket said.

"D'you have a shilling?"

"A shilling? For you to take us to the scene of a crime?"

Missy shook her head. "A shilling t'tell you where it's at. Three shillings t'take you there."

Bristol sputtered. Skarbunket folded his arms. "Three shillings, is it? That seems a lot."

"Three shillings," Missy repeated. "An' three more if I has t'save you from bullybeaters."

"Two shillings," Mayferry said.

"Three!"

"Two," he repeated. "And if we encounter any ruffians, we'll fend for ourselves."

Missy looked at him through appraising eyes that seemed too old for her face. "Done," she said. She held out her hand.

"Mister Bristol, pay the woman, if you please," Skarbunket said.

"Aye, sir, but I will be filing for reimbursement," Bristol grumbled.

Missy led them along a winding path, changing direction and doubling back frequently. Presently, their noses announced they had reached the tannery district.

"Phew!" Bristol said, covering his nose with his arm. "Our man Thaddeus Mudstone Ahmed Alexander Pinkerton lives here, does he? Why would anyone live here?"

"People don't live here because they want to," Mayferry said. "They live here because they have no choice."

"Phew!" Bristol said again through the sleeve of his shirt. "Smells like a fire in a refuse-dump behind an animate shop."

"It was there!" Missy pointed to the narrow building wedged so precariously between the tannery and the textile mill. Both enterprises were in full swing. Thick smoke belched from the tall brick chimney behind the mill, clear evidence that the machinery of commerce was running at capacity.

"What happened?" Skarbunket said.

"I tole you! Three bullybeaters lay about an' jig. Right there." She pointed to the tannery. "They waited fer 'im t'go inside. They all looked t'fig him to a nap."

"What's that?" Bristol demanded.

"She says they planned to beat him to death," Mayferry said.

"Tha's what I said! They all had clubs an' efferything."

"What happened next?"

"'E came right out the window! Right through there." Missy pointed. "Lef' one of the bullybeaters with 'is nob all split open on the stove. 'E ran up the stairs an' one of th' others fell through the step." She pointed again. "An' then 'e ran on the roof. Came down on th' other side."

"What happened to the third man?"

"Fell off th' roof!"

"And you saw all this?"

"I tole you! Posies don' listen too good."

"Hm," Skarbunket said. "We have a report that a crime has been committed here, which, if I'm not much mistaken, gives us leave to enter the premises." He pushed on the door. It opened easily.

Skarbunket stepped gingerly into the tiny space, hand on his truncheon. Bristol followed a step behind, largely owing to the fact that the space was far too small for him to be two steps behind. He looked around, then turned toward Missy. "Young lady, you have been wasting our time. Lying to the police is a crime. I could arrest you right now."

"I ain't lyin'! I tole it all true!"

"I don't see any bodies," Bristol said, indicating the room with a sweep of his arm that threatened to knock over everything on the narrow shelf. "And the window looks just fine to me." He gestured to the undamaged sheet of oilcloth nailed across what served as a window, or at least a crude approximation of one.

"I tole it true!" Missy said. She crossed her arms, frowning.

"Now look here—"

"Hold on a moment, Mister Bristol," Skarbunket said, laying his hand on the man's arm. He knelt, running his fingers over the cold stove. "Looking around, what conclusions would you draw, Mister Bristol, about Thaddeus Mudstone Ahmed Alexander Pinkerton's approach to cleanliness?"

"If he ever owned a broom, he'd use it to hit people with, I'll warrant," Bristol said. "I've seen outhouses in war zones that are tidier."

"My thought precisely. Yet in the midst of all this mess, would you not say, Mister Bristol, that this is the cleanest coal stove you have ever seen?" He swung the door to the firebox open with a squeak. "Inside and out. I would venture, and I say this despite not knowing Mister Pinkerton's religious habits, I would venture that if cleanliness is next to godliness, this stove is in a state of grace." He rose.

"What about the window, sir? Nobody went through that window."

Skarbunket squeezed past Bristol and back outside. He knelt on the ground, examining the edge of the window closely. "No, Mister Bristol, nobody went through that window." He picked something up from the ground, then stood. "But someone may well have gone through the window that was here yesterday."

"You found something, sir?" Mayferry said.

"What does this look like to you?" he said, holding up a small, ragged sliver of brown.

"A scrap of oilcloth, sir," Mayferry said.

"That's what it looks like to me as well, Mister Mayferry." He looked up toward the ashen sky. "There's a missing stair up there." He walked a few steps until he stood directly beneath it and knelt again. His fingers traced through the coarse, gravelly dirt. He rubbed his fingertips together and brought them to his nose.

"This is most perplexing," he said.

"What's that, sir?"

"I do not find it at all surprising, assuming my read of the man's character is correct, his fine taste in clothing notwithstanding, I do not find it at all surprising that someone might want to do violence to Mister Thaddeus Mudstone Ahmed Alexander Pinkerton. I do not even find it surprising that someone might want to do violence to his personage badly enough to send three people after him, which might seem to some to be overkill, if you will pardon the expression, but which evidence suggests might in fact be underkill. What I do find surprising is that someone might, upon attempting this violence and failing, be compelled to go to such extraordinary lengths to conceal all evidence of the crime." He dusted his hands and looked around. "This is neither the sort of crime nor the sort of place that might ordinarily attract an excess of attention. So why bother?"

"I'm not sure I follow, sir," Bristol said.

"When one sends ruffians to do the work of ruffians, one generally tends not to care if other people know. In particular, one does not, I think, send a person out after the ruffians to fix any damaged windows, much less generally tidy the place up. For one thing, that speaks to a level of attention to detail I have rarely found in the head-breaking and—" he shot a glance at Missy, who was watching him with open curiosity— "laying-about-and-jigging trade. Most curious indeed, wouldn't you say, Mister Bristol?" He squinted up at the broken step. "Thank you, young lady, you have been most helpful."

"You see!" Missy said. "I tole you!" She made a rude gesture to Bristol and scampered off without a backward glance.

8

"How's she doing?" Alÿs asked. She gathered her skirt and sat on the chair beside the hearth.

"Furious," Eleanor said. She smiled wanly, sitting in the chair next to Alÿs. They were in Eleanor's quarters, just down the hall from the royal chambers on the second floor of the Palace. The room was decorated in red and green, with ornate fixtures edged in gold. "They won't let her leave her quarters. There are three guards at the door. One of Max's men, one of Julianus's men, and some strange man the Cardinal sent. I've never seen him before. Big fellow, long pike, and I mean the kind with the metal point at the end. I wouldn't know about the other sort. Not very friendly-looking, if you take my drift. They aren't letting most of us talk to her. I'm the only lady they'll allow in and out. You can imagine how she feels about that. Start with livid and go up from there."

"Did she ask about me?" Alÿs asked.

"No. She's too upset. She wants Julianus's head on a pike, and I don't mean the sort that they sing those songs about down in the guardroom. You look terrible! How are you feeling?"

"Like I look," Alÿs confessed. "It's been a long day."

"Oh? Do tell!" Eleanor wrapped her arms around her knees and leaned forward with the hungry look of a shark angling toward a wounded fish. She had caught the scent of gossip, and now the feeding frenzy was nearly upon her.

"I spent all morning answering questions," Alÿs said. "They—"

"Who's they? You're skipping bits. Don't skip bits!"

"The Cardinal, for one. He was there with two people from the Church I've never seen before. You know the sorts. Red robes, funny little hats. Two of Max's guards, one of Julianus's...I think Max sent two because he knew Julianus would have someone there. I'm surprised those two haven't killed each other yet. They had me in one of the sitting rooms and poor Roderick in another room, and they kept going back and forth between us..."

"Roderick? Why? He's just a *guard!*" Eleanor wrinkled her nose at the word.

"He was the only one who saw Shoe Man jump out the door. The only one besides me, anyway. I think they wanted to see if we were telling it the same way."

"Shoe Man. Is that what you're calling him?"

"Yes. They're really keen on finding him. 'If he exists,' they say. I got the feeling that the Cardinal thinks we were making it up."

"I think Her Grace might be of the same opinion," Eleanor said. "If it had been anyone but you, there's no way she would have believed it."

"She doesn't think I was conspiring with Shoe Man, does she?"

Eleanor shook her head. "I don't think she knows what to think. I don't know what to think."

"But I don't—why would I do such a thing? Conspiring against Queen Margaret? I'm engaged to her *brother,* for heaven's sake!"

Eleanor's eyes twinkled. At sixteen, she was two years Alÿs's senior, and she always took a special delight in demonstrating her worldliness to the comparatively naive little princess. "Half brother. Yes, you're to marry her half brother. Who is heir to the Throne, should anything happen to Margaret." She paused dramatically.

Alÿs's reaction perfectly satisfied Eleanor's expectations. Her eyes widened. Her jaw dropped. She stammered for a moment, then finally said, "You can't seriously...that's the most ridiculous thing I've ever heard!"

Eleanor nodded. "Honestly, dear, I agree."

"I'm glad *someone* believes me," Alÿs said.

"If you have a plot, you're smart enough to wait until after you're married to carry it out. Besides, this whole thing is kind of…extravagant, don't you think?" Eleanor leaned in conspiratorially. "You're usually a bit more subtle, aren't you?"

"This isn't a game, Eleanor."

"Of course not." Eleanor nodded sagely and patted Alÿs's hand, slipping with practiced ease from world-wise mentor to innocent friend. "I'm sure it's all going to come right. It's in good hands. But I interrupted your story. Tell me more!"

Alÿs sighed. "The Cardinal said he looked at all the invitations, and everyone was accounted for. No mysterious second cousins once re-moved of the Earl of Gloucester. But the guards would not have let him on without a proper invitation, which means he must have had one. I think that's why he doesn't really believe Shoe Man was there. I told him the whole story, the dance, the kite, everything. Julianus's guy wanted to know everything about the kite. What it looked like, what color it was. I told him I didn't get a very good look at it." She smoothed down her dress. "Everyone is in a tizzy about the ring."

"I don't blame them," Eleanor said. "A spy from the Roman Church! Here, in London! Right on the Queen's airship, even! I bet he was trying to assassinate the Queen. Or steal from her. I bet he dropped the ring by accident. I hope they find who it is and run him through with hot pokers!"

"Yes, well, if there is any—"

"And then hang him!" Eleanor continued. Her eyes blazed with righ-teous indignation. "And after that, they can put him in a cage and throw him in the fire!"

"I don't see how that—"

"And then break his fingers!" Eleanor said. Her mind, having grabbed hold of the image of proper justice for an Italian spy, was reluctant to let go. "And then they could—"

"Yes, yes, alright," Alÿs said. "I think he would be dead by then. If there is a spy."

"There must be!" Eleanor insisted. "I bet it was Shoe Man. He was probably working for the Italians. He looked just like one of them! He had that swarthy complexion like they do, didn't he? I mean, he looked... he looked..." Her brow wrinkled. "He looked like...he had an Italian nose, didn't he? I think he had an Italian nose. I bet he was plotting against the Queen. That would be just like those Roman bastards. Remember what they did after the Schism? They sent their armies to drive all the peace-loving Frenchmen out of Italy and—"

Alÿs leaned back and closed her eyes. "Yes, that was a long time ago," she said wearily. "And I don't think the man I saw was Italian."

"He could be!" Eleanor said darkly. "They're not like us, you know. They're all dark and shifty. And they have those beady eyes. Shoe Man had dark eyes. He must be one of them!"

Alÿs tuned her out. Somewhere in the background, Eleanor went through an extensive catalog of sins, great and small, perpetrated by the Italians since the Schism. It was a list of such length it offered Alÿs plenty of time to think.

The other members of the nobility seemed skeptical of Alÿs. There was overt disbelief of her story, but there was also an undercurrent of paradoxical suspicion: *we don't really believe this man exists, but we think you're probably in cahoots with him...*

The more she thought about him, the angrier she got. Where are you, little man? Where did you go? Little man who can't dance, little man with your hat and your shoes, little man who—

She sat bolt upright, eyes wide.

"...eat babies!" Eleanor said. "What is it?"

Alÿs held up a finger. She chased the thought before it could disappear back down into the recesses of her mind. "Little man with your hat and your shoes," she said.

"What?"

"I have to go." Alÿs stood, so quickly she nearly upset the chair. With a great rustle of heavy silk skirts, she was gone.

"Where are you going?" Eleanor called after her. "You're not chasing the Italian, are you? They do terrible things to women, you know!"

But the door had already closed, leaving Eleanor alone.

✦

Alÿs hurried up to her room, where she shed her corset and heavy skirt for something simpler and, most importantly, less conspicuous. She threw on a plain-looking cloak and hustled through the network of rooms and hallways that sprawled through the underbelly of the palace, the domain of the bustling servant class that made the machinery of royalty function. Few members of the nobility ventured here, among the kitchens and boiler rooms and servants' quarters. Alÿs had explored them all, driven by a curiosity usually absent from people of her station. When you are born into wealth and luxury but you are nonetheless still predisposed to kindness toward your fellow human beings, there are certain gift horses you don't want to inspect too closely if you want to be able to sleep at night—not that any members of the Queen's Court were ever likely to have trouble in that regard.

She slipped out a servants' entrance and hurried across the courtyard to the stables. She searched the stalls until she found who she was looking for. "*Psst*! Henry!" she said.

He turned around. He was a lad of thirteen, all gangly physical awkwardness, with tousled hair and an equally tousled smile, dressed in the green-and-yellow livery of the Queen's stable boys. "Alÿs!" he said. His face broke into a wider-than-normal-grin, revealing teeth like icebergs colliding with one another in a narrow strait.

"Is your brother Rory about?"

"You're not going on one of your adventures, are you?" Henry said. He looked her up and down. "You're on another one of your adventures. The Cardinal said he would box my ears, he did. He said your father wanted him to look after you."

"Well, if he asks, you can tell him I ordered you," she said. "You don't want to disobey a direct order from a lady, do you?"

"I don't know," he said doubtfully. "The Cardinal is a mean old man. I don't want him to box my ears."

"Not even for a shilling?"

Greed lit a fire in the boy's eyes. "Really?"

"I need to go out, and I don't want anyone to know. Is your brother around? There's an extra shilling in it for him, too, if he can drive me."

"I'll go fetch him!" The boy tore out of the stables at breakneck speed.

Fifteen minutes went by. The seeds of doubt in her head began to germinate. Did she really want to pursue a criminal by herself? That seemed rash, even for her. The Queen's Royal Guard was on the case, even if the Cardinal was disinclined to take her seriously. And it was such a tenuous thread…

Henry ran back into the stable, panting. "I found him!" he gasped. "He's not busy anymore. I told him there was half a shilling in it for him…"

"A whole shilling," Alÿs said. "Don't try to cheat your own brother. Family is important." She pressed a coin into his dirty hand. "And don't tell anyone I've gone out."

The hansom cab was waiting in the side yard. Rory stood beside it, tipping his hat as Alÿs approached. He was like a slightly taller version of his brother, the same eyes set above the same warm and easy smile. "My lady," he said.

"I hope I haven't inconvenienced you." She squinted up at the late afternoon sun.

"No more than usual," he said. "Where are we going?"

Alÿs climbed into the hansom. "Do you remember what to do?"

"Aye!" Rory said. "Out the gate, down the street, across the bridge, double back, turn around in front of the fountain, make sure nobody's following. Where to after that?"

"Just like that," Alÿs said. "Then head to Pemmerton Street. Don't tell anyone at the gate I'm here." She crouched on the floor and drew the blanket over herself.

"Pemmerton Street?"

"Yes. I'm going shopping for shoes."

Brundel and Sons occupied a new, stylish storefront at the corner of Pemmerton Street and Lower Cross Way, in the center of one of New Old London's more exclusive neighborhoods. The place was artfully made to look old and shabby, by people gifted in the art of mimicking poverty without approaching it too closely. Fine lumber had been exquisitely crafted to look old and weather-beaten, and new gas lamps were fitted with carefully cracked glass that had been cunningly stained with the finest faux dirt.

Mister Brundel the elder was similarly crafted. His suit looked shabby and old, though Alÿs couldn't help noticing it had the most fashionable of contemporary cuts. The store was designed to look crowded and just a little bit fusty, but if a single speck of dust were somehow to make its way in, it would die of loneliness.

On most days, he worked the shop alone. He had three sons, not one of whom properly appreciated the vast amount of work he had put into building a future for them. On any given day, the three of them could usually be found at one of Mister Spear's establishments, gambling or drinking their future away. There were people, some of them employees of Mister Spear, who made book on how long the sons would be able to evade the workhouse once Mister Brundel shuffled off to the hereafter.

Not that Mister Brundel minded, oh no. He was playing the long game. When, after he passed, they pissed away their inheritance and ended up in the workhouse, then, in the fullness of time, in Purgatory, he planned to smile down on them beatifically from his well-deserved rest in a better place and say, "I told you so!" Timing was everything to Mister Brundel. He was prepared to wait.

When Alÿs came in, he peered at her through eyes almost entirely concealed by the most astonishingly bushy white eyebrows she had ever seen. His face was similarly obscured by a heavy, bushy beard so white it was nearly blinding.

"Welcome to Brundel and Sons!" he said. "My sons are all preoccupied at the moment, but I would be happy to assist you." He gave her the calculating look of proprietors of expensive goods the world over, the one that appraised both her net worth and her knowledge of commerce and arrived through an intuitive mental calculus at the margin of profit she might represent. "Do you have anything special in mind?"

"Not for me," Alÿs said. "I was hoping you might have something for a gentleman friend of mine. I'm afraid he's terribly uninformed about fashion. Something modern, I think. Stylish."

"A gentleman's shoes?" Mister Brundel changed gears. The abacus of his soul shifted the number it had previously calculated one place to the left. "Ah, I know just the thing. High heels are the rage in France right now. Everyone loves a tall gentleman, hm? Hm?" He stood on his tiptoes, peering down at Alÿs.

"I was thinking of something more specific," Alÿs said. "Something flat, with metal points that turn up at the ends. Made of many different kinds of leather. Kind of a patchwork, you know?"

His eyes narrowed. "Such a pair of shoes would be very, hm, expensive," he said. "They are, hm, not just for anyone."

"I was at a ball," Alÿs said. "I saw them there."

"Did you just, then? Indeed, indeed. Likely you saw many, many shoes, hm?" Mister Brundel nodded. "The history of shoes is the history of civilization, my dear. You can tell a great deal about a man by the shoes he wears. And about the city by the shoes it wears, oh yes. Such a pair of shoes, well, such a pair would be made for a very special kind of gentleman, wouldn't it? A very discerning gentleman. A gentleman of considerable wealth and power, hm? A regal man. A man most powerful. A lord. Not an ordinary man at all. Only a very poor businessman would risk the displeasure of such an esteemed and, ah, profitable gentleman, hm? But I wonder, would they necessarily be worn by such a man?"

"That's what I'm hoping to find out," Alÿs said.

"Yes you are, hm? I think you are not here to buy shoes."

"What makes you say that?"

"Look around you." The man flung his arms wide, indicating the many shoes on the shelves lining the room. "Here you are, in a store that sells shoes, yet you haven't glanced at even a single pair. This is most unusual for one looking for shoes, wouldn't you say, hm?"

"Do you know the shoes I'm talking about?" Alÿs asked.

"Oh, I do, I do. Intimately."

"Do you know why I'm asking about them?"

The man waggled his surrealistically bushy eyebrows. "I cannot read minds, young miss. Only shoes."

"Can you tell me who bought those shoes?"

He frowned theatrically. "I am a maker and a purveyor of shoes. Not of gossip, young lady."

Alÿs stamped her foot in frustration. Mister Brundel shrugged. "Will that be all, hm?"

"Wait!" Alÿs said. "You must know other craftsmen, right?"

"Oh, I know some people, here and about," Mister Brundel said.

"Suppose I were looking for a craftsman to make me a kite," Alÿs said. "A very large kite, made of silk and bamboo, intricately designed to fold up into a very small space. A kite of great beauty, but large and strong enough to carry a man. Whom would I be looking for?"

"Oh, now that is a very interesting question," Mister Brundel said. "Most interesting. There is no man in London who can make such a thing as that."

Alÿs's shoulders slumped in defeat. "Oh," she said. "Thanks anyway." She turned to go.

"You do not want a man," Mister Brundel said. "You want a woman. Mistress Chiyo Kanda. Highpole Street, across the Centenium Bridge, in Old New London. You will know her shop when you see it. Look for her kites, hm?"

His eyebrows waggled after her as she left the shop.

9

Her Most Excellent Majesty Queen Margaret the Merciful was seated in a white chair of white wood whose white cushions were covered with white silk of the highest quality, adorned on their edges with small blue flowers whose stitching was so exquisite they appeared painted on. The room around her was so opulent it could bring a blush to the cheeks of the conquering chieftain of one of those nomadic tribes accustomed to raiding cities and carting off anything of value or that looked like it might be of value or was once sitting next to something that might be of value. The moldings along the ceiling were gilt. The paintings on the walls, mostly of somber-faced men standing beside horses while wearing military regalia festooned with an exuberant array of medals or relaxing in pastoral settings while hunting dogs cavorted about in the grass, were mounted in wide, heavy frames, also gilt. The Queen's personal effects, of which there were many, tended toward a gilt motif, with the addition of rubies and other gemstones wherever they could be worked in or, failing that, glued on.

It wasn't that Margaret particularly liked gold, though a casual observer could be forgiven the assumption. It was just that the royal treasury was blessed with an embarrassment of the stuff. It had been arriving night and day from the colonies across the ocean for a very long time, and there was no sign that the flow would be letting up soon.

The Spanish had been the first to reach the New World, and so had been the first to confront the problem of an embarrassment of wealth. The Spanish government, flush with gold, had thought, perhaps reasonably, that the best thing to do with a sudden influx of cash was to spend it, and so had proceeded with great enthusiasm to spend their economy straight into oblivion. The other nations had watched the ruin and, on the idea that it is far less expensive to learn from other people's mistakes than from their own, had taken a more moderate approach to dealing with the gold they brought home from their own colonies.

The British treasury soon established a cartel, carefully limiting the amount of gold released on the market to keep its value up, which left the enviable but nevertheless still knotty problem of what to do with all the stuff piling up in the vaults. Decorating the royal chambers with it was one obvious solution to the problem, and so the Queen's personal effects tended toward a monochromatic yellow theme.

Margaret held a china cup in her hand, its rim edged with gold. Her hand trembled slightly.

"Thank you so much for taking the time from your schedule to meet with us, Your Eminence," she said. "We appreciate the blessing of your presence."

The Cardinal was seated in a chair identical to Margaret's. On the small gold-edged table between them, his own gold-rimmed china cup sat untouched. The Cardinal didn't trust tea. It was a foreign drink, difficult to get and extremely expensive. He had little use for expensive foreign curiosities. When people made a fuss over expensive foreign curiosities, expensive foreign wars often followed.

His face became even more sour. "Sarcasm does not befit one so young," he said.

"You're right, of course. Forgive us. It's much more suited to those with a more ecclesiastical nature."

"Your Grace," the Cardinal sighed, "I am not your enemy."

"Had the Realm more friends like you, we should never want for enemies," Margaret said. "Already the ambassador from the Caliphate is expressing concerns about our nation's stability. Your little show certainly did not fail to make an impression."

"The timing was poor, I agree. Such is the way of crisis." He folded his hands in front of him. "We cannot always schedule them when we would like."

"And yet, from the perspective of the Church, this timing must appear divinely inspired. Anything that pushes us further from the Ottomans must bring us closer to the embrace of France, hmm? You must be pleased. And then there is the matter of the Council of Lords. It meets tomorrow, and here we are, confined to this..." she waved her hand "...gilded cage."

"Alas, the law, as our friend Julianus would say, is very clear. Any person suspected of association with the heretics of Rome, regardless of station, must be placed under arrest until an ecclesiastical tribunal can determine the truth, if there is any, of the matter."

"Yes. Julianus," Margaret said. "We will deal with him in due course. As for the truth of the matter, only a madman, a fool, or a schemer would suggest that the Crown is conspiring with Rome. You are no fool, Your Eminence. We wonder, are you a madman?"

"A question I have asked myself more than once." The Cardinal picked up his cup and glowered at it.

"The Council has reached an impasse. And when the Council is at an impasse—"

"—yours is the deciding voice," the Cardinal said. He cleared his throat delicately. "I am aware. Nevertheless, I am certain we both agree that in a just society, the rule of law is paramount. I have already begun the process of convening the tribunal."

"Your promptness would be notable even for a man half your age. You certainly seem prepared for action."

The Cardinal shook his head. "Allow me to be frank, Your Grace."

"We wouldn't have you any other way."

"We have known one another for a long time, Your Grace. I do not believe even for a moment that you are an Italian sympathizer. It is my desire that the matter of this tribunal be concluded as expeditiously as possible, and I am confident they will see things as I do."

Margaret smiled grimly. "Never let it be said that the ambassadors of the Most Holy Church are anything less than agreeable in their words. Yet here we sit, with guards posted outside my door. We can't help but notice that some of them are yours."

The Cardinal shifted in his seat. "A formality only, Your Grace. It is Julianus, not I, who has confined you. I assure you, I find this state of affairs as deplorable as you do. As you know, the Church has only a limited role in the internal affairs of the sovereign nation of England."

"Yes, of course. Which is why the Church has headquartered its own private army not half a mile from the Royal Palace."

"As protection against any member of the Council of Lords who might take it into their heads to use their soldiers improperly. The true Pope in Paris felt it expedient, in an abundance of caution, to protect the Church's interests after your father brought back private levies." He shifted in his chair. "That is not what concerns us today. I aim merely to facilitate the ecclesiastical tribunal that will adjudicate your guilt or innocence." He coughed delicately again. "Beyond that, I have no direct authority."

"You split some very fine semantic hairs," Margaret said. "Should we ever need the services of a master hairdresser, we shall consult with you."

He inclined his head. "We all have our parts to play. Mine is limited to the matter of the selection of the tribunal and offering it what advice and counsel I may have."

The Cardinal arranged his face into what he hoped was a generous expression. He was having a good day, or at least as close as he ever approached to having a good day. He appeared quite relaxed, which set Margaret's nerves jangling. Few people advanced far in the Church's hierarchy without a generous helping of ruthless opportunism. Religious institutions bred it into their upper echelons. When such men were happy, it usually meant they spied an opportunity for someone else's misfortune.

"Advice and counsel. That's what you call it? Hmm. We should love to be in a position where we have nothing to offer but advice and counsel, if we get to choose the ones we're advising."

The Cardinal picked up the delicate china cup sitting in front of him. He examined it for a moment, sniffed its contents, then set it back down again. "I am certain," he said, "that your allegiance is to the true and rightful Catholic Church, and to the Pope in France, not the corrupt Church in Rome."

"This goes without saying," Margaret said. Her voice was wintry.

"In a case such as this, when one is under a cloud of suspicion, there is little that goes without saying. It is best, I think, to be explicit about where your loyalties lie."

"No doubt you already have ideas about how we might make our loyalties explicit," Margaret said.

"As I've said, Your Grace, I do not believe you are a heretic or a Roman sympathizer. Tomorrow's meeting of the Council of Lords is important. If Your Grace chooses to attend, the Church will register no objection."

"We are relieved to hear it. We thought we had just heard you say that the law requires our imprisonment until the tribunal."

The Cardinal smiled. The overall effect could give nightmares to small children. "The lovely thing about the Law is there is so very much of it, and it so often contradicts itself. One merely needs to look hard enough and one can find a precedent for almost anything. The Church employs the finest lawyers to be found anywhere outside the gates of Hell itself. I have every confidence they can find a compelling legal case for your presence."

"And thus does the Church involve itself in the affairs of the State after all." Margaret took a sip of her tea. "What quo might the Church expect in return for this particular quid?"

The Cardinal leaned back, arms folded. "The Church seeks nothing but the glory of God. The affairs of state are secondary to the salvation of man. What things of this earth could possibly matter more than the Kingdom of Heaven? The state is naught but a foundation upon which

God's works can be built. It is only on those occasions when something threatens to upset that stability that the Church feels called to act. The succession of power in the monarchy is one such occasion. Stability requires—nay, demands—a clear path of succession." He cleared his throat. "When a ruler reaches the age of majority without choosing a spouse or producing an heir, that creates a matter of great interest to the Church."

Margaret's face grew cold. "We hope you are not suggesting that the Church should choose a husband for us in exchange for allowing us to attend a Council meeting."

The Cardinal spread his hands. "I would not dream of making such a suggestion, Your Grace. At most, I might propose an introduction, nothing more. The Marquis de Chambert is without a wife. He is a fine, upstanding man from a noble family..."

"Is he?" Margaret said sweetly. "A God-fearing man, I presume?"

"Yes, he—"

"A man who takes his direction from the Pope? A man who might use his influence over his wife to see things from the Church's point of view?"

"Your Grace, I wouldn't say—"

"No, of course you wouldn't. You're never that direct. You always come slithering in sideways, don't you?"

"Your Grace," the Cardinal protested, "you wound me. I simply think—"

"The answer is no. We will hold no council save our own about this."

The Cardinal shook his head sadly. "This is most vexing, Your Grace, most vexing indeed. On the one hand, it seems inconceivable that your sympathies might lie with Rome. On the other, your intransigence in the face of reasonable guidance from the rightful Church in France will surely raise questions with the tribunal."

"I think you mean to say you will raise questions with the tribunal," Margaret corrected.

"I can only do what my conscience dictates."

"Your conscience or your ambition? The servants of the Church are known for many things, but stupidity is not among them. The tribunal will not be swayed. Refusing to accept a husband you choose for me hardly proves collusion with Rome."

"Nevertheless, I think the tribunal will like to see that you are agreeable to the true Church," the Cardinal said. "It is the appearance of the thing. Even something small, to show—"

"To show that I am an obedient lapdog?"

The Cardinal sighed. "To show that you are not an enemy of the Church." He steepled his fingers in front of him, glaring at Margaret. She waited patiently, expressionless.

Finally, he spoke. "The issue in front of the Council of Lords tomorrow. You are referring to the petition to allow use of animates for military purposes, yes?"

"Yes. What of it?"

"The Serpent of Rome has been clear in his opposition to animates from the moment they were first invented," the Cardinal said. "Life from unlife, he calls it. He sees it as a mockery of God's creation. I believe you share that position, Your Grace."

"We care little for theological debates about the nature of God's creation or how many angels can dance on a pin," Margaret said. "We care more for the consequences of our actions in this world than in the next."

"Then let us discuss the matters of this world. Your nation and mine have been at war with the Spanish and the Italians for hundreds of years. We have fought to a stalemate in both the Old World and the New. This cannot continue. Now, in our time, we have before us an opportunity to turn the tide. We can put an end, once and for all, to countless years of bloodshed. It is within our grasp, if we but have the courage to reach out and take it."

"The pretend Pope in his palace in Rome may be wrong in his reasons, but even such as he may sometimes be right in his conclusions. If the false Pope in Rome said the sky was blue, would you expect us to prove our independence by issuing a royal decree that it is green, merely to spite him?"

The Cardinal scowled. "Your Grace, I don't think—"

Margaret put down her cup. "Obviously."

"It is a small thing, Your Grace," the Cardinal said. "But even such a small thing would send a clear message. You are not in the sway of Rome. You desire, as I do, to defeat the enemies of England and ensure a lasting peace. You stand in opposition to the position of the Roman heretics."

"What about the true Pope in Paris? We hear the theological implications of animate creation are still being debated in the halls of St. Vincent's. We are told he is leaning toward declaring the creation of animates a sinful act. Do you want to put us on the wrong side of both Popes?"

The Cardinal inclined his head. "His Holiness Pope Simon IV has not indicated where his thoughts lie on the matter. This may become a rare point of agreement between the true Pope and the false. But consider the effect that an advantage over the enemies of the true Church might have. Should the animates become the key to erasing the Roman heresy from the world, they would be doing God's work."

Margaret looked at the Cardinal with calculating eyes. "Wheels within wheels," she said finally. "The true Pope is not a young man. How is his health these days? Poor, we hear. If you were to announce a weapon to defeat the Church's enemies, this would no doubt greatly impress the College of Cardinals when the time comes to elect a new Pope."

"All I want," the Cardinal said carefully, "is for our two nations, united, to gain, once and for all, the upper hand against Spain and Italy." He was not accustomed to feeling uncomfortable, and he decided he didn't much like it. "The war in the New World has been going on too long without either side gaining an advantage. Meanwhile, many die in the skirmishes here on the Continent, and for what? Nothing! This stalemate must end."

"Why, Your Eminence, we had no idea you were such an optimist," Margaret said. "Do you know the problem with optimism? Optimists forget the law of unintended consequence. An end to war? Have you learned nothing from history? One's enemies never stay vanquished. They adapt, or new enemies rise to take their place. Animates are mindless monsters. They feel no pain and have no allegiance to anyone save those who know the right words to set them loose or make them stop. They have no honor. They do not understand the rules of war." She leaned forward, green eyes blazing. "They are not people. They are things. Who wages war in such a way, sending things instead of people into battle?"

"Begging your pardon, Your Grace, the history of war is the history of the military arts," the Cardinal protested. "The sword, the pike, the siege engine, the cannon. Would you have men today cast aside their rifles to charge into combat with stone knives?"

"The pike and the cannon are wielded by men," Margaret said. "Men who know when and how to use them. More importantly, men who know when not to. Wars are fought by men. What honor is there in staying out of harm's way many miles from battle and sending things in your place to do your fighting for you? War is a nasty business. The losses we might face sometimes give us pause to look for other ways to resolve our conflicts. When we no longer need to stay our hand for fear of our own casualties, I fear it will make us all the more eager to reach for war as a first resort instead of a last. What will that do to those we oppose?"

"It should make them more agreeable to our desires, I expect," the Cardinal said.

Margaret studied his face for a long moment, then shook her head. "Do you really know so little of the hearts of men? If our enemies understand they cannot hurt us on the battlefield, they will find other ways to hurt us. They will not just bow to our might. Men are too proud for that." She sighed, her expression softening. "If they know that we can hurt them but they cannot hurt us, they will simply look for other places to put the knife. What you propose will not be the end of war. It will make war more ugly. And you're forgetting how delicate things are in the Colonies. Both our nations need the goodwill of the natives to fight the Spaniards. If we bring animates onto the battlefield, we risk destroying our alliance. The natives are superstitious and will not look kindly upon armies of the dead."

The Cardinal shrugged. "That is a question I leave to our generals, and yours," he said. "With the animates, we may no longer need the natives, in war or in peace."

Margaret raised an eyebrow. She opened her mouth, then closed it again. Her mental ledger of reasons to dislike the Cardinal gained a new entry.

"You argue passionately in favor of these new weapons of war. What is it to you?"

The Cardinal inclined his head. "As I have said, it is merely a gesture. A token to show that you are willing to take counsel from the true Church, and oppose the false."

"And if we refuse?" Margaret said. "If we place the good of the nation over our own good?"

"The tribunal will evaluate the facts on the table and reach its conclusion. They might ask why you would decline to pursue every opportunity to press the advantage against our enemies, and why you stand in such solidarity with the false Pope."

Margaret leaned back, studying the cleric through narrowed eyes. Eventually, she shook her head slightly. "You play a dangerous game. We are not without our supporters. The seat of the Church's authority is in Paris, and we are a very long way from Paris."

"Not so far as you might think." The Cardinal shrugged. "It is a small gesture, Your Grace, but small gestures matter."

The two sat for a long moment in silence. When Margaret finally spoke, her voice was tinged with resignation and barely contained bitterness. "Very well. You have your small gesture. We will vote as you suggest. You must be very pleased."

The Cardinal permitted himself a small smile. "I want nothing save the glory of God and what is best for our nations, Your Grace," he said.

"It is unbecoming of you to lie so transparently. But while we are speaking of expedience, I think we are finished with this conversation. If you will forgive us, Your Eminence, it has been a long day, and we must pray you take your leave."

"Of course, Your Grace," he said. He bowed slightly.

"Your Eminence."

The Cardinal left, his face less sour than it normally was.

10

The study of human history leads inevitably to the conclusion that there is no greater entertainment to be had than the contemplation of the misery of another. At no point in space or time had this tendency been more refined than in London, where entire industries had sprung up around the mass dissemination of other people's misfortune. London tabloids traded in misery as their standard medium of exchange, and thanks to the events on the airship, that trade was booming. Newspaper headlines shouted from every street corner. Cries of "News of the century! Queen Margaret under arrest! Read the story!" swirled around Julianus and Max as they shouldered their way through the crowds.

Max growled at a young boy staggering under a load of newspapers. "This is a disgrace," he said. "Look at these people, feeding on rumors and deceit. Disgraceful!"

Julianus looked up, shading his eyes from the hazy midafternoon sun. "This must be close to the place," he said.

"This is a complete waste of time."

"You didn't have to come," Julianus said mildly, looking at the row of shops stretching along the broad street.

"What? And let you prance around with one of my men, filling his head with—hey, I'm talking to you! Filling his head with nonsense and lies about…hey!" He poked a finger in the center of Julianus's engraved golden breastplate. Julianus looked down at the offending digit, then up at Max's angry, sweating face, then back down at the prodding finger, holding his gaze steady until Max withdrew it. "Filling his head full of nonsense and lies about the Queen," he finished. "Someone needs to keep an eye on you. I still don't see why we're here."

"We're here," Julianus said with the patient tone one might use with a particularly recalcitrant and not overly intelligent child who didn't understand why he should have to finish his supper, "because if someone did take a dive out of the Queen's airship, he would probably come down somewhere around here."

"If he flew out on a kite like your man says, he might have come down anywhere."

"Perhaps, perhaps," Julianus said. "But I don't think so. He wouldn't want to risk landing in the river. And it was rainy last night. He couldn't see very far. I think he would want to get to the ground as quickly as possible. Well, not exactly as quickly as possible, but you know what I mean." He strode down the street, moving so fast that Max had to run to keep up.

People parted around the two men the way water parts around the prow of a ship: it doesn't particularly want to, but the ship doesn't care. Julianus looked down each intersection as they crossed.

"What are you looking for?" Max said.

"I don't know," Julianus said.

"Then how the blazes do you expect to find it?"

"I don't know," Julianus said again.

"Disgraceful," Max said. "They will let anyone into the Guard these days."

"So it seems," Julianus agreed. "Shameful, isn't it?"

The machinery of Max's mind processed the statement for a time before the gears whirred and ground into the proper configuration. "Now wait just one minute!"

But Julianus was already several paces ahead, craning his head to peer down every alley. He looked up at the sky, then back down again, muttering. He crossed the street, heedless of a giant four-legged clanker dragging three long iron wagons loaded with coal. The clanker driver was forced to stop so fast that the wagons crashed into each other, sending a shower of coal onto the street. Julianus ignored him, even when the driver sounded a long blast of his steam whistle to express his displeasure. Julianus turned and walked back the way he had come, still looking up. Max hurried after him.

And so they traveled the streets of New Old London, the two of them: Julianus following an erratic route, looking down every street and alleyway; Max trailing behind, muttering impolite things under his breath. They followed an ever-widening path out from the center of the city, through streets crowded with people, horses, clankers, and once, a handful of confused-looking goats being driven by a harried-looking man in blue overalls.

Max complained vociferously about the time they were wasting, about the throngs of people, about Julianus's reckless disregard for traffic. Julianus ignored him. This failed to soothe Max's temper. In Max's world, ignoring him was a capital offense, second only to acts of violence against the Crown, and then only by the breadth of a whisker. Finally, he grabbed Julianus by the shoulder. "What are you doing?" he demanded.

Julianus scanned the roofs of the buildings around him. "I'm talking to you!" Max thundered. "What are you looking for?"

"That," said Julianus, pointing.

"What? Where?" Max followed the direction of his finger.

"Look up," Julianus said. "On the roof."

Max followed his fingers. "Looks like a minor violation of section 103 of the maintenance code of New Old London," he said. "Failure to maintain a roof or other structural element of a permanent structure in good repair. Hardly a thing for the Queen's Guard to—hey, where are you going?" He ran after Julianus, who was already halfway down the alley.

When he caught up to him, Julianus was standing knee-deep in rubbish in a refuse-dump. The side of the dump had broken, spilling its contents across the alley. "Come up here," he said. "Give me a hand."

"What? No!" Max said. "Have you lost your mind? It's undignified, a member of the Guard mucking around in garbage. Show some self-respect!"

"What does that look like to you?"

"A problem for someone else to deal with," Max said. "Are we roofers now?"

"Does that look like a scrap of silk?"

"Maybe," Max said grudgingly. "So what? That doesn't prove anything."

Julianus hopped down off the pile of wet refuse. Max wrinkled his nose. "Congratulations," he said. "You smell like something rotten. It suits you."

"We've never really talked much, have we?" Julianus said. "I don't know a lot about you. Like, how did you get promoted to captain of the Queen's personal guard?"

"I rescued her half brother from drowning in the pond by Queensbury Lane. He was six," Max said. "Why?"

"Ah, no reason," Julianus said. "I thought it might have been your encyclopedic knowledge of building maintenance laws." He was scanning the ground, pacing back and forth in front of the broken refuse-dump. He knelt in the gutter, ignoring the water soaking into his clothes. "What is this, do you think?"

Max bent over and peered at the small object on the ground, curious despite himself. "Looks like a broken stick," he said.

Julianus picked it up, turning it in his fingers. "A broken bit of bamboo. With a metal joint attached. Look." He held it up. The end of the short bit of wood was capped with a gleaming bronze fitting, attached to the bamboo with exquisite care.

"So where's the rest of it?" Max said. He looked up, tracing the path of destruction on the roof, engaged even in the face of his skepticism. "If your kite fellow landed here, looks like he landed pretty hard. So what, now you think your mysterious flying intruder jumped out the window, landed on the roof, fell into the alley, then stopped to pick up all the broken bits before he ran away?"

"If there was anything else here," Julianus said, "scavengers would have gotten to it pretty fast. Something as valuable as silk isn't going to stay put long on the street."

"Okay, so if this was your guy, and I'm not saying it is, but if it was, now what? He's had a long head start. Where is he now?"

"Let's go," Julianus said.

"Where?"

"We're thinking about this the wrong way." Julianus tucked the broken bit of bamboo into his pocket. "We need to work backward. Follow the kite, not the man. I want to know who made this. I think I know just the people to ask."

11

"I don't see why I should have given them my hat," Thaddeus said glumly.

"Would you rather be arrested?" Claire asked. "Just think, you could have the best hat in the cells. All your fellow criminals could admire it while you wait for the Magistrate. What do you care? You looked a complete tit in it anyway."

"It's the principle of the thing," Thaddeus said. "That was my hat!"

"It was," said Claire the pragmatist. "Now it ain't."

Thaddeus and the Bodger siblings were sitting at a workbench that had been cleared of tools and parts. The afternoon whistle had sounded, marking the break for the midday meal. Thaddeus was astonished at how quickly the place emptied out. The swarm of apprentices, journeymen, tinkerers, and other craftsmen stopped as one, all save for the boy who was crawling around in the enormous tracked machine. By the time the last echoes of the whistle blast had faded, the clanging, hammering, pounding, and thumping had ceased, the great driveshaft in the ceiling had spun down to a stop, and the apprentices were already filing out the back door toward the combination kitchen and bunkhouse in the back. In short order, the shop was nearly silent, save for the *tick tick tick* of cooling metal.

Three wooden bowls of rich stew sat on the bench. Thaddeus poked at his suspiciously with a spoon. When nothing moved, he tucked into it.

"Tell us the whole egg," Claire said. "Leave no facts unturned."

"It started in a pub," Thaddeus said.

"Of course it did," Claire said. "And then?"

Thaddeus related the story of his adventures, beginning with how the man he inwardly referred to as "Mister Creepyhands" had approached him in a tavern. The strange and unsettling man had provided him with clothes and a fancy invitation, printed in gold leaf on fine linen. He had told Thaddeus to board the Queen's airship to plant a ring among her effects, and then make his getaway by means of the folding kite that had also been given to him. Details poured back into his memory: the cover story his employer had supplied, his bewilderment at the baffling array of cutlery that accompanied the strange dishes at the buffet, the odd drinks the Queen had supplied...

"What about the drinks?" Claire asked.

"Not beer, not mead, not water, not wine," Thaddeus said. "Well, there was wine, and beer, but those weren't the odd ones. The odd ones were hot. Foreign. One of them was black and tasted like roasted dog rear. Strong. Nasty." He made a face at the memory. "Don't remember what it was called. The other one was called 'tea.' Brown and warm, served with milk."

"What was it like?" Claire asked.

"Liquid heaven," Thaddeus said. "I've never had anything like it before. Why?"

"No reason, just curious."

Claire and Donnie listened to the rest of his story without interruption Thaddeus related how he'd been buttonholed by a rich and inquisitive, if rather short, young socialite in a stupid dress, and how this very same woman and a member of the Queen's Guard later witnessed his dramatic exit from the airship. He told the story of the long, terrifying trip to the ground, hanging beneath a great silk kite that fluttered in the breeze, how he'd been instructed to fly a tight loop lest he end up far from where he needed to be or, worse, in the foul-smelling sludge of the Thames.

He described his close encounter with his employer, and the subsequent unwelcome arrival of three exuberantly beweaponed ruffians at his door. He told of his cleverness and determination in his escape, ending the tale with his late-night arrival at Bodger & Bodger.

When he had finished, Claire sat back, arms folded. Silence filled the space.

Finally, after lengthy internal consideration, she shook her head. "Muddy, that's the most ridiculous story I've ever heard. None of it adds right."

"What do you mean?"

"I mean, how does that make any sense? Hiring someone to plant something in the Queen's quarters? Aboard an airship? And why would someone hire you, of all people? No offense, Muddy, but you're not the first person I'd pick for a secret mission. If someone wanted to plant something on the Queen, there are easier ways. And jumping out of an airship? That ain't exactly an inconspicuous getaway, if you follow my drift."

"Maybe he heard of me," Thaddeus said. "I have a reputation, you know."

Claire looked at him sadly. "Muddy, I like you, but you're dense as lead and not half as bright. Someone set you up."

"What do you mean?"

Donnie leaned forward. "My sister means you ain't very smart."

Thaddeus searched his face, but there was no hint of malice written there, just Donnie's normal open friendliness. It was not an insult, just the facts as Donnie saw them.

"I don't see what you're getting at," Thaddeus said, a trifle defensively. "Why do you think it was a setup?"

Claire sighed. "Oh, Muddy. A person with enough access to get you an engraved invitation to the Queen's airship doesn't hardly not have a way to plant a ring on the Queen himself. And jumping out the back door? They didn't want you not to be seen. You can hardly ask for a less inconspicuous exit. Nobody would really take finding some evidence on the Queen seriously what with you jumping out the window. That's got 'planted evidence' writ all over it. Or maybe 'botched attempt at spying.' Something. People will notice. People won't talk about anything else."

"So if you're so sure nobody would take it serious, why go through all the trouble to get me to do it?" Thaddeus said. "And why try to kill me?"

"'Bout time," Donnie said.

"About time? For what, killing me?"

Donnie shook his head. "No, 'bout time you started askin' the right questions."

"Okay, smart guy," Thaddeus said, "if you're so smart, what are the right answers?"

"Dunno. Ain't got all the pieces yet," Donnie said placidly. "Pretty near obvious why 'e tried t' kill you, though. Yer a loose end. Can't have you runnin' around spoilin' 'is plan."

"What's his plan?"

"Dunno that either." Donnie's massive shoulders moved up and down. "So let's think 'bout what we know." He held up an enormous hand and counted on his fingers. "Number one: my sister is right. Figure whoever hired you wanted you t' be seen. An' remembered, right? Number two, they wanted you t' set up the Queen, but not, like, in a believable way. Number three, they wanted you dead after." He turned his hand this way and that, contemplating his fingers. "So the way I sees it, either you were there as a distraction, t' take attention off what's really goin' on, or you were there as misdirection. That's the way royalty works. Schemes within schemes, and us commoners are the pawns. That's you, Muddy. A pawn. Only yer a pawn who didn't get off the board when 'e was supposed to. That makes you dangerous. Even a pawn can topple a king if 'e's in the right place at the right time."

"That's chess, right?" Thaddeus said. "I don't know anything about chess."

"Best learn."

"So what do I do now?"

"We ain't got all the pieces yet. So you need t' go out an' get more pieces."

"I can't leave here!" Thaddeus wailed. "The police are sure to be looking for me!"

"What makes you think that?"

"There are dead people at my flat! If the posies come looking to talk to me about dead people at my flat, they won't just take my hat and go away."

"True," Claire said. "They already have your hat."

"That's not funny!"

"Yes it is," Claire smirked. "It's a little bit funny, anyway. Oh, cheer up, Muddy. It ain't as bad as all that. Thing is, the police notice dead people more in some places than others. That's the way it is. Some lives matter more than others. If dead people turn up on the porch at the Palace, they'll take note, no question. But in your neighborhood? They might find a guy with thirty stab wounds in his back and be content to write it up as suicide." She smiled without mirth. "So it goes."

"Easy for you to say." Thaddeus's expression was grim. "You're not the one with two or maybe three dead guys on your doorstep. That sort of thing tends to raise uncomfortable questions."

"Perhaps," Claire said. "Maybe. It might depend on what sort of mood the cop is in, or whether someone else found them first. You're in the middle of a game being played by people way above you, Muddy. If they don't want the city police involved, the city police won't be involved." She scratched her head. "Still, I take your point. Probably not wise for you to go back home right now. What say we get Elias to go take a look?"

Donnie nodded. "Perfect."

"Elias? Who's Elias?"

Donnie whistled. It was the kind of whistle that could shatter stone, a piercing sound designed to carry easily over the clamor of the workshop in high gear. In the silence, it was deafening. The boy who'd been half-in, half-out of the strange tracked machine came running at breakneck speed.

"This is Elias," Claire said. "He's the new number two apprentice. Got a job for you, Elias. You good at getting around without being seen?"

"Oh, yes!" Elias nodded with the enthusiasm of a person who likes his lot in life, and is keenly aware there are the multitudes of other

103

apprentices who would gladly step into the shoes of the new number two if given even half an opportunity. "Whatever you need, I'm your guy!"

"See, now that's the spirit we look for in an apprentice," Claire said approvingly. "Here's what we need you to do. Sneak over to Muddy's flat, check around for a couple of dead guys, or maybe three dead guys, or the gendarme asking about dead guys, or anything to do with dead guys. See if the law enforcement types is about or if they ain't. Figure out what's going on. But don't draw attention to yourself, okay? Oh, and see if you can find out whether anyone else is creeping around doing the same thing you're doing. Got it?"

"Got it!" he enthused. "Sounds like fun!"

"You have a strange sense of fun," Thaddeus said dryly.

"Scouting for corpses in the streets of London gets you out of the shop for a while. Not that I don't like it here," he added hastily. "But every now and then it's nice to mix things up."

As he was leaving, Thaddeus called after him. "Hey, number two!"

"Yessir?"

"If a big guy with a club tries to take your money, tell him you're working for Thaddeus Mudstone and he'll have to reckon with me if he doesn't leave you be, okay?"

"Sure thing, Mister Thaddeus!" And he was gone.

"Good kid," Thaddeus said.

Donnie nodded. "Quick study. Might go far."

A thumping came at the door. Thaddeus froze, his spoon halfway to his lips.

"Open up for the Queen's Guard! Open up in the name of Her Majesty the Queen!" boomed a voice accustomed to prompt obedience.

Blood-curdling panic hatched in Thaddeus's toes. It crawled up his body, turning his legs to jelly, twisting his stomach into knots. He knew, somehow, that when it reached his brain he would start shrieking and running in circles, and then it would be all over. How had they found him? To have come so far, evaded all these attempts on his life, and now this…

Claire rose smartly and took his hand. "With me. Donnie, you talk to them." She tugged him to the back of the workshop, where an enormous half-assembled machine lurked, all struts and cables and massive riveted iron. She pulled a large, grubby sheet of canvas off the base of the machine and spun open a hatch. "Climb into the boiler. Pull the hatch shut behind you." The hammering on the door came again.

Heart pounding with dread, Thaddeus squeezed through the hatch and dropped into a narrow, pitch-black space that smelled of rust and iron. He felt his way around carefully. Menacing rivets protruded from the rough metal, looking to snag his clothes or gash his skin. Flakes of rust rained down on him. He tripped on a bolt protruding from the bottom of the boiler and fell, cursing. Slowly, cautiously, he turned around. The hatch was heavier than it looked and protested when he swung it closed. He left it open just a crack, peering through the gap to see what was going on.

Donnie opened the door. Two men came in, both dressed in bronze chestpieces, plumed helmets, and long white cloaks. Thaddeus felt an icy stab of fear through his heart.

"My name is Julianus," said one of the men. "This is my partner, Max." An expression of fury crossed the face of the man beside him. His knuckles whitened around the hilt of his sword. Julianus paid no attention. "Are you Claire and Donnie Bodger?"

Claire bowed. Her clothing cracked stiffly, sending a small cloud of coal dust drifting to the floor. The big orange cat twined in a figure eight around her legs. "Claire Bodger, at your service. This is my brother, Donnie." He nodded curtly.

Max stepped forward, addressing Donnie, his back to Claire. "Under the Crown Directives Act of 1818, all subjects of the Crown are obliged to render such assistance to the Crown or its duly appointed representatives as is necessary and lawful in the service of the security of the Crown."

Donnie smiled. "I'll take yer word for it," he said. "Can the subjects of the Crown be expected any remuneratin' for their service?"

"It is your duty to assist us!" Max barked.

"Thought not." His grin grew wider. "What can my sister and I do in the service of the security of the Crown?"

"The Bodger twins are well known throughout London," Julianus said in a conciliatory tone. "You are highly regarded for your skill in the engineering arts. We are investigating a matter of some urgency for the Queen and need some information. We hoped you might be—"

"Oh, get on with it!" Max said, scowling. He snatched the small bit of broken bamboo from Julianus's hand and gave it to Donnie. "What is this?"

Donnie held up the fragment. He examined the metal fitting on its end critically. "Ain't Bodger & Bodger," he said. "Ain't our style. Too delicate." He turned it over in his huge hand. "Nice work though. I have no idea what it is. Looks broken. What's it from?"

"A flying apparatus," Julianus said. "Possibly a large kite, designed to be folded up small."

"Huh," Donnie said. "Sounds like you already know what it is. Why are you askin' me?"

"We were hoping you—" Julianus began.

"Can you tell us who made it?" Max interrupted, scowling.

Donnie shrugged, his shoulders moving like tectonic plates. "Might ought. Not many folks 'ere in London can craft somethin' like that." He handed the bit to Claire. "Kanda?"

Claire looked at the small broken thing, turning it around in her palm. "Kanda. Yep. Could be. Looks like her work, sure."

"Kanda? Where is that?" Max asked, suspicious.

"Not where. Who. Chiyo Kanda," Claire said. "She has a shop in Old New London. It's on Highpole Street near Riverside."

"Highpole?" Max made an expression of distaste. "I know that neighborhood. Mohammedans and the sons of Israel and other queer folk, all doing God knows what to—" Julianus laid a hand on his arm. Max glared at the hand and jerked away.

Claire handed the fragment back to Julianus. "That all you needed?"

Max pushed past her, eyes narrow. He spun around suddenly. "You having lunch?"

"Yes," Claire said.

"Just the two of you?"

"The apprentices take their meal out back." She waved her hand vaguely toward the back of the shop. "Is the Queen's Guard suddenly interested in the dining habits of the commoners?"

He pointed to the workbench. "Why are there three bowls?"

Thaddeus gulped. His heart stopped. He crouched in the dark, dirty boiler, shaking.

Claire laughed. "The third one is for our new number two apprentice. His name's Elias."

"Who's the number one apprentice?" Julianus asked.

"Where is Elias?" Max growled.

"Sent him out on an errand not half a minute before you got here," Claire said. "Short lad, overalls, 'bout so high. Surprised you didn't run right into him."

"You sent him out in the middle of eating?"

"He's an apprentice," Claire said, as if that explained it.

Apparently it did, at least as far as Max was concerned. He nodded, satisfied, and spun on his heel. Julianus followed him out. Claire watched them go, shaking her head. When the door closed behind them, she said, "There's a couple of complete tossers and no mistake."

"Reckon so," Donnie said. "Don't surprise me much. Job requirement, I think." He scratched his chin thoughtfully. "Hope Kanda's all right. Hate t' see 'er mixed up in all this."

The steam whistle blasted. Apprentices streamed back into the shop, a bit less enthusiastically than they'd left it. The great driveshaft overhead whirred and shuddered back to life.

Claire helped Thaddeus climb back out of the boiler. He was fairly gibbering with fright. Claire dusted off his clothes, sending a great cloud of dirt flecked with small bits of rust to the shop floor.

He jerked his thumb back toward the machine whose belly he had just vacated. "What is that thing?"

"Spider!" said Donnie.

"I'm sorry, what?"

"It's a war clanker in the shape of a giant spider," Claire said. "Some army engineers took a liking to the notion that a giant mechanical spider might be an awesome thing to ride into battle. Impress allies, strike fear into the hearts of the enemy, crush all who stand against them beneath great metal feet, you get the idea."

"Does it work?"

Claire laughed. "Nope. Terrible idea. Too many legs. Too heavy. Too complicated. Way too hard to steer. Military technology is as much about what things look like as what really works, you know? If you're gonna kill a bunch of folks, might as well look good while you're at it. They paid us a huge wedge of cash and it's complete bollocks. But we're very hopeful about this new one." She gestured to the machine Thaddeus had seen Elias working on.

"What is it?"

"Battle machine," Donnie said. "Self-movin' artillery. 'As a cannon up front on this turret here that you can turn to point any way you like. An' see? No wheels! Just these little gears with metal tracks that go 'round and 'round. Like it takes the tracks with it, right? So it always has good footing. Near 'nuff impossible to get stuck, not like wheels or legs. Iron all 'round. Like bein' in a fortress you can take with you."

"Huh." Thaddeus looked at the great iron hulk. "Does it work?"

"Dunno. Ain't finished it yet."

"Muddy," Claire said, "I have a question. What did you take from Queen Margaret's room?"

"Oh! That." Thaddeus shrugged. "I don't know. I just sort of, you know, grabbed the first thing looked valuable. How likely was I to be there again, right? Hold on."

He went up to the loft to retrieve the jeweled case tucked under the mattress. When he came back downstairs, he handed it to Claire.

She opened the case and blinked. Her shoulders shook. Soon she was laughing uproariously. The sound boomed through the vast hall. Apprentices craned their heads curiously to see.

"What? What's so funny?" Thaddeus said.

"Oh, Muddy. Only you." She handed the case to him, shaking her head sadly. "Only you would sneak into Her Majesty's bedroom and come out with a comb. It's a nice comb, I'll give you that. Lots of gold all over it. But still." She giggled. "Limitless opportunity, and you grab a comb. Muddy, that's so very you."

12

Highpole Street was a miniature world unto itself, a place held apart from the rest of London. It was a chaotic, noisy place of bright colors and strange smells and the languages of dozens of far-off places. The street was jammed with people and horses and carts, so many that the hansom was forced to slow almost to a standstill. The crowd swirled around the carriage, creating little eddies and whirlpools of humanity in its wake.

Alÿs stared in fascination at the wash of people flowing around her. A tall, slender man on stilts, dressed in brilliant yellow, walked past, juggling brightly colored balls. His skin was black as night, his eyes two dark pools. He smiled, showing dazzling teeth as white as his skin was black. The horse whinnied and shied. Two men in black with long white beards and black skullcaps almost walked right into the hansom on their way across the street, so intent were they on their conversation. A woman draped in brilliant blue advertised elaborate woven rugs from a small wooden stall in front of an alley. She smiled as they passed.

Alÿs rapped on the side of the hansom. "Let me out here," she said.

Rory pulled the cab up next to the curb. "Should I wait, my lady?" The horse snickered, tossing its head.

Alÿs shook her head. "I don't know how long I'll be," she said. She fished in her bag and handed him a shilling.

"It is not a problem. I can wait."

"Thank you, but I will be fine," Alÿs said.

"It's just that the Cardinal…"

Alÿs folded her arms. "Yes?"

"He would be very upset if anything happened to you."

She laughed. "He'd have to wait in line. It would be inconvenient for many people if something happened to me. Entire nations would fall, I'm sure. Really, I'm fine. I can find my own way back."

"As you wish, my lady." His expression betrayed displeasure at leaving Alÿs in the maelstrom of Highpole.

She watched him navigate the hansom carefully across the streaming flow of people. Before long, he was lost to the crowd.

Alÿs walked down a sidewalk even more crowded than the street, feeling distinctly out of place. She'd heard tales about Highpole, each more lurid than the next, but even the most vivid of them was a pale shadow of the real thing.

A breath of warm, scented air, heavy with opium smoke, drifted from an open doorway. A man dressed in white sat drowsily on a bench in front of it, his eyes heavily lidded, his mouth concealed behind a bushy black beard. Further on, a woman sold grilled meats on long wooden skewers from the back of a horse-drawn cart. She waved as Alÿs passed. "Mutton? Lamb?"

"No thanks," Alÿs mumbled as she hurried on.

She peered into each building as she walked by. She saw a long, narrow shop, open to the street, where rings, bracelets, necklaces, and earrings of gold and silver, copper and gems, were laid out on black cloth. A short, friendly looking man with a wide smile fussed over the collection, arranging and rearranging the jewelry as if looking for some secret combination that would unlock more sales. A tall, burly man stood just inside the door, glowering at the sidewalk throng, his massive arms crossed in front of him like great tree trunks. He had a long sword strapped to his back.

Further on, a haphazard collection of tables and chairs clustered on the sidewalk outside a restaurant that advertised its menu in English,

French, the sinuous curves and dots she recognized as the script the Arabs used, and another language she couldn't recognize, pointed and boxy. She was forced to detour around the nearest table, where two men dressed in clothing that might have been fashionable five years ago were arguing loudly in German. One of them thumped his fist on the table for emphasis.

She stepped out into the street. A group of women in long, floating saris pushed passed her, giggling. In a doorway across the street, a woman with almond eyes danced, her body wrapped in brightly colored silk adorned with bright gold. She locked eyes with Alÿs for a lingering moment. Alÿs looked away, blushing.

Alÿs passed a dressmaker's shop displaying clothing in styles she had never seen before, simple one-piece garments of green and yellow held together with a cunning arrangement of knots.

On the corner of the street, a crowd had gathered around a lanky white man standing on top of an upended wine casket. He was dressed in severe black clothes and a black hat with a wide brim. Curious, Alÿs edged closer. He was shaking his fist at his audience, yelling about spiritual corruption in Paris and Rome. "They are all the same, these false prophets of God!" he shouted. "Fattening their coffers, living in corruption and sin! The final hours are upon us, oh yes, the final hours indeed! It is written that the Kingdom is at hand, and all the unrighteous shall be swept away in fire and blood!"

"How much blood?" a woman's voice called.

"What?"

"How much blood? It takes a lot of blood to sweep someone away."

"Oceans of blood!" the man roared. He raised his hands above his head. "A river of blood!"

"Which is it? A river or oceans? They ain't the same thing!"

"You mean you don't know your river from your ocean?" came another voice from the crowd, this one male. "How can you know about the future if you can't tell a river from an ocean?"

"Maybe," said a third voice, "he's trying to say that there will be a river

112

of blood that flows into an ocean of blood. Or maybe the Thames will turn into blood." A chorus of voices murmured assent to that idea.

"Won't do much washing," the first woman said doubtfully. "The Thames is too slow. Besides, them church types is all up the hill. Ain't no way the river is going to get them up there, even if it does turn into blood."

"In God all things are possible!" the street preacher cried.

"Dunno 'bout that," someone else said. "Seems like rivers always flow downhill to me. Otherwise they ain't really rivers, see?" The crowd laughed.

"What about when the tide comes in?" the second voice said.

"The tide? Well, the tide don't wash you away unless you're just standing there. You ever know a priest to just stand there?"

"Not at suppertime," the first voice admitted. More laughter.

Alÿs kept going, pushing through the crowds.

Eventually, she came to a shop whose front was festooned in ribbons and streamers of every color imaginable. Kites of all shapes and sizes hung from the massive black beams that supported the overhanging wood awning. The beams curved up at the ends, which were carved to look like the heads of dragons, or maybe serpents of some sort. Broad windows displayed all manner of curiosities: elaborately carved wooden boxes, small jade figures wielding curved swords, folding bamboo screens decorated with paintings of flowers. *This has to be it*, Alÿs thought.

She shouldered the heavy door open. A cascade of tiny silver bells on a slender wire tinkled to announce her arrival.

The door closed behind her, blocking the sounds of Highpole. Alÿs blinked. She felt a bit as though she'd stepped through a magic portal in a fairy tale and now found herself in some distant, enchanted place.

Every inch of the small shop was given over to breathtaking beauty. The floors were covered with thick, vividly colored Persian rugs, woven with swirling organic patterns. The walls were hung with silk tapestries covered with strange characters Alÿs could not identify. Shelves of black wood bore treasures from all over the world: small carvings of ivory and jade, exquisitely decorated boxes, dazzlingly intricate jewelry, cunning

clockwork toys. The ceiling, braced with thick, heavy beams, was festooned with kites of every conceivable shape and size: tiny diamonds
smaller than Alÿs's hand, long serpentine dragons with heavy beards,
complex box kites with ribbons hanging from their ends.

"Hello?" Alÿs said, stepping farther into the shop. "Is anyone here?"

There was a short scream from somewhere above her that ended far
too abruptly.

"Hello?" Alÿs stepped still farther into the room. The shop was long
but narrow, with a folding screen at the far end.

"Hello?" She approached the screen cautiously. Still no answer. On
the other side of the screen, the space had been made into a workshop,
filled with tiny tools, small metal fittings, bolts of silk, blocks of exotic
hardwood, pieces of jade and ivory. A rickety set of stairs against the
wall suggested a second-story apartment.

"Is anyone here?" Alÿs called. She started up the stairs, heart pounding. There was a sound of something scraping over wood, followed by
a thump.

There was no doorway at the top of the stairs, only a heavy curtain
of dark wool, woven with an image of a round red sun behind a tall,
stylized mountain. She pushed her way through.

Alÿs screamed in horror.

There was a woman, barely as tall as Alÿs herself, kneeling on the
floor in a dark blue kimono. Her hands were clutched to her throat. A
spray of blood jetted between her fingers, reaching almost to the ceiling.
She looked at Alÿs. Her mouth opened wordlessly.

She heard a thump from the far end of the room. The window stood
open, looking down into a narrow alley behind the shop. Alÿs caught
the briefest flicker of motion. She turned her head just in time to see a
hooded, cloaked figure dart through the window, moving up, not down.
A small shower of gravel fell onto the windowsill.

Something bubbled behind her.

Alÿs turned, eyes wide. The woman had fallen over onto her side.

One hand still clutched uselessly at her throat. Blood was pooling rapidly beneath her. Her other hand pointed directly at Alÿs.

No, not at Alÿs, at something on the floor. A large, elaborately crafted knife, its pommel decorated with leather wound with fine silver wire. It was covered in blood.

Alÿs picked it up. She turned back to the woman. The woman's eyes looked up at her, filled with terror and pain, and then filmed over. Just like that, she was gone.

Alÿs took a trembling step back. The blood pooled on the wood floor, almost to her feet. She screamed and fled down the stairs. She ran, blinded by the horror, until she collided heavily with a man walking in the door.

"Hey now, what are you doing here?" Alÿs looked up with wide startled eyes into Julianus's face, which was almost as surprised as hers. He looked down at the knife in her hands, then back into her face.

Max pushed past them, sword drawn. "Wait here," he growled. He disappeared behind the screen.

Alÿs looked around, eyes wild with panic. "It wasn't me!"

"I'm sorry?"

Max thundered down the stairs. "Seize her!" he cried. "She murdered the shopkeeper!"

"It wasn't me!" Alÿs said again.

"Grab her!"

Alÿs turned, wrenching herself from Julianus's grasp. She spun away from him, plunging through the door and out into the street. The two men chased after her, scattering the crowd on the sidewalk outside.

When she reached the street, Alÿs ran blindly. The look of naked terror on her face caused the crowd to melt away in front of her. Astonished people closed behind her, watching her speedy retreat down the street, so Julianus and Max encountered an almost solid wall of humanity. "Make way!" they cried. "Make way for the Queen's Guard! Make way in the name of the Queen!" But Alÿs had already vanished.

Julianus and Max stood in the middle of the street, swords drawn, looking around in frustration. A space had opened up around them, surrounded by gawkers. Max snarled in fury and started down the street. Julianus put his hand on Max's arm. "Don't," he said. "Don't waste your time. We know who we're looking for. We'll have her by night. What did you see?"

"She killed the shopkeeper," Max said. "Covering her tracks, no doubt. Your man was right. She is in this thing up to her eyeballs. There's no doubt."

"Show me," Julianus said.

A short time later they were back in the small room above the shop. Julianus crouched next to the body, his expression thoughtful. "I don't think the Lady Alÿs did this," he said.

"What? How can you say that? She was right here! She was holding a knife!"

Julianus nodded. "She was. But have you ever known the noble classes to do their own dirty work? And look." He gestured to the woman's throat, which had been slashed so deeply she had almost been decapitated. "Whoever did this was strong. The killer would have been covered in blood from head to foot. Alÿs wasn't."

"I don't care!" Max said, frustrated. "You saw her. She had a knife. The airship, and now here? Once is coincidence. Twice is conspiracy."

Julianus stroked his chin, still thoughtful. "Maybe," he said. "But something's wrong." He went to the open window and looked out. His eyes fell on the small mound of dust and pebbles on the windowsill. He ran his fingers through them, then turned his head to look up.

"See anything?" Max said.

"No."

"What do we do about the Lady Alÿs?"

"Put out the word," Julianus said. "Have her detained if any of the Guard sees her. We need to talk to her. You said it yourself. Once is coincidence, twice is conspiracy." He rose. "Someone is definitely covering their tracks. Still think this was a waste of time?"

Max growled resentfully.

"I'm glad you agree," Julianus said. "Look around. There might be something here that points toward whoever ordered that kite. A journal, a ledger, anything. We'll need to inform the civilian police and bring them in on this. They're going to want to know there's been a murder."

"I don't see why we should have to talk to them," Max said. "Let them find it on their own."

"Call it being good citizens, if you like," Julianus said. "Or, if you prefer, think of it as keeping a hand in. If we bring them in on a case involving Her Majesty the Queen, then we have a legitimate claim to being informed of everything they learn. If it's just a random murder, we can't take an interest without making them curious."

Max considered this. "Huh. Good point," he said grudgingly. "Maybe you're useful for something after all."

13

Alÿs ran for a long time, taking turns at random, fleeing headlong down roads and alleys she didn't recognize. She didn't stop even when she collided with people, ignoring the cries of "Hey!" and "Watch where you're going!" that trailed behind her in an audible wake.

Here, in this corner of Old New London, the streets were narrow and the buildings clustered close together, as if fearing to be too far from their neighbors. The roads tended toward bendy rather than straight, so that even experienced people who often did business in the quarter frequently found themselves lost. So exuberant had London's expansion been once the Centenium Bridge had touched down that little thought had been paid to street numbering, zoning, or any of the other niceties of civic infrastructure that concerned more sober and serious-minded towns. The result was, it was generally agreed, a confusing mess.

Alÿs kept going until her legs gave out beneath her. She crashed to the ground, startling a small knot of pigeons that had been searching the cobblestones for things shiny or edible. When she climbed back to her feet, she leaned against a wall, gulping huge breaths of air that felt like knives in her lungs. The image of the slain woman, the life fading from her eyes, lingered in front of her no matter where she looked. She squeezed her eyes shut. It didn't go away.

When she could breathe again, she set off once more. No matter how fast she ran, that image kept pace with her. So much blood…

She carried on in her headlong flight, without thought or destination, ignoring the concerned looks on the faces around her. The crowds thinned, and the neighborhoods grew rougher. Red and gold touched the sky.

Alÿs heard chanting, long and musical. She plunged on, pressing through a crowd of white-turbaned men gathering before a domed building with great arches of white limestone. The tight cluster of men exclaimed after her in surprise. She tripped and nearly fell, crashing into a muscular man with a long black beard. Concerned brown eyes looked back at her. "Miss? Miss? Are you alright?" he asked, but Alÿs had already regained her footing and was gone.

Eventually, bit by bit, awareness crept back. A rumbling in her stomach made her aware that she had not eaten in a long time. Night was gathering the city beneath its wings. She looked around, seeing the streets and alleys for the first time since the shop, realizing she did not know where she was.

The vision of blood and death faded with the last scraps of daylight. The gathering gloom cast long shadows in the nondescript alley before her.

From somewhere far away, a clock bell tolled seven. The sky was hard and clear, unusual for the time of year. Stars were already appearing in the deep velvety sky.

Alÿs turned around, trying to retrace her steps, but succeeded only in becoming more confused. In the darkness, she stumbled down a blind alley lined with refuse-dumps, and the full enormity of her situation fluttered in to descend on her like a suffocating weight.

She could not go back. The Guardsmen had recognized her. They had been suspicious before. They would be certain now, absolutely convinced she was part of whatever was happening. They might even believe that she had killed the woman in the shop. If she tried to return to the Palace, she would surely be detained. There would be people looking for her, Guardsmen and the police and who knew who else. She faced arrest at the very least, and prosecution for murder or heresy or who knew what else at worst. She was alone, far from home, without allies. Her friends at Court, politics being what it was, had doubtless already started to turn against her.

She slumped down with her back against the wall in the gloom of the narrow alley. The tears came quickly, great wracking sobs that shook her entire body.

She buried her head in her knees and wept, her fists curled into tight balls. In hindsight, running was stupid—possibly the stupidest thing she'd done so far in her short life. In one second, she had confirmed the worst suspicions of those skeptically disposed against her and destroyed all hope of clearing her name. She pounded her hands against the road beneath her as she sobbed, hammering against the rough cobblestone until her palms were raw and bloody.

If only she were as conniving as Eleanor had suggested. If she were a schemer, she could have collapsed in Julianus's arms, begged him to save her, concocted a fantastic but plausible tale to explain her presence… that's what Eleanor would have done. But she wasn't. Her pride and bravado, useful in maintaining her social position as one of the youngest ladies in Queen Margaret's Court, had dissolved. She didn't feel like a courtier or a lady. She felt like a child, in trouble that was way over her head.

Eventually, the sobs slowed. She panted, crouched still in the alleyway. She needed a plan, she thought. A roof over her head, food in her belly, and someplace to think. She would have to get away from the city. She had only the coins in her bag, which…

Fear gripped her heart. The last remnant of purple-black light was fading. There were likely to be bandits and criminals about, and she had no way to defend herself. She would need—

"D'you have a shilling, miss?"

"Wh—what?" Alÿs looked up.

"I said, d'you have a shilling?"

Alÿs wiped the tears from her eyes. The girl swam into focus. She was dressed from head to foot in rags, save for a top-hat that was far too large for her, wrapped with a purple sash…

Alÿs's heart lurched. The despair that had held her moments ago began to slide off her. A flicker of hope, small and fragile, took root somewhere inside.

"That's a very *nice* hat you have," she said, her focus sharpening.

"It's *my* hat!" The girl drew away defensively, like an alley cat ready to bolt. "You can't have it!"

"I'm not going to take your hat," Alÿs said. "Here." She drew a coin from her pouch. "I have a shilling for you. And I will give you another half-shilling if you tell me about your hat."

The girl snatched it from her. "My da gave it to me before he died," she said. "It was his hat."

"Did he?" Alÿs said. "That's a very good story. I'll tell you what. How about another half-shilling if you tell me the truth?"

Missy regarded her for a long moment, sizing her up. Then she held out her hand. Alÿs passed her another coin. It vanished speedily, disappearing somewhere on Missy's person.

"I got it from an odd dog," Missy said. "He gave it t'me. He did! He was being waked by a meerkat tammer. I think 'e meant t'fig 'im t'a nap for sure. They had a rumple spur. Right there." She pointed down an alleyway. "The tammer came back and snapped it right off me nob!"

Alÿs held her breath, hardly daring to move in case the little girl ran away, severing her only connection to Shoe Man. "What's your name, little girl?"

"Missy. Missy Ellington. An' don't call me little girl."

"Okay. Missy Ellington it is." Alÿs lowered her voice. "Missy, I need to find the man who gave you that hat. Do you know where is he now?"

"I tole you! He ran away."

"Did you see which way he went?"

Missy looked at her shrewdly. "D'you have another shilling?"

"Well, that depends," Alÿs said. "How much do you know?"

Missy looked her up and down, eyes narrowed. "How much will you give me t'take you t'him?"

"How much do you want?"

"What's 'e worth t'you?"

Alÿs sighed. "Honestly? I don't know."

Missy snorted. "Don't know? Is 'e yours?"

"Mine?" Alÿs shook her head. "No, he is not mine."

"Oh." Missy nodded. "D'you want to kill 'im? It's more if y'want t'kill 'im."

"No! What? No, I don't want to kill him! You're a strange girl."

"I know," Missy said. She thought for a moment. "Five," she said finally, as if arriving at an answer to a particularly difficult school problem. "Right. Five shillings. I take you t'him."

"I've already given you two shillings! I'll give you three more."

"Four more." The girl held out her hand. "Four."

"Four," Alÿs said. "But not until we're there."

"An' one extra if we have t'run the cake."

"Cake?" Alÿs looked puzzled.

"The cake toppers," Missy said. She rolled her eyes in exasperation. "Coppers!"

"Oh! I told you," Alÿs said, "I don't want to kill him."

"Then it won't matter t'you." Missy folded her arms, her mouth set in a stubborn curl.

"Fine," Alÿs said, resigned. She had trouble shaking off the impression that she had just been out-negotiated by a child. "Four shillings plus one more if we have to run away from the police."

"Deal," Missy said. "This way."

14

The big orange cat crouched near the half-finished battle machine, tail twitching. Muscle rippled under its fur. Its eyes were focused on a spot of empty air about six inches in front of it. It growled, a long, low, menacing growl. Then it tightened its muscles and sprang, front legs outstretched, claws extended. It grabbed a handful of nothing and hit the ground rolling, tumbling to a halt several feet farther away. It stood as though nothing had happened, licked itself for a moment, then wandered away.

"Why does your cat do that?" Thaddeus said.

"Hmm? Oh." Donnie glanced over at the cat, which was now rubbing its face on a drive wheel from a large two-legged industrial clanker that stood partly disassembled against the far wall. The machine looked just humanoid enough for Thaddeus to find it unsettling. "Dunno. Who can know a cat's mind?"

"What's his name?" Thaddeus asked.

"Dunno what 'e calls himself. We call 'im Disorder, on account of 'cos it's what 'e spreads." On cue, the cat leaped into the belly of the clanker. A pile of tools and small metal cogs slid to the stone floor with a crash.

"What am I going to do, Donnie?" Thaddeus said.

Donnie shrugged. The corded muscles in his shoulders and upper arms moved like serpents wrestling beneath his skin. "Dunno. 'Alf of knowin' what to do is knowin' what situation yer in. Dunno what situation yer in, Muddy. Jus' that yer in it good. Wait for Elias to come back. We'll know more then."

"When is he going to be back?"

Another shrug. "When 'e finds somethin' out."

"But I can't go home!"

"Nope," Donnie agreed. "Not if you like livin' anyways."

"What do I do?"

"Dunno." Donnie rose from his chair and patted Thaddeus on the back. "I 'ave work that needs doin'. You want to 'elp with the battle machine?"

Thaddeus slumped in his chair.

"Naw," Donnie said, "thought not. Not the Mudstone way."

Thaddeus spent the next several hours thinking of the string of miserable failures that had led him to this point in his life. First had been the matter of his birth, of course. He had unwisely been born into poverty, rather than wealth and idle luxury as was more properly his due. That had been an astonishing lack of foresight on his part, he thought. From his perspective, the people who did live in wealth and luxury seemed to spend a lot of time mucking up and generally making a mess of things. Had he been given a shot at that role, he could hardly do a worse job.

Compounding that error, he had foolishly chosen to be born to a Muslim woman married to a British man. That was a matter of some scandal, the result of which was her expulsion from her Highpole-born family. The newlywed couple ended up in Whitechapel, London's district for those without anywhere else to go, which was, in Thaddeus's expert opinion, hardly a place to raise a child, what with the muddy streets and the funny smells and all.

He had spent the best part of his formative years attempting to rectify his poor judgment in birth circumstance. The way he saw it, those with wealth and power spent a great deal of their time making everyone else miserable. Attempting to deprive them of their wealth and power was, therefore, a selfless act of public good.

Wealth and power, Thaddeus thought bitterly. Was that too much to ask? He heard people say things like "wealth follows work," but that was clearly a load of tosh. The hardest-working people he knew usually struggled to make ends meet, whereas the truly wealthy, the highest of the social classes, were born to a station that wouldn't know work if it hammered iron ingots into horseshoes right in front of them. Work was a sucker's game. "Wealth follows work" was something rich people said to poor people to get them to work so that the rich wouldn't have to.

But the reality was that because he hadn't had the foresight to be born to wealthy upper-class parents, that left few opportunities for advancement, save for finding the occasional odd item of value in someone else's pocket and transferring it into his own. Unfortunately, most of the pockets he had access to held little in the way of valuables, and so he, Thaddeus Mudstone, was trapped in a life unreasonably beneath his proper place.

For a brief moment, he had sincerely believed things might be turning around. A man in a pub had offered him more money than he normally saw in a year, just to attend a party. How could that go wrong? Then, on the airship, he'd taken the opportunity to pocket a shiny bauble that, by all rights, should be worth quite a lot of money—not riches, sure, but more than he had ever had before. So what if it was a comb? It was a gold and platinum comb in a jewel-studded gold case...

...monogrammed with the Queen's insignia, which guaranteed he would never be able to sell it. Just another of Life's little jokes at the expense of Thaddeus Mudstone Ahmed Alexander Pinkerton. Who in their right mind made combs out of gold, anyway?

Now, as if all that wasn't bad enough, someone was trying to kill him. To Thaddeus, that just felt like piling on.

He climbed the rickety wooden stairs to the loft, looking for a place as far as possible from the bustle of Work and Industry going on around him. Being surrounded by people trying to Better Themselves only made him that much more depressed. He sat despondent on the edge of the bed. The big orange cat followed him up the stairs. It hopped onto the bed next to him, climbed into his lap and pressed its head against his hand.

"Go away," Thaddeus said.

The cat tilted its head, as if struggling to work out what he'd just said. Then, with great deliberation, it bit him on the thumb. Thaddeus yelped and cursed. Satisfied, the cat hopped off his lap and curled up on the floor.

The sun dragged a brightly-colored cloak down over London's restless, smoke-filled sky. The dinner whistle blew. The workshop cleared out with the same rapid efficiency it had at lunchtime. Elias, the new number two apprentice, was still conspicuous in his absence.

The Bodgers sat down for dinner. Thaddeus joined them, looking around anxiously. "Where's your apprentice? Shouldn't he have been back by now? When will he be back?" he asked Claire.

"Can't say," she said. "When he finds something interesting, I suppose."

"What if something happened to him?"

"Muddy, you worry too much," Claire said. "What's the worst that can—"

A rapping came at the door, hesitant at first, then with greater authority. Thaddeus jumped. Claire sighed. Donnie rose from the workbench-cum-dinner-table.

He came back a minute later. "A girl an' another girl with your hat want t' see you," he said.

"What?" Thaddeus said. "My hat?"

"An' a girl an' another girl," Donnie said. "Focus."

Thaddeus rose reluctantly from his stew and went to the door. Sure enough, there was a girl there, dirty and disheveled, caked with mud, her face streaked with dirt and dried blood, her eyes puffy and red. She looked vaguely familiar, in an uncomfortable sort of way he couldn't quite put his finger on. Standing expectantly next to her was another, younger girl dressed in rags. She was entirely too familiar.

Thaddeus glared at Missy. "You," he said. "Back to try to get me killed again?"

She returned his glare levelly, her expression filled with loathing. "You tried t'cleave my qab."

"You tried to kill me!" Thaddeus said. "Before I took your hat! My hat! That's my hat!"

"It's mine," Missy said. "You didn't give me a shilling."

Thaddeus felt a rush of heat creep through his body. "You b—"

"Language!" the older girl said sharply. "I will remind you that you are in the presence of a member of the royal family of France and a lady of Queen Margaret's Court."

"—lack-hearted miscreant," Thaddeus finished lamely. The memory clicked into place. "Wait, you're that girl on the airship!"

Alÿs curtsied. "At your service."

Missy turned to Alÿs, hand out. "'E's here. Pay up."

The older girl dropped a handful of coins into her palm. "I hope we can do business again soon," she said. Missy counted the coins, then tucked them away so quickly Thaddeus wasn't entirely clear where they had gone. She nodded. Then, with one more venomous look at Thaddeus, she disappeared into the darkened street.

"So," Alÿs said. "Man who jumps out of airships, are you going to invite me in?"

"I, er—" Thaddeus opened and closed his mouth several times, flustered. Three assassins sent to his house to murder him? That, he could deal with. A former employer pursuing him down a dark alley with a dagger? Inconvenient, to be sure; perhaps even vexing. But this diminutive girl, with her imperious demeanor, was entirely too much to handle. He looked around for help. Donnie smiled serenely at him. Claire was watching him with an expression of curious interest, and was that a tiny smirk on her face?

"Come in, uh, Your Gr—err, my ladyship," Thaddeus stammered.

Claire was unquestionably smirking now.

"You may call me Alÿs," Alÿs said. She stepped into Bodger & Bodger and managed, somehow, to create the impression that she owned the place. "And what do I call you, Shoe Man? And your friends?"

"I'm Thaddeus, my la—Alÿs," Thaddeus said. "This is Claire and, um,

Donnie. They're twins. Bodgers. Um, the Bodger twins." He shook his head to clear it. "What are you doing here?"

"Looking for you," Alÿs said. "I've been running all over London. I would never have found you if I hadn't happened upon your friend. What did you do to Missy to make her hate you so much, anyway?"

"She set me up. I failed to die. Apparently, she didn't like that," Thaddeus said.

"That must be an interesting story," Alÿs said. "But I'm sure you have many of those."

"You have no idea," Thaddeus said ruefully.

Alÿs curtsied again. "Claire Bodger. Donnie Bodger. Pleased to make your acquaintance."

"Likewise, my lady," Donnie said. He glanced between her and Thaddeus. "Don' get many social callers of th' royal sort here. Mostly folks from your side o' the river come 'ere in a more official capacity. You ain't here to enquire about military clankers. Yet here y'are. That's three times someone's come knockin' and wantin' to know 'bout Muddy an' kites an' airships. What kin we do for you, Alÿs o' the French royalty?"

"Three times?" Alÿs said. "Who else has been here? What have you told them?"

"Such a lot o' questions," Donnie said. He looked Alÿs up and down. "You ain't here as a member o' the Court. You look like someone in trouble. Why are y'here, Alÿs o' Her Majesty's Court?"

Alÿs deflated visibly. "I'm in trouble," she said softly.

Claire nodded. "You look hungry too. Sit," she said. "Have some stew. Tell us about it."

Alÿs sat gratefully on a stool at the workbench. Between bites, the tale came out. She started with her encounter with Thaddeus on the airship, describing the ruckus that had followed his abrupt disappearance: the ring, the arrest, the standoff, the Cardinal's intervention. Thaddeus turned pale when she told him the Royal Guard was hunting for him.

The Bodger siblings listened attentively while she told them how she had followed the trail from the shoemaker's shop to Highpole Street.

Donnie's eyes narrowed when she told them of the murder and her subsequent headlong flight from the Guard.

"Describe the man you saw," Thaddeus demanded. "Black cloak? White bony hands?"

"I don't know. Maybe?" Alÿs said. "I only got a quick look. He dropped this." She pulled out the dagger. Donnie took it from her, examining it closely. He whistled and handed it to Claire, who examined it as well before passing it back to Alÿs.

"You're lucky you're not dead," Claire said. "Go on."

Alÿs finished her story, recounting her encounter with Missy and her arrival at Bodger & Bodger.

"Well then," Donnie said after she had finished. "There's some more pieces."

"Beg pardon?" Thaddeus said. He was still reeling from the news that he was suspected of being an Italian spy of, apparently, the baby-eating variety.

"This is a conspiracy," Claire said. "Think of a conspiracy like a machine. If you want to know how it works, you have to understand all the parts. My brother is saying we have more parts now."

"What parts?" Thaddeus held his head in his hands mournfully.

"We know that you were hired to frame the Queen. It seems the same person who tried to kill you also likely as not killed Kanda. That means we know the mastermind wants to cover his tracks. We know, thanks to your friend here, there's some kind of vote coming up tomorrow that the Queen was supposed to participate in, though apparently that's up in the air now."

"She's not my friend," Thaddeus said sullenly.

"Muddy, m'boy, don't be an idiot. You're needin' all the friends you kin get right now," Donnie said.

Thaddeus looked away, recognizing the self-evident wisdom in Donnie's words. "Okay, so why was I supposed to frame the Queen? To keep her from this vote or whatever?"

"Mebbe, mebbe not," Donnie said. "Conspiracies have layers, like an onion."

"I thought she just said it was like a machine," Thaddeus said. "Now it's like an onion?"

"It's a metaphor," Claire said.

"Mechanical onions? What sort of metaphor is that? I think you two are just as confused as I am. You're making this up as you go along."

Beside him, Alÿs looked pale and withdrawn. Out of her environment, she was nothing like the confident, commanding woman he'd met on the Queen's airship. She also was much younger than he'd thought, and smaller, too. She gave him a flicker of a smile and looked away.

"So what do we do?" Thaddeus said.

Donnie shrugged. "We wait," he said.

"That's what you said before."

"Patience, Muddy. Our enemy is playin' a long game. We need to know more."

"*Our* enemy?" Thaddeus said. His voice was bitter. "He didn't try to kill *you*."

"'E killed Kanda. She was one o' us." Donnie's face was serene. "We will find 'im. We will punish 'im. This ain't just about you anymore, Muddy."

"But we need—"

"Patience."

"But—"

Thaddeus was interrupted by the door crashing open. Elias, the apprentice, hurried inside, breathing hard. He ran up to the four of them. "I'm back!" he said. "I found out...who is she?"

"This 'ere's the Lady Alÿs," Donnie said. "She's in a bit of a spot. We've taken 'er in."

Alÿs rose and curtsied. "And you are?"

"This is Elias," Claire said. "He's the new number two apprentice."

Confusion played across Alÿs's face. "Who is the number one apprentice?"

"What did you find out?" Donnie said.

"No sign of trouble at Mister Thaddeus's flat, sir," Elias said. "No bodies. No coppers. Nothing. No sign that anything happened at all."

"Except for the hole in my window," Thaddeus said.

"No sir, Mister Thaddeus," Elias said. "I mean, begging your pardon, but the window is fine. Brand-new oilskin, all nice and tidy."

Donnie rested his chin in his hand thoughtfully. "Now that is interestin'," he said. "More pieces."

"What do you mean?"

"He means we know more than we did," Claire said. "Our adversary is organized, meticulous, and disciplined. He, or they, don't leave anything to chance. They clean up loose ends. They make sure everything is tidy. Which makes it all the stranger that they hired Muddy here."

"Hey!" Thaddeus said. "I don't think—"

Claire held up her hand. "Muddy, you know I like you. You are undisciplined and disorganized. You are practically a walking loose end. You're brave, I'll give you that. Ain't too many what wouldn't balk at jumping out of the back of an airship. But that ain't why they hired you. You were supposed to be seen, make a big splash. Then you were supposed to disappear. I wouldn't be surprised if your body was supposed to turn up at some convenient time. Or maybe you weren't supposed to not stay gone, dunno. Thing is, you were supposed to be dead and you ain't. Our enemy can't be liking that too much. Our enemy likes things tidy. You got away. Alÿs saw the attack on Kanda. Things are not tidy. That must be worrying."

"So what do we do?" Thaddeus asked again.

"We make things more untidy," Alÿs said.

The Bodgers looked at her expectantly.

"We make things more untidy," she repeated. "You said it yourself. Thaddeus is a loose end. I wasn't supposed to see what I saw. If we both come forward, we put our enemy even more off balance."

"There is a logic t' it," Donnie said slowly. "Risky, too. How do you come forward without bein' arrested? Who do you trust? That's the thing 'bout conspiracies. You dunno who to trust."

"I know who to trust," Alÿs said. "I trust the Cardinal."

"Wait, *the* Cardinal?" Thaddeus sputtered. "You mean, the Cardinal cardinal? Old Sourpuss? That guy?"

"Unless there are other cardinals running around London that I don't know about," Alÿs said. "Why?"

"I don't trust him!" Thaddeus said.

"Oh? Why?"

"Because he…because…because nobody trusts him!"

"I do," Alÿs said firmly. "He is a friend of my father. He looks after me."

Thaddeus crossed his arms, unmollified. "Nobody trusts him," he insisted.

"How many people do you know who know him?"

"Well, I, that is, uh…" Thaddeus scratched the back of his neck.

"That's what I thought," Alÿs said. "We have an advantage. It's a small one, but we should use it. We should go tonight."

"No," Donnie said firmly.

"Excuse me?" Alÿs said.

"No, m'lady."

"No? Why not?"

Donnie shook his head. "Reckless. Need time to think. Go tomorrow, after you get some sleep an' can think with your head clear. Tomorrow evening, when the streets are clear."

"I think we should go now."

"Yer a mess. Yer tired an' scared. Tired an' scared is when people make mistakes. It's like you said. Small advantage. High stakes. Be careful. We will find a way to get you t' th' Cardinal, if that's what you want. Tomorrow. Meantime, I'm goin' out."

That got a look of surprise from everyone, including Claire. "Now?" she said.

"Yep." Donnie nodded. He rose from the workbench, clapping Thaddeus on the shoulder. "I'm goin' t' go put out the word. Someone killed Kanda. This city is filled w' artisans an' craftsmen an' apprentices of all sorts. Nobody notices us. Nobody pays attention. But we are everywhere. So I'm gonna tell everyone. When yer out and about, keep yer eyes an' ears open. Spread the word. Someone somewhere knows who this man is. Someone will see 'im. I'm goin' t' let people know. Twenty shillin's t' whoever tells me where 'e is."

Thaddeus nodded. He could almost feel sorry for the man. If they were looking for someone, Thaddeus suspected he would be found. Then he recalled the dagger whirring toward his face, and the sympathy evaporated. It would serve the bastard right.

"Why not go to the police?" Alÿs said.

"The police? Look, m'lady, no disrespect, but the long arm o' the law doesn't care none 'bout what happens in Old New London an' certainly not 'bout some foreign artisan on Highpole Street. Besides, you said it yourself. How much do you trust the city coppers?"

Alÿs opened her mouth to protest. The look on Donnie's face changed her mind. She nodded.

"Okay then," Donnie said. "You go an' see yer friend the Cardinal tomorrow. I go an' talk t' my friends tonight."

He shrugged on a huge, heavy overcoat and smiled his placid smile. A suggestion of something malicious glinted behind that smile.

When he had gone, Alÿs slumped. "I wish I were back home," she said softly. "I want a nice bath, a glass of wine, and for none of this to have happened."

"Can't help you with that last one," Claire said, "but I maybe can help with the first two. There's a bathtub through the door behind the big mechanical spider. There are two knobs. One on the left is cold water, one on the right is hot. And there is some excellent wine in the storeroom."

"Really?" Alÿs looked skeptical.

"You think only you nobly types like the fruit of the vine?" Claire said. "Darling, those of us born beneath you know more of the world than you imagine. Who do you think makes the wine you drink? Do you imagine that you get the best of it?" She winked. "The nobility gets its culture the same way they get everything else. From other people. Towels are in the cabinet. I'm afraid I don't have any clothes that will fit you. There might be something in the apprentices' supplies that'll do." She looked Alÿs up and down. "Who knows? Overalls might suit you."

15

The sun, which had a long policy of shining on the just and the unjust alike, ascended the sky, doing its best to make the squalor of London just a little bit less squalid.

London was having none of it. The rising sun had to contend not only with the clouds that had settled over the city during the night, but also with the long cloak of soot and coal dust with which London clothed itself. By the time it reached the ground, the light managed to look pale and just a bit dingy.

It shone on a nondescript man with an easily forgotten face and a distinctly Roman nose, who was entering a rental flat just off Highpole Street with a large package under his arm. He wore unremarkable workman's clothes and solid, practical boots. He moved with the caution of a man carrying an armload of explosives, on account of the fact that he was carrying a large armload of explosives. He looked around furtively before slipping through the door. He was annoyed, because the man from whom he'd purchased the black powder he carried had been late in delivering it to him. Harsh words had been exchanged, and they had very nearly come to blows. Normally, that would not bother the man in the least. But his wealthy and very influential patron had insisted that there be no unnecessary complications, even going so far as to suggest such complications might have implications for their future business relationship, and so the man had swallowed his temper, taken the powder, and left. In the ledger book of his mind, there was a new black mark, however, and he intended to revisit the matter promptly upon resolution of his current assignment.

It shone on the head of a young beggar girl in a hat several sizes too big for her, who had just dipped her hand in the pocket of a respectable-looking gentleman in an expensively tailored suit jacket and a top-hat of his own, come down to the docks to inspect a load of timber sent on a steam-powered paddlewheel ship from the New World. So intent was he on the lure of future profit that he paid no notice to the urchin girl asking him for a shilling. So deft was her hand, so adroit in the way she lifted the coin pouch from his waistcoat, that he noticed not a thing, a fact that would cause him some consternation in a few hours' time when he attempted to bribe the dockmaster into releasing his shipment without the normal dreary procedure of customs and tax.

It shone on Commander Skarbunket, dressed in his finest and, not coincidentally, least-comfortable uniform, who glared up at it with no inconsiderable resentment. He had been roused from his bed far too early in the morning by an urgent missive from Lord Gideon Clay of Borneham, demanding an immediate update on what was known of the whereabouts of the Lady Alÿs de Valois and her involvement in a murder. He was groggy and grumpy and not at all happy to be dislodged from his bed. He glowered up at the sun as though it were personally responsible for all the ills of the world, an opinion the sun would, had it the mind to, have considered grossly unfair.

And it shone through the windows of the Queen's private dining room in the Palace. Ah, here it could do what it was meant to do. There was plenty of gold adorning the moldings along the ceiling to gleam off of, and the table was set with gold-rimmed plates it could make sparkle. Yes, this was much more like it. It gleamed and sparkled cheerfully, almost ready to forgive London its sordid grubbiness.

Her Most Excellent Majesty Queen Margaret the Merciful sat on a gilt-edged chair in front of the gilt-edged table. Her expression was that of one not entirely impressed by the gleam and sparkle of the early morning sun. In truth, she scarcely even noticed it. Her mind was more preoccupied with the knowledge that while she was no longer confined to her quarters, representatives of both her own guard and the Cardinal's private forces stood just outside the door, lest she forget the cloud of suspicion that still clung to her like the bad smell that sometimes follows one who's spent the entire evening much too drunk in exactly the wrong company and finds himself waking in the gutter minus his money.

A vigorous knocking came at the door. A moment later, it was flung open. A young boy dressed all in blue and green darted into the room, followed closely by a short, portly man with a round face and a frizz of white hair surrounding an entirely bald dome of head like a bristly halo.

The boy flung his arms around Margaret. "Maggie!" he exclaimed. "My uncle says these men have to follow you around everywhere."

Margaret smiled warmly at the boy. "What do we say around other people?" she asked.

He looked down, chastened. "I'm sorry, Your Grace," he said.

"Your Grace," the man said. "You look well. The Duke here has been inconsolable over this deplorable situation."

"Lord Rathman! We are as well as one might expect. We are pleased you were able to join us for breakfast, despite these unfortunate conditions," Margaret said. She put her arm around the boy.

"I am surprised the Cardinal isn't here," Rathman said. "It seems out of character for him to miss an opportunity to gloat."

"Oh, he's been doing plenty of that," Margaret said. "He has managed to extract his pound of flesh from us in exchange for expediting the tribunal."

The little man pulled up a chair across the dining table from Margaret. Servants appeared silently, bearing platters of roast duck and small gold trays of grapes. A woman appeared next to Rathman's elbow with a gold-rimmed china cup of hot brown liquid. He sniffed it and smiled.

"Expediting it, eh? What does expediting mean, exactly? Bringing back old traditions, perhaps? Trial by combat? Ducking stools? I hear the old techniques for resolving matters of heresy guaranteed quick results."

Margaret smiled grimly. "Nothing so dramatic. He intends to convene the tribunal in two days' time. He seems quite confident they will find that we are not working in collusion with the false Pope. It appears our upcoming repudiation of the heretic Pope's policies will be quite persuasive."

"Repudiation of what?" Rathman's eyes narrowed suspiciously. "What does that mean?"

"It means," Margaret said, "he thinks it will play well with the tribunal if we demonstrate our independence from Rome by supporting the petition to allow the use of animates by the military."

"Oh. I see." For just a second, his face betrayed genuine surprise. "We have had our differences on this matter in the past, Your Grace. I would be lying if I said I'm not pleased that you have found your way to my side. This new technology has great promise. Great promise. Still, I am distressed by the circumstances. I had hoped that reasoned argument alone would prevail. That explains, then, why the Council is meeting today after all. There was talk of postponement."

"Apparently we will be meeting," Margaret said. "In the interests of expediency. Though it is not without protest. It is the opinion of the Crown that this course of action is harmful to the future of the Realm."

"Your Grace, I fail to see why. History shows that those who are quick to adopt new technologies of war benefit greatly."

"This is more than just a new weapon. What about our new citizens, driven to our shores by the Spanish and Italians?" she asked. "They will not take well to these…monstrosities."

Rathman shook his head. "Your open-door policy toward the Israelites and the Mohammedans has earned you some enemies, Your Grace. Not everyone believes in such generosity toward those fleeing the Inquisition."

"And some friends, as well," Margaret said. "Not everyone is frightened of strangers. The traditions of the refugees from the Inquisition have enriched us greatly. The followers of Mohammed have taught us much about medicine and mathematics. Trade with them has increased our wealth. The Israelites have among their number many gifted scholars who have advanced us in the arts and sciences. What would they think of such a thing?"

"Does it matter?" Rathman said. Seeing her expression, he steepled his fingers in front of his lips. "This is still our nation, not theirs. They are here as our guests. Besides, I don't think the Israelites will object. Their traditions are complex, and include tales of rabbis creating living things from clay. Their scholars teach that man may make living things, but only God may give them souls. I think we and they will agree that animates are not in possession of souls. They are mindless things, only alive after a fashion." He leaned forward. "The Mohammedans are less… complex in their views. They oppose all animate creation for all purposes. But no matter. They also understand their position here depends on our good graces. We need only remind them of that and they will soon fall in line."

"So you think we should pay them no mind at all."

"Many people, including some on the Council of Lords, fear strangers in our midst. Resentment for those who live in Highpole in particular runs deep. Poor foreigners are bad enough, but wealthy, influential foreigners…" He shook his head. "It might not be wise to be seen allowing these guests of the Crown to determine national policy."

"We are not of the same opinion," Margaret said. She raised her hand. "But that is not what we should like to discuss this morning. This debate is finished. We are voting in your favor. We would seek your counsel on a more personal matter."

Curiosity made itself known on Rathman's face. "Of course, Your Grace."

"The Cardinal raised the issue of finding a husband."

"Did he?" Rathman sighed. "Let me guess. He already has someone in mind."

Margaret permitted herself a chuckle. "He is predictable, in his dreary way. Still, he does have a point. It is time we are married."

"I agree, Your Grace," Rathman said. "If I may speak boldly, I wouldn't recommend you follow his advice, but what you're planning…well, some would call it madness. Uniting in marriage with a Mohammedan? Mark my words, that will cause an uproar. Please, for your own sake, Your Grace, I would beg you off this course of action."

"Madness? Only if a fox is mad. The Ottomans have much to offer us. Culturally, economically…"

"And their rather formidable navy?"

"Yes, that too," Margaret said. "There is much to be gained from a union between the Crown and the Ottoman Caliphate. Think of it, Lord Rathman!" Her eyes glowed. "We would become a force to be reckoned with. An alliance with the strongest force in the East! Control of the trade routes! Maybe even a path toward ending the war in Afghanistan! Can you picture it?"

"I knew your father well, Your Grace," Rathman said. "He was the most ambitious person I had ever known. I feel that your ambition might surpass even his."

"Thank you."

"I am not sure that's a compliment, Your Grace," Rathman said. "This thing you propose is…well, it will not be well received at home or abroad. I am sure the Ottomans will be no more enthusiastic about it than your own subjects. I will support you as I always have, but if I may speak in confidence, I think you are treading a dangerous path."

"It is already done. The Caliph's son and I will be wed before the end of the year."

"I see." Rathman stroked his chin. "Does the Cardinal know?"

"No."

Rathman nodded. "That is probably for the best. This should be handled gently. The echoes will be felt throughout England."

"If we succeed, they will be felt a lot further than that," Margaret said. "It is trade, not war, that will define the most powerful nations in the future. For too long, we have played second fiddle to the imperial ambitions of the Spanish and the French, taking only such power as they leave to us! What has it given us? Constant war in the New World.

Near-constant war at home. No more! We will build a commercial empire, one unlike anything that the world has seen before. There will be those who do not like it. Let them fall in the ash heap of history."

"As you say, Your Grace," Rathman said. He inclined his head. "I know you well enough to know your mind when it's made up. It seems to me you take only your own counsel. You're a lot like your father that way too." He studied his teacup thoughtfully. "I will admit there are some advantages to trade with the Ottomans."

"Indeed," Margaret said. "Trade in tea alone could become very lucrative, we feel."

"I hope you're right."

"There is no need to hope." Margaret ruffled the hair of the boy, who was sitting at her feet. He gazed up adoringly at her. "Your unwavering support has been invaluable to us."

"Thank you, Your Grace." He looked at the boy. "Your half brother is my last living relative. I would do anything for him, and for you. What kind of world would this be if we could not count on our own? If you will excuse me, Your Grace, I must prepare for the Council."

"Of course," Margaret said. "As must we. Please send the Lady Eleanor in."

"As you wish." Count Rathman nodded to the boy. "If you please, my lord."

The boy looked up at Margaret. "But I want to go to the Council with you!"

She looked down at him, her expression softening. "I know," she said, squeezing his hands, "but that would not be considered proper. You are a lord with standing in your own right. I will see you there."

He nodded solemnly. "Okay." He gave her a quick hug, then followed Rathman out the door.

16

The Council of Lords gathered at regular intervals in the great Hall of Assembly in New Old London, erected on the spot where the Palace of Westminster had once stood. King John the Proud had thought the old Palace far too fusty and, well, Medieval for a modern, cosmopolitan city like London, and had ordered it razed to make way for a grand new Hall that would usher in a new, forward-looking era to shine as a beacon of good governance for all the world to admire. This had, apparently, meant "Do it like the ancient Greeks did, with lots of columns and white marble and stuff, but modern, too, right?"

The royal architects had done their best. The result was grand, no doubt about that. None who saw it could honestly dispute that point.

It had columns, many of them. And marble? Acres of the finest, snowy white marble. It had doorways so grand they could scarcely be opened even with the cleverest of pulleys and counterweights. The architects had debated making them steam-powered, then ultimately decided simply to cut smaller doors, still quite grand in their own right, right through the larger doors. It had balconies from which stirring speeches could be made, though they were seldom used save by pigeons, who rarely had anything interesting to say.

Upon seeing it, the monarch had proclaimed himself quite pleased.

The front of the Hall of Assembly was lined with fountains, because someone had once told King John that fountains gave a building a certain gravitas. The courtyard was paved with marble, because nobody had ever told the King that marble is slippery when it gets wet. In winter, the mist from the fountains, which had to be kept running to prevent the plumbing from bursting, froze on the marble, creating a glaze of ice that sent many an unwary pedestrian tumbling. For that reason, locals referred to the street in front of the Hall of Assembly as "Teakettle Road," for the frequency with which those who walked down it ended up ass over teakettle.

As morning broke, the aristocrats who made up the Council of Lords started arriving at the Hall of Assembly. Sessions of the Council were scheduled to begin at nine in the morning, but this rarely happened. It is a common trait of those who imagine themselves to be irreplaceable that they love making dramatic entrances, and it's hard to make a dramatic entrance if you arrive before everyone else. Over time, the lords acquired the habit of arriving later and later, until it was rare to see a quorum before half past nine.

Lord Wombly was the first to show up. He often was, by virtue of the fact that having reached eighty-four years of age, he no longer felt the need to try to impress anyone. He had a face vaguely reminiscent of a weasel, under an astonishing mass of white hair that spread about his head in a chaotic cloud so large it occasionally wandered into neighboring postal codes.

Wombly's footsteps echoed in the vast Grand Hallway. The walls and floor were covered in dark-colored wood, and the ceiling was all but lost overhead. Rows of statues watched in silence as Wombly walked by. They were all long-dead lords or members of the royal family or something, he was sure; in all the years he'd been on the Council, he had never bothered to look at any of the name plates. One departed politician was pretty much like another, seemed to him.

The guard posted before the entrance to the Great Chamber stood to attention, resplendent in his uniform. It had all the unnecessary ornamentation and ostentatious over-engineering that marked him as a ceremonial guard, rather than the other, more deadly type. "Good morning, my lord," he said. Wombly nodded agreeably and passed through the great mahogany doors, each more than twenty feet tall, cunningly designed to make everyone traveling through them feel small and insignificant. King John the Proud had his own ideas about the proper place of the lords on the Council, and rarely missed an opportunity to inform them of it.

Viewed from above, the building was shaped like the letter T. The vast, fountain-bedecked facade was the top of the T, extending in grand fashion along Teakettle Road. The stem of the T, crowned by a vast marble dome all gilt with hammered gold, was the Great Chamber itself, the enormous space where the Council of Lords took place.

Beneath the colossal dome, which was ringed on its upper floor by curved balconies, the seventy-two seats for the Council of Lords spread out in concentric semicircles, facing toward the throne, where the reigning monarch presided over the gathering. To one side, three tall wooden chairs allowed the representatives of the Church, whose presence was at least nominally more symbolic than legislative, to witness the proceedings. Often they were empty, or occupied by minor ecclesiastical types.

Lord Wombly sat in his assigned seat and put the powdered wig on his head. He fussed with it for a bit. He harbored a deep suspicion that the wigs were some sort of practical joke whose origin and humor had been lost to time. Tradition has a way of making absurdity seem ordinary.

The Great Chamber was huge, in part because regulations required the seats for the lords to be placed apart from one another by the distance of a short sword plus three inches. More than one past experience had proven the utility of these sorts of architectural features.

More aristocrats began streaming in, singly and in groups, all wearing the impractical robes that nobles affected to convince themselves they were more dignified than the common rabble.

The common rabble was already assembling, in its raucous way, in the curved balconies overlooking the Great Chamber. King John the Proud had been a strong believer that all meetings of the Council be open to the public—not because he thought transparency made for good governance, but because it was easier for him to keep an eye on what the public, and the lords, were up to. The commoners had their own doors that led directly into the balconies—normal-sized, because commoners as a general rule need no architectural cues to remind them they are small and unimportant.

Meetings of the Council were, as a general rule, about as exciting as porridge. On most meeting days, the balconies were abandoned save for a handful of people who talked to one another in hushed tones about the importance of civic participation and other things that really only mattered to people who had lots of free time on their hands. There was only so much excitement the working class could muster for committee meetings about the allocation of funds for the Commission on Gardens and Landscaping, given that most of them were far more concerned with allocation of funds for their own dinner tables.

Today was different. Today, those balconies were packed with the city's thronging masses—or such of the masses as would fit, anyway. An air of festivity filled the chamber. News that the Queen would be in attendance had traveled fast, and all of London was hoping to catch a glimpse of her. Laborers, tradesmen, artisans, fishmongers, and deliverymen stood shoulder to shoulder, chattering and back-slapping one another, united by a shared opportunity to witness somebody else's misfortune.

Among those people crowded onto the balcony was Thaddeus, trying—and failing—to look inconspicuous. He was wearing a grubby, dirt-stained shirt and striped overalls that belonged to one of the Bodgers' apprentices. Unfortunately, the apprentice owned only one pair of shoes, and Thaddeus had not thought to ask the new number two apprentice to fetch his own shoes from his flat, so he was forced to wear the unfortunately fashionable shoes he'd been cursed with since the party on the airship. The combination of workman's overalls and aristocrat's shoes was unlikely, he suspected, to set the world of fashion on fire.

Though you never could be sure, when it came to matters of fashion.

The jabber picked up when the Cardinal came in, flanked by two red-robed priests, hands folded in front of them. He moved to the tight group of three plain wooden chairs, frumpy compared with the gold-plated exuberance of the throne next to them, and sat in the tallest. The priests accompanying him sat to either side. Whispers swirled through the assembled spectators. "There he is! Old Sourpuss himself!" "I hear he wants to push the Queen aside!" "Do you think he'll have her hanged?" "I bet he's behind all this."

The Cardinal settled into his seat, paying no attention to the currents of whispers running through the balconies. The younger of the two priests sat behind him: a lad barely old enough to be out of *seminarium*, looking as out of place as a mouse in a cage of wolves. He leaned over to whisper to the Cardinal, who waved him away.

The doors opened again to admit His Excellency the Duke of Byron-on-shire, Margaret's half brother and next in line to the Throne of England. The boy looked out of place among the old men in the grand hall. Sir Marcus of Rhinehelm, Regent to the Duke, followed after. His Excellency the Duke had, by right of title, a place on the Council, which was occupied by the Regent in his place until such time as he reached the age of majority. As far as Marcus was concerned, that day could not come soon enough.

Lord Rathman entered shortly after, his face unusually somber. He nodded cordially to several of the other lords and sat.

Her Majesty the Queen, as reigning monarch of all the lands under the protection of the British Crown, had her own entrance, just behind her throne. This doorway was more conventionally sized, and of course was covered in gold leaf, as befitted her royal status.

An absolute silence fell with the abruptness of the executioner's axe when Her Majesty entered the chamber. Her eyes scanned the crowded balcony. Everywhere they landed, people lowered their gaze.

The assembled lords and the representatives of the most holy French Catholic Church all rose as one. The Cardinal caught Margaret's gaze for a moment just long enough to be uncomfortable. Then, in accordance with tradition, he descended to one knee. The priests on either side of him followed his example. The rest of the hall, lords and commoners alike, genuflected together.

Margaret permitted herself a small, tight smile. She crossed over to the throne and paused there, surveying the silent hall. For a long moment, the stillness of a tomb settled over the space, the people in it as immobile as a Chinese emperor's terracotta army.

Regally, without haste, Margaret sat. Life returned to the hall. The Cardinal rose, followed by his priests. Duty to Crown and God discharged, the lords resumed their seats. Finally, the commoners in the balconies, accustomed in the fashion of commoners the world over to prolonged discomfort, regained their feet. The normal sounds of crowded humanity crept back into the vast space.

Margaret scanned the faces of the assembled aristocrats. Empty seats dotted the hall. Nearly a third of the lords were absent—an astonishing display of rudeness, even by the normal fractious standards of British governance.

Margaret pursed her lips. The Cardinal tapped his fingers on his knee. Murmurs ran through the balcony.

Lord Wombly blinked his rheumy eyes and raised his hand. "If it pleases your lordships," he said, "I would like to get this bloody thing over with. Perhaps we can get started?"

Lord Marlboro rose from his seat. This required some not-inconsiderable effort, as the lord was possessed of that particular combination of florid complexion, prominence of nose, and rotundness of form attainable only through many years of far too much wine. He leaned against the curved table in front of him. "I am sure his lordship, the most eminent Lord Wombly, is aware that we are here to discuss the security of the nation of Britain. I know his lordship's petunias are also a pressing concern." He looked around at the ripple of laughter that passed through the hall. "Nevertheless, I would suggest we wait for the rest of the Council to arrive." He smiled pleasantly at Lord Wombly and sat.

"I am not half as interested in my petunias as your lordship is in the fruit of the vineyard, I expect," Wombly grumbled. A titter ran around the balcony. "If the security of the Realm is in such peril, how come half of us can't be arsed to be here on time?"

"A question I am sure will be answered to your satisfaction in the fullness of time," Lord Marlboro said. "In any event, we cannot come to order until the Lord High Chancellor arrives. Unless I miss my guess, he appears to be among those who, in the lord's vulgar if colorful words, 'can't be arsed to be here.'"

"In the absence of the Lord High Chancellor," Wombly said, "Her Majesty the Queen can call us to order. I would beseech Her Majesty to do so, so that we may get on with the business of debating the security of the Realm, or whatever it is we are supposed to be doing."

"Now see here!" Lord Edward, Baron of Harringworth, said. He rapped his knuckles on the table, then hoisted his tall, angular form to his feet. "This is most inappropriate. Most inappropriate. Lord Marlboro is right. We are here to discuss matters far more grave than your petunias or Lord Marlboro's love of the grape. I say we wait."

Lord Wombly crossed his arms. "And I say we allow Her Majesty to decide. If—"

He was cut off when the great door banged open. A tight cluster of men walked in: Richard Gaton, High Chancellor of the Council of Lords; Lord Clifford, Duke of Barnstaple; Lord Alexander Clay of Borneham; Lord Simon Hamilton of Clovenshire; and an assortment of other noblemen, some out of breath and still pulling on their powdered wigs. Lord Gaton bowed perfunctorily to Margaret. "Your Grace," he said. "My most humble apologies. I was unavoidably delayed."

The latecomers took their seats. Margaret frowned, fingers curling into the ornate gold-plated armrests of her throne.

"About time," Lord Wombly muttered. "Now maybe we can get on with it."

Richard Gaton, Lord Chancellor of the Council of Lords and Keeper of the Royal Seal, regarded Lord Wombly through narrowed eyes. Gaton was a great believer in Civilization. Civilization was what separated man from beast. And the thing that defined Civilization was Protocol. Sure, indoor plumbing had its place. And language. And writing, there was that, too. But above all those things was Protocol, the greatest achievement of the human spirit, the true hallmark of a civilized people.

And Lord Wombly did not properly respect Protocol. He had a distressing and distinctly un-British habit of speaking his mind. Worse, he showed utter disrespect for formality, tradition, and proper procedure. As far as Gaton was concerned, that meant Lord Wombly wasn't a proper lord at all. A true lord recognized the importance of Procedures and Rules of Order and, above all, Protocol. Men like Wombly, with their coarse language and their distressing habit of speaking out of turn, were threats to all that separated humanity from a long, slow slide into barbarism.

But a storm was coming, oh yes. It was very nearly here. And when it arrived, it would sweep away all the Lord Womblys who clogged the arteries of civilization, each and every one. Gaton awaited that day with satisfaction.

In the meantime, there were traditions to be respected and protocol to be followed. Where would man be without traditions and protocol? No doubt in a cave somewhere, banging on the walls with sticks or something.

"Keeper of the Rolls, are you satisfied that a quorum of lords is present?"

"Eh?" said the Keeper of the Rolls, the Very Honorable (and also very ancient) Lord Benjamin Bellingsworth. He blinked and looked around. "Oh. Yes, yes, I'm sure we're all here."

Gaton sighed and gave a silent prayer of thanks for the oncoming storm.

"Very well. By the authority vested in me by the Crown and the lords assembled, I call the Council to order. Keeper of the Records, let the record show this meeting of the Council of Lords has begun at..." He opened his pocket watch. "Ten twenty-six in the morning."

"Aye," said the Keeper of the Records, otherwise known as Lord Prescott Tiffendale of Porridge. He scribbled something in the enormous book in front of him. Each line in that great book, thought Gaton, represented one more rung on the ladder of progress. The choreography of procedure was the dance of enlightenment.

"Thank you, Lord Tiffendale. The first order of business before the Council of Lords is the decision to permit the Ministry of War to evaluate the suitability of artificial living constructs, colloquially known as animates, in the prosecution of war to further the defense and stability of the Realm. I will now open the floor for discussion."

Lord Clifford rose. Gaton smiled. Right on schedule.

"If it please the Council," he said, "I propose we lay this debate on the table. There is a more pressing matter that concerns me: to wit, the disappearance of the French princess Alÿs de Valois and the arrest of Her Majesty the Queen on suspicion of treason."

Margaret sat upright. The Cardinal froze in his seat, still as the dead, his face betraying nothing. In the balconies, murmurs swirled like dust devils on a hot summer day.

Lord Rathman rose. "A motion to interrupt the established agenda requires a second. I don't see—"

"Seconded," Lord Clay said. "I wish to hear what the Honorable Duke of Barnstaple has to say."

Lord Gaton's smile grew. "There is a second. Lord Clifford, you may speak."

"Thank you." Clifford adjusted his coat. "The arrest of a sitting monarch by order of Cardinal de Gabrielli, a citizen of the Kingdom of France, is unprecedented. My lords, we live in troubling times, most troubling times. That the Queen should be accused of heresy and collusion with Italians on such transparently trumped-up charges—it troubles me greatly." He shook his head. "This is clearly an attempt by a foreign power to meddle in the affairs of the British state. I do not believe even for a moment that the Queen is a heretic. And the mere notion that the Crown might collude with the imposters of Rome?" He glared pointedly at the Cardinal. "Only a dupe would fall for such a ruse, sir. Only a dupe."

There was a smattering of applause from the balconies. "Silence!" Gaton roared. "Pray continue, Lord Clifford."

"Thank you, your lordship. Members of the Council, friends of my soul, something is rotten in the state of Britain, yes, very rotten." He nodded vigorously for emphasis. "Very rotten…" His eyes turned misty. "We live in the greatest realm this world has ever seen. The nation of Britain is a beacon of light for the rest of the world, yes it is. We stand strong for peace and prosperity. I am proud, oh yes, proud to be here, proud to represent this greatest of all nations." He sniffled. "Your lordships, we have much to be proud of. But all that we have worked for, all that we have fought for, it is all in peril. We risk losing everything, all because of weak leadership from the Crown!"

Margaret's face darkened. The Cardinal watched Lord Clifford with the curious attention a cat gives to a small rustling in the grass.

"Weakness emboldens our enemies!" Clifford thundered. "They see our weakness, and it has made them strong! We have played right into their hands, yes, right into the hands of those who would do us harm!" He shook his fist at the dome above him, as though counting it among the enemies seeking to harm the British state. "Today, our borders are open to the tides of Israelites and Mohammedans and who knows who else! These people are not to be trusted. They are swarming to our shores from our enemies, Spain and Italy. They come from Afghanistan and Northern Africa and from the farthest East, and we know nothing about them. Can they be trusted? Who is to say? Queen Margaret has seen to it that they are welcomed here, yes, welcomed with open arms! Straight from the very nations we are at war with! Foreigners, pouring into our nation, undermining our ways, skulking about, sneaking in to do who knows what! And what does Her Grace do? She invites the representatives of the Caliphate to dinner! She carouses with them on her airship, while our people suffer! Why has she allowed these heretics and traitors into our land? What good have these foreigners ever done for us?"

A roar of self-righteous outrage rose from the crowded balconies above the hall.

"They built this hall," a small voice said.

Silence fell. Every eye in the Great Chamber swiveled to the speaker. Leo, the young Duke of Byron-on-shire and half brother of Queen Margaret, rose from his seat. "They built this hall," the boy repeated. "My father brought in workers and architects from all over the world. I'm surprised you didn't know that. He always said that we were made stronger when we welcomed outsiders." He waved away Sir Marcus, who was frantically signaling him to sit. "The people coming here from Spain and Italy are fleeing the Inquisition. They are the enemies of our enemies. They are grateful for the safe harbor we offer here. They are loyal subjects."

"The Council does not recognize the Duke," Lord Gaton said.

"I don't care!" the boy replied. "This is stupid. My father was right. You are all a bunch of frightened old men. The Muslims and Israelites are not a threat to us."

"And what does a boy know of the security of the Realm?" Clifford sneered.

"Better than a bunch of frightened old men, seems like," Lord Wombly said, rising. "This boy talks more sense than the lot of you, the way I see it." He cackled. "You're standing in a building built by foreigners asking what foreigners ever did for you. Pray remind us, how much gold do you make from trading with the Caliphate, hmm, Lord Chancellor? I hear you're doing pretty well with the Russians too. And you, Lord Marlboro. You keep a private doctor from the Caliphate on your personal staff, do you not?"

"Many of us do!" Marlboro huffed. "I don't see your point."

"That is quite enough!" Gaton roared. Red mist filled his vision. "We will observe proper protocol here! The floor does not recognize the Duke of Byron-on-shire! Or Lords Wombly or Marlboro!"

"Okay, okay," Lord Wombly said. "No need to get all shouty."

Gaton composed himself with difficulty. "If you have something to say, my Lords," he said, "please do observe the proper procedures. We are not barbarians!"

"Are you sure about that?" Wombly said, looking pointedly at Lord Clifford.

Lord Alexander Clay of Borneham rose slowly from his seat, like a great undersea creature surfacing from the depths to feed. "If it please the Council," he said.

"The Council recognizes Lord Clay," Gaton said.

"As your lordships know," Clay began, "I am a great admirer of the Crown. I have nothing but the deepest respect for everything Her Highness Queen Margaret has accomplished during her brief tenure. It pains me, therefore, to confess that I am troubled by recent events. First, the implication that Her Grace might be guilty of heresy—a deplorable situation, it must be said, and I find myself concurring with Lord Clifford's words on that matter—and now, I have been made aware that the Lady Alÿs is missing, and implicated by none other than the London Metropolitan Police themselves in a murder on Highpole Street." Murmurs ran through the crowd on the balcony. Lord Clay spread his hands. "Yes, yes, the rumors are true. I spoke to the chief inspector this morning. The Lady Alÿs is a suspect in a murder." The murmurs grew louder. "I do not believe our Queen is a heretic. Nor do I believe the Lady Alÿs to be a murderer. But someone wants us to believe these things, my friends, someone who bears us ill. And I ask myself, who benefits from these rumors? Who indeed! Undermining the Queen? Disrupting our alliance with France? This is foreign influence, I say! What do these foreign devils want? They want to see us fall! Now is the time for us to be strong. We will not fall!"

"That's right!" came a voice from the balcony. "We'll show 'em!" A general cheer of assent went up from the crowd.

"For too long, we have let these foreigners into our lands. We have welcomed them openly. And how have they repaid us? By undermining our government! By betraying our trust!" Lord Clay said.

"Aye, that's right!" the voice called from above. "An' have you been down Highpole Street? How do all those so-called refugees have so much money an' so many of us barely get by?" More sounds of assent rose up from the people jammed into the balcony. The Cardinal's eyes narrowed ever so slightly.

"The Lady Alÿs was last seen on Highpole Street by none other than the Royal Guard," Lord Clay continued. "They were there searching for the spy who infiltrated the Queen's airship. This cannot be a coincidence! All roads, it would seem, lead back to Highpole Street. Highpole Street, the foreigner district! Foreigners we allowed in, foreigners who eat away at us from within! We must put a stop to the rot!"

"Aye! A stop to the rot!" came the voice. A cheer went up from the gallery.

"To that end," Clay said, "I propose an emergency curfew on all foreigners and residents of Highpole Street, beginning tonight at six o'clock and lasting until this state of crisis has ended. Until we have gotten to the bottom of this treasonous plot, we must protect ourselves!"

"Do what needs doing!" called the voice from the balcony. "Do what needs doing!" The call was picked up by the rest of the crowd: "Do what needs doing! Do what needs doing!" As the cries grew louder, the owner of the voice that had started them, his face hidden beneath the brim of a hat, slipped out the exit.

Thaddeus watched him go. He was familiar with most of the scams and cons that played out daily in ways large and small all around London. To his eye, the plant in the crowd stood out plainly. It wasn't even particularly well done. The man in the hat and Chancellor Gaton had made eye contact too many times. That was rule one of that con: the huckster and the plant couldn't be seen interacting with any familiarity.

Amateurs.

Thaddeus slipped out the door after him. The man hurried down the short hallway that led to the stairs, and from there to the road perpendicular to Teakettle Road. He was about Thaddeus's size, dressed in an overly large coat. He kept his hat pulled down low over his eyes.

Thaddeus hung back for a moment. The man showed no sign of being aware he was being followed. Thaddeus took a deep breath and, head down, set out after him.

Inside the hall, the Cardinal had similar suspicions. He leaned over and whispered to the elder of the two priests seated beside him. The priest nodded and slipped quietly from the Chamber.

Chancellor Gaton allowed the raucous cries from the balcony to continue. That ought to show 'em, he thought. There was a small but growing number of madmen in the nation who held distressingly untidy ideas about the people's representation in the government. These folks seemed to feel that commoners—commoners, for the love of all that was holy!—should have seats on the Council of Lords. A handful of these lunatics even suggested, unbelievably, that an entire new Council should be created, *populated entirely by commoners*. The madness of that idea was self-evident, Gaton felt, to all right-thinking men, yet there were more of these people every year.

Commoners? Expressing what they wanted in these chambers? Nonsense! Everyone knew the commoners barely even knew what they wanted until you told them. And telling them was so *easy...*

Eventually, when he felt the point had been adequately made, he raised his hands and called for order. "Does anyone else wish to speak?"

Lord Hamilton stood. He was a burly man, broad of chest and still filled with the vigor of youth. He possessed a booming voice that filled the Chamber. "If it please the Chancellor and your lordships," he said, "I wish to contribute my voice to those of our esteemed colleagues. A curfew on the foreigners of the Highpole District seems prudent and measured. Until the Lady Alÿs is safely back with us and, God willing, assuming the worst has not happened," and here he crossed himself, "we cannot afford to be reckless. One murder has been committed already."

He put his hands together in a gesture of pleading. "My lords, you all know the Lady Alÿs, some of you quite well. There are none among us who do not look upon the young lady with favor. The nation of France has honored us by entrusting her to our care. We must allow no harm to come to her. I am informed that she was last seen running away though the Highpole District, seeking, I have no doubt, to escape whoever committed the most tragic murder that took place there. I fear the worst, and would beseech this Council to instruct the Metropolitan Police and the Royal Guard to spare no effort to search every part of the Highpole District for her. Let nothing stand between us and her safe return. Every shop must be searched, every house turned upside down, every house of worship examined, every basement and storeroom investigated until she is safely back with us. Each moment we delay brings us closer to the worst."

A chorus of cheers and calls poured from the balcony. None of the people there knew Alÿs, of course, but that didn't matter. The image of a young and defenseless girl held captive by dark-skinned foreigners in some basement somewhere in Highpole had a way of dislocating reasoned thought.

Gaton smiled his tight little smile. It was all so *easy*. It almost didn't seem fair.

The debate was swift. When it had ended, new emergency measures limited travel and nighttime activity of foreign-born citizens and noncitizens of Britain, effective immediately. The proposal to search every building on Highpole Street was defeated by the slenderest of margins. The rest passed handily, with only Lord Wombly and the regent for the Duke dissenting.

And that, Gaton thought to himself, is how it's done.

The moment the vote was taken, Lord Chancellor Gaton called an immediate dismissal of the Council.

If the Queen or the Cardinal felt any surprise that the main topic of debate never arose, neither of them showed it. They merely rose and left, Queen Margaret through the private door, the Cardinal via the main door. The other lords, save for Lord Wombly, lingered, congratulating one another for Taking Firm Action to Deal With the Matter at Hand.

Margaret caught up with the Cardinal in the hallway outside the great chamber, moving so fast the two men assigned to her personal guard had to run to keep up. "What was that about?" she demanded. Her face was suffused with rage.

"I'm sorry, Your Grace?"

"You went to a lot of trouble to bring us here to this…this…assassination of our character."

"Your Grace, I assure you—"

"Silence!" Margaret thundered. "We will not stand for this attack you have engineered on our person."

The Cardinal's face grew dark. "Your Grace, I assure you this was not my doing. That this meeting was engineered as an attack on your character, I have no doubt. But as to the identity of its architect, I am quite ignorant. I have little to gain and almost as much to lose by this as you do. What possible benefit would there be for me to undermine you before the Council? Damaging the special relationship between the Church and the Crown serves neither of our interests."

The Queen studied him for a long moment. Then, without a word, she gathered up her dress and left. Eleanor, who had been waiting outside the chamber, fixed the Cardinal with a look that spoke ill and followed after.

Wombly, for his part, was eager to get back to his garden. At least petunias didn't stab other flowers in the back, or foment unrest against the hibiscus bush. When you got right down to it, petunias were a better class of people than most people.

17

Thaddeus kept to the shadows, following closely behind the man he'd seen leaving the Hall of Assembly. This was harder to do in New Old London, with its wide streets and uniform buildings, than it would have been in Old New London, in whose windy cobblestone alleys you could be followed by an entire circus parade with brass band and troupe of performing monkeys without being aware of it. The role of the civil engineer in shaping a city's character is often underappreciated by everyone save for the criminal classes. The architecture of a neighborhood shapes the kinds of criminality that take place in it. Broad, open streets point to a higher class of crook, the kind who steal with limited liability companies instead of daggers.

It didn't seem to matter. The man moved with purpose, giving no sign he was even thinking about being followed.

The man Thaddeus was tailing was named Miles Daffern. He moved without regard to being followed because, while he was unquestionably a criminal sort engaged in a criminal enterprise, he was also a True Believer.

There are two sorts of people who commit atrocities: those who know that they're engaged in the business of atrocity, and those who don't.

The first sort are careful. They realize the evil of what they're doing, and they know that other people realize it as well. They tend toward paranoia, these sorts, trusting little, always keeping one eye looking over their shoulder. They understand that the business of evil is one that earns a man many enemies, so they take care not to be caught. They're cautious and pragmatic.

This is not to say that none of the first sort genuinely believe in their cause, of course. But the second sort truly believe destiny is on their side. They don't recognize the moral dimension of their own actions, but see instead only the good that will come about in the end. If people must suffer twixt hither and yon, well, that's just the way it was meant to be. This sort generally rely on divine providence to look after them, which means they're not very good at looking after themselves.

It was fortunate that Miles Daffern belonged to the second sort, as the priest who was also following him knew as little about following a mark discreetly as Thaddeus knew of the inner workings of the Order of the Visitation of Holy Mary. Miles went on his way, completely unaware of the twin shadows following behind.

Thaddeus sent a brief prayer to Saint Dismas that the priest would not spook their target. He felt a churlish sense of resentment at the priest's clumsy shadowing. Generally speaking, Thaddeus steered clear of the business of saving souls, and he felt it only fair that the Church should return the favor by keeping out of matters of petty thievery. Leave the experts to their domains, Thaddeus thought. It helped avoid embarrassing incidents.

The unholy Trinity—the agitator, the thief, and the man of God—traveled in a row north and west toward Westminster Bridge. When Miles reached Old New London, he headed north along Highpole Street, which was jammed with its conventional mix of unconventional people.

They passed through a vast open-air market midway up Highpole Street, a noisy, chaotic mass of unfettered commercialism that filled the air with the scent of spices, incense, grilled meats, and human enterprise. Thaddeus's stomach rumbled a reminder that he hadn't bothered to eat breakfast before leaving Bodger & Bodger. His mouth watered.

He was tempted, for a moment, to call off the pursuit. But no, the priest was following too, which meant the man was of interest to the Cardinal, which made him that much more interesting to Thaddeus.

The crowded streets made following both easier and harder. Easier, because with the crush of people, it would be difficult for Thaddeus to be spotted; harder, because the crowd made keeping an eye on his quarry more logistically challenging.

Fortunately, the strange man was as inexpert at knowing he was being followed as the priest was at following him. That was a strange thing; normally, if one were to hire a plant to rile up a crowd, one would choose someone familiar with the practice of criminal enterprise. This fellow seemed to Thaddeus to be woefully naive in the practical matters of the criminal arts. Thaddeus burned with curiosity. On two occasions, he was worried the priest might lose the scent just through sheer inexpertise. He didn't want that to happen, because he was dying to see what the holy man would do once the man they were following reached his destination. What was it Donnie had said? *Schemes within schemes*—and he, Thaddeus Mudstone, was a pawn.

"I'm getting more pieces," Thaddeus told himself grimly. "I just wish I knew how to play chess."

Thaddeus's quarry, still cheerfully oblivious, turned off Highpole Street just south of the Great Mosque. Here, a block away from the glitz and glamour of Highpole Street, the buildings were older and more shabby. Brick and limestone gave way to wood, most of it sun-bleached to a dull gray color. There were fewer people out on the street, and the priest in his red robes stood out like a haddock in a fruit salad. Thaddeus hung back, keeping well away from both target and priest.

The man headed toward the water and stopped in front of a three-story brick building that looked to have seen better days. Steps led up to a broad porch with a row of doors, all painted different colors. A faded wood sign out front advertised "Flats for Let" in English, French, German, Spanish, Hebrew, and Ottoman Turkish.

The man fished a large brass key out of his pocket. The priest stood in the middle of the street watching him. Thaddeus shook his head sadly at the follies of amateurs outside their area of expertise.

He held his breath, waiting for their quarry to turn around and notice the red-robed priest. It didn't happen. The man opened the door and disappeared inside. The priest stood there for a moment wearing the timeless expression of men everywhere who find themselves with no idea what to do next. Then, he turned and sprinted back the way they had come, as fast as his clerical legs would carry him.

Thaddeus briefly debated following him. But he could only be in one place at one time, and he didn't relish the thought of trying to run after the priest in these ridiculous shoes. He watched the front door of the flat from the shade of a lonely and slightly pathetic-looking tree, curious to see if the man would show a sudden, unexpected burst of sense by leaving once the priest was out of sight. It's what he might do if he were being followed, after all: pick the lock on some suitably dilapidated building, wait for the person following him to either make a move or leg it, then go about his business again. The only thing more satisfying than giving someone the slip was tricking him into thinking you hadn't given him the slip.

The sun beat down. The sad, scraggly tree had little shade to offer. Thaddeus's feet ached. The shoes seemed cruelly designed to try to contort his toes into positions that nature had clearly never intended. He wondered, not for the first time, if "fashion" wasn't perhaps a French word meaning "the vengeance of cobblers and artisans against the rich."

Still no sign of the man. Perhaps he really hadn't spotted either of his tails. Remarkable, that. Thaddeus couldn't remember a time when he'd ever been so unobservant.

Thaddeus crept around behind the building. The rear of the building was enclosed by a low stone wall. He scaled it easily, shoes notwithstanding. Keeping low, approached the grimy, dirt-streaked windows that punctured the shabby sun-bleached building. He crouched beneath what he hoped would be the right one, took a deep breath, held it for a moment, and risked a quick peek inside.

The window was almost completely blocked by a stained sheet of canvas that had been nailed up inside the room. Almost completely blocked, but not completely blocked. The canvas was worn and threadbare, with a convenient rip that allowed Thaddeus to peer inside. Thaddeus gave a silent prayer of thanks to whichever saints might inspire those engaged in criminal enterprises to save money on security. A brand-new bit of canvas might have made his life significantly more difficult.

The room beyond was grubby even by Thaddeus's permissive standards. A filthy mattress was pressed up against one wall, supported by a rusted bed frame that sagged until it nearly touched the floor.

It would be a lie to say the peeling wallpaper had seen better days. It had seen fewer days, certainly, once upon a time—days when it was less peeling, days when large swaths of it did not hang in sad, tattered strips from the plaster wall beneath. But for that particular shade of green, there are no better days.

The floor was littered with a collection of old newspapers, piled so thick and so deep that they formed a rough chronology of the whole of human civilization. Teams of paleontologists could have spent years in that room, exploring the various linguistic strata of newspapers. At the deeper levels, where the papers made up a newsprint Cambrian era, the letterforms might be seen in their simplest forms, the Phoenician alphabet evolving over time, gradually assuming the shape of the characters inhabiting the modern world of written language.

Empty glass milk bottles, dozens of them, lay scattered over the layers of newsprint or piled in wooden carrying boxes. A battered table, one leg missing, leaned uneasily against the wall opposite the bed, an equally battered chair beneath it. Wooden chests, the only absolutely pristine, new-looking things in the room, lay atop the table in neat rows. A pile of clothes had settled in a heap at the foot of the bed but looked ready to scurry off at the slightest provocation. A pair of work boots peeked out from beneath the mound of greasy rags.

The door into the room opened. Thaddeus ducked down, counted slowly to ten, then raised himself up to peer in again.

The man was sitting at the shabby table, balanced precariously on the beat-up chair. Carefully, almost reverentially, he opened one of the small chests. From it, he scooped a measure of fine black powder, which he poured with exaggerated caution into one of the milk bottles. He scooped up a handful of little bits of metal and poured it into the bottle atop the powder. Then he tore a strip from a bit of rag and stuffed it tightly into the mouth of the bottle. Thus prepared, the bottle was placed gently in a wooden box with a handle on it.

He worked steadily, filling bottles with the black powder, adding handfuls of rusty bits of iron, stuffing the mouths with rags, and setting them delicately in the boxes. As he filled each box, he carefully closed the lid, then stacked it next to the door, where a pile of similar boxes already stood.

Thaddeus flattened himself against the wall, heart pounding. He felt out of his depth. *Schemes within schemes.* Here he was playing poker, while all his adversaries were playing chess. And the stakes kept climbing.

He risked another quick peek. The man was still working. He turned his head, and Thaddeus had a sudden, acutely uncomfortable sensation of peering through a mirror into an alternate reality. The man was the very image of Thaddeus—same height, same build, same hair. Thaddeus had the uncomfortable feeling that come dawn, he would be wanted for questioning in connection with something rather horrible.

He fought back an urge to run. It was an impulse that had served him well in the past, but here, it seemed inadvisable. These were extraordinary times. Extraordinary times required an extraordinary response.

Even a pawn can topple a king if he's in the right place at the right time.

What would Claire or Donnie do in his position? Something brilliant, probably. They'd find some clever way to save their skins and also save the day, and everything would turn up roses.

He really wasn't smart enough for this. No point pretending otherwise. In his line of work, smart could get you in trouble. Smart people were easy to fool. Smart meant you could think of all sorts of logical-sounding reasons to believe what you already wanted to believe. Thaddeus preferred cunning to smart. Cunning made you wary.

But this was not his area of expertise. What he needed now was Claire and Donnie's kind of smart, which was a different sort of smart altogether. Thaddeus was cunning, but cunning wasn't good enough. Cunning told you to run; smart told you what to do once you were done running.

A pounding at the front door jolted him out of his self-pity. "Open up! Open up in the name of His Eminence the Cardinal of London!"

Thaddeus peeked into the room. The man was sitting bolt upright, face ashen. The pounding came again. The man bolted from the room, slamming the door behind him.

Voices came through the thin wall. Thaddeus could not make them out, but he recognized their character from personal experience: suspicion and hostility from the Cardinal's men, placatory innocence from their suspect.

Think. Think. What would Claire and Donnie do?

His eyes fell on the work boots. A plan took shape in his head. It probably wasn't a smart plan. Truth be told, it might not even be a good plan. But it was a plan, and dodgy as it was, it had the singular advantage of being the only plan he had.

Carefully, with as little noise as possible, he prized at the window. It resisted. He placed both hands on the jamb and pulled with all his strength, fueled by urgent desperation. It relented, sliding up just far enough for Thaddeus to scramble inside.

The canvas nailed over the window posed a problem. Shabby at it was, it was still quite tough, and it didn't seem disposed to tear easily. Thaddeus pushed and pried at it until he had ripped enough of it free of the nails that sealed it around the edge of the window that he could crawl through. He had a brief moment of panic when he found himself trapped, hanging upside down halfway into the room. Then the canvas gave way with a tearing sound and he tumbled to the floor. His head whacked into the floorboards with a thump. Stars danced in his vision. Outside the door, the voices paused for a second, then continued.

He crept over to the pile of rags and snatched the boots. Fingers fumbling, he pulled off those ridiculous shoes and placed them where the boots had been. Then, with a sudden flash of inspiration, he pulled out the bejeweled box containing the Queen's gem-encrusted comb.

The magnitude of what he was about to do sucked his breath away. He had risked so much to steal the comb. The jewels studding the gold case were probably worth more than anything he'd held in his life. But this was chess, and sometimes, you had to make sacrifices in chess, right? He'd heard something like that somewhere.

Hands trembling, heart aching with the injustice of it all, Thaddeus tucked the bejeweled case just out of sight under the clothes, right next to the shoes. The architect of his recent misery had wanted him to plant evidence? Very well, he would plant evidence.

Barefoot, he padded back to the window. He had just crawled through and closed it behind him when the door into the room opened again.

Throw a spanner in the works. That's what Claire and Donnie would do.

He pulled on the boots. Angry voices came through the wall behind him. They drew closer to the window, becoming clearer as they did, until Thaddeus could make out the words. "What's this, then? These look like the shoes the lady was on about." He heard a protest, indistinct and rapidly cut off. "Right. Let's bring him to the Cardinal. And somebody pass along a tip to the plods about what we've found here. Anonymously."

For the first time in days, Thaddeus smiled.

He hopped the wall and sauntered casually to the street. Three large men in the livery of the Cardinal's personal guard were dragging Thaddeus's doppelganger out the front door. Whistling, Thaddeus walked away, wriggling his toes luxuriantly in the stolen boots.

18

In his office in the London Municipal Police headquarters at Whitehall Place, Commander Skarbunket of the London city police was strongly considering becoming Civilian Skarbunket of Bugger All This.

He held his head in his hands. "With all due respect, sir, this is all going to go sideways."

Sir Benjamin Fieldman, Chief Inspector of the London Metropolitan Police, was harboring similar thoughts about the joys of civilian life. But he had his orders, delivered personally by the Lord Chancellor himself. What could you do?

"Your concern is duly noted," he said. "Nevertheless, this is the way it will be. Your investigation is suspended pending the resolution of this crisis."

"My investigation, sir, is at a critical juncture. I have just returned from Highpole, where the Queen's Guard was assisting me in following up on a murder. One that, I need not remind you, sir, appears to involve the Lady Alÿs, which as I'm sure you're aware, adds a whole layer of political sensitivity to the matter."

"All the same, as of this morning, your investigation is suspended. Sensitive or not." The chief inspector passed his hand over his forehead. "You and your men will be in Highpole at six o'clock this evening, where you will enforce the curfew in accordance with the dictates of the Council of Lords. Am I clear on this point?"

"Very clear, sir," Skarbunket replied. He massaged his temples and thought longingly of a quiet life somewhere far from the mess and stink of London. A farm, perhaps. A farm would be nice. He could raise sheep, maybe some chickens...

"Evening prayers are at six twenty tonight," he said. "Should we try to prevent the Muslims in Highpole from attending their prayer service, sir, they will no doubt interpret this as a deliberate provocation. And I must say, sir, again with all due respect, I must say that I would be inclined to agree with them on this point."

"So tell them to have their prayers before six," Chief Inspector Fieldman said. "Problem solved."

Skarbunket closed his eyes. Chickens, that was the ticket. Perhaps even some cows. Cows were good, right? He'd heard that cows were good. The worst thing he would have to worry about was wolves, barn fires, and attacks from roving bandits or invading Spanish skirmishers or roving Spanish bandits. Piece of cake.

"It doesn't work that way, sir. Their religion is quite clear. They have daily prayers at certain times, and those times are not subject to negotiation. You would know this, sir, if you read the memos you signed. Like the one you signed three months ago, sir, permitting Muslim members of the Force to go on break for prayers."

Fieldman's eyebrows went up. "We have followers of Mohammed on the Force?"

"Yes, sir. Mister Habis, for one. You recently gave him a commendation for excellent service. You know the fellow. Tall, big smile, likes Mrs. Grindle's meat pies..."

"Ah, yes, yes, right. I thought there was something queer about him."

"And Sergeant Nadeem, the one with the crooked nose. I believe you once described him as a 'credit to the Force,' sir."

"Him too? I had no idea we had so many of them!"

Skarbunket sighed. "The point is, sir, they will not just move their prayer service. Nor can I simply order my men to stop them. That would create an irreconcilable dilemma for some of our men, sir, men who are loyal members of our little family. Nobody benefits from such a situation. Sir."

"Oh, I don't know about that." Chief Inspector Fieldman shook his head. "Somebody would probably benefit quite a lot, I suspect. Still, that's neither fish nor fowl."

"Sir?"

"It means it's not your concern, Commander."

"I'm not sure that's what that means, sir."

"Your concern, *Commander* Skarbunket, is enforcing the will of the Crown and the Council of Lords."

"My concern, sir, is also with protecting the peace. Protecting the peace is one of the sacred duties of the Force, sir. In fact, I seem to recall it being part of the oath, sir."

The chief inspector narrowed his eyes. A vein throbbed in his temple. "You will do as you are told, Skarbunket. This is not up for debate. And wear your dress uniform. The people need to see that the police are on the job. Is that clear?"

"As clear as a bell, sir," Skarbunket said. Politicians, he thought to himself, made roving bandits look easy. At least the bandits made their intentions plain. You didn't have to talk to them.

"Oh, and one more thing, Commander."

"Sir?"

"It could be nothing…"

"That's what you said about the thing with the goats, sir."

"Yes, well, I said it could have been nothing, not that it was nothing, Commander."

"Indeed, sir. As I recall, it turned out to be quite a lot of something, sir. There were casualties, sir. And we made quite a number of arrests, sir. And it took days to get the smell—"

"Yes, yes, well, anyway. We have received an anonymous tip."

"Anonymous, sir?" Skarbunket held onto his expressionless expression. "Like the last time, sir?"

"No, not like the last time! That was…complicated. This new tip is about a rental flat just off Highpole Street. And, er, apparently, black powder in some quantity may be involved. In the rental flat. Which you should check out."

"I see, sir. Explosives, you say, sir? In Highpole? On the same day as a new curfew is announced?"

"Precisely, Commander."

"Sounds like coincidence, sir. Not complicated at all."

"Maybe."

"It could be nothing, sir."

"It could be."

"I see, sir." Somewhere in Skarbunket's mind, visions of a peaceful farm faded.

"Put someone on it."

"I will assign it to Officer Bristol at once. And may I request, sir, just in case it turns out to be more 'something' than 'nothing', may I request allocation of funds to hire some animates to clean the place out? You know, in the unlikely event that there are explosives involved, sir, a possibility I mention in passing only because you bring up receiving a tip that explosives are involved. Sir."

"Animates?"

"I find it is best, sir, that if someone is to be blown limb from limb, it be someone who does not mind having it happen. And in fact does not have a mind at all. There are no widows to notify, sir."

Chief Inspector Fieldman opened his mouth to speak, then closed it again. "Fine."

"I will get on it at once, sir."

"Very good. I will leave you to it then, Commander."

Skarbunket watched him go. He shook his head, rose, and walked to the door of his office, visions of pastoral life dancing in his head.

As a commander of the London Municipal Police, Skarbunket had a large office on the top floor of the new police headquarters, built near the river Thames during King John's epic urban reconstruction project. The London Municipal Police was run from a five-story building between

Whitehall Place and Scotland Yard, outfitted with electric arc lights, a central boiler, the kind of indoor toilets that have levers on them, and all the other latest amenities technology had to offer.

It was a severe place, built of brick and stone, with imposing columns and an elaborate facade featuring statues of brave men in immaculate uniforms arresting a wide assortment of miscreants, thugs, villains, thieves, murderers, skulkers-about, Italians, and other ne'er-do-wells. The main entrance was a tall set of mahogany doors set into a peaked stone archway over which the figure of Lady Justice loomed, one hand holding a sword, the other a set of scales. Skarbunket had often wondered, as he passed through those doors, where the lady was off to, and why she was in such a hurry to get there that she had forgotten all her clothes. The whole thing was capped with a tall and somewhat incongruous mansard roof, because someone had told King John that French architecture was where it was at.

During the day, the large window in Skarbunket's office offered him a beautiful view of the river, or it would if the position of his desk didn't mean he had his back to it most of the time. But that didn't matter. It wasn't enjoying the view, it was that he could enjoy it if he wanted to. Knowing it was there, that was the thing. Or so he assumed, anyway. The perks of high office often seemed to be things that people got simply because they wanted to have them, not because they wanted to enjoy them.

At night, the blaze of electric arc lights kept the inside of the building in such a state of brilliance that the windows were all mirrors, reflecting the machinery of law enforcement without actually allowing the many people who made up that machinery to see the city they were nominally protecting.

The whole thing was far too institutional and, well, political for Skarbunket's liking. The old police headquarters had been in Old New London, back when it was still just New London. Back then, the police were still a comfortable distance from the Palace, both literally and figuratively, which meant could go about their business with a minimum of meddling. Now, the Municipal Police felt more like an arm of the government. It was surprising how often the interests of the government didn't exactly align with the peace and security of the city. The business of policing too easily turned away from apprehending threats to the public safety and toward apprehending people politically inconvenient to the upper classes.

He walked into the hall and leaned over the railing. The central core of the building was a huge open space that went all the way to the ground floor, ringed with hallways on each level that opened into interrogation rooms, evidence lockers, and offices. So many offices. King John had felt that people should see what their tax money was paying for.

"Mayferry!" he roared. "Bristol! Both of you! My office!"

The controlled chaos of the station slowed for a moment. From somewhere below him, he heard a "Yes, Sir!" Satisfied, he returned to his office.

London Constabulary Officer Bristol materialized at Skarbunket's door with commendable rapidity. "Sir?"

"Officer Bristol! You look splendid this morning. How are the wife and kids?"

"I'm not married, sir," Bristol said. "A fact of which you are well aware, sir."

"Right. Maybe you should get on that. How do you feel, Officer Bristol, about checking out an anonymous tip involving black-powder explosives in a rental flat in Highpole? It could be nothing."

"It could be nothing? Like with the goats, sir?"

"I expect exactly like with the goats."

"Then I imagine I feel pretty badly about it, sir."

"Good. Smart man. Head over to Highpole. If you find anything that looks like it might go bang, rent some animates and have them clean it out. I don't want to risk the lives of…the lives of anyone alive."

"Yes, sir."

As he turned to leave, he ran into Officer Mayferry, who was slightly out of breath. "You could just use the speaking tubes, sir," Mayferry said, somewhat reproachfully.

"Oh?" Skarbunket considered the suggestion. Finally, he shook his head. "Would it get you here as quickly? I thought not. Do you have any plans for the evening, Mayferry?"

"Now that you mention it, sir, yes. I am—"

"Cancel them. I want you to call in the two dozen or so people you trust the most. Tell them to muster in the yard in two hours. Oh, and have everyone bring their best uniform." He lifted a finger. "Choose carefully, Mister Mayferry. I need men with cool heads. Preferably men who don't harbor unwarranted animosity toward those not like themselves, if you take my drift."

Mayferry blinked. "Is there something I should know about?"

"New orders from their lordships. It seems we are going out to Highpole tonight to enforce a six o'clock curfew."

"What? Why?"

"For the safety and security of the Realm, of course, and shame on you for imagining anything else."

Mayferry gave him a look. "Er, yes, well," he said finally, after a silence that was about two seconds longer than awkward. "Just a small point of clarification, if I may, sir. Does this relate at all to the murder of the artisan we are investigating?"

"A prescient question, Mister Mayferry. And, surprisingly, the answer is not exactly no. Some of the illustrious members of the Council of Lords have taken it into their heads that the Lady Alÿs, our mysteriously absent witness to that matter, must have fallen afoul of the true conspirators, said conspirators probably holding her captive in some basement somewhere doing who knows what to her even as we speak."

"A basement, sir?"

"Yes. In Highpole, naturally."

"And this curfew is…?" Mayferry's eyebrows completed the question.

"As I said, for the safety and security of the Realm."

"Because while we're enforcing it, we won't be looking for the missing Lady Alÿs? Or following up on the murder?"

"You catch on quickly, Mayferry. Have you considered a career in politics?"

"Sir!" Mayferry said. "That kind of language is uncalled for."

"My apologies, Mayferry," Skarbunket said. "My cynicism sometimes gets the better of me." He leaned back in his chair. "As you say, rather than searching for the Lady Alÿs, or investigating the murder, we are to enforce a curfew imposed by men who say they wish to find the Lady Alÿs and get to the bottom of the murder. And shame on you again, Mayferry, for harboring those doubts I can see in your eyes about the efficacy of this cunning strategy devised by their lordships. Now, given that you wish to continue your career as a member of the great city of London's Municipal Force, rather than taking a role in the political sphere, I want you with me and those of the Force we can trust not to be lighting matches in tinder kegs, save for our comrade Mister Bristol, on Highpole Street tonight at six."

"How come Bristol gets an out?"

"Why, would you like to trade places with him?" Skarbunket smiled. "I will arrange it if you like. Simply say the word."

"Er…would you mind telling me what he's doing?"

"Officer Bristol will be following up on an anonymous tip this evening. Could be nothing."

"Oh. A 'could be nothing.' The last one of those…"

"Yes, Mayferry?"

"Um, no, sir, I think I will leave him to it. It could be nothing, as you say."

"Very well, then. Make sure Mister Habis and Sergeant Nadeem are with you. Oh, and that new fellow, what's his name? The Israelite."

"Mister Levy?"

"That's him. Bright lad. A bit wet behind the ears, perhaps, but we all need to get thrown into the frying pan at some point. I want him front and center."

"Why him, sir?"

"Because, Mayferry, things might get ugly out there tonight. The citizens of Highpole have many enemies. I do not want them to number London's finest among them. I want them to see that the constabulary includes some of their own. Everyone in dress uniform. That's from on high. And no swords or firearms. Truncheons only. That's from me."

"Will you at least be bringing your pistol, sir?"

"Absolutely not, Mayferry."

"Sir? I thought you said it might get ugly."

Skarbunket regarded his subordinate for a long moment. "We are not riding into battle, Mayferry," he said at last. "When the police fear the populace, we forget that we are here to protect and serve. When that happens, everyone becomes the enemy. I will not have that, Mayferry."

"Aye, sir."

✦

Two hours to the minute later, the men of the Metropolitan Police were assembled in the Yard.

The Yard was, for want of a better word for it, a yard. It was a large yard, made as impressive as the Royal Architects could make it, given the paucity of material to work with. It was nearly two blocks long, and situated just across the main entrance to police headquarters. Hedges in neat, stepped rows lined its edges, maintained by royal order to mathematical exactitude. In the precise center of the Yard stood a lonely flagpole topped with a bronze casting of a woman, only barely less scandalous in her attire than Lady Justice, holding a trident triumphantly skyward. The whole thing was rather dreary, in its geometrically perfect way.

It hadn't originally been a yard. Once, it had been a school. But then again, New Scotland Yard had been a curved street once. King John could not abide streets that curved for no reason. He also believed that if a street was called New Scotland Yard, there should be a yard on it. He had both of those oversights corrected during the Great Reconstruction. Nowadays, it was noteworthy mainly for the astonishing number of pigeons that called it home.

On most afternoons, the Yard was surrounded by throngs of people on their way to and from the Palace. For the most part, they stuck to the sidewalks, walking around the Yard rather than through it. On most days, there was, as a general rule, nobody on the Yard itself. Almost nobody ever went on the Yard.

Not today. Today, the Yard played host to nearly thirty people, all lined up in two neat rows so tidy as to make King John's heart soar, if indeed he had had a heart, which was purely a matter of conjecture.

Skarbunket paced back and forth, seemingly unaware of the rows of men standing in front of him. Beside him, Mayferry shifted his weight uncertainly. Little gusts of bone-chilling wind blew around them. A light rain drifted down from the ashen sky, the kind of rain that gets in your eyes and sticks to your clothes, just enough to make you uncomfortable but not enough to be worth getting out the umbrella for. Inside Skarbunket's mind, a cold wind howled.

"Sir?" The voice, hesitant, originated somewhere in the second row. The owner of the voice, a thin, gangly man who barely looked a day over sixteen, coughed nervously. He had large blue eyes and a shock of yellow hair that sprouted almost vertically from his head, giving him the perpetual expression of a very surprised duck that had just had an unfortunate accident with a live electrical wire.

"Yes?" Skarbunket said. His eyes refocused on the external world. "Tumbanker, is it?"

"Yes, sir. Peter Tumbanker, sir. Beg pardon, sir, but why are we here?"

"The times are changing," Skarbunket said, more to himself than to the ranked men before him.

"I'm sorry, sir?"

A gust of wind blew a smattering of rain into Skarbunket's eyes. He shook his head. "Most of you have probably heard the news by now. The Council of Lords has ordered a curfew for all residents of Highpole Street, beginning at six o'clock tonight and each night thereafter until such time as the Lady Alÿs de Valois of the French Court is located."

"And she's somewhere in Highpole, is she?"

"Not to our knowledge."

"I don't understand, sir."

"Then I suppose it's a good thing that understanding is not part of your job," Skarbunket said, his face carefully neutral.

"But sir, if we're all out at Highpole tonight, who will be patrolling the rest of London?"

"Who indeed, Mister Tumbanker. London will have to look after itself tonight."

"What about tomorrow night? And the night after that? Won't the crims know we're all in Highpole?"

"You have an admirable way of putting your finger directly on the pulse of the problem, Mister Tumbanker. I do not doubt, and I say this not to discourage you, Mister Tumbanker, but I do not doubt that will cause you no end of trouble as you advance in the Force. Do you have any other impertinent questions for me, Mister Tumbanker?"

"Just one, sir. Won't the people in Highpole be upset?"

"Oh, yes, I imagine they will be. Very upset, I expect. Ask yourself how you would feel in their shoes."

"So what do we do?"

Skarbunket looked at the ranks of tense faces. They were all good men, to a one; perhaps a trifle uninspired, some of them, but good men nonetheless. Each of them had been placed in an untenable position and was looking to him for a way out.

And he had nothing to offer them. Well, nothing beyond the consolation prize of firsthand experience with the twisted labyrinth of the political mind.

"We do as we're told," he said. "We enforce the curfew. Our betters have spoken." He made no attempt to keep the bitterness from his voice. "Effective immediately, all other ongoing investigations are paused. Whatever it was you were doing, you aren't doing it anymore. I am designating Finske, Pipstrin, and Leodsman as acting commanding officers for the duration of the curfew. I want each of you to take a section of Highpole Street south of the mosque and work out amongst yourselves which men you will take with you. Mayferry, Habis, Nadeem, Tumbanker, and Levy, you will accompany me. Mayferry, choose another half a dozen or so people who you trust to keep their wits about them. We will be enforcing the curfew on the north end of the street."

"Me, sir?" Tumbanker's eyes were wide. "Why me?"

"Because you have a keen and inquisitive mind, Mister Tumbanker, and as I said, such a thing may cause no end of mischief if it is not carefully managed. Oh, there is one other thing, if I may, gentlemen. Remember that these people you will encounter tonight are citizens of London, the very people you swore an oath to protect. Some of you number the residents of Highpole among your friends. Some of you live there, or have family there. The people of Highpole will be angry, and this is reasonable. They are not the enemy. I expect to see no less than the highest level of conduct from each of you. If any of you gentlemen here assembled believe you may have difficulty remembering the oath you took when you joined the Force, step forward now. There is no room among us for such men. Anyone?"

He waited for several heartbeats. A field of statues could not have been so still. "Good," he said. "I will see you all reassemble here at four thirty. Mayferry, Habis, Nadeem, Tumbanker, Levy, with me, if you please." He turned smartly and headed back toward headquarters. The other men had to race to keep up with him.

19

"I don't know anything!" Eleanor wailed.

She was sitting on an uncomfortable chair in the guardroom behind a broad, polished-wood table that looked brand new. Behind her, the stone wall was lit by the flickering yellow glow of oil lamps. Her fingers twisted together in the fabric of the long green dress she wore, clenching and unclenching, clenching and unclenching.

King John had personally decreed that the guardroom would be illuminated by oil lamps rather than the modern electric arc lamps that graced most of the rest of the Palace. He embraced the onward march of Progress, but when it came to matters of personal security, his sensibilities took a more pragmatic turn. He had reasoned that if all the light in the Palace came from electricity, then all that would be necessary to storm the Palace would be to cut those slender copper wires that connected the Palace to the great coal-powered generators a mile or so away. It was what he would do, anyway. So critical parts of the Palace could be illuminated by gas jet, oil lamp, or both, should the need arise.

Besides, oil lamps gave the guardroom a more appropriate ambiance.

On the other side of the table, Max the Axe and Julianus sat looking at Eleanor. Max the Axe was angry. This time, his attention was not split.

"Aiding and abetting a fugitive from justice is treason," Max growled. "Treason is punishable by death."

"But I don't know where she is!" Eleanor was near tears. "I told you! I don't know anything!"

Julianus leaned back, eyes half closed. His head throbbed. This day hadn't been the least bit productive so far, and it didn't seem to be on a path toward improving anytime soon.

They'd spent most of the morning in the kite maker's shop in Highpole. The police had whisked away the body to wherever it was they took murder victims. The man in charge of the investigation, Scarbungle or Stambangle or something like that, was one of those sorts who was entirely too clever for his own good. He didn't like the presence of Max and Julianus at his crime scene and had made a show of pretending to conceal his disdain for them without quite going so far as to actually conceal his disdain for them. He and his men did what policemen did, which mostly seemed to be looking around a lot and writing notes in small notebooks.

Chiyo Kanda, the recent and recently deceased proprietor of the shop, had been the sort to keep careful, meticulous, and highly detailed notes in a thin, precise hand on all her clientele, all recorded in a thick ledger book bound in leather. That was the good bit.

And oh, such a good bit it was. The ledger was massive, a thing of extraordinary beauty, wrapped in soft red leather embossed with intricate geometric designs. The edge of the book was painted with a seascape, small black birds soaring high above foam-topped waves. The pages of the book were filled with notes, calligraphy, sketches, a watercolor or two, and ledger entries—hundreds of pages of ledger entries, all neatly organized. The last quarter or so of the book was blank.

The bad bit, at least for anyone other than Chiyo Kanda, was that all her careful records were written in a language neither the two Guardsmen nor the policemen had ever seen before, all boxes and little lines stacked in neat columns. It contained a vast amount of information, all of which was completely inaccessible to the police, the Guard, and all the language experts employed by both.

Julianus's optimism had gradually evaporated, replaced by that throbbing pressure in his head. The ledger book was a dead end. It contained the identity of the mysterious person who had commissioned the kite, he was sure of it. But it kept its secrets tightly locked away behind a wall of strange impenetrable handwriting.

When Julianus proposed they show the ledger book around the Highpole District, in hopes that someone else might be able to read the odd, blocky script, the police commander, Scarbungle or Starbucket or whatever his name was, had insisted on accompanying them, citing "chain of custody" and "verifiable information" and other things that had made Max very angry. His tone and manner suggested he questioned the integrity of the Queen's Guard. If there was one thing that Max the Axe could not abide, it was anyone who questioned his integrity.

If there was a second thing Max the Axe could not abide, it was anyone who questioned his authority. If there was a third thing Max the Axe could not abide, it was anyone who doubted his dedication to the Realm. After that, Julianus stopped keeping count of the things about Steerbundle that Max the Axe could not abide.

He let the two of them argue it out, intervening only a couple of times when it seemed Max might be on the brink of doing something regrettably violent to a commander of the municipal police force, which, while understandable, might have led to a distracting political tangle.

Eventually, they agreed that Max, Julianus, and the police commander would all look in Highpole for a translator for the ledger. That, too, had been a dead end. Nobody they talked to seemed to know how to read the book; in fact, few of the people they encountered seemed to speak the Queen's English at all. A crowd had gathered around the three of them, all whispers and suspicious gestures, but wherever they turned their attention, it seemed to melt away into nothing. And, of course, nobody knew anything.

Typical.

Finally, Julianus had given up. "This is pointless," he said. "We're getting nowhere. We need to come at this from another angle."

"Alÿs," Max said.

"Ah, there it is at last! I wondered how long it would take us to come to a meeting of the minds, partner," Julianus said. "Yes," he continued, ignoring Max's expression, "the Lady Alÿs. We followed the kite to the shop, and there she was. She's connected to the shop, which means she's connected to the kite, which means she's connected to the man who jumped out of the airship with the kite. All these threads tie together. We just need to find the right one. What threads connect to Alÿs?"

"I bet I can find some of those," Max had said. His face was bright with the promise of violence.

Half an hour later, they were in the guardroom with Eleanor in tow.

"I told you already! She didn't tell me where she was going!" Eleanor said. She looked back and forth between the two of them, searching their faces. The Queen's Guard was supposed to protect the Queen, and by extension, that meant they were supposed to protect *her*. Yet somehow, things had gone topsy-turvy. The Queen arrested by members of her own Guard, her ladies being interrogated like common criminals, or Italians...

"You are her best friend," Julianus said.

"Yes! I mean, no! I mean, I don't know! She was...she is...she hardly talks to me!"

"That's not what the other members of the Court say," Julianus said mildly. He examined his fingernails as though suspecting them of collusion with Eleanor.

"Okay! Okay! Yes, we are friends!" Eleanor said. Tears flowed. "But I swear on the life of Her Grace Queen Margaret of Britain, I don't know where she is!"

"She left yesterday afternoon," Julianus said.

"Yes! We were talking about Shoe Man, and—"

"Shoe Man?"

"The man who jumped out of the airship!"

"Did she know him?"

"No! She wanted to go look for him. I tried to warn her that he was an Italian spy, but she wouldn't listen! I told her the Italians aren't like us! They eat babies, I told her that!" She looked up, horrified. "Do you think he caught her? Do you think he—" Her voice choked off in a sob.

Julianus glanced at Max. "Where was she going to look for him?"

"I don't know!"

"What did she say?"

"She didn't say anything! She just stood up and left. She had that look in her eye, the one she gets when she runs off on one of her adventures." Her expression changed, became more hopeful. "Why aren't you talking to that stable boy? He usually helps her when she gets in one of her moods. I bet he knows where she went! You should talk to him!"

"Do you mean Henry? Young lad, about so tall, red hair?" Julianus asked.

"Yes! Henry! You should talk to him!"

"We did," Julianus said. "We spoke to him and his brother not half an hour ago. They were cooperative, but not very helpful. That's how these things go sometimes."

"Did they know where she went?"

"No," Max said. "We were very…persuasive. If they had known, I'm sure they would have told us."

Fear flickered behind Margaret's eyes. "What do you mean?"

"I'm sure the older boy will probably walk again," Max said. "Whether they ever see the outside of a cell again is still open to debate. As I said, aiding and abetting a fugitive is treason. Even if you don't know you're doing it."

Eleanor's eyes widened. "I tried to stop her! I told her not to go, I did! But when she gets that way, you can't tell her anything. It's like when—" She stopped suddenly and clapped both hands over her mouth.

Max and Julianus looked at each other. They both looked back at Eleanor.

"I—I—" Eleanor stammered.

They kept watching her, Max with feral interest, Julianus with clinical detachment. Neither of them spoke a word. Slowly, deliberately, Max folded his arms.

Time stood still. Shadows danced on the stone walls.

Eleanor made a small keening sound. Gradually, it increased to a wail. The sound rose and rose until it transcended the bounds of human hearing. Then, without a warning, she exploded into tears. Words poured out of her in a rush, each one vying with its neighbors to be the first past her lips. "She told me to do it I don't know what the message said she just told me to send it to the Cardinal I think it was in Latin she said it was a secret message it's how he knew to meet the airship after you arrested the Queen she said to throw it in the fire I had to do it because Roderick was watching her it wasn't my idea!"

Max and Julianus looked at each other again.

"The message?" Julianus said.

"The message!" Eleanor affirmed. "The one to the Cardinal! She gave it to me! She wrote it down and told me to give it to the signaling man! I don't know what it said, I swear on my life! I never was any good at Latin. Oh, God, I should have studied more. She said it was a secret message, not for any of the Guard to kn—" She put her hands over her mouth again. "Please don't put me in the cells! I'm not a traitor! I don't even like Italians!"

"You see?" Julianus said, turning to Max. "Follow the threads." He leaned forward, arms around his knee. "Is Alÿs close to the Cardinal?"

Eleanor nodded, sniffling. "He's a friend of her father's."

"The French king?"

"Yes. He asked the Cardinal to keep an eye on her. She goes to the cathedral often, and I don't mean just to pray. She likes to gossip. The Cardinal indulges her. I don't know why."

"I see." He leaned back, stroking his chin. Eventually, as if it had just come to mind for no particular reason, he said, "I seem to recall there's a commoner's Mass tonight. And, unless I miss my guess, the Cardinal will be delivering it."

"I wouldn't know about that," Eleanor said.

"No. I imagine you wouldn't. I don't expect you mingle much with commoners? But the same is not true of the Lady Alÿs, is it? Thank you, my lady, you have been most helpful."

"So I can go then?" Eleanor said, hardly daring to breathe.

"You may leave," Julianus said. "I think I'm feeling a sudden rush of religious inspiration. It's been far too long since I've been to church. Max, how's your relationship with God?"

20

The indecisive rain had finally made up its mind and was now falling with greater confidence. It sleeted down over the Palace, made complex patterns of spreading circles in the great mucky Thames, and fell in sheets over the cobblestones of Highpole Street, where it reflected the light of gas lamps, lanterns, torches, and brightly colored paper lanterns that swayed under the eaves of the complex tangle of shops.

The weather did nothing to deter the crowds of people, many of whom had come from over the bridges to New Old London or streamed in from the slums of Whitechapel. The word was out that the police would enforce a mandatory curfew, and all of London, rich and poor, wanted to be there to see what happened next.

Commander Skarbunket led a small group of perhaps fifteen men over the Blackfriars Bridge toward the Great Mosque. Behind him, the lights of the Cathedral of St. Paul glittered.

On his more philosophical days, he sometimes meditated on the way that the two grand religious structures, mosque and cathedral, were so close to each other, separated only by a few blocks and the river Thames. It seemed fitting that these two houses of worship would be so near, yet separated by that gulf of inky blackness. If he tried hard, he could probably come up with a metaphor or something.

Most of the rest of the two dozen or so men Skarbunket had chosen were entering Highpole from the west, over the Westminster Bridge. He had wanted the men to arrive in small groups, not all marching together in a single column like an army into a conquered land. It had worked. As the sun settled, the number of blue uniforms quietly increased, but at no point could anyone shout "There they are! The coppers are coming!"

The eyes of the crowd were on him. Some watched with curiosity, others with hostility, still others with anticipation. The city of London could tell something historic was happening. Historic usually meant dramatic, and London loved her drama.

"Sir?"

Skarbunket looked in the direction of the voice. The man who had spoken was barely past his nineteenth birthday, though delicate enough of frame that he could still be mistaken for sixteen. His uniform was just a bit too big for him, which added to the impression. He had dark hair and dark eyes, and his skin was that exact shade of olive that suggested the Mediterranean. His expression was miserable.

"Yes, Mister Habis?" Seeing the naked terror on the lad's face, he said more gently, "You have a question?"

"Yes, sir. I mean, no, sir. I mean…this is how it starts, sir."

"How what starts?"

The boy ran his hands through his hair restlessly. "All of it, sir. My jaddah—my grandmum, sir—she told me the stories." He spread his hands, indicating the people around them. "The people here, sir, most of them came here to get away from this. This is how it started, sir, in Spain and Italy, I mean. The Inquisition, well…" He looked around helplessly. "They don't just come for you all at once, sir. It starts small. Little things. Like telling you you can't leave certain neighborhoods, you can't go out at night. The people here, they know. They remember. This is how it starts. My grandmum…" He gulped for air. "The ones who left, who came here, sir, they were given a choice, all of them. Convert, leave, or die. They would not convert, sir. And now…" He trailed off, looking miserable. His dark eyes swam.

"Go on."

"It's just that prayers start at six twenty, sir. The people are going to want to pray. They won't want to hear that they're not allowed to. You're asking me to uphold my vows, sir, and I want to do that, I do. I love this city. But it does not love me. My grandmum, she came here rather than give up who she was. She told us the stories, the ones from before, I mean, when it all started. How we were all rounded up, sir. How those of us who weren't caught had to hide. They found her, her and my grandpa. He didn't make it. He died, sir. He couldn't escape the Inquisition. Now you're asking me to make the same choice. I can't…I can't do it, sir. When the Call to Prayer starts, I won't…" He stood up a little straighter. "I won't be a policeman anymore, sir."

"Why not?"

"I swore an oath, sir, to the London Metropolitan Police. But I also made an oath to God, sir. If I have to choose, well…"

Skarbunket clapped him on the back. "Marvelous, Mister Habis. I am delighted to hear it. This is why I wanted you with me."

"Sir?"

"Mister Habis, I have not the slightest intention of asking you to choose between your secular and divine duties. When the call to prayer comes, I expect you and Sergeant Nadeem to attend worship, together with the rest of the people of Highpole. And when the prayer ends, you will return to your duties for the police, and we will enforce this wretched curfew. After the prayer. Not before."

"But sir, our orders—"

"As your commanding officer, mine are the orders you need to be most concerned with. As Commander of the London Metropolitan Police, I have a certain degree of…let's call it discretion in how I choose to discharge my obligations. Leave that to me to worry about."

"Sir, I don't understand—"

"Again with the understanding. How have I inherited a command with so many subordinates who want to understand what they're being told to do? Don't look at me like that, Mister Habis, it was a joke. I see that disapproving tone of voice in your eyes. I understand this is no time for levity, but tell me this…okay, okay, you're right."

"But sir, I didn't say—"

"You didn't have to. Levy!"

"Sir?" Levy said.

"Ah, there you are. I have a special mission for you. You are acquainted, Mister Levy, with the, the what do you call him, short guy, almost bald, stooped back—the rabbi! You are acquainted with the rabbi of the Highpole temple?"

"Synagogue, sir. Of course, sir. Rabbi Rosen, sir. I—"

"Splendid, Mister Levy. I want you to go talk to him."

"Sir? Right now?"

Skarbunket sighed and rolled his eyes. "Yes, right now. Would I bring you out here on a rainy night to tell you to talk to him next Tuesday? Next I suppose you'll say you don't understand, either."

"Sir, I don't understand, what—"

"Go and talk to him, Levy. Right now. I want you to tell him that the police are not his enemy. We count some of his people among our family in the Force, and it is our intention to treat him and his people with courtesy and discretion. Go! The rest of you, form up! When I said this could be ugly, I didn't mean the Highpole citizens. We are here to protect them from the rest of their fellow Londoners as much as we are to enforce this curfew. Mister Habis is right: this is how many very ugly things start. We are men of the law, and I will have no bloodshed tonight, is that understood? We are here to protect the people of London—all of them. Now form up!"

The police force, now thirty strong, arranged itself in a loose line down the center of Highpole Street, the various small clusters of watchmen spreading up and joining together. As is natural with human beings who see a line, the people on the street sorted themselves out along it, some on one side of the line, some on the other. The Highpole residents ended up, unsurprisingly, on the east side of the line, farthest from the Thames and New Old London; those who had come in to watch ended up on the west. Between them stood a thin row of policemen, all in their dress uniforms. Overhead, the drifting forms of the ever-present zeppelins were lost in the wet and dreary sky. Voyeurs hoping for an aerial view of murder and mayhem would be doubly disappointed this night, Skarbunket told himself. The thought pleased him.

As the sun settled lower, the tension on the street increased. People pointed at the row of police, waiting.

Across the Thames, the clock chimed six. The police stood unmoving.

When the echoes of the last "bong!" had faded, the police remained in place, not moving a muscle. The crowd rippled. They had expected something, and clearly, this wasn't it.

Another minute ticked by. Still, the line of policemen did not move.

Five minutes past curfew. The police remained in place, doing nothing, just standing there.

By ten minutes past curfew, even the dimmest of London's citizens had figured out that Something Was Not Quite Right. And when Something Was Not Quite Right, that usually meant Something Was Up. And that, in turn, meant Drama, with a capital D. Just the sort that the various residents of the city, respectable in their various disrespectable ways, most dearly loved.

Almost imperceptibly at first, the crowd behind the line of policemen, on the Thames side of the street, became restless. It started to press forward, in little fits and surges, before flowing back again like waves at the beach. But the tide was coming in, and the crowd edged closer and closer to the line of waiting men.

On the other side of the line, the crowd was starting to melt away. The residents of Highpole were tense and wary, but for the moment, nobody seemed to want a confrontation. Those people who remained outdoors knew they were violating the newly imposed curfew, but they didn't seem to be looking for trouble; they were curious to find out what the plods would do. Skarbunket couldn't see any weapons, but he had no doubt they were there, somewhere, convenient to hand in case they just happened to be needed.

The evening balanced on a knife's edge. Things could still go either way, he told himself, but for right now, nothing bad was happening.

"Hey!" someone shouted from the river side of the line, emboldened by anonymity and distance from where the action, if there was any, was likely to be. "They ain't doin' nuffin! It's past curfew and they ain't doin' nuffin!"

"Just wait! They'll do somefin!" another voice answered from the gathering darkness.

Mayferry looked at Skarbunket, questions written on his face. Skarbunket held out his hands.

From deep within the mosque, amplified by cunning architecture, came the long, trilling sounds of a human voice. The call to prayer had begun.

"Mister Habis, Sergeant Nadeem, unless I am very much mistaken, and I don't believe I am, that is your cue," Skarbunket said. "Go," he said, addressing a pair of skeptical looks. "Pray. Let your fellow worshippers know we respect their right to be here."

Hesitantly at first, in ones and twos, then in larger numbers, people began to stream from their houses toward the hall of worship. Many of them turned to point at the silent line of policemen, whispering to each other behind the backs of their hands. Not that it mattered; they could speak openly and Skarbunket wouldn't have the slightest idea what they were saying.

Habis and Nadeem left the ranks of the waiting policemen and headed for the mosque. An anticipatory hush passed through the crowd behind them. The worshippers gathering at the mosque looked suspiciously at them.

"Aye, see?" came a voice from the crowd. "'E's going to arrest the foreigners!"

"They're going inside!" an answering voice said. "They're going in to pray! They ain't doin' their jobs! They're in league with the foreigners!"

"Brave words from someone hiding behind his friends," Skarbunket said. "Would such a man, I wonder, be brave enough to say those words to my face? It's easy to sound bold when you can run away. Even my gram can do that."

Laughter swirled in the crowd. Somewhere in the back, the laughter found its target. There was a disturbance that became a pushing that became a shoving. The crowd opened up enough to let three men through. They were all big, naturally, with the squinty eyes and restless dispositions of professional skull-crackers. One was tall, fair of hair and eye, with something rolled under the heavy leather coat he wore. A club, maybe, or a broken bottle. Maybe even a knife, if he was that particular flavor of stupid.

The other two were shorter but broader, covered with muscle, and wore shirts with the sleeves ripped out to advertise it. Their eyes were dark and mean.

Of course it would be three, Skarbunket thought. It can never be just one. And of course they'd all be reeking of gin. One of them would be the leader, unwilling to be shamed in front of his friends.

The fair-haired one stepped closer, until his nose almost touched Skarbunket's. He was at least four inches taller than the commander. Height meant reach. Reach meant trouble, if it came down to it. Probably best to make sure, then, that it didn't come down to it.

"You're in league with these devils!" the man said. The words arrived borne on the wings of gin and halitosis.

Next to him, Skarbunket could sense Mayferry tensing. He smiled slightly to himself. Oh, it had been too long…

"What's your name, son?" Skarbunket said.

"Business," the man replied. He glanced at his friends. "Nonya Business." They laughed dutifully.

"My condolences, Mister Business," Skarbunket said. "It is never a good thing to have parents with an unfortunate sense of humor. Why, with a name like that, sir, a boy might grow up with all sorts of inferiority complexes."

"Har har." The man reached under his jacket. Skarbunket tensed, fingers curling around his truncheon. He relaxed when the man pulled out a rolled-up newspaper, which he unrolled in Skarbunket's face. "What do you think of that, smart guy?"

Skarbunket glanced at it. It was a flimsy tabloid, printed that afternoon. "HIGHPOLE FOREIGNERS ABDUCT PRINCESS," blared the headline. In slightly smaller print underneath, it continued, "IS ANYONE SAFE??" Below that, in type just a little bit smaller, it read, "WHO WILL HOLD THE OUTSIDERS ACCOUNTABLE??"

Skarbunket looked into the stranger's suspicious blue eyes. "I think using two question marks when you only need one is a crime against language, is what I think." He scanned the paper's masthead. "*The Daily Rail*? Isn't that the newspaper owned by Chancellor Gaton?"

The man looked confused for a moment. In his mind, or the bits of it that weren't swimming with gin and the fiery rage of righteous anger, this wasn't the way this conversation was supposed to go. "Who cares?" he said. "What are you going to do about it?"

"The thing is, Mister Business, there's not much I can do. You see, a newspaper editor is free to use two question marks in a subhead if he desires, as much as we all might prefer, Mister Business, and I'm sure you will agree with me on this, as much as we all might prefer he stayed within the bounds of grammatical decency and stuck with only one. Whatever editor approved that headline, I have no doubt that he believed he was doing the right thing. Sometimes, men of good conscience can do things they really ought to know are wrong, Mister Business, though we all might wish it were otherwise."

More laughter from the crowd. The man's face turned red. Skarbunket watched the transformation with interest. It started as a flush of pink in the man's cheeks that spread rapidly, darkening as it went, until the entire visible portion of his head resembled nothing so much as a freshly harvested beet.

"No, not that, idiot!" he said, rage taking hold of him so completely that his hands, and the newspaper, shook. "I mean the foreigners! They abducted the princess! It says so right here!"

"So it does, Mister Business," Skarbunket said. "It is exactly as you say. Well done, Mister Business." Keep the crowd laughing at this fellow, that was the key. If their allegiance shifted and they started laughing with him, well, sooner or later someone would work out that they out-numbered the cops by four to one, and then things might get just a hair too interesting.

"So what are you going to do about it? When are you going to start arresting these devils?"

Skarbunket smiled beatifically at the gin-addled agitator. "Ah, I think I see the problem," he said. "I think, Mister Business, you may be suffering under a misapprehension. A mistaken idea," he clarified at the man's confused expression. "We are not here to arrest the good citizens of Highpole, Mister Business, nor to force people back to their homes. The people of Highpole are honest, law-abiding citizens, Mister Business, who I have every confidence will obey the law without need of any prodding. No, Mister Business, we are here to make sure that the rest of London's citizenry, many of whom, I might add, Mister Business, I hold much less confidence about in the law-abiding department, do not take it into their heads to come to this neighborhood for the purpose of committing unlawful acts."

"But it's past curfew!" he whined. "Six o'clock! It says so right here!"

"I'm sure it does, Mister Business, I'm sure it does. A regrettable over-sight on the part of the Council, I am certain, who, had they known eve-ning prayers started at six twenty, would no doubt have adjusted their timetable accordingly, Mister Business."

"Stop calling me that!" the man said, petulant.

"Why?" Skarbunket said. "It's your name, is it not, Mister Business? You must know your own name. Because, you see, if your name is not Nonya Business, that would mean, Mister Business, that you know-ingly gave false information to an officer of the law when questioned. And that, Mister Business, would be grounds for bringing you in. It's what we call a *tech-ni-cal-i-tee*, you see." He enunciated the five-syllable word carefully.

"You can't arrest me for that!"

"Oh, I assure you, Mister Business, the cells are filled with men who are there on razor-thin technicalities." Skarbunket leaned closer to the man. "Do not test me on this, Mister Business."

The freshly christened Nonya Business glared back at him. Skarbunket knew this was it, the moment when the man would either back down and accept humiliation in front of his friends, or lash out and accept a beating from the police, or a night in the cells, or both. A small, mean part of him, a part he was not proud of, almost hoped it would be the latter.

The two men stared at each other, neither moving, each daring the other to blink. After a long moment, the stalemate was broken by one of the man's friends. "Come on, Nonya, let's go." His other friend sniggered.

The man gave Skarbunket a wide grin as phony as the smile on a banker's face. He turned to go, then spun around, fist speeding toward Skarbunket's nose. Skarbunket stepped smartly out of the way, grabbing the flying fist and twisting it up behind the man's back.

"I'm sure I don't need to tell you this, Mister Business, but assaulting an officer of the law, and that's what you've just done there, is grounds for arrest. Not on a technicality, either." he leaned close, talking directly in the man's ear. "You are testing the bounds of my limitless patience, Mister Business. I recommend you make yourself a lot less visible." He gave the man a push. "Go home."

The three turned sheepishly and were swallowed up by the crowd.

"Impressive. I'm surprised he didn't hit you."

Skarbunket turned toward the new voice. "Chancellor Gaton. What a surprise it is to see you in Highpole on such an unpleasant night. What brings you here?"

"That's *Lord* Chancellor Gaton. I'm sure we're here for the same reason, Officer…Skarbunket, isn't it?"

"That's *Commander* Skarbunket, my lord," Skarbunket said.

"Ah, of course. Commander Skarbunket." The chancellor removed his top-hat and looked at it critically. He flicked some droplets of rainwater from the brim and replaced it on his head. "Indulge my curiosity, if you will, Commander. It seemed to me that you knew that man was about to punch you. How did you know?"

The same way I know you and I are not here for remotely the same reasons, Skarbunket thought. Out loud he said, "He had to do it. If he hadn't, he would be Mister Nonya Business to his friends for the rest of his life. He would never live it down." He shrugged. "He still might not."

"I could not help but notice that you did not arrest him, even though he assaulted an officer of the law."

"What purpose would it serve, my lord? Other than taking some of my men away from their duties here, that is. But surely, my Lord Chancellor Gaton, surely it is not matters of operational procedure that have rousted you from your home this evening and brought you all the way across the river in the rain."

"It is exactly matters of operational procedure that have brought me here, Officer—pardon, Commander Skarbunket. This morning, the Council of Lords passed a resolution calling for a six o'clock curfew on all foreigners in the Highpole District."

"I am aware, my lord. Though I might add, my lord, that it is difficult to know who is a foreigner and who is not, here on Highpole Street. Many of the residents have been here for generations, which makes them British rather than foreigners, does it not?"

"Don't get smart with me, Commander!" Gaton said. "You know exactly what the resolution means."

"Indeed I do, my lord," Skarbunket said. Inwardly, he added an unvoiced *it means you're scapegoating.*

"And here it is, now…" He pulled a pocket watch from his pocket and snapped it open. "Let me see. Can this possibly be right? Unless I am sorely mistaken, it is six thirty-seven, and there are still people on the streets. Indeed, it looks like the mosque is open, and those *foreigners* are still in there praying."

"You are not mistaken, my lord. It is indeed still open."

"Was the resolution not clear, Commander Skarbunket?"

"It was very clear, my lord."

"And is it not already later than six o'clock?"

"Indeed, my lord."

"What is it that you and your men are doing here, Commander Skarbunket?"

"Normally, my lord, we do not bring others in on matters of operational security," Skarbunket said. "But you are the High Chancellor of the Council of Lords, so if you don't have the necessary station to know confidential information, who does?" He looked around at the curious crowd, then lowered his voice conspiratorially. "I would beg you, my lord, to the utmost discretion in this matter."

"Oh?" Gaton leaned in. "What are you up to?"

Skarbunket looked around again, then bent close. "This is not for common circulation, my lord."

"Go on, man, out with it!"

"You see, my lord, at this very moment, and I mean this literally, at this exact moment in time I have, on my orders, my lord, two of my men inside the mosque."

A flicker of uncertainty crossed his face. "Inside the mosque? Right now?" He glanced at his pocket watch again. "Really? Right now?" The uncertainty changed to doubt. He glanced at the mosque, then back at his watch. "Do you think that's safe, Commander?"

"I can't imagine why it wouldn't be, Lord Chancellor. Can you?" He surveyed the man's face. "The presence of the police in Highpole Street provided an opportunity, I'm sure a man of your intelligence can understand, an opportunity to place some of my men within the walls of the mosque itself. Should the missing lady be there, they will find her, you may rest assured of that. But in order for that to happen, my lord, it was necessary to permit the evening prayers to take place. Otherwise, you see, the opportunity would be lost."

Gaton nodded. "Of course, of course." He waggled his finger. "I, ah, I admire your, ah, initiative, Commander. That is, ah, clever. Very clever. Yes, of course. A man in the mosque. Who would have thought of it? You're a smarter man than I realized, Commander."

"Thank you, my lord," Skarbunket said. "You don't know what that means to me coming from a man like you, my lord."

"Do you think they will, ah, unmask the, ah, the conspiracy? Against the Lady Alÿs, I mean." He glanced again at his pocket watch.

"I am absolutely confident, my lord, that my men will find everything there is to be found. Absolutely confident. But I would beg you, my lord, to keep your voice down. It is important, as I know you understand, it is important not to tip our hand, so to speak."

"Ah, yes, of course, of course," Gaton said. He snapped the pocket watch shut and tucked it away. "Well, I will leave you to it. Do keep me informed how things progress?"

"Of course, Lord Chancellor."

Skarbunket watched him depart. The crowd parted before him like a tropical sea before an avenging Biblical patriarch. When he had gone, it closed again, leaving no trace he was ever there.

"Well there goes a complete tit and no mistake," Tumbanker said.

"That's Lord Complete Tit, Mister Tumbanker," Skarbunket said, "lest the likes of us forget." His eyes narrowed. He turned toward the man next to him. "Something stinks, Mayferry. He was expecting something to happen. He wanted to be here to see it himself. Something stinks, and for once it's not the Thames."

"Begging your pardon, sir, I think that is the Thames you're smelling. The Lord Chancellor has already left," Mayferry said.

The doors to the mosque opened. People streamed, apprehensive, into the chill and soggy evening.

"Ah, well, here come Mister Habis and Sergeant Nadeem," Skarbunket said. "I imagine Mister Levy will be along shortly as well. I think that's our cue." He raised his voice so that it boomed out over the street. "Good citizens of Highpole! As you are aware, in the interests of public safety, the Council of Lords has requested you to return to your homes this evening. The rest of you lot, it's a rainy and miserable night, and there will be nothing else to see here. We request that you return to your homes as well. A curfew is now in effect in the Highpole District for everyone in this neighborhood, wherever you may call home."

21

"This is a bad idea," Thaddeus said. "It was a bad idea yesterday. Now that I've slept on it, it's still a bad idea."

He was standing in one corner of the shop, back turned to the great iron hulk of the mechanical spider. Somewhere beneath the tarp, he heard the rustling of Alÿs changing her clothes.

"You don't know him. I do. I trust him." Alÿs's voice floated up from beneath the tarp.

"Well, I don't," Thaddeus said, petulant.

"You don't trust anyone, Thaddeus Shoe Man," Alÿs said.

"I do!" Thaddeus protested. "I trust Claire and Donnie."

"How come?" came Alÿs's disembodied voice. "Why them?"

"Because! They are…well…you wouldn't understand. You're noble and all."

"And that means I can't understand you commoners?"

"Yes! It's just…. Things on the streets are different."

"Different than what?"

"Different than living in a palace! When you're in trouble, you go to Claire and Donnie. They look after you, and they don't expect you to have to pay them back. Everyone knows. If you don't have anywhere to go, they'll help you."

"That's very generous of them," Alÿs said. "London is a big place." The tarp rustled. A bit of bare flesh peeked out from behind it. Thaddeus looked away, embarrassed. "What do they do with all these strays they collect?"

"Well, you know," Thaddeus said. He looked up, catching a glimpse of an exposed leg, and hastily looked down again. "Some of them become apprentices. You know, if they have the talent for it."

"How did you meet them?"

"I came here after my parents...it's not like I had anywhere else to go, is it?"

"But you didn't become an apprentice."

"No. Never got the hang of it."

"Why do they call you Muddy?"

"On account of my name," Thaddeus said. "My friends can call me that. Nobody else."

"The Bodgers are your friends? Is that why you came here?"

"Yes. They helped me. They help everyone. That's why *you're* here, after all. And they know things."

"Things?" Alÿs said. "What kind of things?"

"Everything!" Thaddeus said.

"That's not a very informative answer, Shoe Man." Even from under the tarp, her voice sounded prim.

"Everything!" Thaddeus said again. "They know what's going on in London. They have people who tell them things."

"Like you?"

"Like me, and like lots of other people. Claire and Donnie have friends in high places and not-so-high places. And they take care of their friends." He ran his hands through his hair. "Not like the Cardinal. How are we going to get in to see him without being recognized, anyway?"

"Easy. They're looking for a lady of the Court, not a commoner apprentice." She stepped out from behind the tarp. Thaddeus goggled.

She was dressed in shabby but unremarkable clothes and a striped pair of overalls, the universal uniform of the working class. Her mad tangle of unruly hair had been tightly disciplined with comb and pins, and was tucked up under a hat. She looked...looked...

"You look like a boy!" Thaddeus blurted. The instant the words were out of his mouth, he realized how stupid they sounded.

Nevertheless, Alÿs looked pleased. "Thank you," she said. "I learned some tricks when I was back home in Paris. My father never let me leave the house without a full entourage, so I had to get creative if I wanted to go out on my own. Even the guards at the gate didn't recognize me if I was careful to keep my head down."

"The house?"

"Well, the palace, I suppose. He is a king."

"Of course he is," Thaddeus said, with more bitterness than he intended.

"Hey, don't be that way. We can't help how we're born. I've always wanted to be a commoner," Alÿs said.

"No, you haven't!" Thaddeus said.

"Sure I have! The freedom—"

"Freedom to starve, or be sent to the workhouse—"

"—being able to come and go as you please—"

"—never knowing where your next meal is coming from—"

"—not having to get permission to leave the house—"

"—not having a house…I get it! You don't like being hemmed in. But you don't want to be a commoner. You want to play at being a commoner and then go back to your nice safe palace and your banquet tables and your friends in high places."

Hurt registered in Alÿs's eyes.

"I'm sorry," he said more gently. "Some of us can't be commoners only until it's not fun anymore."

"Aye, what's goin' on 'ere?" Donnie rumbled.

"Nothing," Thaddeus said. "I was just telling Alÿs that this is a really bad idea."

"You don' haf t' go with her, Muddy my boy," Donnie said.

"Of course I do!" Thaddeus protested. "I'm in it good, you said so yourself. I need to work on getting out of it."

"Speakin' o' that, where are your fancy shoes, Muddy?" Donnie's eyes flicked down to the work boots on Thaddeus's feet and back up to his face.

"I got rid of them," Thaddeus said sullenly. For reasons he didn't really understand, he hadn't told anyone what he'd done in Highpole. He still wasn't convinced his spur-of-the-moment frame had been the right thing to do. A pawn can topple a king, but it helps if the pawn knows the rules of chess. Pawns that act impulsively probably create all kinds of trouble.

"You two know the plan, then?" Donnie said.

"Yes," Alÿs said. "Lucky for us King John decided to hire you when he wanted to add bell towers to the cathedral. And lucky you kept the key for the service entrance."

Donnie smiled his placid smile. "Luck ain't got nothin' t' do with 'ow things get done 'round 'ere. Surprised you don't know that by now, my lady."

"Does the Cardinal know you have this key?" Alÿs held up the key in question, a heavy iron thing with a startlingly complex shape.

Donnie's smile grew a fraction wider. "Run along, you two. Sun is down. Street should be safe now."

✦

"This is a bad idea," Max said. "We have no idea if the lady is going to try to talk to him. If she wanted to, wouldn't she have already done so?"

"Why don't we ask him?" Julianus said.

"Because he has no reason to tell us the truth."

"If they're as close as the Lady Eleanor says, he will be concerned about her disappearance."

"Unless he's involved in it."

"True," Julianus said. "But I don't see him commissioning a murder in Highpole. Especially not from the Lady Alÿs. I'm sure a man in his position has plenty of his own men he can use for that kind of thing."

"You really think she'll show?"

"It will be interesting to find out."

The two men were sitting across the street from the main entrance to the great Cathedral of St. Paul. It was a grand building, made of white stone with a pale blue roof, crowned by a modest dome from which sprouted a tall spire that ascended to the heavens in steps and that had earned the whole building the affectionate name "the Wedding Cake" from Londoners.

It was a grand building, its face dominated by great arched windows of exquisite beauty, but since its construction in 1702, it had suffered one minor but nevertheless quite perturbing flaw: it completely lacked proper bell towers. This absence was not lost on King John, who, upon embarking on his ambitious civil program, sought to rectify that issue by ordering construction of two great bell towers equipped with modern, steam-powered, automated bells. At the same time, he had added two new wings, one of which became the cathedral's new chapel house, and the other of which made up the living quarters of the Cardinal.

He did these things without the input or oversight of the Pope in France, which led to a certain amount of tension between the Papacy and the Crown. King John pointed out that the French clerical hierarchy paid the Crown no rent for use of the cathedral, an oversight he would be pleased to revisit if the Church so desired, but meanwhile, given that it technically belonged to the Crown and not to the Church, he would make such improvements as he bloody well pleased, thank you very much.

The French Pope, upon considering the potential impact to the church's treasury from a different arrangement, reconsidered his objections.

From where they sat, Max and Julianus could see everyone entering the church. The great doors were brightly illuminated by electric arc lights that bathed the courtyard in fierce blue-white light. The bells pealed the start of the evening Mass. Worshippers streamed through the doors.

"Any sign of her?" Max growled as the last stragglers entered the church.

"No. Let's go." Julianus hopped off the low wall he'd been seated on and headed for the church.

Max shook his head. "This is a waste of time."

"So you keep saying. You have a better idea?"

"No."

"Then what are we waiting for?"

✦

The last ringing echoes of the bells had long faded to silence by the time Thaddeus and Alÿs reached the cathedral. Alÿs started across the street. Thaddeus grabbed her by the hand. "*Psst!*" he said. He drew her into the shadows behind the tavern that stood, in defiance to all that was holy, directly across from the main entrance. The sign over the door proclaimed it the Stumbling Stoat, with a carved picture of a drunken mustelid beneath, just to make the point. Thaddeus knew the place well; it was frequented by his sort of people, for some definition of "his sort." There were those who might say that conducting criminal enterprises in the shadow of the cathedral might be taking camouflage just a step too far, but where such people saw danger, others saw opportunity. It was surprising how often proximity of the criminal elements became a matter of ecumenical convenience.

Besides, it made going to confession that much easier.

"What?" Alÿs said. "It is not polite to grab a lady."

"You're a boy, remember?" He released her hand. "What is it with people just charging about without looking to see if they're being watched, anyway?"

"Huh?"

"Look. See?" He pointed across the street. "Notice anything funny? The Queen's Guard doesn't normally stand in front of the door. We can't let them see us."

"I'm a boy, remember?"

Thaddeus snorted. "Sure, until someone gets a look at your face. They know you, right? And they're the ones looking for you, right?"

"Okay, fine. What do you think we should do, Mister Criminal Mastermind?"

"Criminal Mastermind." Thaddeus turned the phrase around in his head a few times. "I like the sound of that. I think we should make sure nobody is watching the service door."

"Why would someone do that?"

He shrugged. "It's what I would do, if I were looking for you and I thought you might go see the Cardinal."

"So what now?"

"Now I look for guards around back and make sure this key fits in the lock. Then I come back here and get you."

"If it doesn't?"

"Then something has gone very wrong with the world," Thaddeus said. "Claire and Donnie always come through."

"But—"

"Always."

Thaddeus scurried away, leaving Alÿs huddled under the eaves where the light but steady rain could not reach. Behind her, in the tavern, she heard angry voices. The angry voices were followed up by angry thumps, then a crash of breaking glass. She shivered, wishing for her ermine-fur coat. She usually preferred to go on her adventures on more comfortable days and head back to the Palace if the weather grew too unpleasant.

Thaddeus materialized by her elbow, so silently that she yelped with surprise. "There are a couple of the Cardinal's private guard at the front," he said. "Nobody around the back. We can go in the service entrance without being seen. Try to be quiet, okay?"

They scooted across the street, evading the water flowing along the gutter. In this part of town, the storm drains were particularly good, and hardly anyone dumped raw sewage into the streets. Whatever else you could say about them, the clerical classes of London had access to a better class of smell.

They soon made it to the service door, tucked around the back of one of the bell towers. From the other side, they could already hear the chords from the pipe organ signaling the start of Mass.

Thaddeus put his finger to his lips and swung the door open. Inside was darkness. He closed the door behind them, and they stood for a moment, letting their eyes adjust.

Clockwork machinery filled the bottom of the bell tower. Long cables and thin metal rods ascended into the darkness above. A huge toothed wheel, mounted horizontally atop a large metal box, turned slowly. Its surface was studded with holes, some of which were filled with metal pegs about the size of Alÿs's thumb.

Thaddeus quietly opened the inside door and ushered Alÿs through. He closed the door noiselessly. They were in the vestibule of the cathedral, once an open-air courtyard, enclosed with marble walls hung with enormous windows when the bell towers were built. Ahead of them, the tall, narrow doors led into the nave.

Thaddeus opened the door just wide enough to allow them to slip through. Inside, the church was less than a third full, with worshippers crowded together in pews that stood in neat ranks before the altar.

During the renovation, the church had been outfitted with electric arc lights inside as well as out. The lights over the altar were burning, casting a brilliant glow around the Cardinal, resplendent in his gold-trimmed red cape. The rest of the lights were dark, creating dramatic shadows that filled the aisles along the sides of the nave. Dozens of tiny candles in small glass containers flickered in the gloom, creating uncertain pools of yellow light around the statues of the Blessed Virgin and Christ the Savior.

Thaddeus melted into the shadows. Alÿs watched him fade, seeming to merge into the darkness until he was part of it. "How do you—"

He reached out and drew her into the shadow.

"I will remind you, I am a Lady of—" she started. Thaddeus put his finger to his lips again. He crept forward, flitting silently and effortlessly from shadow to shadow, keeping the pillars between himself and the

Cardinal. Alÿs crossed herself and followed, feeling loud and clumsy by comparison.

Bit by bit, darting quickly from the cover of one column to the next, Thaddeus moved forward, keeping always in the shadow at the outside edge of the nave. Alÿs did her best to emulate him. When they had worked their way about halfway down the length of the church, Thaddeus paused, his back to one of the enormous round pillars. The pews closest to him were all vacant; the cathedral usually wasn't filled for a midweek Mass under the best of circumstances, and tonight a lot of folks seemed far more interested in whatever was going on out in Highpole Street than in the disposition of their immortal souls.

"What now?" Thaddeus whispered.

"What?" Alÿs whispered back. "Why are you asking me?"

"This was your plan, remember?"

"I wouldn't call it a plan," Alÿs said. "More of an intention, really."

Thaddeus shook his head. "We can't exactly walk up to the Cardinal right now. So what do you want to do?"

"Actually, I can walk right up to the Cardinal," Alÿs said. "I am going to sit in that pew. When it is time to take Communion, I can tell him it's me and I need to talk to him. Nobody will look twice at me. I look like a boy, remember? What? What is it?"

Thaddeus was gesturing urgently, pointing toward the worshippers seated in the pews ahead of them. He jerked his thumb toward the congregation, then waved his hand in front of his throat.

"What?" Alÿs said. "I don't understand."

Thaddeus jerked his thumb frantically toward the seated worshippers.

"I still don't—oh!" Alÿs pressed back against the cold marble, willing the shadows to swallow her. That was unmistakably the broad form of Max the Axe, seated not thirty feet away. She scanned the seated figures. Yes, there was Julianus, several rows ahead, toward the center of the throng. They both seemed to be paying more attention to the other members of the congregation than to the sermon.

"Now what?" Alÿs whispered.

Thaddeus shrugged. He jerked his head toward the exit.

Alÿs shook her head. "No. We wait here until after the service. When they leave, we'll talk to the Cardinal."

"You want us to wait here and hide until the end of Mass?" Thaddeus's tone was incredulous.

"Yes! They're not looking for you. As long as I keep my head down, they won't recognize me. Just relax and try to stay out of sight, okay?

✦

"It took you long enough, Mister Levy," Commander Skarbunket said.

"Yes, sir. Sorry, sir. Rabbi Rosen was very interested in talking to me, sir. We had a long conversation."

"About what?"

"About you, sir. I—" He gulped. "You are known to the people around here."

"I imagine I would be doing a rather poor job if I weren't, Mister Levy."

"Yes, sir." Levy nodded vigorously. "It's just…well, you are seen as a friend to the people of Highpole."

Night had well and truly set. The candles guttered in their paper lanterns along Highpole Street. Commander Skarbunket had already made a complete circuit of the district, north to south and back north again. The rest of the police were still there, patrolling in twos and threes, but there was nothing to patrol. Everyone had evaporated, driven off by the rain and the lack of violent confrontation. Skarbunket's boots squished on the wet cobblestone. Other than policemen, nobody was in sight.

"Thank you, Mister Levy. That means a lot to me."

"And he says to tell you, sir, that you have friends here too. People who have seen you stand up for them many times, sir. It has not gone unnoticed. You are respected here, sir. People are still scared. There are a lot of folks wondering what's going on. They are looking to us, to you, sir, for answers."

"A question on my mind as well, Mister Levy. I will admit, and I say this without making any statement about her guilt or innocence, I will admit that I would very much like to know where the Lady Alÿs is."

"So would a lot of people here. Do you believe the newspapers, sir? About someone in Highpole kidnapping her?"

"Not even for a moment, Mister Levy."

"So what's going on then, sir?"

"An excellent question, Mister Levy. Keep asking those. They will either make your career or destroy it."

"No offense, sir, but that sounds awfully cynical."

"Thank you, Mister Levy. None taken. Ah, and here is our Officer Bristol," he said, nodding to the man jogging toward them, puffing and out of breath. "May I presume, Mister Bristol, from your tightness of mouth and the considerable quantity of dirt I see on your shirt, that our 'could be nothing' was not, in fact, nothing?"

"It was something alright, sir. Rented flat full of enough black-powder bombs to take down yonder mosque, I'll allow."

"Hm. Did you apprehend the owner?"

"No sir. Nobody in sight. Just a flat full of black-powder bombs."

"Really." Skarbunket folded his arms. "That is most curious. Do go on."

"I made enquiries, sir. The locals were...less unhelpful than usual."

"That's an interesting number of negatives."

"It seems the renter wasn't much liked. Quiet, they said. Kept to himself. Didn't talk to anyone. And..."

"Yes?"

"Apparently he was arrested this morning. Or so the locals say."

"Even more curious. Not by us?"

"No, sir. Definitely not by us."

"That doesn't leave very many people," Skarbunket said.

"No sir. Nobody seemed to know who did the arresting, though."

"So they were not very helpful."

"Like I said, sir, less unhelpful than usual, but still a bit reticent."

"And Mister Levy here was just telling me how much the people of Highpole like and respect us."

"Oh, that they do, sir," Bristol said. "Doesn't change the fact we're outsiders. Outsiders you like are still outsiders, come the end of the day."

Skarbunket squinted up at the rainy night sky. "Which it is, literally. And what of the explosives? Please tell me you didn't simply leave them where they were."

"Safely removed from the flat, sir, courtesy of animates rented from the day labor place over on Jasper Street."

"One of the few times the local laborers won't complain about their jobs being encroached, I imagine. What did you do with them?"

"I briefly considered storing them at the bottom of the Thames, sir," Bristol said, "but I reckoned you might like to inventory them for evidence. So I had them loaded into a paddy wagon, sir. Said paddy wagon currently being in the warehouse off Yeardling Street down by the river, on the theory that if it explodes sky-high, we won't lose anything but a sodding big building full of files. Win-win, either way."

"How did you get it there, if I may ask?"

Bristol blinked in surprise. "Why, I drove it there, sir. How else?"

"You drove a wagon filled with black-powder bombs to a warehouse in the middle of the night? Sometimes I marvel at how your mind works, Mister Bristol. Remind me to recommend you for a commendation for bravery. Did you get a description of the lodger?"

"Oh, yes, that I did, sir. And that's where it gets even more curious, sir."

"Oh? I didn't think that was possible. Bombs and nobody to throw them isn't curious enough?"

"Well, it's just that, from the description, sir...I think we've met him. At the ironworkers' shop, sir. The suspect in the hat-theft case, sir."

"Well. Well, well, well." Skarbunket sat back on his heels. "Isn't that interesting?"

22

"What do we do?" Thaddeus said. At the altar, the Cardinal, flanked by two priests in red, was delivering the homily. He spoke in English, the better for the faithful to understand him. Shortly after the Schism, the French Catholic Church had broken with tradition and begun giving Mass in whatever language the congregation was most likely to speak, under the notion that it was easier to save souls if the souls you were trying to save knew what you were on about. The Italians, who reasoned that if salvation was so valuable you really ought to be willing to work for it, continued to address the flock in Latin. This was just one of the many differences of opinion between the two Popes, and much blood had been spilled in their attempts to reach a meeting of the minds on the matter.

Tonight's homily concerned, apparently, the entwined sins of pride, ambition, and greed. Thaddeus was only half paying attention, but he got the general impression the Cardinal was generally disposed against them.

"Let's sit in the back and wait," Alÿs said.

"But—"

"Nobody will look twice at us. Nobody knows you, and nobody will recognize me. Just keep your head down and don't act suspicious."

"Don't act suspicious? What does that mean?"

"I don't know, act casual! Lurking in the shadows is not casual."

"Who's lurking?" Thaddeus said. "I'm not lurking! I'm casual! Look at how casual I am. I'm just standing here casually by this pillar. Hey!"

Alÿs had already moved into a pew. Thaddeus chased after her. He slid, as casually as he could manage under the circumstances, into the pew beside her.

The priests brought two covered silver trays, each trimmed with gold, toward the altar. The Cardinal began a prayer. The entire room, save for a hooded figure in the middle of the congregation, knelt. Alÿs crossed herself, lips moving in a silent prayer.

"When do we—*oof!*" Thaddeus said, the last part a rebuttal to Alÿs's elbow in his ribs.

The congregation rose. Operating automatically, Alÿs rose with them. Thaddeus put his hand on her arm. "Stay here!" he hissed.

One by one, the worshippers lined up to receive communion. Thaddeus and Alÿs remained where they were. A handful of other people did the same. Julianus turned, scanning the crowd. Alÿs ducked her head, hands clasped in front of her. Thaddeus's heart skipped a beat. He held his breath until that roving stare turned away from them.

One by one, the people accepted the bread and wine. One by one, they returned to their seats. Julianus scanned the crowd once more, his gaze lingering for a moment on Thaddeus and Alÿs. Thaddeus felt his knuckles crack, so tight was his grip on the pew in front of him.

He relaxed slightly when everyone was sitting once more. They went through the motions of the rest of the service, Thaddeus preoccupied, Alÿs rather more pious.

The Cardinal gave the concluding rite. The pipe organ played. The choir sang. The Cardinal, flanked by his attending priests, left the altar.

Thaddeus heaved an enormous sigh of relief. He'd been to many a tense Mass, but never had he so longed for it to be over—not even when he knew there would be cakes afterward. He smiled and turned toward Alÿs. "We can..."

His heart froze. Julianus was standing near the front of the church, looking right at him. Their eyes met. Thaddeus forced himself to smile.

Act natural! he told himself. But what was natural, anyway? "Natural" for Thaddeus Mudstone was suspicious as hell, because he was naturally a shady character. His encounters with the law usually followed a simple dynamic: he was doing, or had done, or was about to do, something that was illegal, against civic order, or both; and they, naturally, wanted to stop him from doing it, or apprehend him, or both.

That was the natural order of things. The part where he just sat there without running was precisely the opposite of natural.

What did normal people who weren't criminals do, anyway? Thaddeus had no idea. Did they wave? Had he seen people wave to the Queen's Guard? Thaddeus wasn't sure if he could wave. And didn't that mean the Guardsmen were supposed to come over? He could not remember a time in his life when he'd ever wanted a guard to come closer. Was that something ordinary people did?

He ventured a small nod. That seemed safe enough.

The Guardsman appeared to accept the nod as some kind of commoner slang for "I'm not a criminal, please don't come arrest me," and looked away, bored. For the second time in only a few seconds, Thaddeus ventured another enormous sigh of relief.

Maybe the evening was going to be okay after all.

"Are you alright?" Alÿs asked. "You look a bit shaken."

"Yes! Yes, I'm fine. Guards make me nervous, that's all," Thaddeus said.

"Oh? Why?"

"Why?" Thaddeus exclaimed. He looked around, eyes wild, then lowered his voice. "Why? Why do you think? You know what I do for a living, right?"

"Besides jump out of airships in the middle of the night? No, I don't. What do you do, exactly? My friend Eleanor is convinced you must be an Italian spy."

Thaddeus laughed. "An Italian spy would probably have more money than I do. Do Italian spies make a lot of money? Where do you go to be an Italian spy? You don't really have to eat babies, do you? I might take the job if there's no baby eating."

"Shh!" Alÿs said. "Keep your voice down. Let's go."

They started toward the front of the cathedral, then stopped. The worshippers were thinning out. Here and there, people lit candles in front of the statues or remained at the pews in silent meditation, but Max and Julianus were striding with a purpose toward the Cardinal's chambers.

"Oh sh—" Thaddeus began.

"Language!" Alÿs said sharply.

"—allow shambling misfortune," Thaddeus said. "They're going to talk to him!"

"Then we will wait," Alÿs said. "We need to blend in." She rose, slipping out of the pew.

"But what are they—"

"I don't know. Follow me."

"Where?"

"To light a candle for the Virgin." Alÿs knelt in front of the statue of Mary, crossing herself as she did. She picked up a candle and looked back over her shoulder at Thaddeus. "For a man who didn't want to see the Cardinal in the first place, you sure are impatient, Shoe Man."

Thaddeus knelt beside her, shaking his head. "I don't like this. I don't like this at all. What if they arrest him?"

"Arrest him?" Alÿs looked perplexed. "The Cardinal? Why would they arrest him?"

"I don't know, they're the Queen's Guard! It's what they do!"

"You have strange ideas about the Guard. Now hush."

✦

"Your Eminence, a moment of your time, please," Julianus said.

The Cardinal paused, halfway through the door to the right of the altar that led to his private chambers. "Ah, my excitable friend Julianus. Splendid to see you at Mass. And Max, too. How are the two of you getting on?"

Max growled.

"We have some questions for you, Your Eminence," Julianus said. "If you don't mind. Some time-sensitive questions. They concern the missing Lady Alÿs."

"I see." The Cardinal's long face contorted into a grimace. "Well, in that case, I imagine you should join me in my office. If you please."

He ushered them through the door, into a long but very narrow hallway tiled in marble. He opened the first door on the right. It led into a small study, equipped with a desk and several chairs. The desk was filled with papers, all neatly constrained inside soft leather folders to prevent them from running around and causing mischief. He had eschewed electric arc lights in favor of more conventional gas jets, and the tiled floor gave way to a thick woven rug. "Please," he said, "sit down. What can I do for you?"

Julianus sat. Max remained standing, arms crossed in front of him.

"I'm sure you're aware the Lady Alÿs remains mysteriously unaccounted for. She was last seen in a shop on Highpole Street—"

"Yes, so I have been told," the Cardinal said. "By the two of you, no less. Fleeing the scene of a most grisly murder, if I am to believe the report."

"That is correct, Your Eminence," Julianus said.

"Ah." The Cardinal leaned back in his chair behind the desk, fingers steepled in front of him. "I must confess to some incredulity regarding this tale I've heard. You are here, I am sure, to ask me if I have seen or been in contact with the Lady Alÿs, no doubt under the assumption that I am her friend and therefore her sanctuary in times of trouble?"

"Something like that, Your Eminence," Julianus said.

"It took you rather longer than I expected to arrive at my doorstep to ask me these questions," the Cardinal said. "I was beginning to question my decision to put you on the task."

"We've been busy," Max said.

"So I've heard, so I've heard. In any event, the answer is no. No, I have not seen or heard from the *Princess* Alÿs. No, I have no knowledge of her whereabouts." He leaned forward. "A situation I find intolerable. I do not like not knowing these things. I am very distressed by her absence. I am not a man who takes distress kindly. What, may I ask, have you done beyond bothering me to locate her and ensure her safe and speedy return? There is a diplomatic sensitivity to the state of affairs as they are now."

"So?" Max said.

"While I appreciate the sensitivity of the current situation," Julianus interjected smoothly, "our task is to find out what happened on the airship. Alÿs was there, and then she was at a place where a lead in that investigation was murdered moments before our arrival. I'm sure you can appreciate we would like to speak to her very much indeed. The diplomatic aspects of the investigation are best left in more diplomatic hands than ours."

"Diplomatically put," the Cardinal said. "Should you ever find yourself growing tired of a life dedicated to watching the moneyed class eat and exchange gossip, please come see me."

Julianus shot a glance at Max. "Thank you, Your Eminence," he said. "I will consider your proposal."

"Again, diplomatically put." He rose. "Unfortunately, as I said, I have neither seen nor spoken to the princess, nor do I know where she is. I've set some members of my private guard to making enquiries, which have so far been uncharacteristically fruitless." He passed his hands over his eyes. "Now that I have answered your questions, I would ask you to continue your enquiries." He sagged. For a moment, he looked less like the second most powerful person in London than like a tired old man. His voice softened. "Please. Find her. Bring her back." Then the moment passed, and he was the Cardinal again. "Good night, gentlemen."

The two men left the office, Max annoyed, Julianus thoughtful. They walked across the cathedral to the side entrance at the far end of the nave, their footsteps echoing in the enormous space. "Do you believe him?" Max said.

Julianus thought about the question for a moment. "Yes," he said finally. "I do."

"I thought you didn't trust anyone."

"I don't," Julianus said. "Not even you. Certainly not him. But I don't think he knows where she is. He seems genuinely worried about her."

A priest in red robes showed them out. A scraping sound told them the door had been locked behind them.

Max looked up, through the steady drizzle into the blackness above. He blinked rain from his eyes. "Another dead end. What now?"

"We've been on our feet all day," Julianus said. "There's a pub across the street. I could use a hot meal in front of a warm fire. I still want to keep an eye on the place. I'm not giving up on Alÿs coming to see the Cardinal just yet."

✦

Thaddeus nudged Alÿs, who was still kneeling before the statue of the Virgin Mary. Candlelight flickered on the Blessed Mother's face. It made Thaddeus nervous, the way the light seemed to make the statue's eyes follow him. "They're leaving!" he said.

Alÿs rose. From the shadow of the pillar in front of the Blessed Virgin, they watched Max and Julianus cross the nearly empty transept, talking to each other in low voices. The side door creaked open, then closed. A priest moved around, tidying up after Mass.

The hooded figure still seated in the pew rose. Alÿs and Thaddeus started forward toward the Cardinal's office. The figure turned.

Time stopped.

Thaddeus clutched Alÿs's hand, so tightly she cried out. "You're hurting me!" she said. "What—"

Thaddeus pointed. Alÿs gasped. Somewhere under the hood, the man who had tried to kill Thaddeus, the man who had murdered the shopkeeper and then fled through the window, smiled.

Things happened very fast after that.

Thaddeus turned to flee. His feet felt like they were dragging through molasses. The hooded man's smile grew wider. His hands came out of his pockets. In one hand, a long, wicked knife gleamed. *He's fast,* Thaddeus thought, *so very fast...*

The main door to the cathedral might as well have been miles away. It seemed pointless to run.

"Yes, Thaddeus Mudstone," the man hissed. His voice writhed and squirmed in Thaddeus's head. "You remember me. So nice to see you, Thaddeus Mudstone." He moved toward them, not hastily, gliding with eerie silence over the floor. "We have unfinished business, Thaddeus Mudstone."

Thaddeus backed up a step, then another. Alÿs kept pace with him, her hand clutched tight in his.

"There is nowhere for you to run this time, Thaddeus Mudstone. We will conclude our business, Thaddeus Mudstone."

Thaddeus watched the glittering knife, unable to tear his eyes away from it.

The priest walked back into the nave. "I'm sorry, the cathedral is closing," he said, moving toward the man. "You will have to leave."

"Father! Look out!" Alÿs screamed.

"What?" He turned toward them. "I—"

The knife flashed. Surprise crossed the priest's face. A jet of blood described a graceful arc through the air, landing in long dark streaks on the snowy white tile. He fell to his knees, hands on his throat, eyes wide.

"Run!" Thaddeus said. He pushed Alÿs away from the man in the cloak and bolted toward the transept, straight toward his attacker, the eyes of the Blessed Mother following him.

The priest slumped forward on the floor. The paralysis that had gripped Alÿs left. She fled, running as quickly as she could between the pews toward the opposite side entrance.

The hooded man darted between the pews toward them, as quick and graceful as a hunting cat. Alÿs flung herself sideways, landing with a painful jolt on the hard floor. He held the knife in front of him, smiling. His eyes met Alÿs's.

Thaddeus sprinted down the aisle and collided with the man, taking advantage of his instant of distraction to throw his entire body weight against him. The man staggered for a moment, off balance, but recovered almost immediately. The knife flashed.

Thaddeus was already gone, running toward the altar as if his life depended on it, his speed made all the greater by the fact that his life did in fact depend on it. The hooded figure turned in pursuit, padding catlike after Thaddeus, careful and deliberate.

Alÿs scrambled to her feet and darted across the aisle. The figure turned at the sound. She dove forward and slid beneath a pew, then wrapped her arms tightly around her body and rolled, coming to a stop beneath another pew.

Thaddeus darted up the raised platform directly beneath the dome and crouched behind the altar, breathing hard. The hooded man turned back in his direction. He padded lightly down the aisle, looking between each row of pews as he passed.

He mounted the steps to the platform, knife in front of him. Thaddeus leaped up, snatching a heavy, elaborate candlestick from the altar and swinging it with all his might. It connected with the man's head with a satisfying thud.

Beneath the hood, the man smiled again. He grabbed the candlestick and wrenched it from Thaddeus's grasp, flinging it away to clatter on the floor. Thaddeus circled the altar. The man followed, wary.

Thaddeus grabbed the other candlestick and threw it. The man evaded it easily and was already lunging across the altar, quick as a snake, before it had even hit the floor.

Thaddeus turned and ran, heading for the gloom of the tiny chapels lining the transept. The man followed slowly, stalking his prey like a cat. "Thaddeus Mudstone!" he called in his slithering, sibilant voice. "Thaddeus Mudstone, would you like your reward? Thaddeus Mudstone, I have something for you! Thaddeus Mudstone, come and collect your payment!"

Alÿs crawled under the pews, moving forward toward the altar. Her cap caught on a footrest and came off. Her hair spilled free. The man turned.

"Thaddeus Mudstone, why won't you come play with me? Thaddeus Mudstone, will your friend play with me?"

Thaddeus flattened himself against the polished wood wall of the tiny chapel. A carved statue of John the Baptist regarded him mournfully over a field of tiny candles and a small, sad handful of flowers, their dry petals crumbling into gray dust.

Thaddeus pressed back further, wrapping the shadows around him, quieting his breathing. He looked around the space for a weapon. Nothing.

Alÿs crept forward another inch, then another, flat against the floor beneath the pew. Something hard pressed painfully into her chest. She reached beneath her borrowed apprentice's coveralls and pulled out her handbag. Hands shaking, she rummaged through it.

There it was! The dagger from the shop in Highpole. She stared at it, warm and heavy in her hand, hypnotized.

"Thaddeus Mudstone," the hooded figure said. He passed the knife from hand to hand. "Thaddeus Mudstone, where are you going? There is nowhere for you to run! Will your god save you from me, Thaddeus Mudstone?"

Alÿs slid forward, angling toward the voice. Her heart pounded. She slowly crawled across the smooth marble floor, willing herself to invisibility beneath the pew. Another inch, another…

Her foot caught on the prie-dieu. The kneeling bench fell with a thump. The man whirled.

"Thaddeus Mudstone! Is that you, Thaddeus Mudstone? What will you say to your god, Thaddeus Mudstone? What questions will you ask him when you see him?"

Thaddeus crept out of the far side of the chapel and ran to the door. He pulled on the handle. The lock did not budge.

"Are you frightened, Thaddeus Mudstone? Do you know what is coming?" The man moved slowly down the aisle, between the rows of pews. "Do you think you will go to heaven, Thaddeus Mudstone?"

Alÿs held her breath. She could see the man's shadow, coming closer and closer. From under the pew, she saw the hem of his cloak, almost reaching the floor. His foot descended, right next to her, his skin white and withered and covered with blue blotches. He wore simple sandals made of leather, his toes long and tipped with thick, downward-curving nails.

Alÿs closed her eyes. Sweat formed on her skin. Her body shook.

She opened her eyes again. Then, with every ounce of strength, she stabbed outward, aiming for his exposed heel.

His skin was surprisingly tough, but the dagger was well made and exquisitely sharp. It pierced that mottled flesh and came out the other side. She sliced sideways, twisting as she pulled. The blade came free, severing the man's Achilles tendon.

Thick blue fluid splattered on the tile floor. The man fell heavily to the ground without a sound. Alÿs shimmied backward. Already, his knife was whirring through the space she had just vacated.

She scrambled out from under the pew and climbed to her feet. The man tried to rise, and fell again. He grabbed the edge of the pew, hauled himself upright, and lunged at her. His knife blurred through the air. Alÿs screamed and leaped aside, her knee colliding hard with the edge of the pew. The man fell again, hissing.

And then Thaddeus was there, charging down the length of the aisle like an avenging banshee. The tip of his heavy work boot smashed into the man's hooded chin. The man grabbed the boot with both hands, his dagger skittering across the floor. He pulled and twisted. Thaddeus crashed heavily to the ground.

The hood fell. Alÿs's eyes grew wide.

Beneath the hood, the man's face was a patchwork of scars, assembled from parts of a dozen people. His mouth was filled with needle-sharp teeth. His eyes, deep set in his scarred and bone-white face, were the eyes of a cat, not a human, golden-hued, the pupils vertical slits.

Alÿs screamed.

Thaddeus shook his head, stunned. The man, or creature, whatever it was, picked up his fallen knife, his motions graceful and unhurried. He—it—smiled broadly. "It is time, Thaddeus Mudstone," it said.

Alÿs screamed again.

The door to the Cardinal's quarters slammed open. The Cardinal stood there, framed in the rectangle, a rifle at his shoulder.

The creature turned. Its mouth split into a horrifying expression of triumph. It crouched and sprang, scrabbling toward the Cardinal on hands and knees.

Thaddeus twisted away toward Alÿs. "Run!" he said.

His eyes locked with the Cardinal's. An expression of surprise and recognition flashed across the Cardinal's face.

The creature snarled.

The gun spoke.

In the enclosed space of the cathedral, the sound was like the thundering voice of God. Thaddeus cried out in pain as spikes of agony drove themselves into his ears. Alÿs covered her ears with her hands. It looked like she was still screaming, but Thaddeus could hear nothing save the agonizing roar in his ears.

"Run!" he tried to say. The words were swallowed up in that dreadful noise that was not noise.

A hole bloomed in the creature's back. It fell backward in a slick puddle of blue fluid. "Run!" Thaddeus screamed again.

The main doors of the cathedral, so very far away, opened. Two men rushed in, dressed in the uniform of the Cardinal's guard, already unslinging their rifles.

The creature rose on hands and knees. It whirled toward the Cardinal and sprang again, far faster than any biped on all fours should move. The Cardinal dropped the gun and drew a knife of his own.

Thaddeus staggered over and grabbed Alÿs by the arm. She started toward the side exit. He shook his head. "It's locked!" he said. "This way!" He pointed toward the other exit on the other side of the transept.

The thing flung itself at the Cardinal. It jumped, propelling itself at the Cardinal's face with its working foot. He stabbed at it with his knife, striking only empty air. It knocked him to the floor. Its knife came up and descended, once, twice. Blood erupted across marble. The creature let out a triumphant hiss. "This is how you will end too, Thaddeus Mudstone!" it said.

Alÿs screamed again and stopped dead, eyes fixed on the Cardinal, lying motionless in a grotesque, impossibly vivid mixture of red blood and blue ooze. Thaddeus followed her gaze. "Come on!" he shouted. "We can't help him!" He ran, half-leading, half-dragging Alÿs. He could hear distant shouts, somewhere on the other side of a thick layer of cotton.

The creature turned and fled in the opposite direction, moving fast on all fours toward the door to the chapter house.

One of the Cardinal's men raised his gun. An explosion of sound filled the cathedral. The creature collided with the chapter house door, which slammed open, sending a spray of splinters and bits of broken lock in all directions. It darted through the large octagonal room without slowing, crashing through the door on the far side and out into the damp London night.

In the courtyard, the creature bowled through a small group of people, dressed in the overalls and caps of apprentices, huddled together beneath the overhanging roof. It hissed angrily, scrabbling on the wet ground. A large black coach sat waiting in the alley behind the cathedral. Its driver opened the door. The creature flung itself into the coach.

One of the apprentices watched the driver close the coach door. His name was William, and he was, those who knew him would agree, a nervous sort of lad, generally respectful of his elders and reliable enough in his way, but lacking that essential ingredient of initiative that made for an outstanding assistant in the artisanal trades. That made the next thing he did quite extraordinary.

In the cathedral, Thaddeus threw his body against the side exit. *If this is locked,* he thought, *it's all over...*

The door slammed open. They stumbled into the wet rainy night. Somewhere behind him, a thousand miles away, he could dimly hear the pealing of the cathedral's alarm bell. Soon the fury of the Cardinal's en-tire guard would swarm the cathedral, looking for answers and revenge.

"Run!" Thaddeus said. "Move!"

Alÿs froze. Thaddeus dragged Alÿs after him, charging across the cathedral lawn toward the pub and the streets beyond.

Across the street, the two members of the Queen's Guard were racing toward the cathedral, Max two steps in front of Julianus.

For the second time that evening, Thaddeus locked eyes with Julianus. Max and Julianus stopped dead in their tracks. Thaddeus heard angry shouting voices behind him. "Stop them!"

Thaddeus shook his head, just a little bit. "No," he said. "No."

The two Guardsmen started to move. "Alÿs," Thaddeus said. "Run!"

23

Commander Skarbunket's boots were soaked through. The rain showed no sign of wanting to let up anytime soon. The candles under the eaves had long since gone out. The gas jets hissed and spat under the steady assault of the rain.

He had sent some of the men home. The streets were quiet and, save for patrolling officers, utterly deserted. Skarbunket gave a silent prayer of thanks for the weather. People were, by and large, much less interested in standing up to The Man when doing so meant being cold and wet.

Mayferry, Levy, Tumbanker, and Bristol were accompanying Skarbunket along the cold, wet streets. The five of them had already made a complete pass of Highpole Street from north to south and back north again, and were nearing the mosque once more. He'd assigned the remaining police, the ones he hadn't sent home, to patrol the side streets in groups of two.

"You kept watch on the flat?"

"Yes, sir, for most of the night after we cleared it out. Nobody came, nobody went."

Skarbunket snorted. "I sure would like to know who left that 'anonymous' tip."

"I've thought that very same thing, sir," Bristol said. "We should have taken Mister Thaddeus Mudstone Ahmed Alexander Pinkerton into custody for a more formal chat. I have a feeling there are a lot of dark places he might be able to shed light on."

"Tread lightly with that thought, Mister Bristol," Skarbunket said. "The Bodger twins have friends in high places. They do business with the finest members of the body politic that the military and genteel classes of London have on offer. And when I say 'finest' I mean 'most politically connected,' not that other kind of finest."

"But they're commoners! And not even that, they're blacksmiths!"

"Even so. The thing about the Bodgers is—"

Across the water, the bells of the great cathedral began to peal.

The policemen looked at each other.

"Is that—" Levy started to say, but the others had already started at a dead run toward the bridge.

They arrived, panting and out of breath, to a scene of absolute chaos. All the lights around the cathedral blazed brightly. Men wearing the colors of the Cardinal's guard swarmed the cathedral grounds, shouting orders at each other. A group of four grim-faced men with rifles held up their hands at the policemen's approach.

"Commander Skarbunket, London Metropolitan Police," Skarbunket said. "Behind me are Mister Mayferry, Mister Bristol, Mister Levy, and Mister Tumbanker, also of the Metropolitan Police. What's going on?"

"Platoon Commander Hans Gisler, Pontifical Swiss Guard." The man who spoke was tall and fair, with brilliant blue eyes set above a thin nose and the sort of lips better suited to barking orders than whispering sweet words of tenderness. He was dressed in the red robe of the Cardinal's personal guard but had dispensed with the peaked steel helmet in favor of a flat beret of red velvet. "What can I do for you, Commander Skarbunket?"

"We heard the alarm bells. What happened?"

"There has been an attack in the cathedral," Platoon Commander Gisler said.

"Against?"

"Father Henri Angier and Cardinal de Gabrielli." Behind him, two men loaded a stretcher into the back of a carriage. The stretcher was covered with a bloody sheet.

"Suspects?"

"Escaped. Only…"

"Yes?"

Gisler paused for a moment, looking the dripping, out-of-breath policemen up and down. He nodded. "Maybe you'd better come inside, Commander."

Inside, all the arc lights were blazing, lighting the whole of the cathedral bright as day. Father Angier's body lay where it had fallen, unseeing eyes staring up at nothing. The pool of blood around the body had started to congeal, red-black beneath the harsh electric glare. Near the open doorway to the Cardinal's quarters, more blood had pooled on the floor. Levy turned green and looked away, hand over his mouth.

Skarbunket knelt next to the body. The man's throat had been slashed so deeply that the cut nearly exposed his spine. "Remind you of anything, Mayferry?" he said.

Mayferry got on one knee beside him and examined the body curiously. "The shopkeeper. It takes a lot of strength to cut that deeply with one stroke."

"Or a lot of rage." Skarbunket stood. "Are you okay, Mister Levy?"

Levy glanced over at him, then immediately looked away again. "Not really, sir."

"Good man. Where's the Cardinal?"

"We summoned his personal surgeon," Commander Gisler said. "He's badly wounded. We're taking him to the Turkish ambassador's physician, who is reputed to be the most skilled physician in London. He's going to need it."

"He's alive, then?"

"For now. It doesn't look good, Commander. He's lost a lot of blood. But that's not what I wanted you to see."

"What is it, then?"

"Over here, Commander." Gisler pointed to the floor between the pews. What do you make of that?"

Skarbunket looked down at the pool of viscous blue ooze, already turning gelatinous. He knelt and touched it with his fingers, then brought them to his nose. "Whew! Ugh. This is the stuff they use to make animates, isn't it?"

"That's exactly what it is, Commander."

"So the perpetrators brought an animate with them to attack the Cardinal?"

"Not exactly, Commander."

"'Not exactly?' What, exactly, does 'not exactly' mean, Platoon Commander?"

"It appears, Commander…well, if eyewitness accounts are to be believed—"

"And they rarely are," Bristol muttered.

"—that the animate was the perpetrator," Gisler finished.

"Excuse me, what?" Skarbunket said. "What does that mean?"

"There were two guards stationed outside the main entrance. They responded to screams and gunfire inside the cathedral. They ran in to find Father Angier dead and the Cardinal on the floor with an animate over him holding a knife. They shot the animate, which appeared to be wounded. It fled, along with two people, a man and a young woman dressed as a boy. Only—"

"Yes?"

"One of the men, Sergeant Tobler, swears he heard it speak, Commander."

"The animate? Speak? Nonsense. Animates are mindless. They can't speak," Skarbunket said.

"Precisely. There was a great deal of noise, confusion, bells, gunfire. I am not sure I put a lot of stock in it. He is not entirely clear on what it said. But still, something isn't right."

"You mean other than an animate running around the cathedral slicing people up?"

Gisler shot him a cryptic look. "Other than that. The guards stationed outside say they heard a woman scream, then a gunshot. That would be from the Cardinal's gun, which has been fired." He gestured to where the weapon lay on the ground. "They came in to find the animate over the Cardinal. Sergeant Tobler fired his weapon, striking the animate. The two suspects fled through the north transept exit. The animate made its escape through the chapter house and out the back exit."

"I see," Skarbunket said. "Did anyone see it leave?"

"No, Commander. The exit through the chapter house is barred from the inside. We do not normally station anyone outside that door unless there is a meeting in progress."

"An oversight I'm sure you will be addressing in the future," Skarbunket said. "Curious the perpetrators and the animate exited in different directions. There was nobody else in the cathedral when your men came in?"

"Other than Father Angier, no, Commander. Father Brisson had already retired to his quarters across the way after Mass. He left Father Angier to clean up and lock up."

"Wait," Tumbanker said. "Something doesn't make sense. Why would the woman scream if she was one of the perpetrators?"

"You'll have to forgive Mister Tumbanker," Skarbunket said. "He has a habit of placing his finger directly on the problem. I fear what it may do to his career. Please continue."

"Your Mister Tumbanker has spotted exactly the thing we're curious about," Gisler said. "And there's another problem as well."

"Really? Oh, good. I was thinking there weren't enough of those. I await this news with bated breath," Skarbunket said.

"Sergeant Tobler believes he recognized the woman," Gisler said. "He swears it was the Lady Alÿs, dressed as a boy. She comes here often."

"Chickens, perhaps a couple of pigs…" Skarbunket said dreamily.

"Sir?"

"Nothing, Mayferry. Just contemplating the path not taken. A career I might have had. One that did not involve a princess of the French royal family turning up at the scene of not one but two grisly murders in about as many days." He surveyed the cathedral. "Platoon Commander Gisler, I must commend you on your openness. It has been my experience in the past that the Papal Guard is rarely so willing to accept assistance from the outside."

"The first priority of the Pontifical Swiss Guard is the safety and security of the officers of the Church," Gisler said. "We pride ourselves on our willingness to reach out to our brothers in local law enforcement to work together to—"

"You have no idea what's going on, so you need our help," Skarbunket cut in.

"I wouldn't precisely use those words, Commander."

"Ah, I imagine not. And the involvement, or possible involvement, of the Lady Alÿs adds a political wrinkle that puts you in a very dangerous position," Skarbunket continued. "The Cardinal is quite close to the French royal family, is he not? So doing anything indiscreet might bring down the wrath of both the French Crown and His Eminence on your head, which is a formidable combination for one head to take."

"Again, I wouldn't put it quite—"

"Not to mention Her Majesty the Queen," Skarbunket mused, "who is quite fond of the lady, from all accounts, and not exactly noted for her kind and gentle disposition."

"While there is a political dimension—"

"Best just to hand it off to the local plods, so if we make a mess of things, it isn't your neck on the block, eh, Platoon Commander?"

"We understand each other exactly, Commander Skarbunket."

"Splendid. Glad to be of service," Skarbunket said. "Well then. Since we all understand each other exactly, let's get started. Take me through the action as you believe it unfolded, Platoon Commander."

"We believe that the assailants entered the cathedral with the animate before or during Mass. After Mass, the Cardinal retired to his quarters, as he usually does. Father Angier was slain about this time, probably while he was cleaning up."

"And he was standing here." Skarbunket walked over to the body.

"Correct, Commander. Then the Cardinal came out of his study…"

"With his firearm?"

"Correct."

"Why?"

"Commander?"

"Why did he come out with his firearm?" Skarbunket said. "Is he normally in the habit of carrying a gun about the church with him?"

"No, Commander. He probably picked up his weapon when he heard the scream."

"So the animate killed Father Angier. Then the Lady Alÿs, if it was she, screamed. This aroused the Cardinal's curiosity, so he picked up his gun and came to investigate."

"Yes."

"Hmm," Skarbunket said. "That seems, and I mean no offense, Platoon Commander, but that seems a very odd thing, does it not? Why not simply go into his quarters and kill him there, where he could be taken unawares? Why warn him and allow him to arm himself?"

"Perhaps you can tell me, Commander."

"I don't know yet." Skarbunket paced over to where the Cardinal had fallen. "Go on, please."

"The Cardinal fired his weapon. The two guards outside the cathedral rushed in and saw the animate stabbing the Cardinal. The Lady Alÿs and the unidentified man fled through the transept entrance. The animate departed through the chapter house."

"I see." Skarbunket walked back and forth between the body of Father Angier and the place where the Cardinal had fallen, lost in thought. He paced the circuit several times, then spun around. "Those candlesticks on the ground there, Platoon Commander. Where did they come from?"

"I believe those are normally on the altar, Commander," Gisler said.

"Did any of your men approach or disturb the altar?"

"I don't believe so, Commander."

"So if the animate was here," Skarbunket said, walking over to Father

Angier's corpse, "and then it approached the Cardinal here," he continued, walking to where the Cardinal's blood still pooled on the floor, "then it would go nowhere near the altar. How did the candlesticks end up on the floor?"

"What are you suggesting?" Gisler said.

"Suggesting? I'm suggesting nothing. I'm observing, Platoon Commander. What next?"

"That's it, Commander."

"Hmm." Skarbunket walked back and forth. "The animate was damaged by the Cardinal's shot. That's the puddle of gunk here," he said, pointing to the floor in the central aisle between the pews.

"We believe so, Commander."

"And there is another puddle of gunk here, near the place you say the Cardinal was attacked. That would be your man, Sergeant…"

"Tobler."

"Of course, Sergeant Tobler. So if the animate killed our unfortunate Mister Angier over there, what was it doing in the aisle here?"

"No idea, Commander."

Skarbunket walked up and down the aisle. He bent over. "Mister Mayferry, Mister Bristol, what does that look like to you?"

Mayferry and Bristol bent over. "A bit of animate ichor, sir," Bristol said.

"Animate ichor? Is that what it's called?" Skarbunket said. "I had no idea. Hm. There's no end to the things you can learn every day. So if the Cardinal shot the animate over there," he pointed, "and Sergeant Tobler shot it over there, then how did it end up bleeding over here?"

"No idea, sir," Mayferry said.

Skarbunket got down on his hands and knees. He looked under the pews. "Huh. What's this?" he said, fishing the cap out from beneath a pew.

"It looks like an apprentice blacksmith's hat, sir," Mayferry said.

"And this?"

"A long black hair, sir."

"Platoon Commander Gisler, remind me again what kind of hair the Lady Alÿs has?"

"It's long and black, Commander. What are you thinking?"

"I am thinking I will need to talk to Sergeant Tobler, if you could be so kind as to direct me."

"Of course. Allow me to go fetch him." The Platoon Commander scurried off with the expression of one relieved that his problem was turning into someone else's problem.

"So what are we thinking, sir?" Bristol said. "Were Thaddeus Mudstone and the princess here?"

"Oh, yes," Skarbunket said. "I would bet money, that is, if I weren't on a civil servant's salary, I would bet money on it."

"So what is it? French conspiracy? Italian conspiracy?"

"I'll wager you they were here, Mister Bristol, but not that they were involved."

Mayferry looked taken aback. "That hardly seems plausible, sir. Why do you think they weren't involved?"

"That candlestick," Skarbunket said.

"Sir?"

"It doesn't add up. When things don't add up, it means you're missing something. When you imagine what happened here, Mister Mayferry, can you account for why that candlestick is on the floor over there, or why there's that bit of animate ichor here?"

"No, sir."

"Exactly. That means whatever it is we think happened, we're wrong." He looked down at the cap in his hands. "We met Mister Thaddeus Mudstone at the Bodgers' shop, and lo and behold, the Lady Alÿs, or a person who may be the Lady Alÿs, shows up in the company of Thaddeus Mudstone dressed as a blacksmith's apprentice."

"Begging your pardon, sir, lots of different apprentices wear that sort of cap," Tumbanker said.

"Indeed, they do, Mister Tumbanker. But since I seem in a wagering mood, I'll wager I know where this cap came from. I would very much like to speak to Thaddeus Mudstone again. And to the Lady Alÿs as well. And I will further wager I have a good idea where I might find them. I suspect they can tell us quite a lot about what happened here, and I further suspect that what they can tell us about what happened will differ quite remarkably from what our Platoon Commander thinks happened."

"And you got all that from a candlestick?" Tumbanker looked doubtful.

"Don't be silly, Mister Tumbanker. I got all that from a candlestick and a bit of animate ichor. And now I want to pay a second visit to the blacksmith's shop. Perhaps we should hear what Sergeant Tobler has to say, and then we should—"

The main doors crashed open. Max and Julianus came in, panting. Their cloaks were wet and muddy, and they were both thoroughly rain-soaked. Max leaned against the wall to catch his breath. His face was a study in rage.

"And here I thought this day couldn't get any worse," Mayferry said.

"Don't say that," Bristol said. "Never say that. What's wrong with you?"

"Judging from the expression on yonder Guardsmen's faces, I think this day might be about to get much worse," Skarbunket said. "Chin up, lads. I'm sure the joy we feel upon sight of them will be matched only by the joy they feel when they see us. Let's go have a talk, shall we? Mister Tumbanker, it's time you got a lesson in interorganizational politics. Try not to be clever. After that, we'll speak to Sergeant Tobler."

✦

Thaddeus ran until he couldn't run any more, then kept running some more anyway. He kept his hold on Alÿs's hand, forcing her to keep up with him. They darted through alleys and down narrow gaps between buildings, always turning and twisting, never keeping to a straight line for more than ten or twenty yards. Thaddeus gave silent thanks that King John's ambitious reconstruction project had not extended past the place where the Thames bent to the east; if they had been in the new parts of New Old London, the bits with the straight roads at perfect right angles to each other, their odds of escape would have been very small.

Leave it to King John. Civil engineering really did have an impact on crime.

The two Guardsmen pursued them with a tenacity that Thaddeus would have found admirable were it not for the fact that should they succeed in catching him, he might have a short drop and a sharp jerk to look forward to.

If he was lucky. Offenses against the Crown often ended beneath the headsman's axe.

Not that it really mattered that much, he thought. Axe or noose, dead is dead, when it comes down to brass tacks. Still, he preferred to the extent humanly possible to keep his head about him, so to speak.

Down an alley, across a road, between those buildings, down this other alley, then double back, push through this yard, duck behind the refuse-dump, then around again.

"He's dead, isn't he?" Alÿs said.

"Don't know. Got to run," Thaddeus said.

"The Cardinal, I mean. That thing, it…it killed him."

"Looks that way. Talk later. Run now." Thaddeus pulled her into a narrow space between two tall buildings, one brick, one wood. "Up the fire escape. Up! Go! Go!"

He pushed her toward the narrow iron steps. She climbed, unresisting. They ran out across the roof. Below them, Max and Julianus pounded past.

"This way," Thaddeus said. "Down here. Come on! Bit of a jump, not too far, you can make it. Okay, ladder here. Now run! Run!"

"Stop," Alÿs said. She bent over nearly double. "Stop."

"We can stop when we're dead. Which might be sooner than we like if we stop now."

"I…" She panted, gasping for breath, then vomited profusely in the alley.

Thaddeus looked around, frantic. "Okay. Back here. Try to stay hidden."

They crouched in the back of the stinking alley, cold rain falling on their faces. Someone opened a window three stories above them and emptied a chamber pot, pouring a foul-smelling deluge over both of them. Alÿs cried out.

"Still want to be a commoner?" Thaddeus said, wringing out his shirt.

Alÿs shook her head. She seemed numb, her eyes only barely registering what was happening around her.

"I think we shook them," Thaddeus said. "We need to get back to Claire and Donnie's place. They'll know what to do. They always know what to do."

"But...I can't..."

Thaddeus risked a peek out of the mouth of the alley. "Come on. You can. It's time to go."

They arrived at Bodger & Bodger about an hour later. The vast work space was still, the apprentices having gone off, Thaddeus supposed, to wherever it is apprentices go when they aren't apprenticing. Alÿs had passed through mere misery and horror and come out the other side somewhere else, in a place where misery and horror took on a transcendent quality. Claire took one look at her and hustled her into the bath.

"Muddy, my boy, you look like death an' smell worse," Donnie said. "Phew! What happened?"

"You aren't going to believe it," Thaddeus said.

"Try me."

Thaddeus spoke without interruption for so long that by the time he was finished, Claire and Alÿs had returned, the latter significantly cleaner but no less morose.

"Alÿs has been telling me a remarkable tale," Claire said. "About a talking animate that's as smart as a person."

"Muddy 'ere 'as told a similar tale," Donnie said.

"Yes," Thaddeus said, "that sounds about right. Did she get to the bit where it tried to kill us? And then it killed the Cardinal and a priest?"

"Father Angier," Alÿs said softly. "I knew him."

"She did mention that bit," Claire said.

"A most perplexin' conundrum," Donnie said. "Talkin' animates w' a taste for murder. Alÿs, is this creature the same one that killed Chiyo Kanda?"

"I don't know," Alÿs said. "I think so."

"Be sure," Donnie said. His voice was low and dangerous. "Think. Be sure. Was it the same creature?"

Alÿs closed her eyes. "Yes. Yes, it was. I'm sure. Why?"

"Someone made it. Someone set it after Chiyo. A smart animate, someone knows o' such things. We will find 'im." His normal placid smile was gone. He spoke without anger, and somehow, that was even more frightening.

"Why kill Kanda?" Thaddeus said.

"Don't know," Donnie said.

"Why kill the Cardinal?"

"Don't know. Somethin' big is 'appenin'. Attackin' the Cardinal at the cathedral, that is very risky. Dangerous. Someone wanted 'im dead pretty badly."

Alÿs shrank a little, drawing herself into the oversized shirt and trousers Claire had found for her. "I can't believe he's dead," she said. Her voice was small.

"Believe it. They will be lookin' for you."

"Who?"

"Everyone. Yer like Muddy 'ere. A loose end. Muddy says the Queen's Guard was there. Did they see you?"

"Yes," Alÿs said.

"Did they recognize you?"

"I—I don't—"

"Did they recognize you?" Donnie said again. His voice was soft, but beneath it there was an edge of steel.

"Yes. Maybe. Yes, I think they did."

"Problems. You got big problems," Donnie said.

"What are you going to do?" Alÿs looked around in alarm. "Are you going to turn me in?"

Claire put her hand on Alÿs's shoulder. "No," she said softly. "We are not going to turn you in. You are a friend to us. We take care of our own."

"An' if we can't do that, we avenge them," Donnie said.

"If it's all the same to you," Thaddeus said, "I prefer the saving to the avenging."

A quick, light rapping sounded at the door. Claire and Donnie exchanged glances, then Claire unhooked her crossbow from its customary hanging place on the wall. She moved toward the door cautiously. Donnie picked up a heavy iron hammer and followed after her.

"What do we do?" Alÿs said.

"Get ready to run if we need to," Thaddeus said. "You'll get used to it. Part of your glorious new life as a commoner. Out the back, around the side, through the alley that comes out on Hammersmith Street. There aren't a lot of gas lights, so you can stay out of sight. Head toward the river, take a left on Pinback Road; there's even fewer gas lights and lots of places to hide."

"Is this really how you live?" Alÿs said.

Claire and Donnie came back in toward them. Thaddeus tensed. Between them was a young boy, perhaps nine or ten, wearing the striped working clothes that identified him as an apprentice to a blacksmith or ironworker.

"Who's he?" Thaddeus said.

The boy took off his cap and clenched it in front of his chest. "My name is Will. William Hughes, sir. I'm, I work over in, I'm apprentice for…I'm an apprentice smith on Pentuttle Street, sir. I work for Mister Blakesley, sir. He's a smith." He turned to Donnie. "You came and talked to him, sir."

"I did," Donnie rumbled. He folded his arms. "An' what do you want to tell us, Will Hughes?"

"Well, sir…" The boy twisted his cap in his hands, looking down at the floor. "I remembered what you said, Mister Bodger, sir. About the man who murdered the woman in Highpole, sir. This evening, I went to Mass. Mister Blakesley, he thinks we should go, sir. He says it is important to be close to God."

Donnie nodded. "'E's a good man." The big orange cat, Disorder, wandered through the workshop and stopped in front of Will. He made a quizzical *brrp?* sound and rubbed up against the boy's legs.

Will fidgeted, eyes still downcast. "After Mass was over, I stayed outside the cathedral, sir. I was talking with some of my mates. Mister Blakesley doesn't like when we do that, sir. He says idle hands are the Devil's work. I just…it's the only, I don't get a lot, I don't get to talk to my friends very much, sir." He twisted his cap like he was wringing out a dishrag, his face contorted with misery.

"It's okay," Claire said reassuringly. "We aren't going to tell anyone you were talking to your friends. Here, sit down."

The boy sat, hugging his arms tightly to his chest. The cat hopped up in his lap. "Thank you, ma'am," he said.

"What 'appened next?" Donnie prompted.

"Well, sir, I heard a lot of shouting and noise. My friends, they ran away, sir. And then this man came out of the door. I remembered what you said, sir. White skin, strange looking. He had the cloak and the hood and everything, sir. I thought, this must be him. And people were shouting, sir, and there was so much fuss."

"Did you see where he went?" Claire's voice was low and urgent.

"Yes, ma'am. He got into a big black carriage. It was behind the church, ma'am. I think it was waiting for him. It was one of those rich people's carriages. All big and posh. He got in and closed the door, ma'am. And I remembered what Mister Donnie said, we all need to be the eyes and ears, and…and…"

"Yes?" Claire prompted.

"I…well, you see, ma'am, when he got in the coach, I wanted to see where he was going to. So I…it might have been wrong, but I jumped on the back of the coach. It had one of them things on the back, like a big trunk, see, and it wasn't latched or anything, so I put myself in it."

"You 'id in the coach?" Donnie said.

"Yes, sir. I know it was bad. I shouldn't have done it…"

"You did a brave thing," Donnie said.

"Really?" Will looked up, hopeful.

"What happened next?" Claire said.

"We traveled for a while, ma'am. I don't know which way we went. It was a pretty nice road. Not a lot of bumps. Then we stopped and I heard men talking—"

"Talkin'?" Donnie said. "'Bout what?"

"I don't know, sir. I was too scared to open the trunk and look, sir."

"Okay, go on."

"We started moving again, sir. But only for a little while. Then we stopped. I heard the man get out of the carriage and the driver get off, sir. People came and unhooked the horses. Then I didn't hear anything for a long time. So I opened the trunk just a little bit, sir. I didn't see anyone. So I crept out, sir." He stopped and stared at his hat.

"Where were you?" Claire asked.

"In a stable, ma'am. The carriage was in a stable. A big one, with buggies and carriages and a lot of stalls. And there were a lot of creatures, ma'am."

"Creatures?" Claire asked.

"Creatures. Big ones, like those things that sometimes bring iron to the smith. They were horrible! They were all in a line in the back of the stables, ma'am. They were just standing there, not doing anything. Like they wasn't even alive. Just standing there."

"So what happened next?"

"I crept out of the stable, ma'am. I think I was in one of those big country estates the rich people have, with the big house and walls around it and stuff. It was dark. There was no lights in the stable. There was a big stone tower by the stable. Lots of lights in it. And there was a big house, with all those new electric lights around it and everything. And a big yard out front. And…" He stopped.

"Yes?" Donnie prompted.

"I saw a lot of men in the yard," William said, so quietly the others could barely hear.

"Men?" Donnie said.

"Soldiers," the boy said. He twisted his hat so tightly Thaddeus feared he might rip it to pieces. "Lots of them. There was this huge house, and grand, sir. So grand. Like a palace, sir. And a great yard in front of it, with fountains and things. It was all lit up, sir. And there were lots of soldiers. Maybe hundreds, sir. They were all lining up. They all had guns. There were people shouting things. I couldn't hear what they was shouting. Horses too, sir. But mostly soldiers. I was scared. So…so I ran, sir. They didn't see me. I ran away. The gate, it was closed, sir. And there were more soldiers at the gate. I climbed over the wall. I'm good at climbing, sir. And then I ran."

"And you came 'ere?" Donnie said.

"Yes, sir. You said to, sir! You said if anyone finds out anything, they should come see you, sir. So I did."

"You did the right thing," Donnie said. "Thank you for comin' to me."

Alÿs leaned forward. "The estate, where was it?"

"North, ma'am," the boy said. He unfolded his hat and smoothed it out. "Along Treban Road. A long way, ma'am. It took me hours to get back." He twisted the hat in his hands again.

"Describe the estate," Alÿs said.

"Big!" The boy's eyes grew wide. "There's a stone wall all 'round. The house, it has all them pointy arches and funny peaks at the top. There's a huge yard out front, ma'am, so big you would never believe. Stables on one side. There's a big round tower at the end of the stables. And another house, ma'am, on the other side. Brick. It has gas lamps out front, and square windows with big chimneys."

Alÿs sat back. "Rathman. That's Rathman's estate."

"Is it now." Donnie crossed his arms.

"I don't get it, though. Why would Rathman send an animate to kill the Cardinal?"

"That's the wrong question," Donnie said.

"What? Why? Seems like exactly the right question to me!" Alÿs said.

"The right question," Claire said, "is why is Rathman marshalling an army in his courtyard in the middle of the night?"

"Why is—"

"Because 'e's movin' ahead," Donnie rumbled. "'E 'as a goal. Whatever it is, 'e don't want yer friend the Cardinal involved. Decapitation."

"Decapitation?" Alÿs said.

"Cut the 'ead off the snake an' it can't bite you. Cardinal's got an army, right?"

"Well, yes," Alÿs said doubtfully.

"Can't use an army if there ain't no one t' give it orders," Donnie said. "Pity 'bout the weather, though."

"Why?"

"I think we need t' go out an' pay this Rathman fellow a visit."

"Really? Wait, are you serious? You can't!" Alÿs said.

"Why not?" Donnie's face bore no expression.

"He's—he has an army!"

"So I've 'eard."

"He's the Queen's uncle!"

Donnie nodded. "That's what they tell me."

"He has a murderous animate that's already killed three people!"

"Ah, yes," Donnie said. His expression darkened. "An' that is exactly why we will see 'im. 'E killed Kanda, or knows who did. My sister said it. We take care of ours."

"So go to the police! Tell the Queen!"

Donnie shook his head. "She was one of ours."

"What are you going to do? You can't just ride in there!"

"Why not?"

"What are you going to say?"

"Suppose that depends on what we find when we get there," Donnie said. He rose and padded over to a large bench hidden in the dusty corner near the gigantic mechanical spider. He pulled a huge, grubby tarp off the bench.

"What are those?" Thaddeus asked, curious in spite of himself.

Donnie hefted a heavy-looking contraption, all round tanks and straps. "Now the problem with an animate, Muddy my boy, is it don't feel pain, right? You can shoot 'em all you wants an' if you don't hit something vital they just keep comin'. This 'ere's a new invention. Workin' on it fer th' regular army. Shoots a jet of fire out of the end. They ain't been field-tested yet. Should work good though. Ain't really made for use on animates, but they ought t' work better'n most things we got lyin' around here. 'Cept maybe the armored clanker an' that ain't finished yet."

"You're really serious about this," Alÿs said.

"Yep." Donnie's face, dark before, was now positively grim. "We'll take the new number two apprentice an' some o' the other apprentices. Muddy, you want t' go pay a visit t' the men who are tryin' t' kill you?"

"I don't have anything better to do tonight," Thaddeus said.

"I'm going too," Alÿs said.

"No y'ain't." Donnie's voice held a note of steely finality.

Alÿs stamped her foot. "Yes, I am!"

"No, y'ain't," Donnie repeated. "This ain't yer fight."

"Because I'm a girl?"

"Ha! My sister's a girl an' she's goin', ain't that right, Claire? It's because yer French royalty. This ain't the place for you."

"Then where is the place for me?"

"Queen's yer friend, right?" Donnie said. "Someone needs t' let 'er know what's goin' on. Who else but you?" He handed her an apprentice's cap. "Try not t' lose this one."

"They'll arrest me if I go back to the Palace," Alÿs said.

Donnie shrugged. "Mebbe. So don't get caught." He looked at Thaddeus, who was halfway to the front door. "Where you goin', Muddy?"

"To find a friend," Thaddeus said. "If I'm not back here when you leave, I'll catch up with you."

24

Winston Clark, His Honor the Judge of the Police Court of Greater London in service to Her Majesty the Queen, was not having a good evening.

He turned the piece of paper on his desk over and over again, as if willing it to say something else on repeat examination. When it failed to do so, he scowled at it. He turned it over one last time, and when it again failed to change its meaning, he directed his scowl at the police officer standing in front of his desk.

"Commander Starbunket—"

"Skarbunket, Your Honor."

"Skarbunket. Well, that's hardly an improvement, is it? Commander Skarbunket, do you know what you're asking me for?"

"Yes, Your Honor." Skarbunket shifted his weight, hands clasped behind his back. Beside him, Mayferry snickered. "I am asking for a warrant, Your Honor, to allow myself as representative of the London Metropolitan Police, together with such members of the Force I may deem appropriate, to search the premises located at 112 Hammersmith Street, said premises being an establishment known as Bodger & Bodger Iron Fittings, Your Honor, for the personages of, or any indication of the personages of, (a) The Lady Alÿs de Valois of the French royal family, and/or (b) a man who calls himself Thaddeus Mudstone Ahmed Alexander Pinkerton, such indications of their personages in question including but not limited to a pair of distinctive shoes made and/or sold by Brundel and Sons of Pemmerton Street, said shoes described in detail in Attachment A, and/or any evidence of the presence of a particularly aggressive animate, possibly badly damaged, described in detail in Attachment B, Your Honor."

"Remarkable," Judge Clark said. "You've got it verbatim." He straightened his wig, which itched something fierce, and squinted at the paper in front of him.

"He does that, Your Honor," Mayferry said.

Judge Clark sighed. He closed his eyes for a long moment. When he opened them again, the police commander was still standing there, wearing that earnest, guileless look he had come to associate with officers of the law who were Up To Something.

On any normal night, he wouldn't be here. On any normal night, he would, at this hour, be abed, snuggling in close to the warm and ample bosom of Mrs. Clark, perhaps playing a rousing game of Judge and Jury with her. With luck, there might be strenuous cross-examination, and if things went very well, maybe even a hung jury.

Instead, he was behind the desk of the night judge in a small office off the main floor of the headquarters of the London Metropolitan Police. Someone well above him had expected something big this evening, involving lots of requests for warrants and investigations, and he'd experienced the sinking sense that Judge and Jury would have to wait for another night. So here he was, commanded to make himself available all night long by order of the office of the Lord Chancellor himself.

The evening was quiet. Whatever the Powers That Be had expected to happen was conspicuous in its failure to have happened. Judge Clark had been sitting in his office all evening long, far from the close and warm embrace of Mrs. Clark, forced to content himself with nothing beyond the more ordinary sort of judge and jury.

Less than the ordinary stream, in point of fact, given that there was an excess of judicial types handling a paucity of cases. Despite the entire police force being tied up in Highpole, London's criminal classes appeared to have declared an unofficial criminal holiday of sorts. The holding cells were nearly empty. All of London, it seemed, wanted to see what would happen.

Commander Skarbunket could have popped into any office. There were half a dozen judges in the offices that lined the south wall of the police building, three times as many as would ordinarily be here at this hour, and with that embarrassment of choices, he had walked into this office. And now, Judge Clark was fearing for his job.

"You do realize what you're doing, Commander Skarbunket?" he said. "Not that I would cast aspersions on your choices, career-limiting though they may be."

"I'm applying for a search warrant, Your Honor."

"At Bodger & Bodger."

"Exactly so, Your Honor."

Judge Clark peered at the warrant. "Claire and Donnie Bodger have certain...connections, Commander Skarbunket."

"So I've heard, Your Honor."

"Are you aware, Commander, that Admiral Mellon is a big fan of theirs? He invited them to his birthday party last year. Every British ship of the line carries a Bodger & Bodger autoloading device fitted to each of its cannon, did you know that?"

"Really?" Skarbunket said. He looked at Mayferry. "I can't say I was aware—"

"Brigadier General Sir Lawrence Flatiron personally insisted they attend the wedding of his daughter. He is quite fond of the Bodger & Bodger Automatic Rotating Heavy Gun. He seems to think it might finally bring an end to the deplorable situation in Afghanistan, you see."

"Is that so? How interesting, Your Honor. I had no idea—"

"The point I am trying to make here, Commander," Judge Clark said, "is you are proposing to search the shop of some very well-connected and influential people for—for—" He blinked once more at the paper, as if trying by force of will to make the letters written on it change shape.

"For a member of the French royalty, whom you suspect to be involved in a murder…"

"Two murders, Your Honor," Commander Skarbunket corrected. "And one case of assault that may yet become a murder."

"Ah, right, yes, of course, that's much better. *Two* murders. And one assault. Yes, yes, it says that here." He shook his head. The heavy wig stayed in one place as his head rotated beneath it, creating an effect that suggested his head was being attacked by a great, strangely shaped parasite consisting entirely of white curls. "You wish to search Bodger & Bodger Iron Fittings for a missing member of the French royal family, who you believe to be implicated in at least two murders, with, er…" He squinted. "With a knife. This is rather an unusual thing for members of the French royalty to be involved with, don't you think?"

"Not really, Your Honor," Skarbunket said. "In fact, I might say that it's a very common thing for French royalty to be involved with—*oof!*" Mayferry elbowed him sharply in the ribs. "It's the knife I find unusual—*oof!*" He glared at Mayferry, who had just elbowed him again.

"And the reason you believe this is, as I understand, relates to a hat and a pair of shoes?" Judge Clark put his hand over his forehead. He'd heard stories about Commander Skarbunket, with his reputation for brilliant results achieved through distressingly lateral means.

"I'm not sure which would be worse, Commander," he said, "if you find your missing princess or if you don't. Humor the man who's being asked to put his name on your search warrant. If you find the missing French princess in the custody of the politically influential artisans, what do you propose to do then?"

Commander Skarbunket gave the judge his best guileless, I'm-not-up-to-anything grin. "We would very much like to bring the Lady Alÿs in for questioning, Your Honor," he said. "Purely police procedure, you understand."

"Ah. I was afraid you might say something like that." He scratched his head, setting the wig to bouncing. "And should she express reluctance to this idea?"

"Well, Your Honor," Skarbunket said, "I don't really think—"

"So I gather," Judge Clark said dryly.

"Begging your pardon," Mayferry said, "I hardly think that's—"

Judge Clark raised his hands. "Relax, Officer." He rearranged the papers on his desk. "I didn't say I wouldn't grant the warrant. Though if it were anyone but you, Commander Skarbunket, I might not be so inclined. Your reputation precedes you." He picked up his fountain pen and twiddled it between his fingers. "I want you to understand, Commander, that if you should come up empty-handed, the consequences for your career will likely be severe."

"Thank you, Your Honor—"

"I'm not finished. The consequences for my career will likely be severe as well. Perhaps not as terminally so, but severe nonetheless."

"Thank you, Your Honor. I will—"

"I'm still not finished. The Bodgers have powerful friends. My name is on this warrant. If you make them angry, and any of that anger spills over onto me, I will make it my life's mission to see to it that it is transferred where it properly belongs, by which I mean onto you. And I am a very patient man, Commander, very patient indeed. In light of that, Commander, do you still want me to sign this warrant?"

Skarbunket inhaled. "Your Honor, I believe—"

"I don't care what you believe, Commander. Only what you can prove. Now tell me, Commander, considering the hellfire I will rain down on your head if you're wrong, do you still think I should put my name on this warrant?"

"I do, Your Honor," Skarbunket said. "What's the worst thing that could happen? I've always wanted to try a more pastoral career."

"You may get your wish, Commander." The judge scribbled on the paper in front of him. "Tread lightly. I hear Claire tends to answer the door armed if she isn't expecting guests. And she's the gentle one." He passed the papers over the desk to Skarbunket. "Out of curiosity, Commander Skarbunket, what do you propose to do if they say no?"

"Use my charm," Skarbunket said. He paused. "Wait a minute, Your Honor. How do you know about my reputation?"

"Get out of my office," Judge Clark said. "And God help us both."

On the way out, Skarbunket nudged Mayferry. "Are Bristol, Levy, and Tumbanker still about? Let's get them and go pay the Bodgers another visit. By the way, what was all that about with the elbowing of the ribs?"

"Nothing, sir," Mayferry said. "Just concerned that you might be about to have one of your moments, sir."

"Moments, Mayferry? I have no idea what you mean."

"Of course not, sir. It must have been a tic, sir. I'll talk to the doctor about it. Will we be stopping to collect your sidearm, sir?"

"Tell me, Mayferry, if the Bodgers turn out to be reluctant to speak to us, do you really think it will make any difference?"

"No, sir, I don't reckon it will," Mayferry said.

"My thought as well, Mister Mayferry" Skarbunket said.

As they walked through the hallway, Bristol fell into step beside them. "Did you get him to sign off on it, boss?" he said.

"I did. It seems we might be in danger of being stricken off Admiral Mellon's party list, though."

"I wasn't aware we were on it, sir."

"No? Seems the Bodgers are. Where are Levy and Tumbanker?"

"Outside with the carriage, sir. If we're going to do something that will get us off Admiral Mellon's party list, we might as well be warm and dry while we're about it."

"Ah, good," Skarbunket said. "Remind me to put you in for a promotion if we get through tonight."

"Kind of you to offer, sir, but I don't want your job," Bristol said. The three men passed beneath the silent stone statue of the underdressed Lady Justice and out into the chilly rain.

As promised, Levy and Tumbanker were waiting with a carriage out front. Levy sat in the driver's seat, soaked through. Tumbanker opened the door as they approached.

"Great night to make powerful enemies, huh?" Skarbunket said to Tumbanker as they climbed into the carriage.

"I wouldn't know, sir. I'm still new to making political enemies," Tumbanker said.

"Don't worry, Mister Tumbanker, I'm quite confident you'll take to it like a duck to water. You have the gift."

"Thank you, sir," Tumbanker said.

A short while later, they were pulling up in front of Bodger & Bodger Iron Fittings. All the windows were dark save for a solitary spark of dim yellow light from a single lonely square of glass near the door.

"No time like the present," Skarbunket said. He hopped down from the carriage, his boots squishing in the mud. "Any of you who don't want to risk your careers, speak now."

"Um, sir?" Levy said. "Since you're asking and all, I think I'd rather not risk my career tonight, if it's all the same."

"So noted. Go knock on the door," Skarbunket said. "What? Don't look at me like that. I said you can speak now. I didn't say it would make a difference. Life lesson, Mister Levy."

Levy hopped down in the mud beside Skarbunket. He rapped on the door. Nothing happened.

"Mister Mayferry, care to show him how it's done?" Skarbunket said.

"Of course, sir." Mayferry strode up to the door and hammered on it with his fist. "Open up! London Metropolitan Police! We have a warrant!" he thundered. He turned to Skarbunket. "You do have the warrant, right, sir?"

Skarbunket waved his hand. Mayferry hammered on the door again. "Open up in the name of the police!"

Rain poured down around them. The metal sign reading "Bodger & Bodger Iron Fittings" swung, squeaking in the breeze. Inside the building, nothing stirred.

"What this situation requires," Bristol said, "is more insistence." He slogged up to the door and kicked it several times with his boot. "Open up at once in the name of the London Metropolitan Police!"

The door opened a crack. Bristol looked in, then down. "Who are you, boy?" he said.

The boy looked up at him skeptically. "I'm Will Hughes, sir. I'm an apprentice for Mister Blakesley on Pentuttle Street, sir. Are you really a policeman?"

"Yes. We are all policemen. We are looking for Claire and Donnie Bodger."

"I'm sorry, sir. They aren't here." The boy moved to close the door.

Bristol stuck his foot in the rapidly closing gap. "Now see here," he said. "We have a warrant to search these premises."

"A what, sir?" Will said.

"A warrant. It means we can search this place and you can't stop us."

"Oh." Will considered this for a moment. "What does it look like?"

"What does what look like?"

"The warrant, sir."

Skarbunket passed the paper to Bristol, who handed it to Will. The boy looked at it. "This is just a piece of paper," he said.

"Yes," Bristol said. "It's a warrant. Read it!"

"I don't know how to read, sir."

"Oh, for heaven's sake." Bristol put his shoulder to the door and pushed. Will yelped and scrambled out of the way.

The five officers pressed their way into the workshop. The blinds were drawn on all but one of the windows, and the arc lamps were off. A lonely oil lamp jet provided a small yellow glow beside a cot that had been set up between two workbenches. Vague dark shapes lurked in the gloom.

"Where is everybody?" Bristol said.

"I told you, sir. They're not here. Donnie, he, he told me I could spend the night. I have to go back home to Mister Blakesley tomorrow."

"But where are they?" Bristol demanded.

The boy remained silent, eyes downcast.

"I said, where are they?" he repeated.

Will took off his cap and twisted it silently in his hands.

Skarbunket got down on one knee beside the boy. "Do you like apprenticing for Mister Blakesley?"

"I suppose so, sir," Will said.

"What are you learning how to be?"

"A smith, sir."

"A smith." Skarbunket nodded. "I guess our jobs are still safe then, eh, men? That's a pity. Speaking of which, Mayferry, remind me to put you in for a promotion."

"I don't want your job either, sir," Mayferry said.

"Huh. I can't even give it away," Skarbunket said. "Now, Will, is it? Will, I really need to talk to Claire and Donnie. And to Thaddeus Mudstone, if he's around. Is he with them?"

Will nodded. "Yes, sir."

"Ah. And what about the Lady Alÿs? Is she with them?"

"The noble lady?"

"Yes, the noble lady."

He nodded. "Yes, sir."

Commander Skarbunket raised his eyebrows. "They always doubt me," he said. "Why do they always doubt me? No matter. Now, Will, it is very important that I talk to Claire and Donnie. Can you tell me where they are?"

Will looked down, twisting his cap, saying nothing.

"Do you like Claire and Donnie? Do they treat you well?"

"Yes, sir," Will said.

"There are bad men about, men who want to hurt Claire and Donnie. I fear what might happen if we don't talk to them. Do you want that?"

Will twisted his cap. "No, sir," he said quietly.

"Do you know where they are?"

The boy nodded. "Yes, sir."

"Are Thaddeus Mudstone Ahmed Alexander Pinkerton and the Lady Alÿs de Valois with them?"

"No, sir. I mean, yes, sir. Well, Thaddeus is, sir. The lady went back to the Palace, sir."

Mayferry's eyebrow rose. Skarbunket sat back in surprise. "Really? How very interesting. Did they take the animate with them?"

"No, sir." Will put on his cap, then took it off again. "They're going to go kill the animate, sir."

"This keeps getting better and better," Skarbunket said. "Mayferry, make a note. We need to interrogate young children more often. Now Will, why are they going to kill the animate?"

"Because it killed Kanda, sir. In Highpole. She was one of us, sir. Donnie said so. She was a tinkerer, like us. The police, they...they don't...I'm sorry, sir, but they don't care about us, sir. When someone hurts us, we take care of our own. Donnie says so, sir."

"And just like that, the pieces begin to come together," Skarbunket said. "Now Will, this is the most important question. Where did they go?"

"To the estate, sir. The one where the animate lives. The lady says it belongs to Lord Roth—Count Rich—"

"Lord Rathman?" Bristol said.

"Yes, sir. Lord Rathman, sir."

"Oh." Skarbunket stood. He turned to the other policemen. "Which one of you said this evening couldn't get any worse?"

"That was him, sir." Bristol pointed to Mayferry.

"Right. Mister Mayferry, your promotion is rescinded."

"Thank you, sir," Mayferry said. "In light of recent events, I am now doubly certain I don't want your job. I'm not entirely sure I want my job just at this moment."

"That's what's wrong with people today," Skarbunket said. "They lack ambition." To Will, he said, "How do you know the animate belongs to Lord Rathman?"

"Because I seen it!" The boy's eyes grew as big as saucers. "I saw it. I was at Mass! It came running out the door right by me. There was lots of noise and so much commotion, sir, and it got into a big fancy carriage, sir! So I hid on the carriage. Donnie Bodger, sir, he went around after Kanda was murdered, he told all of us to be on the watch for it. So I hid on the carriage to see where it was going, sir. When we got there, there was a big stable and lots of them creatures all lined up on the wall. So I came here to tell Donnie. Did I do a bad thing? Are you going to cut my head off?"

"That's not my department," Skarbunket said absently, stroking his chin. "When did they leave?"

"Not even an hour ago, sir. Donnie, he was real upset. And there were soldiers, sir, lots of them, all at the estate. The lady, she went to warn the Queen, sir."

"Mister Mayferry, Mister Bristol, Mister Levy, Mister Tumbanker," Skarbunket said, "how do you gentlemen feel about paying a visit to the third most powerful person in the Realm?"

"Tonight? Can't say I feel very good about it, I imagine," Bristol said. "It would be nice if we had something more than just these truncheons if we're going up against animates, sir."

"A salient point, and one I'm surprised our Mister Tumbanker didn't arrive at before you," Skarbunket said. "Where did you say you parked that carriage full of black-powder bombs, again?"

The big orange cat wandered over, sat down at Skarbunket's feet, and meowed up at him.

25

Alÿs crept silently through the rain-slicked streets, doing her best to remain in the sheltering embrace of the shadows. The miserable cold drizzle kept anyone with sense and money, which are often the same thing, off the street. The only people about either had no choice but to be, or were there to prey on those who had no choice but to be. Most of the former were too wrapped up in their own misery to notice a tinker-er's apprentice skulking about; the latter knew from experience that an apprentice seldom had anything worth stealing.

Not that Alÿs was skulking, precisely. In truth, neither creeping nor skulking were within her normal repertoire of skills. Her brief associa-tion with Thaddeus had so far been entirely insufficient for his talents to rub off on her.

She skulked as best she could, navigating toward the Palace by the most direct route that was also consistent with keeping out of sight. The overalls provided little protection from the rain, and before long her teeth chattered. She hugged her arms tightly around herself, trudging over uneven cobblestones made treacherously slippery by the rain. Water swirled around her shoes, seeking its union with the great undi-lutable stink of the Thames.

Once she crossed the bridge, the roads became wider and more level. The clever network of drains that had been part of King John's ambitious civil engineering plan carried the rainwater away with the efficiency made possible by massive public spending. She was still soaked through, but nevertheless there was some small measure of joy in not having to wade through pools of filthy water.

She was able to move more quickly down the wide, flat roads of New Old London. She rounded a corner onto Kingsferry Way and nearly collided with a well-dressed gentleman in a top-hat, carrying a large umbrella. He scowled at her. "You're in the wrong place, laddie," he said.

Alÿs opened her mouth to reply, then closed it again and nodded. Abashed, she turned down the nearest alley, lined on both sides with re-fuse-dumps. A man sat smoking a cigar in the cage of an idling clanker, eyes hidden in the shadow of a wide-brimmed hat. Black fumes trailed from the clanker's stack. He sniggered at her.

Alÿs moved more quickly, feeling the eyes of the clanker driver on her back. She was unaccustomed to traveling through the alleyways, which tended to be narrower and significantly more odiferous than the streets. Thankfully, they were also more dimly lit, and she felt a tangible sense of relief for the sheltering darkness. A part of her wondered if this was how people like Thaddeus always felt.

A lumbering animate came down the alley, a tall human-like figure dressed in simple canvas clothing. Its head was misshapen, and one arm hung lower than the other. Alÿs pressed herself back against the wall, heart pounding. She slid her hand into her handbag. The dagger was still there, reassuring in its weight. The thing passed her without a glance. Still, it was several minutes before her heart slowed enough that she could move again.

✦

"Ah, there y'are, Muddy," Donnie said. "I 'bout gave up on you. Thought you weren't gonna show."

Thaddeus shook the rain from his hair. "I said I'd catch up." He moved in beside Donnie and Claire, who were leading their small group of apprentices down the wet and muddy cobblestone road. "That the fire-throwing machines?" He gestured to the heavy canvas bag slung over Donnie's shoulder. Several of the small group of apprentices carried similar bags.

"Yep," Donnie said. He waved his hand at the bulky man shadowing Thaddeus. "Who is that?"

"This is Jake," Thaddeus said. "Jake, meet Donnie and Claire Bodger. Jake's a good man to have in a fight."

"Yeah, that's right," Jake rumbled. "Muddy says you're lookin' to tangle with some nobly type. That true?"

"No," Donnie said. "I'm lookin' t' finish a tangle some nobly type started."

"Good 'nuff," Jake said. He jerked his thumb over his shoulder. "Who're they?"

"Apprentices," Donnie said.

"Right. Where we goin'?"

"Does it matter?"

"Naw. Just makin' small talk."

They slogged on for a while in silence. Then Jake said, "How'd you drag Muddy into this, anyways?"

Claire laughed. "You got it all wrong. He dragged us into this. Well, him and his friend."

"She's not my friend," Thaddeus said.

"Oh, Muddy, don't be daft," Claire said. "Anyhow, Thaddeus showed up on our doorstep talking about being hired to sneak onto the Queen's private airship. When he told us some people were trying to kill him and some other people were trying to steal his hat, we were, you might say, intrigued and all."

"You mean that stuff about dancin' with them nobles was real?"

"Seems like," Claire said.

"So what do we do when we get where we're goin'?"

"We see what there is to see," Claire said. "We go looking for talking animates with murderous predispositions. If we find one, we kill it."

"Ain't no such thing as a talkin' animate," Jake said.

Donnie grunted. "So they say."

Outside the city proper (or the city improper, depending on whose view you accepted), the cobblestone gave way to dirt. The moon shone wetly off the slick brown mud. Around them, so far from the city's arc lamps and gas jets, the landscape was composed entirely of vague shapes and dark shadows. Donnie's face was set in a grim frown.

"So there's no plan, then?" Thaddeus said.

"That is the plan," Claire said. "We go in, we find the animate, we destroy it, we leave."

"Like it's going to be that simple," Thaddeus said.

Claire shrugged. "We can always hope, eh, Muddy?" She unslung the crossbow from behind her back. "'Course, we might need to be persuasive."

"Why do you carry that thing, anyway?" Thaddeus said. "It was an antique before you were born!"

Claire nodded. "It's good for quiet persuasion, you know? Like, when you want to make a point all eloquent-like but you don't want to draw a crowd."

Beside Thaddeus, Jake chuckled. "Yeah, I know what you mean. I use a sock full o' lead shot for that."

"Means getting up close and personal," Claire said.

"That's the way I like it," Jake said.

They saw the lights before they heard the sound—bobbing yellow lanterns, dozens of them. Then came the sound, horses and men, lots of both, marching in formation down the muddy road.

A man on horseback, wearing a uniform of red and black, trotted up to them. He had a face that looked designed and built to wear arrogance: a long, hawkish nose, dark eyes cast in a permanent squint. If an expression of anything other than boredom or anger had ever crossed his face, it had certainly left no mark there. "Stand aside!" he barked. "Make way! Make way!"

Donnie smiled placidly. "Of course," he said. He and Claire drew off the side of the road. The rest of the motley band followed suit. Thaddeus and Jake melted into the shadows.

"Who are you?" the man demanded. His thin lips pressed with practiced ease into an expression of disapproval.

"Donnie Bodger, of Bodger & Bodger Iron Fittings, at yer service," Donnie said. "This 'ere's my sister, Claire. These are our apprentices. An' you are?"

"Donnie Bodger, eh? *The* Donnie Bodger? I've heard a lot about you." His face betrayed no hint of his opinion on what he'd heard. "Major Charles Archibald, officer commanding, Fourth Lord's Levy Battalion, Squadron A, at your service." Behind him, the columns of men marched by.

"Pleased t' make yer acquaintance, Major Charles Archibald," Donnie said. "Fine night to be out an' about."

"Routine drills," Archibald snapped. He scowled at the tight cluster of people behind the Bodger twins. "What are you and your apprentices doing on the road at this time of night?"

Donnie's smile widened. "Oh, y'know, just testin' some new ideas."

"In the rain? In the middle of the night?"

"Our equipment 'as t' work in the rain," Donnie said. "Ain't much good equippin' soldiers w' gear that only works on sunny days. We have a reputation t' uphold."

"Yes, of course," Archibald said. "What's in the bags?"

"A Bodger & Bodger original," Donnie said. "Multifunction controlled long-distance temperature elevation device. Good fer startin' campfires in wet conditions an' keepin' people warm. All with the Bodger & Bodger guarantee."

"Let me see it," Archibald said.

"Sure thing," Donnie said. He slid the canvas bag to the ground. "Now the secret 'ere," he said, bending over to open it, "is in the Bodger & Bodger two-way pressure regulatin' valve. It feeds a constant stream into the turboencabulator, see, an' prevents backdrafts through the Mynard regulator. Can't have backdrafts through the regulator or y' foul th' spline gate, see? But the real secret, y'understand, is the special retainin' ring on th' mix box inlet manifold. That prevents—"

"Fine, fine, whatever," Archibald said, eyes blank with boredom. He waved his hand dismissively. The gesture was so perfect, composed as it was of equal parts contempt and disinterest and assembled with the precision of a pocket watch, Thaddeus found himself wondering if the man practiced it in front of a mirror. A gesture like that, you couldn't just extemporize. It spoke of a degree of haughtiness attainable only through long hours of work. "You fellows have a good night," the major snapped, in a tone that suggested he hoped they'd have exactly the opposite.

"I thank you, sir, an' wish you success on yer maneuvers," Donnie said. By the time he picked up the bag again, Major Archibald had already trotted off to rejoin the column of men heading toward London.

They set off down the road once more. Thaddeus and Jake appeared beside Donnie as if birthed by black magic from the darkness itself. "That was close," Thaddeus said.

"Naw," Donnie said. "'E wants power, not knowledge. Likes t' throw 'is weight around. No patience fer th' details. Dealt with 'is kind a thousand times. Easy if y'know how."

"Donnie, what's a Maynard regulator?"

Donnie shrugged. "Dunno."

✦

The yard in front of the warehouse was a sea of mud. Commander Skarbunket scraped rather a lot of it off his boots, then sighed at the futility of it all and gave up. "Remind me again," he said, "why you thought it was a good idea to pile a mountain of black-powder bombs into a carriage and park it here, instead of perhaps putting them at the bottom of the Thames?"

"Evidence," Bristol said. He pulled open the door on the crude lean-to that had been built as an afterthought against the side of the warehouse some years ago, revealing the carriage in question. Beside it, a placid-looking horse munched nonchalantly from its feed bag. It seemed totally unconcerned about standing next to a mountain of improvised explosives, demonstrating in its dim animal way that ignorance truly is bliss.

"You couldn't keep maybe just one bomb as evidence? You wanted to keep the whole, and it is with some reluctance I put it this way, Mister Bristol, but you wanted to keep the whole shebang?"

Bristol winced. "I thought it best to retain the option of impressing the Court with the magnitude of the situation, sir."

"Mm, yes, of course," Skarbunket said. "Remind me to put you in for a promotion."

"Sir! I don't think—"

"Relax, Mister Bristol, I wouldn't really do that to you. Though we may, if we are not exceedingly careful over the next little bit of time, find ourselves involuntarily promoted to the hereafter. Do any of you gentlemen smoke?"

A chorus of *No, sir!*s rose from the small group of policemen.

"Good. If I hear so much as a heated word from any of you, you're all—and again it is with reluctance I phrase it quite this way—fired. Mister Bristol, get the carriage hooked up." He peered into the coach's windows. "Looks like three of us will be riding inside with the explosives, and two up top over the explosives. Anyone here got a morbid fear of dying?"

"I do, sir," Tumbanker said.

"I'm sorry to hear that, Mister Tumbanker. You're driving."

"What? Why me, sir?"

"Because that very natural and reasonable fear, Mister Tumbanker, should help encourage you to drive with appropriate discretion. The last thing I want, Mister Tumbanker, is to be riding inside a carriage full with explosives driven by a man who does not fear death. I would think that to be obvious to a person of your formidable mental acuity."

"Very good, sir," Tumbanker sighed.

"Excellent. Now then, gentlemen, if there are no further concerns, I think we should all make our peace with the powers that be and go pay a visit to Lord Rathman. Mister Mayferry, I trust you will have no further foolishness to say about how this evening can't get any worse?

No? Good. Mister Levy, you will ride up top with Mister Tumbanker. Let's be off."

✦

Alÿs circled around the side of the Palace toward the stables, still keeping to what few shadows could be found loitering in these parts of London. Her disguise offered at least one advantage: dressed as she was, she would attract little attention using the servants' entrances.

She sidled quickly across the street and darted in through the stable door, pausing to let her eyes adjust to the gloom. "Henry?" she hissed. "Henry, you here?"

"Who's this, then?" came an unfamiliar voice. Alÿs froze, heart jackhammering wildly.

A man she'd never seen before, perhaps twenty years old, approached her with a lantern. He had a narrow, hard face and was dressed in the livery of a stableboy. He looked her up and down. "Who are you?"

"Where's Henry?" Alÿs said, trying to keep the quaver out of her voice.

"In prison with his traitor brother, Rory. They helped the traitor Alÿs escape. What do you want?"

"Nothing. Nothing, I…I was just looking for him, because, uh, I had something for him."

"Do you? Give it to me," the man said.

"What?"

"Give it to me," he repeated. "If you have something for the stablemaster, then whatever you have is for me. If you have something for Henry personally, then you're in league with traitors and I will turn you over to the Guard." He held out his hand. "Either way, whatever you have, hand it over."

"I…" Alÿs looked around. "I don't…"

"That's what I thought." He grabbed her wrist. "Right. I'm taking you to the Guard."

The next thing that happened seemed to do so of its own accord, without the intervening of conscious thought.

Alÿs twisted her arm sharply. Her foot came up, catching him be-tween his legs. A remote, detached part of herself took note, with no small measure of satisfaction, of the way his expression changed, his eyes getting big, his face contorting into a cartoonish grimace. She pushed with all her strength and was a little surprised at how violently he flew backward. The lantern fell. She turned and ran, dashing through the door before it had time to hit the ground. Behind her, she heard him start to cry out in surprise, but by then she was already back on the street, darting past a surprised-looking clanker driver dragging a wheeled cart full of coal. She reversed direction, keeping the coal cart between her and the stables.

The man ran out of the stables, roaring with rage and pain. He looked both ways down the street, then tore off down the street, disappearing around the side of the Palace.

Alÿs kept pace with the clanker for a few yards, then slipped around behind the coal cart. She took a deep breath and darted across the street and into the stable. Heart still pounding, she moved quickly between the rows of stalls until she found the servants' entrance to the Palace. She tried the door.

Locked.

She looked around wildly. A lantern hung from a hook on the wall, shedding a soft pool of yellow light over the stable's work table. A pile of horseshoes and nails were scattered haphazardly across it. A torn saddle strap hung over the edge. And there…

Alÿs picked up the hammer. She turned it over in her hands, then brought it as hard as she could against the edge of the door, swinging with both arms.

The door never had a chance.

Wood splintered. The door, or what was left of it, slammed open with a bang. Instantly, Alÿs was through. She pushed it closed behind her. The latch was ruined, and the door would not stay shut. She wedged the hammer under the doorjamb as best she could, then looked around.

She was in a long hallway that led through the heart of the servants' part of the Palace, the part where those of high birth seldom trod. By a blessing of fate, there was nobody in the hallway. Gas jets hissed quietly in their wall mounts.

Alÿs hustled down the hallway, wary of approaching footsteps. The staff would not trouble her, but coming to the attention of the Queen's Guard could create problems she didn't know how to solve. Kicking and running might work with a stablehand, but against a Guardsman? Expecting to evade the Guard that way struck her as perhaps too optimistic.

Nerves jangling, she crossed the invisible dividing line between the servants' palace and the palace inhabited by the royal Court. She felt conspicuously out of place. If anyone saw her, dressed in the clothes of a blacksmith's apprentice, she would almost surely be detained. She kept to the less-traveled passageways as much as she was able, moving quickly over floors of rare marble and exotic wood.

She stopped in front of a gold-trimmed door and rapped on it with her knuckles. "Eleanor? Eleanor, let me in!"

Voices down the corridor set her heart racing again. She rapped once more on the door, more urgently this time. "Eleanor! Open the door!"

A sleep-blurred voice came from the other side. "What? Who's there?"

The voices came closer. In a moment, their owners would round the corner, and all would be lost.

"Eleanor! It's me! Alÿs! Let me in!"

"Alÿs? It can't be you. You're supposed to be missing!"

"Open the door!"

A small group of ladies rounded the corner. The door opened. Alÿs pushed through and closed it quickly, breathing hard.

Eleanor shrieked.

"Eleanor! It's me!" Alÿs took off her cap.

"Alÿs! Are you okay? They said you were taken by foreigners!" Eleanor threw her arms around Alÿs. Then she released her and stepped back. "You aren't a heretic, are you? Julianus and that other one, they said you're a heretic! They told me that associating with you would be treason! I heard you were there, when the Cardinal was attacked! You weren't there, were you? They're saying all kinds of terrible things about you! Please tell me they aren't true!" She burst into tears.

Alÿs put her arms around her. "They're not true," she said. "I was there when the Cardinal was killed. I didn't have anything to do with it."

"Was it Shoe Man? I bet it was, wasn't it? I told you not to go, I did! They aren't like us. Italians are monsters! I bet he killed the Cardinal, didn't he?"

"It was a monster, but it wasn't Thaddeus," Alÿs said, then instantly gave herself a mental kick.

"Thaddeus? Is that the Italian's name?" Eleanor sniffled. "That doesn't sound like an Italian name."

"He's not Italian," Alÿs said. "Listen, I need your help." She tucked her hair under the cap and pulled it back on.

"My help?"

"Yes. I need to see Margaret. Something bad is happening. I need to talk to her."

"She thinks you're a traitor!"

"I don't care. I have to talk to her."

Eleanor shook her head. "No! No no no. The Guard already questioned me. And those stableboys who helped you, they're down in the cells! If they find you here, they'll put me in the cells too!"

Alÿs sighed. "They're not going to put you in the cells."

"You don't know that! Everyone got really angry after you left. They're saying things about you that you just wouldn't believe!"

"Do you believe them?" Alÿs said.

"No! Well, I don't think so. I don't know what to believe!"

Alÿs took Eleanor's hands. "We've been friends for a long time. Margaret is my friend too. She's in trouble. I know who's causing all of this. The ring, everything. It's all part of a plot, and you're the only one who can stop it. Can you get me in to see her?"

✦

Roderick shifted his weight back and forth, shivering in the cold. Ever since that ridiculous man with his ridiculous shoes had flung himself from the back of the Queen's airship on that ridiculous night, Roderick had found himself assigned to the late-night shift in the guardroom. Most of the Palace was fast asleep like reasonable human beings, but not Roderick, oh no.

He was standing in the small alcove in front of the great iron gate placed exactly in the center of the high fence surrounding the Palace. He held his gun, a standard-issue Bodger & Bodger Model 301 Cartridge-Loading Rifle, at his side, ready to defend Queen and country against the incursions of a couple of very fat rats and the occasional wayward moth. High overhead, the blazing arc lamps atop their tall towers filled the courtyard with false day.

He wasn't even entirely sure what he was being punished for. He was certainly being punished, that much seemed plain. Word was, Margaret herself had ordered him out here, standing in this tiny guardhouse next to some other equally unfortunate fellow as a mark of her displeasure for his involvement, accidental and peripheral as it was, in the dreadful mess on the airship. Now whoever was normally in this place at this hour was sleeping in a nice warm bed, while Roderick shivered.

It was hardly fair, was it? He'd been in the wrong place at the wrong time and seen someone jump out a door, and now here he was.

Cold, damp air caressed him with icy tendrils. Little squalls of rain, blown by eddies of wind, slapped him in the face, dripped down his collar, soaked his cape.

"Guardsmen! Stand aside!"

Roderick wiped the rain from his eyes. A man on a horse, wearing the red and black uniform of a levy officer, approached him. He swung down off his horse and walked up to the booth. Behind him, a column of mounted men swung round and took positions along the fence. A long line of soldiers on foot came to a halt.

"Excuse me?" Roderick said. "Who are you?"

"Major Charles Archibald, Lord Rathman's Fourth Lord's Levy Battalion. We have urgent business with the Queen."

Roderick's eyes narrowed. The mounted horsemen formed up outside the gate, facing toward the street, rifles ready. Major Archibald's hand rested on the pommel of his sword.

"What is the nature of your business?" Roderick said.

"That is not your concern, Guardsman. We were sent by Lord Rathman himself. Stand aside."

"At this hour?"

"It's okay," Roderick's fellow Guardsman, a bloke named Bellingsworth or Birmingham or something like that, said. He moved the lever that opened the gate.

Major Archibald gestured. Foot soldiers began marching through the gate, two abreast.

"Hey! You are not authorized to enter the Palace grounds," Roderick said.

"Stand aside, Guardsman." Archibald's hand tightened on his sword. "This doesn't concern you."

"What are you doing?" the other guard—Bremmerton, that was his name!—said. "He's a levy officer!"

"He isn't authorized," Roderick replied. "Major, recall your soldiers. I will consult with the captain of the Queen's Guard."

Archibald drew his sword with a metallic scrape.

Roderick leaped, catching the major square in the chest before the man's sword had cleared its scabbard. The major went down with a surprised *oof!* Roderick swung his rifle. The butt and Archibald's head connected with a satisfying crack. He leaped over the fallen man and darted through the gate toward the Palace.

"Get him! Kill him!" Archibald cried.

Roderick scrambled toward the Palace, running across the courtyard as fast as his legs would take him. Behind him, he heard shouts and the sound of running feet. A group of four men, alerted by Archibald's cry, turned to cut him off.

Adrenaline surged through him. Ahead of him, the soldiers were already drawing their swords. He slowed, sighted along his rifle, pulled the trigger. Sparks flew. A cloud of acrid smoke poured into his face. The gun roared, kicking savagely against his shoulder. The closest man fell.

Roderick lowered his head and charged.

✦

The door to Margaret's chambers was flanked by two men, one wearing the white cape of the Queen's Guard, the other in the red cape of the Cardinal's Pontifical Swiss Guard. They turned toward Eleanor, surprise registering on their faces.

"Her Majesty is not receiving visitors," the white-caped man said. He was tall and broad of shoulder, but his red eyes spoke of too many hours standing in front of a door watching an empty hallway.

"She will see me," Eleanor said firmly. "She always sees me. Stand back, Percival Goldsworth, or I will see to it that you get such a thrashing."

He glanced over at the Cardinal's guardsman. "My lady, it's late," he complained. "Her Grace is asleep. She left word not to disturb her." He looked over Eleanor's shoulder. "Who is this boy?"

"He's from the stables," Eleanor said firmly. "There is a problem that needs the Queen's immediate attention."

"In the stables?" Percy Goldsworth rubbed his eyes. "Can't it wait? She will have my head if I let you wake her up. Maybe literally."

"She might have your head if you don't," Eleanor said. She drew herself up to her full height, marched up to the door between the two men, and knocked loudly.

The Cardinal's guard grabbed her by the wrist. "Let me go at once!" Eleanor shrieked with all the outrage she could muster, which, as it turned out, was quite a lot. A lifetime among the upper classes is excellent training for the mustering of outrage.

"My lady, it is late," he said. "Please return to your quarters."

"Who do you think you are, to lay your hand on a lady?" Eleanor demanded.

"Rudolf Hunziker, Swiss Pontificate Guard. And the Cardinal will have my head if you go in there. Maybe yours as well."

"Very well. Maybe you're right," Eleanor said. She looked back at Alÿs. Alÿs felt her heart sink. She shook her head slightly.

Eleanor stomped on the Cardinal's guard's foot. He let out a cry, half surprise, half pain. Eleanor jerked her arm free and knocked on the door again. "Your Grace! It's Eleanor!"

"Seize them!" the red-caped man said. He seized Eleanor's arm tightly. Percy grabbed Alÿs's arm with a steel grip.

The door opened to reveal a rumpled monarch in her nightclothes. "What is going on here?" Margaret demanded.

"Your Grace!" Alÿs said. She snatched off her hat. "It's me, Alÿs! It's Rathman! His army is coming! I think he means to do something terrible!"

A commotion rose from the end of the hallway. Max and Julianus tore around the corner, followed by the stablehand and a small cluster of Guardsmen. "There he is!" the stablehand said. "That's him!"

"Arrest them both!" Max said. "Eleanor and the traitor Alÿs!"

26

"There it is," Claire said. "That must be the estate."

The roadway leading up to the estate was narrow and flanked with tall trees, crowded close together as if afraid to be out alone on such a night. It ended at an enormous, imposing iron gate set in a tall stone wall. Inside the gatehouse, two men watched them warily.

"What now?" Elias asked.

Donnie smiled. He walked up to the gate, stopping just short of it. "Evenin'," he said. "I'm Donnie Bodger. I have business with th' lord o' the house, Lord Rathman."

The guards stepped out of the gatehouse, blocking his path. One of them gazed levelly back at him. "Lord Rathman is not presently in attendance," he said. "Now I suggest you and your—" He scowled at the loose cluster of apprentices. "Whatever they are, turn around and go."

Claire came up beside Donnie. "We've come a long way on a miserable night. Seems inhospitable to not welcome us in."

"Maybe we ain't feeling hospitable," the second man said. He cradled his gun in his arms, not exactly pointing it at them, but not exactly pointing it away either. "His lordship ain't here. Come back some other time."

"Gentlemen," Donnie said, smiling his most disarming smile, "let's be reasonable."

"I ain't going to tell you again. Get los...*unh!*" The man blinked once and sagged to the ground.

"Hey!" the first guard said. "Wha—*unh*!" His eyes glazed over and he fell forward in the mud.

Thaddeus and Jake appeared out of the shadows behind the fallen men. Jake tapped a wet, heavy-looking sock in his hand, grinning wickedly.

"Nice," Claire said.

Thaddeus picked up a lantern from the small table inside the gate-house. "Now where is…ah, got it." He hauled on a length of chain. Slowly, ponderously, the gate swung open.

"That was easy," Claire said. "Tie them up. Take their guns."

"Mind if I take their coins too?" Jake asked.

Claire shrugged. "Suit yourself. Just do it quickly. Leave the gate open. We might be in a hurry on our way back out."

They headed through the gate, leaving Jake and Thaddeus to deal with the guards. The two of them bound the luckless men with leather cords and dragged them into the gatehouse.

"We should just kill 'em," Jake said.

Thaddeus shook his head.

"They're gonna wake up and come after us, you just watch," Jake said.

"That would be really dumb. Claire'll shoot them," Thaddeus said. "Though I'm a little surprised they were so easy."

"I ain't," Jake said. He removed the money pouch from each unconscious guard and looked inside them. "Pfaw. Hardly any coin on 'em." One of the men groaned and started to move. Jake punched him. He went still. "Guys like this never expect trouble, you know? You spend night after night an' nothin' happens, you start to expect nothin' to happen. Take off their clothes."

"What? Why?"

"You take away a man's gun, he might come after you with his fists. You take away his clothes, he ain't runnin' after you in his underthings."

"Ah, right," Thaddeus said. "Clever."

When they were satisfied the two men were unlikely to cause any trouble, Thaddeus and Jake scurried after the others. The estate yard was dark. The main house was also dark, with but a single window glowing.

The shadow of the great tower loomed overhead, with light pouring from its uppermost windows. Nothing moved.

"Weird," Jake said. "Don't like this none. Place like this, I'd expect more folks to be about."

They kept to the shadows near the wall, where the darkness was almost complete. Donnie gestured them to stop. "That must be the stable," he said, pointing ahead at the long, low building, a vague dark shape in deeper darkness at the foot of the tower.

He dropped the canvas bag to the ground and unzipped it. He lifted the apparatus inside and started strapping the heavy, cumbersome thing to his back. Behind him, five of the apprentices did likewise.

"Hey Muddy," Claire said. "You know how to use this?" She held up one of the guns they had taken from the guards.

Thaddeus took it from her and examined it. "Nope." He looked curiously at the symbol engraved in the hilt, a stylized "B&B" in a square. "This is one of yours?"

"Yep. Hold it against your shoulder here, pull this bit here, and hang on. Kicks like a mule, but that ain't half so bad as what happens to the other guy. You reload it here, move this bit, pull on this, cartridge comes out, put a new one in, close it all back up. Spare cartridges are in this little case here on the strap, see? If you run out or don't have time to reload, you can stab with the pointy bit on the end here. Hey, number two! You get the other one." She tossed the second rifle to Elias, who snatched it gracefully out of the air.

Donnie finished adjusting the straps. He picked up a long metal nozzle attached to the device on his back. Thaddeus saw sparks, then a tiny blue flame, smaller than the flame from a gas lamp. More flames winked into existence as the apprentices readied their weapons.

"That thing really work?" Thaddeus said.

"Dunno. I think so. Let's find out," he said.

Under cover of shadow, they moved single file toward the stable, Donnie in front, then Claire, Thaddeus and Jake behind, and the apprentices taking up the rear.

"I don't like this. Where is everyone?" Thaddeus said.

Donnie grunted. He moved forward cautiously toward the stables.

There was no visible sign of humanity inside. Most of the stalls were empty, with only a single horse, black with a white star on its nose, in evidence. It regarded them with dull, incurious eyes.

"What is that?" Elias hissed. He pointed to the far wall of the stable.

There, the normal stalls had been removed and replaced with tall, narrow alcoves, far too small for a horse. Each alcove contained a single, horrifying occupant, a grotesquely misshapen, leather-skinned *thing* in the approximate shape of a human being. Each of the creatures was held tightly against the wall by wide iron bands locked around its arms and legs. Many of the creatures bore wide, jagged scars on their arms, legs, and necks. A complex tangle of tubes descended from the ceiling, entering the creatures at neck, shoulders, chest, and arms. Their eyes were open but unseeing, registering nothing. They did not move or breathe. A cloying stench rose from them, made of equal parts swamp and spoiled meat.

"I thought animates were ugly," Jake said, "but these things are a whole new kind of ugly."

"Someone's been up to no good," Claire said.

Jake walked up to one of the creatures and prodded it with his club. "It ain't moving," he said. "It ain't doin' nothing."

"Get out of there! Are you crazy?" Thaddeus said.

"What?" Jake said. He prodded the inert animate again. "See? It ain't moving at all. I don't think it's alive. Or whatever those things are."

"Muddy," Donnie said, "are any o' these the one that tried t' kill you an' Alÿs?"

Thaddeus examined the row of silent animates, hand held over his nose. "No."

"Hm. I think we burn 'em anyway. Move away. Elias, get th' horse out of here." He brought the nozzle from his device up toward the row of creatures standing motionless in their alcoves.

Elias opened the stall. The horse seemed disinclined to move. He

272

slapped its side. It looked at him reproachfully and ambled out of the stable.

"Stand back in case this explodes," Donnie said.

"What? Is that a possibility?" Thaddeus said.

Donnie shrugged. "Prototype. Y'know how it is."

"Wait! How is Lord Rathman going to feel about you setting fire to his stable?" Thaddeus said.

"I'll ask 'im if I see 'im," Donnie said placidly. "Might want t' move back now."

The apprentices took several cautious steps back out of the stable. Thaddeus took more than several steps back, until he was well into the courtyard. Jake watched Donnie curiously. Claire smiled.

The nozzle in Donnie's hand made a dull roaring sound. A geyser of flame gushed forth. A blast of heat, intense as a furnace, poured over Thaddeus.

He didn't know what to expect. A part of him thought the animates might do something—wake up, scream, tear free of their bonds and attack them, anything. The result was anticlimactic. The creatures did nothing at all as the flames consumed them.

Within seconds, the stable was an inferno. Donnie smiled with grim satisfaction. "Let's go find the other animate an' finish this," he said.

"Where do you think it is?"

"Dunno. It's 'ere somewhere. Let's start wi' that tower. If it ain't there, we keep lookin'. If there is anyone here, the fire should keep 'em busy an' out o' our way while we look."

Donnie and Claire led the group away from the burning stables toward the tower. They had not even covered half the distance to the tower's base when, with a loud metallic *chunk*, the courtyard was flooded with the harsh blaze of electric arc lights. Thaddeus froze. The shadows fled, leaving nowhere to hide.

A door opened. A man of medium height in a white smock stepped out onto a balcony just above the tower's gate. "Well, I'll be a son of a ring-tailed lemur," he said. "Donnie Bodger, is that you? I haven't seen you since the Admiral's birthday. And Claire, too! My, my. This is a surprise. Why are you setting fires in Lord Rathman's estate?"

Donnie shielded his eyes and looked up at the figure. "Doctor Franken—"

"Please, call me Victor. We're all friends here. At least I thought we were. Am I mistaken?"

"We're lookin' for a murderous animate. You been buildin' animates that talk, Doctor?" Donnie said.

"I prefer to think of it as building the future," Victor said. "The future is here, Donnie Bodger! The days of clankers are over. Science has moved beyond such crude artifice. You still hammer things out of black iron, while I build with the very stuff of life itself! Isn't it amazing?"

"Amazin' is a word," Donnie said. "Your animate killed one of us."

Victor spread his hands dismissively. "The value of my triumph is independent of the uses to which it is put. You know that. Donnie and Claire, the famous Bodger twins. How many people have your creations killed?"

"Don' matter," Donnie said. His face was placid. "We're 'ere to settle up."

"You came here to destroy one of my creations out of some misguided sense of loyalty? Oh, Donnie, Donnie, Donnie. The world must be a terrible place for someone like you. No. I don't think that is going to happen."

"Ain't askin'," Donnie said.

"My dear fellow. You may have rudely set fire to some of my laborers, but no matter. Did you think it would be so easy to come here and undo what I have created? You have absolutely no idea what I've accomplished here." Victor spread his arms expansively. "Haven't you figured it out yet? You are the past. I am the future. See what I have wrought!"

The gate at the base of the tower opened. A shrill, inhuman scream rent the air. Nightmares poured forth.

✦

The impact was greater than he had expected. The bayonet caught the red-uniformed man mid-chest. The shock of it ran up Roderick's

274

arm. The gun was wrenched from his grasp. The man screamed and fell, spouting blood.

Roderick unfastened his cape and, in one fluid motion, slung it at the next man. It caught him in the face. The man flailed wildly. The bayonet on his rifle connected with Roderick's side. Pain blossomed. He kept going, knocking the thrashing man aside.

He reached the main gate before the soldiers. He opened the hatch next to the gate and pulled savagely on the lever inside it. A hundred tons of counterweight, free of the mechanism that held it in place, started its inevitable descent. Gears ground. Pulleys turned, protesting under the stress. The great iron portcullis began to fall.

High overhead, operated by a cunning arrangement of winches and ropes connected to that same counterweight, the alarm bell began to sound.

Somewhere far behind him, Major Archibald screamed with rage. "Stop that gate! Get him! Now!"

Guns spoke. Stars of pain erupted in Roderick's body. He turned toward the gate, which was still descending, creaking and groaning in its track. Two of the soldiers darted through it, then another, and another. Roderick drew his sword. He staggered, holding on to the wall for support. Another man dove toward the narrowing opening. Roderick lunged. His sword connected with the man's neck. Jets of red decorated the ground.

Another round of thunder came from behind. Something slammed hard into Roderick's back. His legs stopped operating properly. He stumbled sideways and fell.

All around Roderick, running men were cursing and shouting, but they seemed far away, unreal. Someone shoved the lever back into place. The portcullis ground to a halt halfway to the ground. Darkness closed around him, and all was still.

✦

"No! Wait!" Alÿs said. "You're making a huge mistake! It's Rathman! He's behind it all! He—"

"Alÿs de Valois, Eleanor de Revier, I am placing you under arrest on suspicion of high treason and murder," Julianus said. He grabbed Alÿs tightly by the arm. "Your Grace, please return to your quarters. We have reason to believe this woman is involved in multiple murders, including the attack on the Cardinal this evening."

Margaret gave Alÿs a long look. "I thought we were friends," she said.

"We are!" Alÿs said. "You have to listen to me! It's not me, it's Rathman! He—"

Outside and above them, the alarm bell started tolling.

"Take them!" Julianus said to the Guardsman at the door. "Bring them to the cells. Your Grace, get in your quarters and lock the door. Max, come with me. Something—"

All the lights went out.

✦

Most of the things had probably been human once.

They ran on two legs, many of them. Some of the legs were human. Some were large and covered with fur, powerful muscles rippling beneath. A couple of them carried weapons, long curved machetes that glinted in the harsh light. The rest had arms that ended in claws or hooks or slashing blades of bone. One had four arms, the two long ones ending in talons, the shorter ones in sharp, piercing spikes.

And they were fast, so very fast.

"What the f—" Thaddeus said.

"Language," Donnie said. A column of flame poured from the nozzle of his device. The closing swarm of creatures dodged aside, evading the roaring gout of fire easily.

Claire's crossbow twanged. A bolt appeared in the center of the chest of the closest creature. Blue ichor dripped from the wound. The creature ignored the wound, closing the distance in great bounds of its legs, claws spread wide.

The animates crashed through the group. People screamed. Thaddeus twisted aside, narrowly evading a slashing claw. Behind him, one of the apprentices, a boy barely fourteen years old, cried out in anguish and died, a ragged hole in his chest.

Tongues of flame licked out. One of the animates went up like a torch. It continued on in the direction it had been heading, colliding heavily with the apprentice who had ignited it. The apprentice spun out of the way, frantically stripping off the heavy tank and his smoldering clothes.

Jake's club whistled through the air. It connected with the head of a creature whose disturbingly human eyes looked out from over a large pair of grasping mandibles. It chittered and slashed at him. He twisted away.

"We can't stay here!" Jake said. "They'll tear us up."

"Back against the wall," Claire said. "We need to keep them from coming at us from all directions."

The small group broke out in a run. The animates circled around behind them, slashing and clawing. Another apprentice went down with a cry. Donnie spun around. Flame erupted. The animates scattered.

The apprentices formed up, turning to face backward. More hungry flame licked out, hungering for a target. The animates hesitated, wary.

"I don't like this," Claire said. "They're smart."

The group edged back toward the stone wall surrounding the estate, cautious. The animates followed, staying just out of reach of the fire throwers. The fire had spread through most of the stable. Thaddeus could feel its heat.

"Now what?" he said.

"One problem at a time," Donnie said. The device on his back roared. Flame jetted.

Claire's crossbow thwanged again. A human-looking animate with quills all over its body looked down at its chest where the bolt had appeared in a splotch of blue ichor. It pulled the bolt out, then looked at Claire and smiled. Its teeth were pointed like a shark's.

"What do we do now?" Thaddeus said.

"We kin only 'old 'em off 'til we run outta fuel," Donnie said. "Best make fer the gate before that 'appens. We need t' run. "

The animates, on some unspoken signal, pulled back. They fanned out in a loose semicircle around the small group of people.

"That's weird," Jake said.

There was a dull rumble from above. Thaddeus looked up.

The thing might have been an alligator, once, in some distant past. It had a long, scaled body and a triangular tail. But alligators don't ordinarily have wide, leather wings, like the wings of a bat, if perhaps that bat were the size of a horse.

It circled once, pinned in the glow of the arc lamps, then folded its wings and dove, front claws outstretched. It had a belt of some sort fastened around its body, ringed with small round protrusions…

The claws opened. A small round object fell. There was a crack, like a mug shattering. A ball of fire spread up from the ground, engulfing an apprentice and his bulky fire thrower. For a second, his eyes locked with Thaddeus's.

Then he was gone, somewhere behind a pillar of flame. Thaddeus heard screaming. The pillar jerked and was still.

"Back t' the stables!" Donnie called. "We 'ave t' get under cover."

"But the stables are on fire!" Thaddeus said.

"You got a better idea?"

The creature rose, soaring in the rainy air, front legs scrabbling at the belt around its waist. A second, nearly identical creature lifted off from within the tower, wings beating fast as it climbed rapidly to join its fellow.

✦

Julianus felt his way along the wall to the nearest gas lamp and pressed the button. The igniter popped. The lamp glowed. Glints of light danced on the gold leaf that decorated the ceiling. "Your majesty, are you alright?" he said.

"Yes, we are." There was a steely tone in Margaret's voice. "What is happening?"

Gunfire sounded, somewhere below and far away.

"Your Majesty, please go into your quarters and bar the door," Julianus said.

"No!" Alÿs said. "There are too many of them! There's an entire army down there!"

"How do you know that?" Max's voice had an edge.

"Because an army left Rathman's estate earlier this evening."

"Lord Rathman?" Margaret said. "Nonsense. He has always supported us."

"He doesn't!" Alÿs cried. "He means to do something terrible! Your Grace, we have to get you out of here. It's not safe. They are too many." She tugged at the hand on her arm.

"Is that your idea, my lady?" Julian said. "To draw her out of the Palace, where there are fewer guards to protect her?"

"No!" Alÿs said. She stamped her foot impatiently. "Your Grace... Margaret! It's me! You know me! Please, we have to get you out of here!"

The booms of gunfire sounded again, closer this time.

"We are friends!" Alÿs said. "When I came here, I was alone and frightened, and you were kind to me. You've known Eleanor your whole life. You know neither one of us is a traitor. Why would we turn against you? Please, we're running out of time. They will be here soon. I don't know what they mean to do, but I know you're in terrible trouble. Margaret, it's me! We need to run! Please!"

Margaret looked back and forth between Alÿs and Julianus. She made a decision. "Very well. We will go. Release Alÿs and Eleanor. Max, Julianus, you will come with us. You," she said, pointing at Percival, "find my brother. And you," she said to Rudolf, "stay here and cover our escape."

"Begging your pardon, Your Grace, but this is a terrible idea," Max said. "If you mean to go with the Lady Alÿs, let me find your brother."

"No," Margaret said. "You are the captain of the Queen's Guard, and you will accompany us, in the event that Alÿs is a traitor."

"Your Grace," Julianus said, "I don't think that's—"

"We have made our decision," Margaret said.

In the great courtyard, a large group of soldiers in the red livery of Rathman's levy had taken up positions in rows along the walls, rifles at the ready. In front of the gate stood a small triangle of mounted soldiers, alert and wary. Lord Rathman had assured them they would encounter no resistance from the regular military, though he had been vague on details. In principle, the whole affair would be concluded within the hour, and the sun would rise tomorrow on a new Britain.

But one thing any veteran of any military service knows is that the only thing you can rely on is you can't rely on anything. So they waited, attentive, ready to defend their compatriots inside the Palace. They were sowing the seeds of a brave new world, and sometimes, the seeds of a brave new world required liberal watering with blood. The men in the courtyard were determined that should that eventuality arise, the blood would belong to someone else.

In the Palace, the Queen's Guard had had little time to react. The alarm bell was unfortunate, but Lord Rathman had thought to kill the electricity to the Palace, plunging much of it into darkness. His men carried lanterns. The gas jets required manual intervention to ignite, exactly the sort of oversight common among those who try to plan for contingencies they don't really believe will happen.

The attackers had a considerable advantage, alarm bell be damned. The guards in the guardhouse had had time to grab their rifles, but after a short exchange, they had been overrun. Now it was down to hall-by-hall fighting. The defenders were disorganized, sleepy, and uncoordinated. They had set up hasty barricades and were blocking off access to the upper quarters of the Palace, but the attackers held numerical superiority and better organization. It was, at this point, merely a matter of time.

One group of attackers formed a column, headed for the wide, sweeping stairway that would take them to the living quarters above. As those in the front of the column fell to gunfire, those behind returned fire, their rifles roaring in the enclosed space. They gave the defenders no time to reload, closing quickly with sword and bayonet, swarming over the improvised barricades, slashing and stabbing. Blood flowed, creating a slick glaze on expensive marble, soaking into exotic foreign rugs brought at great expense from the lands of the Ottomans.

The column moved relentlessly, stepping over the bodies of fallen defenders and, sometimes, its own, but relentlessly nonetheless.

The Duke opened his eyes, blinking. There were loud noises coming from outside his door, and screams. He turned on the gas lamp near his bed.

The sounds outside were loud, and frightening. He curled up, clutching his blanket. Somewhere outside his door, he heard screams. There was a loud thump, then silence.

He stayed in his bed for a long minute. The silence was almost more frightening than the screams had been.

Eventually, he rose and padded in his nightshirt to the door. He pressed his ear against it.

Nothing.

He turned the knob and crept cautiously into the hallway. It was dim, with just a single solitary gas lamp flickering uncertainly in its lamp-house on the wall. The hall was empty.

He walked down the hallway and turned the corner. There were many men there, lying on the ground in awkward positions. The floor was covered with something sticky that clung to his bare feet. He put his hand over his mouth, recoiling in horror.

There were men carrying lanterns a little way down the hall, and all were wearing the uniforms of his uncle. Relief poured through him. "Hello!" he said. "Over here! Help!"

Two of the men turned toward him. He recognized one of them from days he had spent at his uncle's manor house out in the country. He smiled with relief. "Edmund! What's happening?"

"It's the Duke! There he is!" Edmund said. He raised his rifle.

There was a bright flash and a sound that hurt the Duke's ears. He felt something hit him very hard. He blinked. The floor seemed a very long way away. It came closer, floating up to meet him. The world went black before it reached him.

✦

Claire brought the crossbow up and fired. The bolt caught the thing in the neck. It twisted, hissing angrily, and fell toward them. Donnie swung the nozzle of his fire thrower toward it. Flames leaped out to catch the falling monster. They met. There was a dazzling flash and a loud bang, so deep it was felt rather than heard. The creature crashed to the ground in a flaming wreckage of once-almost-living flesh, scattering the small group of people huddled against the wall.

"We 'ave t' get under cover," Donnie said. "Move! Now!"

They moved as a group toward the stables, clustered in a tight knot. Long tongues of fire sprouted in all directions, warning the twisted creatures on the ground to keep their distance.

Half of the stable was completely consumed by flames. Thick black smoke poured into the night sky. The far end had already collapsed, thick wooden beams glowing with heat. Fire danced atop them. A couple of the apprentices, unequipped with the fire-spouting machines, grabbed burning sticks from the rubble, waving them in front of them. The creatures around them seemed unwilling to press closely, either because they'd seen what happened to their companions caught by the fire throwers or from some vestigial, instinctual fear of flames.

Not that they needed to. Time was on their side, and they appeared intelligent enough to know it.

Thaddeus felt the heat close around him. He pressed back as far as he could beneath the overhanging roof. Outside, something crashed to the ground and blossomed into flames. He heard Claire's crossbow thwang again.

"We can't stay here," Thaddeus said.

"Nope," Donnie agreed.

"When the stable burns down, those flying things will kill us."

"Yep."

"And as soon as the fire-shooters quit working, those monsters will tear us to pieces."

"Yep."

"So we're all going to die!"

"Looks like," Donnie said.

"That it? No plan to rescue us all? No clever idea to get us out of here?"

"Nope," Donnie said. "Look out!" A section of the ceiling collapsed to the ground, trailing smoke.

"What do we do?"

"Keep fightin' 'til we can't," Donnie said.

"Thaddeus Mudstone!" The call came from outside the burning stable. "Thaddeus Mudstone!"

Thaddeus shook his head and peered out into the courtyard.

"Thaddeus Mudstone! I know you! I see you! You killed me, Thaddeus Mudstone!"

It was there, standing just outside the range of the fire throwers, a creature that... Thaddeus wiped sweat from his eyes.

It wore a face he recognized, a face that belonged to a man who had tried to kill him, a man who had burst into his flat carrying a heavy mace, only to fall through the steps during Thaddeus's mad climb to safety.

"I know you! I know who you are!" the thing said. "You killed me!"

"You should have stayed dead!" Thaddeus shouted.

"You killed me!" it repeated. It held up its arms, and they were not arms, but two long, curved lengths of bone that ended in wicked points. Something oily dripped from those needle-sharp points.

"You killed me, Thaddeus Mudstone! Now I am going to kill you!"

It screamed an inhuman scream of pure hate and sprang on powerful legs that were not even remotely human, and it was fast, oh so fast. Flames leaped out to meet it, passing through the empty space where it had been. Thaddeus lifted the heavy rifle he carried. He sighted along the barrel and pulled the trigger. A cloud of smoke burned his eyes. An elephant hit him in the shoulder, knocking him back. The rifle fell. A hole opened in the creature's chest. Blue goop poured out. The creature's face twisted with rage. It scrambled to its feet and leaped again.

Thaddeus felt it collide with him. It stank. Its skin was dry and hot. The arms closed. Twin points of agony flared in Thaddeus's sides where those evil points dug in. He felt something pour into him, burning like hot acid. His legs stopped moving. His vision narrowed.

"How does it feel, Thaddeus Mudstone?" the creature said. "How does it feel to know you are dying?" It leaned close until its face was almost touching Thaddeus's. "You did this to me."

Then Jake was there, his club rising and falling over and over until it was covered with blue gunk. The creature stiffened and slid off Thaddeus. Jake's face filled Thaddeus's vision. "Muddy!" he said. His voice sounded far away. "Muddy, can you hear me?"

The world faded.

✦

"Where are you taking her?" Julianus said. Suspicion and anger battled each other for control of his face.

"Down the hallway and left. There's a servants' stairway. It leads into the laundry. On the other side is a hallway that goes all the way through the Palace. There's an ale storehouse and a side entrance that goes out to Bosington Street. Nobody uses it much."

Another gunshot came from the end of the hall.

"Very well," Julianus said. "Move!"

Julianus and Rudolf dragged a large, heavy table, edged in gold, from the Queen's chamber into the hallway. They flipped it on its side, blocking the hallway. Rudolf crouched behind it, propping his rifle over the edge. Julianus extinguished the gas lamp. Gloom descended.

Max led the way away from the sound of approaching gunfire, with Alÿs behind him, then Eleanor, then the Queen. Julianus took up the rear.

They moved in a tight group, keeping low. The hallway was dim, the light uncertain. Alÿs had passed this way countless times before, but tonight, it felt like she was moving through alien, hostile terrain. The lone working gas lamp hissed and sputtered, sending shadows slinking down the walls. Alÿs found herself wishing Thaddeus were there. This seemed like the sort of situation his talents were uniquely suited for. What would he do, if he were here?

Run, most probably. She hadn't known the life of a commoner involved so much running.

Max paused at the corner, where the hallway intersected with another that led toward Eleanor's bedroom and the quarters where Alÿs had, until two fateful days ago, lived. He paused for a moment, darting a quick glance around the corner, then waved them forward.

Heart beating fast, Alÿs followed him. Shadows lay heavily on every wall and in every corner. Light spilled into the end of the hallway from around the corner. "The servants' stairway is at the very end," Alÿs said. "Doorway on the right, just before it turns 'round the bend."

Max held out his hand, gesturing for the others to remain where they were. "I don't like this," he said. "Who lit the gas lamps around there?" He crept forward cautiously, his gun ready.

Shouts echoed up the hallway behind them. A gun roared, setting their ears ringing.

"We need to move now," Julianus hissed. "It won't take them long to realize Her Grace is not in her quarters."

They raced down the darkened hallway, keeping low and quiet. More gunfire boomed up the hall behind them. There was a scream, abruptly cut off.

"Something's wrong," Julianus said. "We should be hearing fighting outside. The regular army should have responded by now."

"I don't think the cavalry's coming to rescue us," Alÿs said.

"Well, then," Margaret said, "we will rescue ourselves."

"It would be easier if the Palace weren't so big," Eleanor said.

"It would be easier for them to find us too," Julianus said.

Max stopped, so suddenly that Alÿs nearly ran into him.

"What's—" she said. Max put his fingers over his lips, a dark shadow in the dim light.

"People ahead," he said quietly. "I hear them."

"How many?" Julianus said.

"Hard to say." He crouched on the floor and laid his rifle down quietly. He took off his cloak. "Give me your breastplate."

"Why?" Julianus said, already unfastening the straps.

Max wadded up his cloak, placed it over his breastplate, and strapped Julianus's over his chest atop it. "Did I ever tell you," he said, "how I was promoted to captain of the guard?"

"You said you saved the Duke from drowning in the lake."

"I did," Max said. "I just left out the assassins. Three of them. Italian sympathizers. They were waiting for us on Queensbury Lane." He picked up his rifle. "They tried to run him through with a sword. I knocked him in the water and killed 'em all. Her Grace felt that advertising the fact that the Italians came so close to succeeding would only embolden the rest of them, so we never talked about it."

"I had no idea," Julianus said.

"Get the Queen out of here," Max said. "Make sure she's safe."

"What are—"

Max was already gone, fast and, for such a large man, eerily silent. He was silhouetted briefly in the light that shone from around the corner. His gun roared. He drew his sword and disappeared.

Answering gunfire boomed around the corner. Eleanor crouched in the hallway with her arms over her head, sobbing. Margaret touched her shoulder. "It will be okay," she said. She squeezed Eleanor's hand. "It's almost over. Just a little way left to go. You can do this."

There was a scream that ended in a hideous gurgle. Another gun spoke. A shower of plaster rained from the ceiling ahead of them. There was a scream, followed by a metallic crash.

"Stay here," Julianus said. "If you see or hear anyone coming up behind you, make for the servants' stairway as fast as you can. Alÿs, you know the way."

"Wait!" Alÿs said. "We can't—"

Julianus was already halfway down the hall.

He stopped just before the corner, back to the wall, and risked a quick look around. Then he waved frantically, gesturing them forward.

Alÿs ran toward him. Margaret followed behind, leading Eleanor by the hand.

Julianus held out his arm. "Don't—" he began. Alÿs evaded him easily and ran around the corner.

Max was lying on his back in a tangle of red-uniformed bodies. His sword was in his hand. Blood pooled on the floor and decorated the walls in long wet streaks. His rifle lay beneath him, the bayonet on the end covered with—

Alÿs looked away.

Max coughed. His breastplate—both breastplates—were dented and perforated. "Go!" he whispered.

"Hang on," Julianus said. "We'll get—"

"Go!" he said again. His voice was a scratchy rattle.

"I'm not leaving—"

"Go!" He coughed. His eyes filmed over.

Julianus's face hardened. "Let's move," he said. "Alÿs, you first."

A groan came from beneath the pile of bodies.

Julianus reached down. His hand came up gripping the arm of a boy of perhaps seventeen. His face was battered, his uniform torn.

Julianus dragged the boy to his feet, twisting his arm behind his back. "Move!" he hissed.

Alÿs opened the door to the servants' stairway quietly. She darted a look down, then slipped through. Margaret and Eleanor followed. Julianus dragged the dazed soldier through and closed the door soundlessly behind him. "What's down there?" he said.

"The laundry," Alÿs said. "A hallway to the servants' quarters. Storerooms. There's another hallway that goes all the way to the alehouse."

"Move."

Looked at from above, with the roof peeled off, the Palace was in many ways two entirely different buildings that shared the same space. There were ballrooms and grand dining halls and opulent living quarters appointed with luxuries from every corner of the globe, all connected by wide hallways with marble floors, just as you might expect from the domicile of the wealthy ruling class.

But there were also storerooms and laundry rooms and boilers and passageways through which food, supplies, and coal were carried, and the small, cramped spaces in which the servants lived, often two or three to a bed.

These two places coexisted in the same space but rarely touched each other, separated as they were by the architect's arts. There were few places where these two entirely different buildings opened directly into each other. It is a truth understood by the best architects that the more your existence depends on other people, the less you want to see of them.

The laundry room was one of those few portals between the two worlds.

The portions of the Palace reserved for the servant classes were lit by gas lamps and oil, rather than the newfangled, expensive electric lights. This second Palace, the one inhabited by the working class, was still brightly lit.

The servants' palace was also a great deal more porous than the palace of the aristocrats. Servants rarely need to make Grand Entrances, after all. They do, however, have to contend with moving food and drink and cloth and bricks and all the other thousand essentials necessary to support other people in a life of luxury in and out, so there were far more doorways from the outside world into the servants' palace than into the aristocrats' palace. That made it far easier for the servants to escape, even as those above them in the accidental social hierarchy imposed by birth were trapped in their chambers.

The people who labored in the laundry had long since fled, abandoning great piles of clothing in enormous tubs of hot water. Rows of coal-fired stoves still glowed with heat, driving steam from the just-washed laundry drying on wooden racks in front of them. The air hit the tiny band in the faces as they descended, hot and humid as a tropical jungle.

Alÿs led the way down the steps. Julianus half-led, half-dragged the soldier, eyes wide with terror, after her. When they reached the bottom, he shoved the man down onto his knees. "What's your name?" he growled.

"Bertie, sir. Bertie Meaker."

"What are you doing here, Bertie Meaker?"

Bertie looked down, lips pressed tightly together.

"I asked you a question," Julianus said.

Bertie shook his head. "I can't tell you. He'll kill me!"

"Who? Lord Rathman?"

Bertie remained silent.

"Is he here in the Palace right now?"

The silence continued.

"Is he in this room right now, with a sword in his hand, talking to you?"

"No," Bertie said.

"I am," Julianus said. "And I am becoming impatient. Whatever you imagine Rathman might do to you if you talk to me, believe me, it is nothing compared to what I will do with this sword, right now, if you do not."

"I can't!"

"I suppose you are of no further use to me, then," Julianus said. "Bertie Meaker, for the crime of taking up arms against the Crown, and by the authority vested in me by Her Majesty the Queen, I hereby sentence you to death for treason." He raised his sword.

"Wait!" Bertie cried. "It was orders, sir! Direct from his lordship the Earl. He says…" He darted an anxious look at Margaret. "He says the Queen is corrupt. He says she is betraying the Realm. It's the Turks, sir! It's bad enough that she allows all the Jews and Mohammedans in our land, but now she wants to marry a Turk!" He clamped a hand over his mouth, red-faced.

"What were your orders?"

"We were told to take the Palace, sir. We were told to find the Queen and the Duke and…"

"And what?"

"And kill them."

"Did you think you would be able to just run through the Palace, just like that?"

"He said the Queen's Guard would not be ready, sir. It's late. They would not have time to react. And there are those among the Guard who believe as we do, sir. They pledged to help us."

"What about the army?"

"He said…" Bertie glanced up into Julianus's face and looked down again. "He said the army wouldn't be a problem. He said he had made an…arrangement. And he said the Pontifical Swiss Guard would not get involved either. He made sure of that."

"How?"

"I don't know, sir."

"What were you supposed to do when you had killed Her Grace and the Duke?"

"We were told to flash a light out the windows, sir. Two from the Duke's window. Three from the Queen's. And then listen for trumpets, sir. When we hear trumpets, we are to withdraw to the courtyard."

"Why?"

"I don't know, sir."

Margaret rose, her face white, hands clenched tightly into fists. "Is my brother still alive?"

"I don't know, Your Grace!" Bertie said. "Please, you have to believe me, I don't know anything else!"

Julianus looked down at him for a long moment. "I believe you," he said finally. "Thank you, Bertie Meaker. You have been very helpful. The sentence stands."

He lifted his sword and, in one quick motion, shoved it through Bertie's neck. The boy's eyes widened in surprise. His lips moved. A wet bubbling came out. He slumped to the floor, still gurgling.

Eleanor cried out in horror, her hands over her face. Margaret nodded curtly. "We must send that signal. We have to make them believe the Duke and I are dead."

"Your Grace, I don't think that's a good idea," Julianus said.

"They are killing us!" Margaret said. "Go upstairs. Find a lantern. Send the signal. Then find my brother."

"Your Grace—"

"That is not a request, Guardsman. You are a member of the Queen's Guard, are you not? We have given you a command."

Julianus nodded. "Yes, Your Grace. What will you do?"

"Your clothes," Alÿs said. "We need to get you out of your clothes."

"What?" Margaret said.

Alÿs waved her arm. "Look around, Your Grace. There must be servants' clothes that will fit you. Eleanor, you too. If we dress as servants and go out the servants' entrance, we have a better chance of getting away."

Margaret looked Alÿs up and down, examining her own blacksmith's outfit. "Very well," she said. "Eleanor, Alÿs, find us some clothes." She gestured. "What's through that door over there?"

"Boiler room for hot water," Alÿs said.

"We will change there. Alÿs, you will assist us."

Julianus sheathed his sword. He picked up his gun. "Where will we meet?"

"Hammersmith Street," Alÿs said. "There's a place called Bodger & Bodger Iron Fittings."

"I know it," Julianus said. "I'm a little curious how *you* know it."

"It's a long story," Alÿs said.

Julianus regarded her. "When this is all over," he said, "you and I will have a conversation about that." He turned to Margaret, bowing deeply. "Godspeed to you, Your Grace. We will meet again soon."

27

Commander Skarbunket picked up a milk bottle and turned it over in his hands, admiring its deadly efficiency. It was filled with a coarse black powder. The neck was stopped with a bit of rag. "Somebody was up to no good," he said. "Curious. I'd really like to know who it was. Does anyone have a tinderbox, or perhaps some matches?"

"No, sir," Mayferry said, "and might I add, sir, I find your question a bit alarming, given the present circumstances."

"Hm," Skarbunket said. "It would be a shame to ride heroically into battle with a carriage full of black-powder bombs and no means to ignite them. It does take away a bit from the dramatic flair, don't you think, Mister Mayferry?"

"Um, sir?" Bristol said. He'd been looking out the window for most of the trip, lost in thought.

"Yes? Something to add, Mister Bristol?"

"I don't think lack of matches will be a problem, sir."

Skarbunket leaned over and peered out the window. A flickering glow lay ahead and to one side of them, reflecting against the low-lying clouds.

"Looks like someone's got quite a fire going over yonder."

"Indeed, sir."

"I can't help but notice, Mister Bristol, that the source of that rather lovely glow seems to lie in roughly the direction of our destination."

"Indeed it does, sir."

"Would you say, Mister Bristol, in your professional opinion, would you say that it seems probable that Lord Rathman's estate is on fire?"

"In my professional opinion, that does seem likely, sir."

"Ah." Skarbunket rapped on the top of the carriage with his truncheon. "Mister Tumbanker, a bit more alacrity, if you please! We don't want to be late for the festivities."

"Sir," came a voice through the ceiling, "need I remind you that the carriage is full of explosives?"

"A fact I cannot help being cognizant of, Mister Tumbanker. Still, the situation is urgent. Drive faster carefully!"

The carriage picked up speed. Skarbunket set his bottle down. "You look like a man having deep thoughts, Mister Mayferry," he observed.

"I'm wishing we had firearms, sir," Mayferry said.

"A man with a gun is incautious, Mister Mayferry."

"A man in a carriage full of black-powder bombs is incautious, sir."

"You make a wise point."

The carriage slowed to a halt. "Gate's open, sir. Do I just drive right through?"

"Good Lord, Mister Tumbanker, are you waiting for the Earl to extend an invitation? If there's a fire, that gives us cause to investigate. Go!"

The carriage moved forward and stopped again. "Oh my G—" Tumbanker said.

There was a crash. Something heavy landed on the roof. The carriage shook.

Skarbunket tried to open the door.

✦

Julianus opened the door at the top of the stairs. The hallway was deserted save for the tangle of bodies. He knelt beside Max for a moment, crossing himself, then closed the man's eyes. He picked up an oil lamp that had fallen beside the body of a boy who looked no more than fourteen. The lens was cracked, but the tank was still half full. He pulled the striker lever. A small point of flame flared to life.

He encountered no resistance until he reached the corner that led toward the Queen's chambers. There were voices in the hallway. A quick look revealed a group of red-coated soldiers going from room to room, kicking open each door. They had dragged several women out of their bedrooms, still dressed in their nightclothes. The women were huddled together on the floor in the center of the hallway. Two men with rifles stood over them. He saw none of the lords who made their residence in the Palace.

Julianus withdrew around the corner, thoughts churning furiously. There was a door next to him, edged in blue and gold. He turned the knob. It opened. He slipped inside.

It was a dressing room, furnished with richly upholstered chairs, a table with a long mirror, and, in a row in the back, stalls for sleek modern water closets in white and green porcelain.

He pressed his ear to the door. He heard voices, coming closer.

He dragged the table with its mirror across from the door. Then he set his stolen lantern on the ground, facing toward it. He extinguished the gas lamp in the dressing room.

When he was satisfied, he thumped on the wall. "Help me!" he called. "What is going on out there? Help me at once!"

The voices came closer. He stood against the wall next to the door and held his breath.

The knob turned. The door opened. Two men wielding guns burst in. They raised their weapons toward their reflections. "Do not move!" one of them barked.

Julianus's sword flashed, once, twice. Blood splattered the walls. The men buckled and folded gracelessly in a tangle of arms and legs.

Julianus stepped around them. Both of the men were too preoccupied with dying to react. He risked a peek down the hall.

Still too many.

He closed the door quietly and relit the gas light. One of the men looked up at him, hand on his throat. Julianus ignored him.

He turned to the other man, the one whose soul was already flitting toward its final reward. He unbuttoned the man's jacket and stripped it off. By the time he was pulling the dead man's trousers off, his compatriot was likewise winging his way to the hereafter.

Julianus rose, dressed now in the uniform of the intruders. He picked up the dead man's rifle. He adjusted the dead man's hat, then stepped out into the hallway.

He straightened, took a deep breath, then ran around the corner toward the cluster of Rathman's soldiers, waving his arms urgently over his head. "Oi! This way!" he shouted. "Over here! The Queen! This way!"

✦

Alÿs led Eleanor and Margaret, now dressed rather frumpily in clothing that had been patched to the point where it seemed it was more patches than original, down the hallway toward the storeroom. She had, much to Eleanor's dismay, chosen the most nondescript, most shabby clothes the laundry had on offer. Eleanor had complained about that. She had complained about how the clothing fit. She had complained about it bunching up between her legs, about how the fabric felt on her skin, and especially about the rag Alÿs tied over her hair. Finally, Alÿs had had enough. She took Eleanor by the hand and led her to where Bertie Meaker's lifeless remains still stared up at the ceiling. "Do you want to end up like him?" Alÿs said. "Because that's what the soldiers will do to you if they know who you are."

Eleanor, face white, had not uttered another peep.

The hallway was narrow and floored with heavy timbers, stained and rough from long use. Gas jets hissed quietly along the stone walls. In stark contrast to the rest of the Palace, there was not so much as a single fleck of gold to be seen.

They still heard occasional muffled gunfire from somewhere a very long way away. The distance didn't reassure Alÿs much.

The hallway ended in a massive wooden door, as wide as the entire hall. "That's the storeroom," Alÿs said. "Stay here."

She put her shoulder to the door and pushed. It groaned open. On the other side were rows and rows of great wooden casks, stacked in heavy brackets of solid timber that reached from floor to ceiling.

Alÿs beckoned. The other two women followed her into the room.

She crept cautiously through the narrow aisles, each only barely wide enough for the barrels. "That's the door up—"

"Who's that now? Come out here or I will shoot you!"

Alÿs felt her blood freeze. She peeked around the last row of barrels.

A soldier stood in front of the door, eyes alert, holding his rifle in both hands. "I see you there!" he said. "I won't say it again! Come out or I will shoot you!"

Eleanor shoved her knuckles in her mouth, her eyes wide as saucers. Margaret jerked her head urgently back the way they had come. Alÿs shook her head.

She reached into the borrowed blacksmith's shirt she wore and touched her handbag. A thought formed in her head.

"It's only me, mister!" she said. "There's no need o' shooting anybody!" She came around the corner. "Who are you, mister?"

The soldier looked at her. "Move away from the barrels."

"D'you have a shilling, mister?" Alÿs said, moving toward him.

"A what?"

"A shilling. D'you have a shilling, mister? Please?" Alÿs held out her hand. "I'm ver' hungry, mister. D'you have a shilling?"

"No!" he said. "I do not have a shilling. Stop right there! I—hgk!"

Alÿs was surprised at how easily the dagger entered his chest. He was taller than she was. She stabbed upward, from under his ribs. The blade sunk deep. Something hot and wet poured down over her hand. His body shook. He looked at her, face frozen in an expression of surprise and horror. His lips moved soundlessly. He twitched. Life fled his body.

A moment later they were outside, running fast, keeping to the shadows of the Palace wall until they reached the street behind the great stone building. Alÿs's fingers were curled so tightly around the dagger that her hand hurt. She ran, Margaret and Eleanor beside her, until she could not run anymore.

Then the tears came, a great ocean of them, and she was convulsing with sobs that left her gasping for breath, and Margaret's arms were all that kept her from falling.

✦

From the pandemonium Julianus had unleashed, a casual observer might be mistaken for believing he had just tossed an angry wolverine into a chicken coop. "Show us!" a soldier with the fringes of an ensign on his shoulder demanded.

"This way! Down here!" Julianus said, voice urgent. "Quickly!"

"You men! After him!" the ensign said.

Julianus ran down the hall at breakneck speed. He turned the corner before any of the other soldiers had caught up to him. "She's here! Look out!" he cried. He opened the first door he came to and darted inside, closing it quietly behind him.

Soldiers raced by. Many of them stopped when they encountered the bodies of Max and their brothers. "Watch out!" someone called. "The Queen's Guard is here!"

The soldiers slowed, raising their guns to their shoulders, made cautious by the warning. Julianus held his breath as he waited for them to pass.

When they had gone, he quietly opened the door and moved quietly back down the hall toward Margaret's quarters, sword in hand.

The ensign was still there, watching over the group of women. Behind him, the overturned table lay where it had fallen. Percy slumped behind it, eyes wide and unseeing.

Julianus snapped to attention. "I have news, sir!"

"Well, soldier? Did you find her?"

"Not exactly, sir. Look at this!" He held up the sword. "I think this belongs to one of the Queen's Guard, sir!"

"And? So what?"

"I think he's still holding it, sir!" Julianus thrust the sword through the man's chest. His eyes bugged. He sank slowly to the floor like a collapsing zeppelin.

One of the women shrieked. She was tall, of operatic build, the wife of Lord Pottsmatter, second cousin of the Duke of Barnstaple. The shriek built rapidly in volume and tenor, encompassing the entire litany of horrors of the evening, beginning with her being dragged out of her bed in her nightclothes and ending with the murder of a man right before her eyes.

Julianus put his finger to his lips. "My lady, all of you. I am Julianus, of the Queen's Guard. Find a place to hide. Wait until you hear trumpets in the courtyard. When you hear them, the soldiers should withdraw. Until then, stay out of sight." He looked around. "Blast. I've forgotten the lamp. Do any of you have an oil lamp?"

The shriek cut off. The Lady Pottsmatter's eyes remained wide, and her expression suggested she was open to the possibility of carrying on shrieking at the slightest provocation. She shook her head.

"Move now. Go!"

Julianus opened the door to the Queen's quarters. There was a soldier in her sitting chair, going through her drawers, stuffing their contents into his pockets. He had, Julianus was relieved to see, a lamp at his feet.

He looked up as Julianus entered.

"May I use your lamp?" Julianus said.

"Why? And what was that dreadful screaming?"

"The screaming? Oh, that. Some lady somebody. She saw something she didn't like. You know how women are." He bent over to pick up the lantern.

"What did she see?"

"She saw me do this." Julianus straightened and, with a flick of his wrist, impaled the man on his sword. There was a ghastly burbling sound that ended with an abrupt finality.

That left one task to do.

He opened the shutters and held up the lantern. One. Two. Three.

Outside, a trumpet began to blow.

The carriage door opened halfway. Something outside slammed it shut again, sending Commander Skarbunket careening across the small space inside. Then it wasn't so much opened as entirely ripped off its hinges. Then a *thing* tried to scramble in. Skarbunket noted, in some small corner of his mind, that it looked like something from one of those medieval paintings designed to warn men away from the path of wickedness. It was horned, and its mouth was entirely too wide and filled with entirely too many teeth. The thing's face was quilted with scars.

It reached a black-taloned hand toward him. Mayferry's truncheon came down hard on its head. It shrieked, claws slashing. The truncheon rose and fell again. Blue gunk splattered across Skarbunket's uniform. The third time it struck, the creature jerked and stopped moving.

"Thank you, Mister Mayferry," Skarbunket said.

"My pleasure, sir. What have we got into here?"

"I don't know. Better grab a bomb. Wait, on second thought, grab several."

They stepped out of the carriage into chaos. They had stopped about thirty yards from the burning stable, of which little was now left. There was a group of people huddled together in the remains of the stable, though it seemed clear they would soon inevitably be forced out into the open, where all the denizens of Dante's *Inferno* appeared to be having a class reunion.

"Mister Mayferry," he heard himself say, "where are Mister Levy and Mister Tumbanker?"

"We're under here," came a voice from beneath the carriage. "I think Tumbanker's hurt."

"Ah, good, good," Skarbunket said. He felt like he was looking at himself from a long way away. Things were happening around him, remote and unreal.

There was a low, guttural noise from overhead, and the flapping of great bat wings. Something heavy struck the top of the carriage and shattered. The driver's chair burst into flame.

"Thank you," Skarbunket said. "That was most handy." He held the rag on one of the bottles up to the flame, admiring the way the fire leaped and danced along the scrap of cloth. Then he threw.

A host of things from the darkest nightmares turned their faces, or in some cases what they had that passed for faces, toward him. There was a blinding flash of light. The crude bomb exploded.

It was far more effective than he had expected it to be.

Creatures screamed as they were torn to pieces. Thick blue glop splattered the side of the burning carriage.

"Nice throw, sir," Mayferry said. He hurled a makeshift bomb of his own.

The creatures screeched and fled, running away from the carriage toward the stable. Enormous gouts of flame jumped out to welcome them. The ones that hesitated took the full force of the blast, jagged bits of glass tearing withered flesh from anatomically improbable bone. The ones that didn't, burned.

Skarbunket threw another bomb, and, just for good measure, another after that. Creatures burned, exploded, and died, if "died" was the right term to apply to something that perhaps wasn't quite alive in the first place, technically speaking.

The great scaly bat-winged thing overhead circled and swooped. Fire bloomed on what little was left of the roof of the stable. One of the small cluster of people raised a gun and fired. The force of the recoil knocked him off his feet.

A hole opened up in the flying thing's side. It flapped, trying to gain altitude, but Skarbunket could see it was in trouble. The wing on that side had stopped working properly. Unable to steer, unable to remain airborne, it twisted in the air and fell, crashing into the roof where it had dropped its firebomb. There was a crackling sound and a dull whoosh as it was consumed by flames.

The roof of the stable groaned and collapsed. The group of people huddled beneath it ran out into the courtyard. Skarbunket recognized Claire and Donnie Bodger immediately. Claire and a man Skarbunket didn't recognize were dragging the inert form of a man, wounded or dead, behind them. Skarbunket needed no introduction to know the type: a ruffian, a common criminal who preyed largely on fellow commoners in a rude, mean mimicry of the acquisitional urge of the aristocracy.

"Good evenin', officer," Donnie said. "Nice to 'ave you 'ere."

"Glad to be here," Skarbunket said. He gestured to the limp form. "If it isn't Thaddeus Mudstone Ahmed Alexander Pinkerton. Can't say I'm surprised. Is he alive?"

"Only just," Claire said. "I think he's been poisoned. We have to try to draw the poison out."

Levy crawled out from beneath the wreckage of the carriage. "I think we better move, sir," he said. "I'm sure I don't need to remind you of the explosives and all. I hate to sound urgent, but—"

"Right," Skarbunket said. "Grab Mister Tumbanker's other hand, if you please. The rest of you, I have many questions for you, but this carriage is about to make a disturbing noise and I think it best we get to some remove."

They scrambled away from the stricken carriage as fast as they were able. They had just reached the fountain in the courtyard when the explosives went.

It was everything any of them could have hoped for, only louder.

Shrapnel and debris pattered against the fountain, sending a nubile and entirely unclothed stone nymphet crashing into the suspiciously jocular fish that had been spitting water at her. Behind them, the windows in the manor house shattered.

"Well," Skarbunket said after his hearing returned. "Mister Bristol, remind me to put you in for a formal reprimand for stacking explosives in a publicly owned carriage. I am certain there will be paperwork. How is Mister Tumbanker?"

"I'll be okay, sir," Tumbanker said. "That thing clawed me up pretty good, though."

"Glad to hear it, Mister Tumbanker. I'm told women fancy a man with scars. Mister Bodger, if you would be so kind as to tell me what the hell's going on, I would be most appreciative."

"Dunno," Donnie said. "'E does." He pointed to the tower, where Victor had ducked back inside from the balcony.

"Right. Well, let's go have a word with him, then. Mister Levy, you stay here with Mister Tumbanker and tend to his wounds. Mister Mayferry, Mister Bristol, with me, please."

"I'm goin' too," Donnie said.

"What? No! This is a police matter."

"We ain't done what we came t' do," Donnie said. "Besides, you ain't equipped fer this. If you run into any more o' them things in there, yer gonna need somethin' more'n clubs, an' I think yer outta bombs. Interestin' t' see how well they worked, though. Might need t' put some more thought t' that. Claire, you comin' with me?"

Claire looked up from where she was tearing Thaddeus's shirt off. She produced a small knife from her overalls and made a cut over each of the two wounds in his side. "Muddy's in a bad way," she said.

Donnie nodded. "Right. You stay 'ere, then. Number two, the rest o' you, let's go finish this."

28

At the sound of the horns, a set of doors opened in a row of black carriages parked along Derby Lane, two blocks away from the Palace.

Lord Rathman stepped out of the lead carriage, dressed in his finery, an expensive top-hat atop his head. Behind him, Lord Clifford, the Duke of Barnstaple, exited his carriage, carrying a cane with a silver knob on the end. Behind him, more lords emerged onto the street from their carriages: Lord Hamilton of Clovenshire, Lord Clay of Borneham, Lord Brandstetter of Cherring, Lord Marron of Lowcastle, Lord Wittonbury of Thrush-in-Pine, Lord Urston of Franningham, Lord Fiske of Kent—members of the Council of Lords, every one.

They walked in a row down Derby Lane and turned toward the Palace. Major Archibald met them at the gate. "My lord," he said, "the Palace is yours."

"Thank you, Major," Rathman said. He gave the man a curious look. "Are you okay? You're walking strangely."

"Battle injury, my lord. Nothing serious."

"Your men have cleared the courtyard of bodies?"

"Yes, my lord."

"Casualties?"

"Thirty men killed or not accounted for, my lord."

"Good, good." Rathman nodded curtly. "Have half a shilling sent to each of their families." He took a deep breath and closed his eyes, savoring the moment. So many plans, so many machinations, so many contingencies thought of and accounted for, all had led to this one, perfect instant in time. The rain had stopped, and a glow was gathering on the eastern horizon. Even the weather seemed to conspire to make the moment perfect.

The Palace was his.

He opened his eyes again. In a moment, he would step through those gates as the new ruler of the Land. But first, he would inform the commoners.

✦

Victor was waiting for them at the arched stone entryway leading into the tower. "Oh, bravo! Bravo!" he said. "Splendid! The brave police swooped in at the last moment to rescue the trapped heroes! How wonderful! The information you have given me has been invaluable. We had been planning to do some field testing, of course, but you brought the opportunity straight to us. Magnificent!"

"As a Commander of the London Metropolitan Police, I am placing you under arrest on suspicion of conspiracy, assault, and murder," Skarbunket said. "Any and all animates on the premises will be seized and taken as state's evidence."

"You? Arresting me?" Victor said. "Oh, my. My, my, my. Commander Skarbunket, words cannot express how mistaken you are."

Skarbunket pressed his hand to his head. "Normally, I would ask you why you think so," he said, "and then you would tell me you have powerful connections and you are above the reach of the law, at which point I would retort that nobody is above the reach of the law and maybe offer a witty quip, but frankly, it's late, I'm tired, and I have had a very, very long day. Let's go." He took Victor by the arm.

A gunshot rang out from the manor house. The police officers flattened themselves to the ground. A hole appeared in the sleeve of Donnie's shirt. Donnie looked down at it, then shook his head. "Always 'as to be somethin' else," he sighed.

"Second window on the left, sir, by the door," Bristol said.

"Mayferry, Bristol, with me." Skarbunket started a low run toward the house, hugging the wall.

"Number two," Donnie said, "watch Victor. If 'e moves, shoot 'im. If 'e looks at you funny, shoot 'im. You others, follow me." He set off on a loping run toward the manor house.

"Well, this is exciting, isn't it?" Victor said. "Such bravery! They're so dashing! Do you have a cigarette?"

"Shut up," Elias said.

Skarbunket reached the door first. He charged through the foyer and into the sitting room beyond. The intricate teak floor was littered with broken glass that caught and reflected the bright glare from outside in a thousand points of light. The fine velvet curtains were already darkening with rain.

A man in a butler's uniform leaned against the window. He was busy with an antique flintlock pistol, carefully pouring powder from a small silver container into the flashpan.

Skarbunket tackled him without slowing down. He went down quickly with an *oof!* Mayferry and Bristol ran in just behind him.

"Are you okay, sir?" Bristol said.

"I'm fine, Mister Bristol. Just contemplating a change of career, and not for the first time this evening." He lifted the man to his feet, holding on to his arm tightly.

Donnie charged into the room, shattered glass crunching beneath his massive feet. "Where is it?" Donnie said. His face was dark.

"Where is what?" the butler said.

"The creature that killed Chiyo Kanda. The animate."

"We destroyed all the animates in the courtyard," Skarbunket said.

Donnie shook his head. "No. It wasn't there." He leaned close to the butler. "Where is it?"

"The tower!" the man said, his eyes wide as saucepans. "In the tower!"

Skarbunket and Donnie looked at each other.

✦

The dawn gathered itself just below the horizon, working up the energy to spring forth. London was already awake. Of course, London was always awake, or at least bits of it were; the great engines of civilization turn night and day. But by this time of the morning, London was *properly* awake, her citizens flowing through the streets and alleys as befitted their station doing…whatever it was that citizens of a great city did. Rathman didn't particularly care. He merely cared that they were present.

"Citizens of the Realm, friends, hear me," Rathman said. He spread his arms wide. "On this night, a great wrong has been righted. Through your work and sacrifice, you have prevented disaster. A calamity that loomed before us, threatening to destroy our way of life, has been averted."

He was standing in the middle of Tenpenny Square, the spacious public square in front of the Palace. When King John had had the Palace constructed, he had felt that a good palace needs a proper public square in front of it, filled with statues and a big arch. Tenpenny Square had been a small and, in his opinion, sad little space before the Reconstruction, all meandering pathways and babbling brooks and not even a single statue, but he had sorted that out. He'd also renamed it King's Square, but the original name had stuck.

Rathman's back was toward the Palace. In front of him, the surviving soldiers from his levy stood at attention in neat ranks. The other lords were arranged in a semicircle behind him. They had each brought five members of their own personal guard, who were arrayed to the sides, in case the peasantry decided they wanted to get too close. There were many unpleasant things about the peasantry, like the fact that they were always so grubby, and they got you grubby when they touched you. Behind them, the mounted units still stood at the gate, situated there to create all the more grand an impression when he took possession of his prize.

A curious crowd of onlookers formed rapidly. The Queen's arrest had been the appetizer, whetting the city's desire for drama, and now, at last, the main course had arrived.

"As you know, these are dark and troubled times," Rathman said. "We are beset by enemies on all sides. The pretender in Rome, driven by his rage against the True and Holy Church, makes unending war upon us. He sends spies and assassins against us. He drives his unwanted, criminals, cutpurses, and murderers, to our shores. We have tried, my friends, to welcome those fleeing his tyranny, to offer them refuge in our lands. But what has it brought us? Only our own misery! He hides his spies in these people. They live among us, but who here can say we trust them? They do not adapt to our ways. They seek only our downfall."

He raised his hands high, warming to the speech. "And as if that is not enough, we have enemies from within, too! The Queen herself, Protector of the Realm, arrested for treason! For collaboration with the enemy! Mad for power, she cooperates with our enemies! We already suffer from the depredations of the foreigners who fill our cities, and she would invite more! Because of her, these foreigners have become so brazen, they openly kidnap and murder even the highest among us! Who is safe? I ask you, my friends, do you feel safe among them?"

Murmurs spread through the crowd. People pressed forward as those behind them tried to move closer to hear.

Rathman smiled. So much work, so much planning, and in the end it had been so easy.

"I bring news!" he said. "Grave news! The Queen, in her shamelessness and deviance, sought to marry one of these foreigners, a foreign prince of the Caliphate! She said it to me herself! And as her bride-price, she means to allow these outsiders, these foreigners, to dock their warships in our ports!"

The murmurs became gasps.

"I have tried, my friends, to persuade her away from this path. I tried so very hard. But she would not listen. She is blind, my friends, blind to the suffering of her people, blind to our needs. She would place foreigners over us, over those of us who have been her loyal subjects all these years. And so, on this night, my heart heavy with sorrow, I came here to urge her to step down, to yield the Throne to her brother, who understands the needs of the people better than she. But she would not hear it! She set her Guard upon us. When it was clear that she could not defeat us, she murdered the Duke! Her own flesh and blood! She ordered her Guard to kill him, so that she would not lose the Throne! So corrupt were they, they obeyed this evil order. And, I regret to say, Queen Margaret herself is dead, perished in the struggle to save the lad."

He looked out at the widening crowd and permitted himself a smile. Make the lies audacious, that was the key. A small lie might be doubted, but a great lie…a great lie was a mighty thing.

"And so her actions have left the Realm without a leader in the moment of our greatest need. I have conferred with my colleagues here. You will recognize them from the Council of Lords. As you know, King John the Proud, who loved this nation of ours from the deepest part of his soul, was my brother. I myself have never wanted the Throne, but the lords have come to me, beseeching me, and none of us may escape the call of duty. It is with great reluctance, but also with hope for our nation, that I have accepted their call. As God is my witness, I will bring Britain back to greatness!"

✦

Meow.

The sound came from down below Elias. He looked down. A large tabby cat with bright green eyes sat looking up at him expectantly.

Meow, it said again, and rubbed against his legs.

Only…

Only the cat was wrong. It had too many legs. Two too many, to be precise. There was a second set of legs just behind the first, and its back was shaped…oddly. Elias stepped backward, recoiling in horror.

"Prometheus, kommst hier! Ich brauche dich," Victor said.

"What?"

The animate came fast, cloaked in a robe, face hooded. It moved soundlessly down the stairs and was on Elias before he could blink. The knife flashed. Elias stumbled, clutching his throat, the gun falling from his grasp.

"Thank you, you're too kind. I think I will take that," Victor said. He picked up the gun and turned to the hooded figure. "Let's go before our heroes return," he said. He looked down, where blood spurted in a fine mist from Elias's throat. His nose wrinkled.

"Yes, master," the thing said. Its voice crawled and slithered.

"You know," Victor said, "it's a shame they burned down the stable. I would quite prefer to ride than walk. Ah, well, at least the rain has stopped. Let's go out through the back of the power generator, shall we? Stay behind me, and if anyone tries to follow us, please tear his throat out."

"Yes, master," it said.

Victor took a look around. "I do hope they don't do too much damage to my lab before they leave. I am so looking forward to an end to this strange reluctance to appreciate the magnitude of my work. Still, eggs and omelettes and all that." He unlocked a heavy steel door in the base of the tower and, followed by his creation, he left.

✦

"I'm sorry," Alÿs said. She was gasping for breath. "We need to keep going. It's a long way to Bodger & Bodger. If we can get across the bridge without being seen, I think we'll be okay. We—what are you doing?"

Margaret was moving toward the square. Alÿs took her arm. "Your Grace, we need to go!"

Margaret shook off her arm. Her face was a mask of rage.

"Your Grace!" Alÿs said.

She might as well have been talking to the Thames. Margaret heard nothing but Lord Rathman, standing in *her* square, speaking lies. Her hands tightened into fists. "Filth!" she spat. "Filth and lies! And those lords with him, I will have their heads, every one."

"Your Grace!" Alÿs said. "Please, we need to go! If anyone sees you, they will kill you!"

Margaret would not be moved. She stared at Lord Rathman, willing him to spontaneously combust.

People started accumulating behind them, jostling for position, pushing them closer to the row of soldiers flanking Lord Rathman. If one of them recognized Margaret or Alÿs, it was all over. Alÿs felt in her handbag for her dagger. It was still there, warm and slick with blood. She looked down. The sleeve of her borrowed outfit was stained dark red, nearly black. "Margaret!" she hissed.

"He's dead," Margaret said. Her voice was wooden. "They killed my brother."

"You don't know that!" Alÿs looked around frantically. It was getting harder and harder to move.

"I know," Margaret said.

"Your Grace," Eleanor said. "We can't stay here."

✦

Lord Rathman was on a roll. He swept his arms expansively to encompass the Palace and all around it. "A new day is dawning, my friends!" he said. "A day bright with possibility. This day, we sweep aside the rot and corruption that has infected us from within. This day, we say goodbye to weakness and insecurity. We move forward with a new resolve to make our land great once more!"

As if on cue, the sun peeked above the horizon, touching the sky with red and gold. The soldiers in the courtyard cheered.

Rathman smiled. A man could be seen commanding the sun to rise, if he planned carefully enough. And the peasants would eat it up. A bit of cheap theatrics, a nudge to people's fears, the promise of a brighter future where all their problems would disappear...it was all so easy. Tomorrow, the peasants would still be peasants, the farmers would still be farmers, the poor would still be poor, the starving would still be starving...the only thing that would be different was the head that wore the crown. But right now, they believed. They believed in a Utopia that was just around the corner, and all they needed to do was put the right head under the crown.

They were so very predictable, every one of them.

Rathman cast his benevolent smile at his new subjects.

And then it all went horribly, horribly sideways.

They came in groups of six, two abreast and three deep, each group following the one in front of it by about ten feet. They came up Derby Street. They came up Bosington Street. They marched right up the main plaza itself, hundreds of them, wearing the red capes and steel helmets of the Swiss Pontifical Guard.

The group in the lead knelt, aimed, and fired. The men farthest from Rathman, caught entirely unaware and shot in the back, screamed and fell.

The Pontifical Guard kept marching, the soldiers behind the front ranks flowing effortlessly around the ones who had just fired and were now on one knee reloading.

Another volley of gunfire rang out. More soldiers from Rathman's levy fell.

The ranks broke. The soldiers in front of Rathman dove for cover. A third volley sounded. Around Rathman, men screamed and fell.

"Men!" Rathman roared. "To arms! To arms!"

The remaining men in his levy scrambled to ready their weapons. A few of them returned fire, but they were disorganized and uncoordinated.

The crowd of Londoners who had gathered to watch Rathman speak fled like rats from a burning building. Londoners, like people everywhere, liked drama, but only from a distance. Hearing about killings and insurrections was one thing; being present when the bullets flew was quite another. Historic events are far more popular to the common man at sufficient remove to make them entertainment rather than personal experience.

This wasn't right at all. With the Cardinal dead, the Swiss Pontifical Guard should be inert, leaderless. Its loyalty was to the Church, not the Crown. There was no reason for it to be here! Rathman felt a surge of frustration at the sour man with his sour face, intruding here in this place from beyond the grave. For an instant, Rathman wished the old man weren't dead, just so he could kill him again.

And what did they hope to accomplish, anyway? With Margaret and her half brother gone, Lord Rathman was the only legitimate heir to the Throne. A handful of foreign men in ridiculous helmets wouldn't change that! He had the backing of the Council of Lords! Rathman fairly sputtered with rage. He had worked so hard to craft the perfect symbolic moment, and they were cheapening it!

He turned toward the Palace. Let them come, he thought. Once he was safely inside, they could do nothing but mill about in the courtyard. When he was confirmed as King, his first order would be to have the whole lot of them sent packing, back to Paris or Switzerland or wherever it was they came from.

"My lords, follow me!" he said. "Soldiers, advance! Drive off these foreign dogs!"

He had hoped his words would rally his personal levy, inspiring them to stand together to rout these intruders, or at least hold them back. Instead, most of them ignored him, scrambling for cover behind marble figures of half-naked women and cherubs with ridiculous wings.

No matter. He could still make the Palace.

He ran. The lords, flanked by their private soldiers, ran with him. They jammed up at the iron gate in front of the courtyard for a bit. Rathman found himself pressed against Lord Clay as they both tried to squeeze through the entrance at once. He snarled and bit Lord Clay's arm. The lord yelped and pulled away, and Rathman was in the courtyard, speeding toward the Palace gate.

Which was closing.

It landed with a heavy thud fully ten seconds before Rathman got there. He stood outside the portcullis, breathing hard. On the other side of the square lattice of iron bands stood a man dressed in the colors of his levy.

"You there!" he said. "I command you to open this gate!"

"I don't think I will, my lord," Julianus said.

29

The morning air was what writers of lurid romance novels call "crisp" and normal people call "chilly." An early snow had fallen the night before, draping the world in a beautiful, crystalline whiteness.

But this was London, and London had things to do. It didn't take long for the beautiful shroud of white to become a squelchy, muddy mess, streaked with coal dust and other, more questionable stains. London was a practical town, and silent shrouds of crystalline white get grubby very quickly in practical towns.

Still, in the space behind the Palace, some bits of it remained lovely and white, at least for the moment. Not far away, children ran around throwing handfuls of the stuff at each other, laughing. The adults in attendance were far more somber.

Queen Margaret the Merciful sat in her chair in a hastily erected enclosure just behind the Palace. The Ladies Alÿs and Eleanor sat to her left. On her right, in a chair nearly as tall as hers, the Ottoman ambassador was seated, dressed in heavy robes of gold and green. Behind them both, Julianus stood with his arms folded, wearing a white cape bisected with a red slash. The plume on his helmet was red.

Henry and Rory, recently offered a royal pardon for the part they had played in helping the Lady Alÿs thwart the coup, arguably unintentional as it may have been, sat wide-eyed in wood chairs beside the ambassador. They seemed, on the whole, still resentful over the regrettable matter of their interrogation and incarceration and were disinclined to look Alÿs in the eye.

The chairs to the left of Alÿs and Eleanor were occupied by the Bodger twins, who were freshly scrubbed for the occasion. The two of them were dressed in finery that would not be out of place among the most aristocratic of the Queen's Court. Alÿs was frankly astonished, once she recognized them, which took rather longer than she felt it really should have. Behind them, Commander Skarbunket stood ramrod-straight in his nicest dress uniform, which was also his only dress uniform. He looked as uncomfortable as Claire and Donnie were comfortable, and neither Mayferry nor Bristol, likewise dressed in their finest, seemed any happier than he to be there.

The ambassador leaned over to Margaret. "I am pleased you have dealt with the problem in your Court, Your Highness," he said. "The Caliph looks forward to a prosperous future of trade between our great nations." He leaned closer and gestured toward the empty seat that had been reserved for the Cardinal. "I cannot help but notice your man of the Church is not here."

"It would seem he has other matters to attend to," Margaret said.

It had been a month and a handful of days since the Queen's brother had been laid to rest in the mausoleum. The event had been attended by thousands of Londoners, jamming the great broad street in front of the Palace. The Queen had called for a week of mourning. Even now, there were mounds of flowers along the front fence of the Palace courtyard, their petals rimmed with frost.

All the ceremony of the young Duke's funeral stood in contrast to the simple way Max and Roderick and the other members of the Guard who had fallen were put to rest. There was no week of mourning for them, no spectators crowding every available space just so that they could one day tell their grandchildren they had Been There When It Happened. Just a brief ceremony, with rows of silent Guardsmen watching.

And the Cardinal. The Cardinal had been there, still bandaged up and walking with a cane, to pay his respects.

After the week of mourning was over, the trials had started. Now, on this snowy day, the sentences would be carried out.

As the lead conspirator, Lord Rathman was, naturally, the first in line. And quite a line it was, representing in total nearly a third of the Council of Lords, plus every commissioned officer of all the levies that had participated in the failed coup. Margaret generously commuted the sentences of the enlisted men in the Levies to life in prison, though the considered opinion of those close to the Throne was that this had more to do with the logistics of finding enough headsmen to deal with that many heads than any uncharacteristic fit of mercy.

In fact, simply coping with all the lords and officers whose necks were scheduled for the block had presented a considerable challenge, requiring construction of a whole new platform in the field behind the Palace just to make room for everyone. That in turn had meant constructing many new benches for the audience, which was quite considerable in its size, and a new shelter for the Queen and her party. Extra iron manacles for all the prisoners had been requisitioned from Bodger & Bodger Iron Fittings, commissioned directly by the Crown. In every human civilization, it has always been true that the business of governance involves more small details than most citizens imagine.

The headsman led Rathman to the block and forced him to his knees. He glared at Margaret, his face showing nothing but hate. She watched him expressionlessly. "Any last words?"

"Yes!" he said. "This nation is on a path to destruction. You, Your Grace, have invited foreigners into our midst. These foreigners care nothing for our traditions or our culture. They will—"

Margaret yawned behind her hand. "Heard it already," she said. She made a small gesture. The headsman swung his axe. Rathman's head rolled, face frozen in an expression of surprise.

One by one, the rest of the people in line went to keep their appointments. Some wept, some pleaded for mercy, some were stoic, but they all went just the same. The snow turned red, then black. By the end, the headsman was panting for breath behind his pointed black hood.

Later, Alÿs and Margaret were in the sitting room sipping tea from gold-rimmed mugs beneath the watchful gaze of the various painted portraits of the lords in their gold-leaf frames.

"I still don't understand why you have to marry that dreadful Frenchman," Alÿs said. "I thought you'd already decided who you were going to marry!"

"That was before," Margaret said. "You were to marry our brother to seal our alliance with France. With the Duke gone, that duty falls to us."

"But you're the Queen!" Alÿs protested. "You can do whatever you like!"

Margaret smiled. "If only that were so. We all have our parts to play, even the Queen. We will marry the man the Cardinal has chosen for us and bear an heir to the Throne who will unite the Kingdoms of Britain and France, because that is what we must do. And you will go home to Paris until your parents find someone else for you to marry, because that is what you must do."

"But it's not fair!" Alÿs said.

For a moment, Margaret looked tired and sad. "I'm not sure I know what that word means," she said softly. "Was it fair my brother was killed and I wasn't?" Then the regal Margaret was back. "We are members of the nobility. The world we live in cares nothing for fairness. This is politics. We owe a great deal to the Church. The Church wants this marriage."

"So what?" Alÿs said. "You have the entire Council of Lords now! There is nobody left who opposes you. You've made the lords disband their private armies. You don't need the Cardinal or anyone else!"

Margaret smiled a small, humorless smile. "Yes, we are more power-ful now than we were before. But the Church will not soon forget how the Pontifical Guard carried the day. The Throne may be more powerful, but so is the Church. The balance remains. Politics."

Alÿs crossed her arms. "What if I refuse to go back to France? What if I say I won't get married at all?"

"Then," Margaret said, "you will probably be carried back, kicking and screaming if need be. Where would you go where you won't be known? You are not a commoner, for all you enjoy pretending to be one." She raised her hand at Alÿs's protest. "And yes, we are grateful. But you cannot be something you are not, Alÿs de Valois. You are the daughter of a king. It is your role to marry the man who is chosen for you and bear his children. You are a woman, not a child. It is time to put the ways of childhood behind you. You will understand in time." Her smile turned dark. "And if it becomes too much, you have shown you know how to deal with men who stand in your way. I do not doubt you will manage."

✦

The Cardinal surveyed the outside of the building and shook his head. It was long and low, and made of cut blocks of limestone. Outside, the hustle of Highpole Street showed no sign of slowing despite the snow. Inside, the air was hazy. Small cubicles, each separated from its neighbor by low wooden walls decorated with intricate carvings, formed a maze that would be difficult to navigate even without the smoke that hung heavy in the air. The Cardinal's eyes watered.

He still moved with exaggerated caution. The animate's knife had done considerable damage, meaning injudicious activity was punished promptly. He had awoken when the alarm bells sounded, surrounded by Ottoman physicians, all of whom had done their best to keep him in bed. Which was, of course, exactly the point. If there was one universal failing of the human spirit that really irked the Cardinal, it was the inability to see the bigger picture.

He waved the smoke away from his face and moved farther into the gloom, flanked by two of his guards. Finally, he found the man he was seeking, curled up on his side on an elaborate rug woven in reds and golds, the end of the hookah trailing from his fingers.

"Lord Chancellor Gaton," he said.

The chancellor opened his eyes. "Yes? Oh, it's you. I heard you were dead. Then I heard you weren't."

"I very nearly was, my lord," the Cardinal said.

"How did you find me?"

"It wasn't difficult, truth be told. Your predilection for the opium pipe is not so hidden a secret as you think." The Cardinal looked around. "It's all so predictable, isn't it? You hate Highpole and everything it stands for so much, and yet, here you are."

Gaton sat upright with some effort. "What of it?" he said. "Why are you here?"

The Cardinal sat down cross-legged on the rug across from Gaton, cane across his lap. "They carried out the sentences on the conspirators this morning," he said.

Gaton waved his hand. "So? I wasn't there that night. I had nothing to do with it."

"Well, one of those things is true, certainly," the Cardinal said. "Even so. Did you know that even today, more than a thousand people a year come to our shores fleeing the Spanish Inquisition? Such a terrible waste of life. To think it's been going on for centuries. How many people do you think the Inquisitors have tortured and killed in the last three centuries, my lord?"

"I'm sure I wouldn't know," Gaton said. "Why do you ask?"

"Officers of the Church question all the refugees who arrive on our shores," the Cardinal said. "The Spanish and Italians have tried to sneak spies into France and Britain disguised as refugees. They've never succeeded, of course."

"That you know of."

The Cardinal inclined his head. "That we know of. These refugees are valuable to us as sources of intelligence, however. We have learned far more about what's going on in Italy and Spain than I think either nation would be entirely comfortable with, merely by speaking with those they drive from their lands. It's funny, don't you think?"

"You still haven't said why you're here," Gaton said.

"Ah, yes, my mind wanders. Do permit an old man his failings. I was coming to that." The Cardinal looked around the shabby room. "The Spanish and Italians are inferior to us in many technical respects, but there is one area of engineering endeavor where they have handily surpassed us, and that is the invention of new and ingenious devices

318

to extract information from those reluctant to part with it. I'm told their devices are of such efficacy that they can make a person confess to crimes he did not even know he had committed." An expression rather like a smile tried to cross his face, like a dandelion attempting to sprout on bald granite. "In any event, we have been keeping up with some of their innovations in this area, a fact I mention because we recently had leave to make use of them during a conversation with a person we found stockpiling bombs in a flat in Highpole. A person who, with some persuasion, eventually told us he was working for you."

Lord Gaton blinked several times, trying to clear his vision. "Nonsense. Hearsay and nonsense. A person will say anything if you torture him enough."

"True. Though I did not say we actually tortured him. Torture is such a blunt instrument. It turned out that merely showing him the devices and explaining their use was enough. No matter. He told an interesting tale. A tale of being commissioned to start a violent riot in Highpole, pin the blame on the Italian spy who snuck aboard the Queen's airship, and then use black-powder bombs in a place of worship. It was all very…oh, what is the word I am looking for? At my age, we sometimes lose words. Ah, conspiratorial, that's it."

There was a long silence. Then Chancellor Gaton shook his head. "You are bluffing. If you had any proof, my head would be disconnected from my neck right now. You have nothing."

"It is true that the Church would, for reasons I prefer not to go into just now, rather not reveal the existence of the prisoner of whom I spoke," the Cardinal said. "So you see the dilemma. I cannot turn you over to the Queen, for then I would be faced with inconvenient questions about how I know of your involvement, a matter the Church feels some eagerness not to discuss."

"What is it, then?" Gaton said. "Blackmail?"

The Cardinal laughed. The sound was as unnatural coming from him as a quack from a dog. "Nothing so crude. I merely wished to inform you that I am aware of some tales that have been told about you."

"Tales."

"Tales. But the day grows late. I have many things to do, and if I am not mistaken, the proprietor of this establishment is attempting to signal to us that he would like to close." He rose and bowed slightly. "Lord Chancellor Gaton, my men will help you to your carriage."

The Cardinal left. His men remained behind. One of them offered Gaton a hand. He brushed the man away angrily. "No, no, no. I don't need your help."

He rose unsteadily. The guards put their arms around him to support him. They led him from the opium den into the alley, where a carriage waited.

One of the men opened the door for him. Gaton started to climb aboard, then paused halfway through the door. "This is not right!" he said. "You imbeciles! This is not my carriage! You've taken me to the wrong carriage! I say, do you realize what you're doing? What is wrong with you? Stop! Fools! Cretins! This is not my carriage!"

The door closed, cutting his protests short. A lock clicked. The driver shook the reins. The carriage drove off.

✦

"Muddy! You have a visitor!" Claire called.

Thaddeus swung his legs out, climbing painfully to his feet. He'd spent the entire month sleeping on the cot formerly belonging to the old number two apprentice. There was considerable gossip about who might be the new number two apprentice, a role the Bodgers had been uncharacteristically slow to fill.

He pulled a shirt over his body, wincing as he brought it down over the bandages. The wounds were already forming two large, puckered scars, almost perfectly circular, one on each side. It looked for all the world like someone had run him straight through with a skewer, in one side and right out the other.

He leaned on Claire's shoulder. She guided him across the flat expanse of grass, strewn with bolts and rivets and small incomprehensible bits of iron that Thaddeus didn't recognize, into the workshop.

It was, for midafternoon, unusually quiet. The apprentices were all gathered about one of the long workbenches, goggling at the man seated beside it. Thaddeus joined them in goggling. Disorder, the big orange cat, hopped on the workbench and pressed his head against the Cardinal's hand. A tabby cat with six legs twined around Donnie's leg.

"Ah, just the person I wished to see" the Cardinal said. He rose and bowed. "Thank you for agreeing to meet with me."

"Don't recall agreeing to any such thing," Thaddeus said.

"No? Well, here we are. Let us make the most of it. Mister Bodger, may I have a moment with Mister Mudstone, if you please?"

"You 'eard the man," Donnie said. "You lot, clear out."

The workshop emptied quickly. Soon, only Thaddeus and the Cardinal remained.

"You are Thaddeus Mudstone," the Cardinal said. It was a statement, not a question.

"My friends call me Muddy, Your Eminence. You can call me Thaddeus."

"No need for petulance, Thaddeus." The Cardinal looked him up and down. "It really is remarkable."

"What is?"

"Beneath the Pontifical Guard's barracks there is a cell, and in that cell is a man who looks exactly like you. We caught him making explosive bombs."

"Are there any other kind?" Thaddeus said.

The Cardinal bowed his head slightly. "Quite right. My mind is not as sharp as it once was."

"Is that so?" Thaddeus narrowed his eyes. "You came a long way to tell me all this."

"Yes. It seems you've been a very naughty boy, Thaddeus Mudstone. First, you implicated the Queen in a conspiracy involving the false Church in Rome, then you set out to commit acts of violence and terror in Highpole Street. After that, you were scheduled to play the role of dead Italian spy, as a testament, you see, to Rathman's success at stopping the foreign agents in our midst." He smiled thinly. "You look rather hale for a dead man."

"So do you," Thaddeus said. "I saw you get killed."

"They tell me had the blade gone an eighth of an inch in any direction, that would indeed be the case. I'm not sure what was more surprising, seeing a man I knew to be locked up in my cell turn up at Mass, or having an inhuman creature leap at me with a knife." He coughed. Pain flickered across his face. "But that's not why I'm here."

"Whatever it is you're about to ask, the answer is no," Thaddeus said.

The Cardinal looked genuinely surprised. "What makes you think I'm going to ask for something?"

"If you weren't, you wouldn't be here," Thaddeus said. He was, all in all, feeling more than a little testy and saw no reason not to allow it to show. "You've come here to talk to me, instead of summoning me to talk to you. That leads me to think there's something you want from me, something you don't want to ask for in a precisely…official capacity."

The Cardinal looked at Thaddeus for a long moment. He seemed oddly pleased. He nodded. "Quite. Well, as I mentioned, we have, in our cells, a man who looks uncannily like you. That man has been very forthcoming in helping us put all the pieces together. He has confessed to a number of things, including entering the Queen's airship under a false name using an invitation procured for him by a person or persons unknown for the purpose of planting evidence to implicate her in a conspiracy, thereby setting the stage, so to speak, for…well, you know the rest."

Thaddeus's face registered no surprise. "Has he?"

"He has. It was the shoes that did it. The shoes and the comb."

"I'm sure I don't know what you mean."

"No, I'm sure you don't. Because only the person who had boarded the airship would have possession of those items, and since the man in our cells had them in his possession, the inescapable conclusion is that he must be the guilty party. Indeed, it can be nobody else. Which means everything is neatly wrapped up."

"I'm glad you have it all sorted," Thaddeus said.

"There is just one thing that doesn't quite fit," the Cardinal said. "He seemed sincerely surprised to see both shoes and comb. In my line of work, you develop a special affinity for reading people, you see."

Thaddeus waited.

The Cardinal nodded again, as if to himself. "If there were someone else, someone with the courage to jump out of an airship and the wit and resourcefulness to recognize an opportunity to leave a comb and a pair of shoes where they would become someone else's problem, such a person could be of value to me."

"Could he," Thaddeus said, careful to keep his voice neutral.

"He could," the Cardinal said. "He wouldn't even have to do very much. Just go about his life, doing...well, whatever it was he did, and while he was about it, collect the occasional stray bit of information."

"What kind of information?"

"Oh, nothing, really. Gossip. Things overheard. Such a person would probably know the pulse of the city far better than an old man sitting in a church office."

"And when you say such a man is valuable..." Thaddeus prodded.

"I think that I would like to offer such a man a stipend," the Cardinal said. "Three shillings a week, payable a month in advance. Bonuses to be negotiated for special assignments." He drew a heavy pouch from his robe and placed it carefully on the workbench in front of him. "In exchange for weekly conversations. Conversations to be had, shall we say, after the midweek commoner's Mass?"

Thaddeus's eyes flitted back and forth between the bag and the Cardinal's face. "If such a man existed," he said.

"Yes. If such a man existed." The Cardinal rose, leaning heavily on a cane. He left the bag on the workbench. "Thaddeus Mudstone, I look forward to seeing you in church. Much as I would love to stay longer, duty calls."

He walked out the front, between the stacks of iron ingots. The sign over the door creaked.

323

Epilogue

The man read the letter silently. When he was finished, he read it again. Then he set it down and regarded the youth who had handed it to him through skeptical eyes.

The workshop was a mess. It had the look of a place that had been built in haste by someone who did not intend it to be a permanent structure, and then, over the years, it had...settled. The walls, made mostly of scrap wood and bits of old barn, had been replaced piecemeal as they fell or rotted away. New rooms had been added in an ad hoc fashion wherever they were needed or could be worked in, giving the place a chaotic, confusing layout. Holes had been cut in the makeshift walls to allow for windows, each of a different size. The entire building spoke of a fearsome dedication to utility above all else.

There was an anvil in the corner, and a second under the largest window. Outside, seagulls spiraled through the air, filling it with the sounds of their cries. The surf rolled in from the harbor toward the rows of clapboard houses lining Boston's beachfront.

A large coal-fired forge took up most of the space in the back half of the workshop. The benches, of which there were many, were littered with bits of iron and machine parts, of which there were also many. A small, crude clanker, barely four feet high, sat half-disassembled in the center of the workshop. It looked like it had been sitting there long enough for a family of rats to have built a nest in its innards.

"So," the youth said, "is it true? Did you really apprentice under Claire and Donnie Bodger?"

The man pointed to the door. Over it, mounted on two iron brackets, was a blacksmith's hammer. The head was stamped with a stylized "B&B" set in a square.

"Oh."

He crossed his arms. Finally, he said, "You're a bit old for an apprentice…" He squinted at the letter. "Alex?"

"Yes, that's right," the youth said. "Alex."

"Y'ain't foolin' anyone," the man said.

"What?"

"Y'ain't no apprentice, because if you were, you would've said 'yes, that's right, sir.' And no offense intended, but you're a terrible liar… Alex." He looked back at the letter. "Claire an' Donnie says you're a quick learner. Says here I should give you a job."

"Thank you, sir, I—"

"Hang on, I didn't say I was gonna do it. I ain't got no use for you."

"What?"

"Look at you! You got soft hands. You barely look strong enough to swing a hammer. This ain't like London. We don't make fine things here. It's heavy work what takes a lot of muscle. Asides, I got all the apprentices I need. I ain't got nothin' you can do that needs doin'."

"Please! I can't go back, and I don't know where else to go."

"Well, now, calm yourself down. I ain't gonna turn you out in the cold neither. You got Claire an' Donnie vouching for you an' that's no small thing. How do you feel about electricity, Alex?"

"Beg pardon?"

"There's a fellow up in Manhattan who's makin' a name for hisself doin' all sorts of stuff with generators an' whatnot. Says electricity is the wave of the future. Says it'll replace gas for lightin' an' maybe even steam. He's lookin' for people with quick wits an' small hands. Claire an' Donnie says you got the first, an' I can see you got the second. Let me do some introducin' and we'll see how it goes."

There was an order underneath the chaos. It was visible, even from the deck of the ship, if you knew how to look. The pier swarmed with people, all rushing about pushing, moving, loading, unloading, hauling, and rolling crates and boxes in unbelievable variety. If you looked at each individual man, focused on just one person out of that mad bustle, his actions might look random. But when you looked at it as a whole, oh, then the patterns came together, yes they did. How clear, how *obvious* the underlying order was.

That had always been his gift, he knew. Seeing things that nobody else could see didn't always make him popular with the slow and the stupid, and there were so very many people around him who were both slow and stupid. You could spot them; they were the ones who rejected the gifts you offered them.

No matter. This was a bold new world, and on the frontier, he would find people who were not afraid of new ways of doing things.

"Can I give you a hand with your things, Doctor Frank—"

He sighed and turned. "Please, call me Victor."

The captain of the ship was polite to the point of obsequiousness, which was as it should be, considering how much money he'd paid to book passage. He was also insufferably dull, and Victor had tired of him almost immediately. The captain had little to offer in the way of conversation or personality. He'd insisted that Victor join him for dinner every evening. Victor had come to loathe those meals, filled as they were with insipid gossip and dreary stories about people in faraway lands who were of no use, and therefore no interest, to him. Even worse was the nonstop stream of crushingly dull anecdotes about life at sea, most of which revolved around headings and sails and weather. Endless, endless talk about weather. Now he found himself unable to remember the man's name.

No matter.

"Thank you, Captain," he said. "I can manage."

He rolled the huge trunk and its precious cargo down the gangplank to the pier. The trunk was imposing in its size, but lighter than it looked. For the first time since the disaster at Lord Rathman's estate, he felt cheerful. A new world awaited.